Hot Futa Tales

Collection 2

Hot Futa Tales

Collection 2

by

Reed James

Naughty Ladies Publications

Copyright © 2021, 2023 by Reed James

All rights reserved. This book or any portion thereof may not be reproduced or used in any manner whatsoever without the expressed written permission of the publisher except for the use of brief quotations in a book review. Published in the United States of America, 2021, 2023

All characters depicted in this work of fiction are over the age of eighteen (18).

Cover Photo © prometeus | Depositphotos.com

Logo © Anton Brand | Dreamstime.com

Naughty Ladies Publications

www.NaughtyLadiesPublications.com

ISBN-13: 9798872838128

Table of Contents

Hot Futa Tales	1
Corrupted by the Futa Succubus	7
Awakening Ellie's Innocent Desires	8
Inflaming Ellie's Innocent Desires	32
Tantalizing Ellie's Innocent Desires	56
Claiming Ellie's Innocent Desires	80
Unleashing Ellie's Innocent Desires	104
Transforming Ellie's Innocent Desires	128
Pandora's Naughty Futa Box	151
Pandora's Naughty Gifts	152
Pandora's Futa Passions Awakened	176
Pandora's Naughty Curiosity	198
Pandora's Futa Satisfaction	222
Pandora's Envious Passion	244
Pandora's Naughty Passions	268
About the Author	289

Awakening Ellie's Innocent Desires

Corrupted by the Futa Succubus 1

by

Reed James

Awakening Ellie's Innocent Desires

Ava Heart – The Futa-Succubus Shamshiel

A shudder ran through me as I stepped across the barrier from the Black Earth into the mortal world. I shuddered as I took on a human form, clothed my essence in flesh and blood. I sculpted myself: large and perky breasts, plump lips, a round face, green eyes, fiery hair, curvy hips, lush thighs, and a bubbly butt. The form of an eighteen-year-old temptress.

A sex goddess.

Clothing flashed over me next: black, thigh-high stockings clinging to those long and gorgeous legs, a thong that slid between my butt-cheeks and hugged my shaved pussy, a black bra that cupped my breasts but didn't quite cover my nipples. Oh, no, I want those rubbing into my blouse. A short and tight mini-skirt gripping my rump and ass. And, last, a tight and stretchy belly shirt clinging to my tits.

I marched forward on my stiletto heels as I settled on a name. Ava Heart. I enjoyed it, my blood on fire as I strolled into the small college to have my fun. An excitement brimmed in me. A quickening in my nethers.

I sensed a virgin.

My clit throbbed to become my dick. All the naughty denizens of the Black Earth were hermaphrodites. Futanari. Oh, the fun I would have in this world. My pussy grew juicier and juicier as I followed the tingle of that virgin to my first ever college class.

~~*~~

Eloise "Ellie" White

The new girl settled down in a seat at the end of my row, her large breasts bouncing in her belly shirt. I couldn't believe what she was wearing. Thigh-high stockings? To class? And that miniskirt... She looked ready to go clubbing. Her fiery hair swept around her shoulders. She crossed her legs. I could almost hear the whisk of nylon on nylon.

Guys were glancing over at her, drooling. She ignored them and glanced at me. She flashed me a sultry smile. I blinked at how direct it was. Smoldering. Her green eyes flicked up and down me. I squirmed in my seat and looked away from her, confused by this tiny itch it stirred in my nethers. Why would her looks do that?

"Oh, my god," my best friend, Jennifer, said as she sat down beside me, blocking the new girl from my sight. "Did you see how she's dressed?"

"How could I not?" I asked. I was wearing a pair of jeans and a pink t-shirt. I pushed up my glasses. "I could never wear something like that to class."

"Right?" Jennifer asked. She had short, black hair that framed her heart-shaped face. Her hazel eyes flashed. "It's like something a skank would wear out clubbing. Geez, and all the guys are drooling over her."

"I know," I said, worried. I looked down at my pink t-shirt. It wasn't tight, but baggy, hiding my small bust.

"Worried about Shane drooling over her?" Jennifer asked.

My cheeks warmed more. "No. I mean..." I leaned forward to gaze past Jennifer at the new girl. The redhead was sitting there preening, three guys standing over her and hitting on her. Her gaze shot to me. I jerked my head back. "There's plenty of guys drooling for her."

"Mega-skank," Jennifer said.

"Jeez," Scarlett said as she swept in and took the seat in front of me. She sat on her desk and faced me, her legs pressed tight. She wore a jean skirt and a red halter top, her nose stud flashing for a moment. Dyed-purple hair spilled about her face. "I can't believe she's wearing that."

"No longer the hottest girl in class, eh?" Jennifer asked, a big grin on her face.

Scarlett scowled. "I'm way hotter than her, right?" She glanced over at the new girl. "God, men are such pigs. Look at them snuffling around the slut-trough."

"Yep." Jennifer leaned back and squirmed. Once again, I could see the new girl. She glanced at me again. Her lips pursed for a moment, her eyes considering me.

Why did she keep looking at me?

"Hey, Ellie."

I turned my head and smiled as my boyfriend, Shane, approached. He was a tall guy and so handsome. A giddy thrill ran through me that we were dating. Jennifer was so jealous that I landed Shane. He had a big nose, one of those bold, Roman ones, and his dark hair gave him such a strong vibe. He wore a t-shirt that fit tight to his chest and a pair of worn blue jeans. Not old or ratty, but worn.

"Hey," I said, smiling at him.

He leaned down and I gave him a quick kiss on the lips, too embarrassed to do more in class. He took the seat on the other side of me, putting him as far from the new girl as possible. I glanced at him, smiling.

"Looking forward to Friday?" he asked me. "I got something special planned. Something that will knock your socks off."

The way he smiled at me made me sure that he wanted to knock more than just my socks off. A nervousness ran through me. He would push harder for sex. I wasn't sure I was ready for it. All the girls were all throwing themselves into it. My friends all had had multiple guys by now. None of their relationships lasted. Especially

Scarlett who was getting a reputation.

It seemed to cheapen sex. At least to me. I wanted my first time to be special with someone special. Maybe that was Shane, but how could I know. We'd only gone on one date so far. He was a great guy, made me feel so giddy inside. I knew I was in college now, that I shouldn't be so uptight, but I just didn't agree with everyone else.

Our professor, Britney Jenkins, strolled in. The older woman wore her black hair in a bun, giving her a severe, disciplinarian look. She had glasses perched on her nose, the style of her frames were bigger than mine. She wore nylons and a long pencil skirt with a notch slit on the left side. Completing her outfit was a silk blouse with a scoop neckline and wide collar. She swept her gaze out.

"I see the new girl is here," she said. "Boys, you can drool over her after class is done."

The guys around the new girl bled away. She stood up and looked around. Everyone stared at her. She had a presence. I swallowed, the tingle spreading through my nethers. Why would a girl do that to me at all?

"Damn," muttered Shane.

"Hi, everyone," the redhead purred. I could see her nipples poking at the front of her belly shirt. Her tits thrust out before her, the work of a push-up bra. "I'm Ava Heart, and I am so looking forward to getting to know you all." Her eyes flicked to me. "So well."

I snapped my head away.

"That's nice," the professor said. She licked her lips. "You can sit down now. I hope you can keep up. I'm surprised the school let such a late-term transfer happen."

"Maybe I bewitched the office with my good lucks," Ava said in a joking manner as she sat down. Giggles burst through the room. I smiled for a moment. What a ridiculous idea.

"Damn," I heard Scarlett whisper.

The English class dragged on. I kept feeling Ava's presence on the other side of the room. I kept catching her glancing at me. I squirmed all through class like I'd sat on an anthill. My cheeks were burning. I couldn't believe it. I was glad to get up and head to my next class.

Shane walked with me. As I left, I spotted Ava surrounded by a group of guys, and felt her eyes on me. I shivered and was glad that I was no longer the focus of her attention. I clung to Shane's arm, feeling his strength, my breasts rising and falling.

"You okay?" he asked. "You're out of breath. Was hearing Mrs. Jenkins talk about dangling participles that invigorating?"

"Yeah," I said and chuckled. "Don't want to dangle them, do we?"

"You definitely don't," he said, grinning, a dirty look in his eyes.

I gave a nervous giggle as I got his meaning. I might be a virgin, but I wasn't *that* unaware of things.

Throughout my next class, I kept thinking about the new girl, Ava Heart. I was pretty good at math, and today we were just having a recap of a test we had yesterday. I did great on it, so I wasn't paying too much attention as the professor went over the questions that the most got wrong and what mistakes were made. Why was that girl lingering in my mind? Why did she have such an electrifying presence?

I had to use the little girls' room after that. I headed to the nearest one to me and slid in. The first five stall doors were occupied, other girls at the sink. I reached the last one, the door mostly shut. I pushed it open.

Froze.

"Oh, my god," whimpered my friend Scarlett. She stood there, her jean skirt shoved up above her waist. Her red panties were bunched around her right ankle. She had one hand squeezing a breast through her halter top while her other held a fistful of red hair.

Ava Heart's hair.

I gaped at the lesbian sight. It was clear that Ava was going down on my friend. Licking her. Devouring her. Scarlett's eyes were squeezed shut. She hadn't realized that I'd seen them yet. Her breathy moans echoed through the stall.

"Get that tongue in me, Ava," groaned my friend, her hips undulating.

This wave of shocked heat rippled through me. It washed from my nethers. I could hear Ava's tongue swiping through my friend's pussy lips. The new girl licked with such enthusiasm. Then she moaned as if she enjoyed the taste of Scarlett's twat. My heart burst into a wild rhythm, pumping wild blood through my veins.

This could not be happening.

I closed the stall door and stumbled back. I hit the counter. A girl touching up her lipstick gave me a weird look. I just blushed and spun around. I stared at my flushed face in the mirror, my glasses askew on my narrow features, my blue eyes wild. I pushed back a lock of my blonde hair, my hand shaking as I tucked it behind my ear.

I did not just see that.

How could they be doing that at school?

They just met! I knew Scarlett was one to hook up easily, but with a girl? How? Why? They were in there doing lezzie things. My cheeks burned. I turned on the faucet, filled my hands with cold water, and splashed it on my face.

It did nothing to quench my fires. My need to pee had evaporated. I fled out of the restroom confused. The sounds they made, the moaning and whimpering, echoed through my mind. The look of passion on Scarlett's face seared into my memory.

She had felt so good from Ava's licking.

I burst into the hallway and rushed to my next class.

~~*~~

Ava Heart – The Futa-Succubus Shamshiel

My tongue swiped through Scarlett's shaved pussy, my nose nuzzling into her landing strip of brown hair. I loved the ticklish feel of her curls as the virgin closed the door behind us. Ellie came in at just the right moment.

Eloise White. She was perfect. So uptight. So virginal. So achingly pure. Not like the slut grinding on my face. It took hardly anything to get her to come in here, drop her panties, and let me eat her pussy. Just a tiny touch of my lust, and she was mine.

My tongue swirled through her while my clit throbbed and ached. I needed to feel hot pussy around my dick. I felt the turmoil in Ellie's mind as my tongue danced through her friend's pussy. The confusion in the virgin was delicious.

She fled.

"Oh, god, Ava," moaned Scarlett, her head throwing back, her purple hair dancing. Her hands grabbed her blouse. She squeezed her tits through it. She groped herself. "That's it. That's what I need. Oh, yes, yes, just right there."

I flicked my tongue to her clit and showed her she needed something else. I sucked on her bud, her tart juices soaking my lips and chin. Mortal pussy—human cunt—was such a delicious thing to enjoy. It had been centuries since my last jaunt to this world. My last freedom from the doldrums of the Black Earth.

I swirled my tongue around her bud. I nibbled on it. She gasped and bucked. Pulled down on her halter top and her round tits popped out. Perky and delicious, dusky-pink nipples so hard. I groaned at the sight of them. I sucked with hunger on her clit.

"Yes, yes, yes!" she moaned, her orgasm building.

I hiked my miniskirt up and shoved my thong to the side. As Scarlett came and showered me in her tart juices, I rubbed my clit. A sharp tingle shot through me. I drank down the flood of passion for the sexy girl, her tits bouncing and heaving over my head.

"That's amazing!" she gasped. "Ava!"

I savored the delight of making her cum. This was no virgin I was corrupting, but even a slut's passion fed my soul. I devoured her ecstasy as hungrily as her pussy cream. Her body bucked. Her purple hair flew.

"Mmm, you haven't experienced anything," I told her and rose. "Look."

"I know you're hot," she panted, staring at my body. She looked down at my pussy, my hand stroking my clit. "I'll go down on you. I've done it to a girl before."

"Not one like me." I smiled as I let it sprout. I birthed my futa-cock.

My clit swelled out of the folds of my pussy. A thick shaft. She gasped as she watched the pink clit shift into my pale-beige cock. Her breasts rose and fell faster as her breath quickened. She clapped a hand over her mouth, her tits jiggling.

"Holy shit," she groaned as she realized a cock was forming. I could feel the lusts shifting in her. The realization of all the delights she could have. Her hips squirmed from side to side. She fanned her face. "That's impossible."

"Not if you're a futa and have a sexy girl before you," I purred.

"And you're cute," she moaned. "Bigger than that Black guy. God, what was his name?"

"Dante," I purred, seeing him in her mind. "Turn around, bend over, and prepared to get fucked like the dirty slut you are."

"God, yes!" she moaned and whirled around. Scarlett bent over, grabbing the plumbing of the toilet. "I'm a dirty fucking slut for big dick."

I smiled as she wiggled her rump at me. Her pussy glistened between her thighs. Juices dripped down her legs. Her tart scent filled my nose. I licked my lips, savoring the flavor as I brought my clit-dick to her cunt.

I pressed it against her flesh, shuddering at the hot and wet contact. I rubbed my thick tip up and down her shaved folds. The eighteen-year-old whore wiggled her hips, moaning in delight. She gripped the plumbing, aching for me to ram into her. To be filled by my big futa-cock.

"Fuck me, Ava!" she moaned. "Oh, god, fuck me with that huge dick."

I smiled, loving how she begged. The heat swept through me as I pressed forward. Her pussy lips spread and spread to swallow my girl-dick. She groaned, her cunt clenching down on my invading shaft, increasing the friction.

It melted down to my juicy pussy. Then the heat radiated through me, brushing my ovaries brimming with my futa-seed. It swept up to my breasts. My nipples throbbed and ached. I threw back my head, my red hair dancing, as I penetrated deeper and deeper into her pussy. I savored the feel of her pussy engulfing my dick.

"Yes!" I groaned. "Oh, god, yes, that's so good." Centuries

without human cunt... I would enjoy this.

"Fuck, you're stretching me out!" whimpered Scarlett. Her back arched, her pussy squeezing so tight about me. "I love it. Oh, my god, you have a monster dick, Ava! A monster girl-dick!"

"You're going to be singing my praise to all your friends, aren't you?" I cooed as I drew back. "But don't tell them about the cock. Let that be a surprise."

"Yes, yes, yes!" Scarlett moaned. "You ate my pussy so good. And now..." Her hips stirred her cunt around my dick. "You're going to make me explode."

Yes, I would.

I drew back my hips. I savored the wet heat massaging my futa-dick. Her silky twat gripped me. The delicious friction swept through my body. My breasts jiggled in my belly shirt, my nipples throbbing and aching against the material.

I slammed into her. I fucked my hips into her cunt with powerful strokes. I savored burying back into her. my crotch smacked into her rump. Her butt-cheeks rippled. She moaned, rocking forward, her purple hair swaying. Then I drew back. She gasped, her passion echoing through the stall.

I pumped away at her. I slammed into her hard and fast. I savored fucking the slut. Her cunt squeezed about me. That silky heaven wreathed my clit-dick in paradise. I gasped and moaned, hair dancing.

"Yes, yes, yes!" Scarlett groaned. "I'm so glad I sat beside you in astronomy. You were so much hotter to look at then dumb stars."

"Yes!" I gasped, burying into her. "Squeeze that twat around me. I'm sending you to your math class dripping in cum!"

"Oh, god, yes!" the eighteen-year-old coed gasped. Her pussy clenched around my clit-dick. Her twat went wild.

I drank her orgasmic passion, glutted on the slut's climactic rapture, while her pussy convulsed around my futa-cock. I buried hard into her. Fast. I rammed my dick into her spasming depths, the pleasure spilling down to my twat.

My cunt drank in the heat and fed it to my ovaries. Pussy juices trickled down to my thigh-high stockings. The pleasure surged through my body. I trembled, my tits heaving in my halter top as I buried over and over into her twat.

"Cum in me!" she moaned. "Flood me! I want your girl-spunk in me!"

"Yes!" I moaned and erupted.

That wonderful moment of climactic release swept through me. I pumped into her over and over again. I flooded her with my girl-spunk. Every eruption sent the pleasure slamming through my body. It crashed into my mind. My thoughts melted beneath the onslaught.

I savored it. Reveled in it. The heat rushed through me. I quivered, tits jiggling in my blouse and bra. My pussy convulsed, juices spilling hot down my thighs. The waves of rapture and jolts of ecstasy reached my mind. Mixed. Swirled.

"Yes, yes!" I moaned, free of the Black Earth. I was in a world of color. Passion. Delights. "Take my cum!"

Scarlett milked me. She worked out my jizz with her hungry twat. She felt amazing, but she was just an appetizer. That true main course lurked out there. That virgin delight. I shuddered, spurting that final blast of cum into Scarlett's twat.

What fun I would have corrupting Ellie.

~~*~~

Eloise "Ellie" White

I couldn't get the image of Scarlett shuddering in delight on Ava's mouth. It stayed with me through my last morning class, Intro to Philosophy. I should have been learning about Aristotelian virtue ethics, but my mind was swimming with that sight.

Why would any girl want another to go down on her? In a college bathroom! How had Scarlett hooked up with Ava so fast? When did they even talk? She just showed up to the school. My mind reeled at these questions.

My phone beeped. I pulled it out and saw a text from Shane. *"Couple of buddies need my help on a project. Got to skip lunch."*

Not wanting to be a controlling girlfriend, I swallowed my annoyance and texted back, *"Oh, sure. Have fun."*

He sent me a GIF of a guy rolling his eyes. I giggled at that.

I swept into the school's common area and spotted Jennifer. She slid up to me in line at the Mexican station. The school made a good taco salad. As she came up beside me, talking about nothing important, I debated if I should tell her what I saw today?

Just thinking about it had that naughty itch building in my nethers. I hated thinking about such things. I wanted to get them out of my head, but they swam through my thoughts. It was so crazy. I sighed as I paid for my lunch with my student ID. Even though I commuted, I did have a lunch allowance as a student.

"And Professor Donovan was like, 'That is the most illogical thing I have ever heard,'" Jennifer was saying as we headed to a table. "He sounded just like Mr. Spock."

"What?" I frowned. "Who said what?"

"Weren't you paying attention?" Jennifer huffed. We took our seats at a small, round table. "What has your head in the clouds?"

"Well..." I swallowed. Should I tell her?

"You have something juicy!" She leaned in. "What, what? Is it about the new girl? Every guy seems to be buzzing about her."

"Yeah," I said slowly. I stirred my fork through the lettuce, tomatoes, cheese, and taco meat of my salad. "I saw her—"

"Oh, my god," Scarlett gasped as she sat down with us, her face flushed. "Ava Heart went down on me. It was the fucking best."

My jaw dropped.

Jennifer whipped her head around and stared at our purple-haired friend with what had to be a mirrored look of shock on her face. Scarlett had a veggie burger on her plate and was squeezing ketchup on it with a packet like what she had said was the most nonchalant thing in the world.

"Wait, what?" Jennifer spluttered. "You and Ava? When?"

"In the girls' bathroom," said Scarlett. She put her bun back on her soy patty. She brought it up to her mouth. "It was just the best. That girl knows how to eat pussy."

"But... but..." Jennifer shot me a look and her eyes widened. "Is that your news. You knew?"

"I, er, saw them going into the stall," I muttered, not wanting to reveal I actually saw Ava eating out Scarlett.

"Did you?" Scarlett said with a mouthful of soy. She swallowed it. "You should have joined us. Ava could have done wonders to that little cherry pie you got."

My cheeks blazed hot. I crossed my thighs tight, my jeans rasping together.

"I don't need to do things with girls," I muttered and stabbed my fork into my taco salad. I took a large bite to avoid having to say anything else.

"Are you sure?" Scarlett shuddered. "It was the best sex ever. The orgasm I had on her... on her tongue was amazing. Out of this world. You two need to try her out. Just beg her to go down on you. It's transformative."

"Not gay," Jennifer said. "I tried kissing a girl. Like kissing my mother or something. It did nothing for me."

"Ava's not like other girls." Scarlett glanced at me and smiled. "You know what I'm talking about, don't you, Ellie?"

I almost choked on my food as I swallowed. I shook my head and grabbed my diet coke, taking a long sip of it to keep from dying.

"Yeah, you know," Scarlett said and took another big bite of her veggie burger.

I swallowed and panted, "No, I don't. I have a boyfriend. I'm not gay, either."

From behind me, a presence swept past. Ava Heart took the seat to my right, a chicken Caesar salad on her plate dribbled in white sauce. It coated the spinach and lettuce mixed with cherry tomatoes and slices of cucumbers. Slices of white, grilled chicken decorated it. she glanced at me and winked.

"I was just telling them how great it was when you went down on me," Scarlett said. "Told them that they all should give it a try."

"Mmm, isn't that sweet of you." She leaned in and kissed Scarlett. Their tongues flashed together, lips working.

A guy wolf-whistled.

My cheeks burned. What was Ava doing here? Were her and Scarlett dating now? They broke the kiss, Scarlett out of breath and looking half-dazed. Ava turned to me, her ruby lips gleaming wet. The moans I heard replayed in my mind.

"So, uh, you're a lesbian?" asked Jennifer, picking at her taco salad. She sat across from Ava.

"I only like women," she said, her eyes flicking to me again.

I couldn't help but feel her staring at me. Was she trying to ogle me? I was glad I wore a baggy t-shirt. I stabbed my fork hard into my taco salad. If she was dating Scarlett or something, she shouldn't be eyeing me like that.

"The only dicks I like are the ones they have to don," said Ava.

"And they can don some pretty big ones," groaned Scarlett, a look of aching lust in her brown eyes. She smiled hugely.

"You, uh, left an impression on Scarlett," Jennifer said. She took a bite of her taco salad, lettuce crunching.

"I hope so." Ava groaned as she ate her salad. She had white dressing on her lips. Her tongue flicked out, licking the pearly liquid up. "I always want to please a girl."

"You've had a lot of girls?"

I swallowed at the question. I glanced over at Jennifer. Her cheeks were utterly flushed. She squirmed in her seat. I gave my best friend an inquiring look, but she was ignoring me and staring across the table at Ava.

"I've had so many." Ava placed her hand on mine. Her eyes didn't look at me, but her words seemed to caress over me as she said, "I've never met a girl that I couldn't seduce and pleasure."

I yanked my hand away. "I doubt that. Not every woman is a lesbian. Not even by a long shot. Jennifer and I are straight."

"Are you?" Ava pursed her lips. Then she stood up and leaned over the table. She whispered something into my friend's ear.

Jennifer gasped. I couldn't tell if it was in shock, indignation, or delight. Ava whispered something else and my friend let out a groan, almost a schoolgirl squeal. Then Ava straightened, her large breast jiggling beneath her top, nipples poking at the black material. She walked around the table and took Jennifer's hand.

My best friend stood up, her eyes locked on Ava's. My jaw dropped as Ava strutted away, not quite pulling my friend along, but leading Jennifer straight for the ladies' room. My fork fell out of my hand and landed in my taco salad.

"They're not," I groaned, my voice tight.

"Oh, they are," Scarlett purred. She took a huge bite of her veggie burger and let out a groan of delight.

What was going on? This couldn't be happening. Why would Jennifer go off with Ava? Just a few minutes ago, my best friend was saying she was straight, and now she was going to go have sex with Ava? I shot my gaze to Scarlett.

"What did she say to Jennifer?"

Scarlett shrugged, her mouth full of her burger. She took another bite and let out a sinfully decadent moan. She looked almost orgasmic eating her lunch. I stared down at mine, my appetite utterly evaporated.

Who was this Ava Heart? Who transfers to a college in the middle of the fall term? I glanced at the ladies' room just in time to see my best friend vanishing in there. I squeezed my thighs tight. I wasn't about to do *that* with Ava.

No way.

My mind itched. Just what was going on in there?

~~*~~

Ava Heart – The Futa-Succubus Shamshiel

I pushed Jennifer into the stall, the black-haired girl panting. She was straight, it was true, but she had nothing armoring her against my desires. She had no maidenhead shielding my influence from inflaming her lusts.

"Do you really..." Jennifer bit her lower lip.

"Yes," I cooed and kissed her.

I pinned her against the wall. I savored the feel of her against me. She groaned as my tongue thrust into her mouth. I swirled around in her, tasted her sweetness. My clit throbbed, my thong soaked with my juices.

Ellie... Ellie... Ellie...

That cute, innocent blonde with her dainty glasses and vivid, blue eyes blazed in my mind. I wanted her so badly. I kissed Jennifer with such hunger wishing it was her friend. The things I would do to Eloise White...

Ecstatic things.

I thrust my hands up beneath Jennifer's skirt as kissed her. I slid up and found her bra. I squeezed her round breasts through her bra. It was plain. Nothing special. What a shame. A girl should wear sexy things beneath their clothing.

It made unwrapping them more exciting.

Jennifer kissed me with hunger, her hand boldly shoving between our bodies and pressing my skirt into my crotch. She rubbed at my pussy, my clit. She felt at me. I felt her confusion for a moment. She squeezed at my cunt, groping me.

I broke the kiss and purred, "Patience."

"I'm not good at that," she panted.

I winked at her and then shoved up her baby doll t-shirt. She thrust her arms in the air and let me peel it off. Her bra was a light beige color, a fleshy tone not much different from her skin. My hand slid along her back and found the clasp.

I released them.

Perky and round, her nipples pointing up. They were small and cute. I grabbed them both, twisting them between my fingers. She gasped and shuddered, her moans echoing through the bathroom stalls. These were such convenient places.

And women wore such naughty things in his era. Watching from the other side had nothing on being here, enjoying these delights.

I darted my head down and sucked on her nipple. She gasped, her hand grinding hard into my crotch. My thong rubbed against my clit and pussy lips. My skirt rustled, sliding up my flesh as she pushed hard against me.

"Oh, wow, Ava," she moaned. "But where is it? You said you had a huge cock."

I nipped her nipple and then popped my mouth off. "Patience." I licked her nub. "You'll get to enjoy it. Let me have my fun stripping you." I sucked on her pink delight again, nursing on it with hunger.

"I'm not patient!" she moaned and then she knelt down before me, ripping her nipple from my mouth in the process. Her lust swept through her. This fiery heat. I straightened up and smiled as she grabbed my skirt and yanked it off of me. The stretchy material slid over my curving hips and bubbly butt. It whisked down my stockings and ended up at my feet.

With a moan of need, she grabbed my thong and ripped it down next, peeling the material from my pussy. She exposed my shaved folds. The spicy musk of my twat filled my nose. I savored it, reveling in that wonderful musk. A hot shiver raced through me.

She buried her face into my dripping cunt. I gasped as her tongue stroked through my folds, her impatience seething through her. She brushed my clit. I gasped at her stroking touch sweeping over my aching bud.

She sucked on it.

"Tch, tch," I clucked with my tongue. "Impatient girls get punished."

"Don't care. I want to see this clit-dick that made Scarlett into your slut!"

I peeled off my belly shirt as she sucked. Her eyes stared up at my bra lifting up my tits but leaving my nipples exposed. She groaned, her lust sweeping through her. She nursed on my clit as she ogled my tits, her lusts shifting inside of her, my perfect body awakening her to new and delicious desires.

"Here you are," I moaned. "You better suck me off and make me cum, though."

I relaxed my bud and seized her head. I held her to my pussy as my clit blossomed. My cock birthed into her mouth, growing thicker and longer. Her eyes widened as she felt it swelling into her mouth.

"Yep," I cooed as her tongue explored my pulsing clit. With the next beat of my heart, it became a cock, the spongy crown fully formed. "That's my clit-dick. Mmm, I'm a futa. Now you're going to suck me off."

Jennifer moaned her agreement and sucked.

I shuddered, my growing cock throbbing in her delicious

mouth. She nursed on it, her tongue sweeping around my crown. The pleasure surged through me. My pussy drank it in, my ovaries brimming with the cum I would fire down her throat.

She moved her head back as my growing clit-dick brushed the back of her throat. Her eyes were so wide, a vivid hazel, brown with flecks of green. Her tongue danced around it as her mouth opened to her limits.

"Yes, yes, that's going into one of your holes," I purred, sliding my fingers through her short, black hair. My tits jiggled in my push-up bra. "Lucky you, huh?"

She moaned and nodded her head, suckling the entire time.

"Yes, yes, lucky you."

I savored her sucking and nursing on my futa-cock. Her head bobbed, sliding her lips up and down my dick. She was no stranger to sucking dick. She loved it, in fact. I felt her lust, nibbled on it as it swelled in her. She wanted my cum flooding down her throat.

My ovaries tensed every time she sucked. The pressure built in them. She'd get her wish. The pleasure flowed out of me. This wicked heat that would consume me. The bliss swept through my body. A pulse-pounding heat that would consume me. I groaned, my dick twitching and throbbing. Her mouth felt incredible about my dick.

"That's it," I panted. "Ooh, you're going to get so much cum. I'm going to flood your mouth."

She squealed in delight and sucked hard. The pleasure swept through my body. My heart pounded in my chest. The heat rippled over me. I groaned, savoring every moment of it. A big grin spilled over my mouth.

She nursed with hunger. She bobbed her head, working her mouth up and down my dick. Her suckling hunger felt incredible. My pussy clenched. The delight dribbled down my thighs. I wiggled my hips back and forth, savoring the hunger she gave me.

"Yes, yes, just like that," I groaned. "Mmm, you're going to make me explode, aren't you?"

She nodded, her eyes so hungry for my cum. They sparkled, just bursting with delight that would explode out of my girl-dick. The pressure rose to the tip from Jennifer's naughty sucking. My pussy clenched, juices trickling down my thighs.

Her tongue swept around the crown of my cock. I gasped at how naughty that felt. The stimulation rippled through my body. I threw back my head and squeezed my eyes shut. My large breasts jiggled in my bra.

"Just a little more," I groaned. "And I'll flood you."

She squealed. Her hand moved. She cupped my shaved vulva. I smiled as I felt her lust surging. She plunged two digits into my pussy. She sank them into my depths. My cunt clenched about those digits. I savored them in me.

They were incredible.

A wave of heat swept through my body. She wiggled her fingers around inside of me. It was amazing. The bliss swept up to the tip of my cock bathed in her warm, sucking mouth. She nursed.

I erupted.

"Colorless passions!" I moaned as my cum fired out of my girl-dick. "Oh, yes, yes, swallow my spunk."

My pussy went wild around her finger while my futa-spunk flooded her mouth. Jennifer's lusts swelled through her as she gulped down my girl-cum. She loved it. Her hazel eyes grew dewy with delight. She sucked hard, drawing out all the cum.

The bliss swept out of my pussy and erupted from my cock. My tits, cradled in my bra, heaved. I grabbed a pink nipple, twisting my nub as I moaned through my bliss. I savored every spurt. Every eruption of cum into her mouth.

"Empty rapture, that's good," I moaned. "Mmm, you know how to suck a girl's cock."

She popped her mouth off my dick. I felt lust surging through her. It was something she'd always wanted to do. She held a mouthful of my cum. She rose up and kissed me hard. She thrust my own salty jizz into my mouth.

I savored it as I attacked the fly of the jeans she wore. I ripped it open while our tongues swabbed my delicious futa-jizz back and forth. We snowballed the cream, the thick and creamy flavor melting over my taste buds. I tore her jeans down then shoved her panties off her hips, my futa-dick rubbing into her belly. Our tits pressed together as she clung to me.

Nipples kissed.

I broke the kiss and hissed, "Bend over. Time to get fucked!"

She panted, cum on her lips. "You can go again so soon?"

"I'm not a man! I'm a futa!" A futa-succubus! Shamshiel, Heart of Fiery Corruption, the Sun of Blazing Sin, and wielder of the Flaming Sword of Womanly Passion.

She spun around and bent over, jeans around her ankles, beige panties bunched around her knees. She thrust her ass at me, her rump toned and gorgeous. Her pussy covered by a trimmed bush of black gleaming with her passion. Her sweet musk tickled my nose.

I aimed my fleshy sword straight at her crack. I plunged my cock between her butt-cheeks, her spit and my precum soaking the tip. She gasped and threw a look over her shoulder. Her eyes widen in shock as I pressed against her asshole.

"Ava?"

"You were bad," I purred. "Impatient girls get ass-fucked!"

I thrust against her anal ring.

Her sphincter stretched and stretched, surrendering to my passion. Her head snapped forward. Her short, black hair swayed. Throaty moans burst from her lips as her asshole opened wider, yawning to engulf my futa-cock's thick and sensitive crown.

I popped into her velvety sheath and savored the hot grip. The wild friction swept up my cock as I probed deeper and deeper into her bowels. Her body shuddered. My breasts jiggled as I delved into her anal sheath's furthest reaches.

My hand slid along her side and grabbed her round tits. I squeezed those firm mounds as I buried to the hilt in her. My pussy lips rubbed into her butt-cheeks. She gasped and moaned in shock. Her first time with anal.

"Good, right?" I asked, her bowels clenching and relaxing around my clit-dick.

"Yes!" Her head tossed. "Oh, my fucking god, that's amazing!"

She squeezed about me the entire time I drew back, the friction incredible. It sent such rapture flowing through my body. I groaned, savoring every inch of her velvety grip. This bliss washed through my body. I reveled in it as I slammed back into her depths.

She gasped as our flesh smacked together. The heat rose through my body. My cunt clenched, my breasts jiggling. The bliss was intense. It flooded through my pussy. My ovaries drank it in, another load of girl-cum just ready to be unleashed in her.

"Fuck! Fuck! Fuck!" she gasped, as I fucked her. She braced her hands on the tiled wall as she took my dick over and over in her bowels. "That's incredible, Ava!"

"Told you that you'd love my futa-cock!"

"Yes!"

I savored her lust swelling in her. I nibbled on the edges as I pounded her bowels with my big futa-dick. The pleasure shot through me. The bliss that swept through my body. It rushed through me. It made me ache and throb. I slammed so hard into her. I fucked her with powerful strokes. With mighty thrusts of passion.

The pleasure rushed through me with every stroke into her bowels. I filled her up again and again. Her asshole clenched around me. She felt so incredible. the pleasure swept through me. My tits heaved. I gripped her round breasts and kneaded her boobs as I plundered her bowels.

The heat swelled. Her orgasm grew. She thrust her ass back into me, moaning and gasping. The ache swelled at the tip of my cock. My ovaries grew tighter and tighter. They brimmed with all that jizz.

"Fuck!" she gasped. "Ava!"

"Empty rapture, I know!" I buried hard into her bowels. "Don't hold back. Let it all out of you! Explode!"

"Yes, yes, yes!" she howled and came so hard.

Her bowels rippled around my futa-dick. The sweet scent of her pussy swelled in the air. I groaned as I plundered her spasming asshole. I devoured her lust-filled energy. I feasted on it—far more filling than a salad—as I buried my cock to the hilt in her bowels.

Erupted.

I flooded her asshole with my cum. Hot spurts of jizz that sent rapture firing through me. I threw back my head, my fiery curls dancing. My big boobs heaved in the cradle of my push up bra. The pleasure swept through my body. It was incredible. The heat blazed through me.

"Oh, my god, you're cumming in me!" howled Jennifer as her

asshole milked me.

"You're getting every drop!" I moaned, squeezing her tits. Stars danced across my vision. I couldn't wait to do this to Ellie. "Work me dry!"

"God, yes!" she moaned, her bowels sucking at me.

I hit the peak of my orgasm. I fired the last of my cum into her bowels. Pussy juices soaked down my thighs to my stockings. My spicy musk mixed with Jennifer's sweet delight. The heady aroma of feminine passion. I loved it.

Loved this world.

"Tell every girl, especially your best friend, just how amazing I am," I purred as I came down from my climactic high. "But leave out my futa-cock."

Jennifer's asshole clenched around my dick. "I will, Ava."

I shrank my clit out of her asshole, missing her velvety grip, and left Jennifer panting, my cum leaking out of her asshole. I didn't bother dressing myself normally. I let my magic re-clothe my body and strutted out. My heels clicked through the bathroom, my body buzzing.

I shuddered when I stepped out of the restroom and spotted Ellie lurking nearby. She gasped when she saw me and looked frozen, unsure if she should run or hide. Her blonde curls spilled about her cherry-red face. I could feel her desires, that itch for me.

"Your friend's going to need a few minutes," I purred.

"What did you do to her?" Ellie demanded, folding her arms. Anger swept through her soul, fending off her lust. She hated how I made her feel. Fought it.

"Made her cum. Several times." I smiled. "She was delectable. How you've avoided not taking Jennifer into your bed, I don't know."

"Because I'm not a whore," she hissed.

"You will be," I purred and winked at her.

"I'll never."

"Oh, you'll be begging for me to take your cherry."

A wave of lust washed out of her virgin pussy. She swelled up and hissed, "I have a boyfriend. I'll never, ever do anything with you."

"Talk to Jennifer. I'm sure she'll help you understand."

I sauntered off, my hips swaying. I felt Ellie's glaring eyes on me. I shuddered, my pussy on fire. Her corruption would be such a sweet and delicious thing. I couldn't wait until she was utterly mine. I would drive her wild with lust.

I would seduce every woman in her life. Through them, I would corrupt her. I couldn't wait. It would be glorious. I was so glad to be out of the dreary Black Earth and into the real world. The mortals were so vibrant. So colorful. Female lust abounded.

I could use another snack. Maybe Asian?

To be continued...

Inflaming Ellie's Innocent Desires

Corrupted by the Futa Succubus 2

by

Reed James

Inflaming Ellie's Innocent Desires

Eloise "Ellie" White

I marched away from that disgusting Ava Heart, shock still reeling through me. I couldn't believe my best friend just up and had sex with the new girl at our college. Jennifer had declared she was straight and then all it took was the redheaded Ava whispering in her ear and they were off to the bathroom.

There was no way *I* would do that. No matter what Ava promised. I would never, ever beg to have sex with her. I was a virgin. I was saving myself for the right guy. I hoped that was my boyfriend, Shane. I liked guys.

Not busty, redheaded sluts who dressed like they were at a rave and not a college. Who wore thigh-high stockings to college classes? And that skirt? It barely covered her ass. Her belly shirt showed off her large tits, her nipples poking against the material. She had practically every guy in school drooling over her.

And she'd had sex with two of my friends now. First Scarlett and now Jennifer.

I burst into the college's bathroom. Maybe this was just a big prank. That was it. Jennifer liked to tease me. She thought it was weird I was still a virgin at eighteen and a freshman in college. She'd been having sex for years.

As I moved through the little girls' room, clutching my hand to my chest, a nervousness rippled through me. What would I find? My glasses slipped on my nose while my blonde hair swayed about my face. I trembled, hating that itch that burned between my thighs. My nethers ached. Dripped.

I scanned the bathroom, searching for my friend. Several of the stalls were occupied. I swallowed and then from the last stall, Jennifer emerged. Smooth cheeks flushed, forehead gleaming with sweat. Her short, black hair a tousled mess about her heart-shaped face. She had a huge smile on her plump lips. Relaxed and buzzing.

The smile of someone who just had sex.

"You really did it," I gasped as I rushed over to her. "You don't even know her."

"I really did," she said, not a hint of shame. She plopped her purse down on the counter and opened it. She pulled out a tube of lipstick and casually retouched her mouth. "It was just the best. You need to try her out, Ellie."

"I have Shane," I muttered, pushing up my glasses.

"She's got a bigger cock," my friend said. Then she gasped. "Oops, I shouldn't have said that."

"What? She's got a... a... penis?"

My friend rolled her eyes. "A cock, Ellie. Grow up." Then she turned to me and gave me a tight embrace. I felt her body against mine. There was something different about this hug. Her breasts rubbed against my small tits through our clothing. Her hands were on my lower back, her cheek against mine. It was so intimate. Her lips brushed my ear. "You should try her out. She'll change your life."

"No thanks," I muttered, anger swelling in me. I pushed out of her hug. "I'm not into girls."

"Neither was I," Jennifer said and then pulled out her compact and touched up the rouge on her cheeks. "She'll change you. It's amazing."

I backed away, shocked. A cock? There was no way Ava had a cock. She was gorgeous. All woman. She couldn't be trans, right? Where could she even hide a cock in her skirt? She'd have a bulge. She looked so feminine. So pretty.

Jennifer snapped closed her compact, and then hooked my arm and dragged me out of the bathroom. I stumbled after her, dazed by everything that had happened. Was this a strange dream? How could this Ava just swoop in and seduce two of my friends with no effort?

Our friend Scarlett waited at our table. She'd finished her veggie burger and had a big grin. She stood up and rushed to Jennifer. They broke away from me, the pair giggling and whispering. No doubt comparing notes about doing things with Ava. I slumped down into my seat, staring at my half-eaten taco salad.

I'd lost my appetite.

I spent the rest of the day in a haze of shock. I squirmed, the image of Ava with a cock blazing in my mind. That big titty girl with a large cock. Bigger than Shane's? I wasn't experienced, but I had felt Shane's bulge on our first date when he kissed me. He had wanted me to do things with him. But I said no, to his shock.

I don't think girls turned him down often.

His size had scared me. How could Shane's big bulge fit in me? And Ava was bigger? I wanted to believe this was all some sort of prank they were playing on me, but I caught Ava going down on Scarlett earlier today. Just eating her pussy out.

When my final class let out, I spotted Scarlett talking with a girl I didn't know. My purple-haired friend had her elbow leaned against the wall the girl stood against, her hand resting on the girl's hip. They were clearly flirting. Had Scarlett gone fully lesbian?

Then I froze when I spotted Ava leading a Hispanic girl named Juana off towards the restroom. Another girl? How many had Ava taken into the restrooms to fuck today? Juana had a cross around her neck. A Catholic girl. I thought she was straight, too.

I rushed home. I was halfway there when I realized I wasn't walking with Jennifer and hadn't given Shane a goodbye kiss. I texted them both my apologies as I passed through the park near my home, a shortcut. Joggers passed me as I stumbled along in a daze, my panties sodden. I had to put on a fresh pair.

I reached my home and headed upstairs to my room. I changed into new panties, a pair of flannel shorts, and a tank top. I put my hair in a ponytail and struggled to do my schoolwork. I battled against this heat that Ava had sparked in me.

Her cock filled my mind.

She couldn't have that. Jennifer had to be messing with me. Or maybe Scarlett had a dildo. Lesbians used those on each other. Strap-ons, right? Yeah, that had to be it. A big, fleshy strap-on. I bit my lip. The urge to masturbate grew in me.

I was scared about what I would think about if I did it.

My step-mom called me down for dinner. I stumbled down there and found my dad already settling down. Mom placed the bowl of peas next to the salad bowl. She had made a crockpot roast for dinner, the meat sliced up and on another platter.

I ate quietly, my thoughts distant. My dad and step-mom were talking about their days, things they heard about, politics and news and stuff. I hardly notice. That darn Ava Heart dominated my thoughts. Her promise to me echoed through my mind.

I would *never* beg to have sex with her. Never.

As I was clearing my plate off in the trashcan beneath the kitchen sink, my step-mom sidled up to me. "Are you okay, Eloise?"

She never called me Ellie. She thought Eloise was a beautiful name. I was named after my father's grandmother.

"Fine," I muttered.

"No, you're not? Is it Shane?"

I shook my head. "Just this new girl at school. She transferred in."

"In the middle of the term?" my step-mom said, sounding surprised by that.

"I guess," I said. I finished scraping my plate. "I have a lot of homework to do."

"Okay." She gave me a kiss on the cheek and then a motherly look, her green eyes soft. She might not be my biological mother, but she'd raised me since I was three. "If you need to talk about it, let me know."

"Sure, Mom," I said. For my step-mother, she was great. I had always gotten along with her and was glad Dad had met her.

I headed up to my room and threw myself on my bed. That itch was growing as Ava filled my mind. The ache to masturbate. I bit my lip and then thrust a pillow between my thighs. I squeezed tight around it and grabbed my phone. I started texting Shane to distract myself. He was eager for our date on Friday. He had something big planned.

He wouldn't mention it. I knew he would want to have sex with me. Maybe I should go all the way with him. Maybe that would stop this itch. I told him I was excited. I even hinted I might be willing to do things with him. I was eighteen. Maybe it was time to grow up and lose my virginity.

Get Ava Heart out of my mind.

She never really went away. It was later that night, as I neared my bedtime, when I got a text from my English professor, Mrs. Jenkins. It wasn't unusual to get a text from a teacher. Sometimes they would send out mass emails or texts to let us know about homework or tests or changes to the class. She wanted me to come in early and see her before her class tomorrow morning. Something that she needed to talk to me about.

Sure, I sent back. *I'll be there thirty minutes before class.*

Perfect, Ellie, she sent back. *Have a good night.*

I brushed my teeth and changed into my PJs. I lay in my bed for hours thinking about Ava seducing all the girls in my school. Just taking them one by one into the restroom and turning them into lesbians. Then they all begged me to be the next one. When I fell asleep, they haunted my dreams.

Images of her going down on girls. Eating pussies. Sucking on their tits. They gasped and moaned and begged her to fuck them with her big cock. She did. She pounded them hard, just driving her dick into their pussies.

I even dreamed of her fucking Mrs. Jenkins. She was at home, in her bed, her husband standing in the corner watching and stroking his cock. He had this look of humiliation and lust on his face. She was on her hands and knees, her big breasts swaying as Ava fucked her from behind. The redhead's big tits heaved, too, her red hair flying as she plowed into my teacher.

"I did it!" Mrs. Jenkins moaned. "Just like you asked. I sent her the message. Yes, yes, she'll be there."

"Good!" Ava moaned, thrusting harder and faster into my teacher's pussy. "You can cum. You've earned it."

"Yes!" my English teacher howled.

When my alarm clock went off the next morning, set thirty minutes earlier, I felt groggy. I slept, but I didn't feel rested. I felt hot and sticky. I peeled off my panties. I had soaked them while sleeping. I took a shower with grateful need, washing my body clean.

I struggled not to keep washing my pussy with the loofah. I was so turned on. I bit my lip, flashes of Ava popping into my mind. That scared me enough to pull the sponge away from my nethers. I was really, really hating what the girl did to me.

I texted Jennifer to let her know I had to go in early, and then devoured a quick breakfast of peanut butter on toast. I darted out the door in jeans and a t-shirt, the morning air cool even as the rising sun promised another nice day.

I cut through the park, the early morning joggers and dog walkers out. I hurried, trying to outrun these lusts that beset me. Ava kept springing into my mind from every direction. She ambushed me every time I thought I had distracted myself.

I started walking and staring at my phone, browsing the news and seeing what was trending on Twitter. There was outrage over something an actor said twenty years ago. It seemed silly for something that old. I was browsing Reddit, staring at some funny memes as I walked through the college's hallway to my English class.

I knew the way by muscle memory. I headed right to the door and opened it.

"Yes, yes, you're going to cum all over my face, aren't you?" slammed into me the moment I stepped in.

I froze to see Mrs. Jenkins kneeling naked on the floor. The black-haired teacher had her hair pinned up in her usual bun, her glasses perched on her face. She had her hands squeezing her large, naked tits around...

Around a cock.

Ava's cock.

Ava Heart lounged in the teacher's chair, one leg thrust up on the desk, the other over the armrest of the chair. Her large breasts jiggled as she squirmed in delight. Her red hair framed her gorgeous face. Her green eyes flicked to me. A smile grew on her lips.

"I'm going to fire so much cum on your face, Mrs. Jenkins," purred Ava. She arched an eyebrow in invitation at me. Meanwhile, Mrs. Jenkins's large breasts worked up and down the new girl's big dick.

Ava had a cock. It looked huge. Thick and long. Mrs. Jenkins's wedding ring flashed as her fingers gripped her large and soft tits. She stared down at the cock, oblivious to my presence. I stood stunned. Rooted in place. This couldn't be happening.

"Mmm, going to splatter your face with all my jizz," cooed Ava. "Then I'm going to lick you clean." Her green eyes never left me. She pursed her lips. She wanted me to join her.

A powerful surge of lust rippled out of my pussy. A cold fear seized me as I soaked my panties. I bolted from the room and ran down the empty hallway in a panic. What was going on? What was up with Ava Heart?

~~*~~

Ava Heart – The Futa-Succubus Shamshiel

I smiled as cute and sexy Eloise White fled the room. But she had seen my cock. Witnessed it in all its glory. I had felt the virgin thinking about me all day yesterday. I knew she dreamed about me fucking Mrs. Jenkins last night, pounding her pussy while her husband watched.

I loved cuckolding men. It was such a treat seeing them witness the lust their women had for my superior dick. My big, throbbing clit-dick. I loved being free of the Black Earth. I savored being in this world of colors and passions and sensations.

I would never go back. Not if I could help it. This world was a paradise for a futa-succubus.

"Mmm, cum all over my face," begged Mrs. Jenkins as she worked her tits up and down my futa-cock, stimulating it.

My shaft throbbed and ached in between her pillowy breasts. Her silky tits slid up and down faster and faster. She massaged my cock, giving me this aching pleasure. My toes curled in my stiletto heels. My nylons rubbed on the desk's surface as my leg twitched. I leaned back in the chair and savored this wonderful treat.

Warm, soft, silky breasts massaging my cock. A married woman's tits. Her delicious voice begging for my cum.

Heaven.

As her boobs slid up to the pinnacle of my tits and engulfed my spongy crown, my orgasm burst through me.

I came all over her face.

My jizz spurted out of me. Blast after blast of my spunk fired from my cock and painted her features. The married woman moaned, her lust boiling out of her. As she opened her mouth to feast on the spurts of my girl-cum, I devoured the pleasure spilling out of her soul. I feasted on the wonderful treat.

My pussy convulsed, juices gushing out to splash the bottoms of her boobs and her torso. More and more ropy lines of my cum painted her face. They spilled over her. She moaned in delight and swallowed the spunk that had landed in her mouth. I could feel how much she loved it. Savored it.

Being a futa-succubus was such a delight. I reveled in every moment of it. There were so few women armored against me. Virgins were immune to my powers. I had to use other means to enjoy them.

Corrupt them.

But women like Mrs. Jenkins took only a nudge to influence. Then they were on me with ravenous hunger. When I showed up at her house, it wasn't long before she was begging me to fuck her in front of the man she loved. A little kiss on his cheek, and he was jerking his little dick in the corner watching as I made his wife into my whore.

"Oh, god," she moaned, staring up at me with cum dripping on her face. "I love your cock, Ava."

Ava Heart wasn't my real name, that was Shamshiel, but it was a delicious nom de guerre for this world.

"And you look so sexy dripping in my cum," I purred. I stood up and grabbed her hands. I pulled her to her feet, her large tits swaying. Then I turned her and pressed her down on her desk. I licked at my salty girl-cum running down her neck.

She shuddered as my tongue lapped at her flesh. I savored my taste. My seed had such vibrancy in this world. On the other, it had hardly any taste. Nothing did. So bland and boring. A prison for naughty entities.

My tongue slid up to her cheek. I caressed over her face, gathering up more and more of my seed. It piled on the tip of my tongue. I held it there and offered it to her mouth. She sucked the spunk off, her lips sealing about my tongue. As she nursed, my futa-cock throbbed.

I gathered more cum to feed her. I lapped up that wonderful, salty jizz while she quivered. Her hands grabbed my breasts. She squeezed them. A heat washed through me, shooting down to my pussy and then up my clit-dick.

I kissed her again, swapping that jizz as I sank down on her body. The sexy, married teacher groaned into my kiss, our tits squeezing tight. Her hands slid around my sides to my back. She stroked me while my cock throbbed and twitched. They were so ready to bury into her. Just slam into her cunt and fuck her hard.

I kissed her as my dick pressed into her black bush. Found her pussy lips.

She squealed into the kiss. I broke it and hissed, "Let me hear you beg for me to fill that married cunt again."

As I licked the cum off her forehead, she moaned, "Please, please, ram that big futa-dick in me again. Just fill me up. You're *sooooo* much bigger than my husband's little cock. Fuck me."

I slammed my clit-dick to the hilt in her. I buried hard and deep into her flesh. She gasped, her pussy squeezing around my cock. Her cunt clenched tight about me. The heat of her flesh swept over me. It was incredible.

"Yes!" she moaned.

I ached and throbbed as I pumped away at her cunt. I thrust into her with hard strokes. Powerful strokes. I buried my clit-dick into her depths. I churned her up. She groaned, squeezing her cunt down around my futa-dick. Her moans and gasps echoed through the classroom as her married twat swallowed me.

I kissed her again, thrusting more cum into her mouth. Her

busty form trembled beneath me. She squeezed her twat around me. She held me tight. Her cunt squeezed about me in just such a delightful way. I savored it as her tongue danced with mine. I kissed her with passion. Then I lapped up more cum to share with her.

I pumped away at her. I fucked her hard and fast. I pounded her juicy twat as we snowballed my jizz back and forth. Our nipples slid over the other's boobs, sometimes brushing. I savored that moment as I buried my clit-dick into her twat.

"Yes, yes, yes!" she moaned as I licked my girl-cum off her forehead. "Ava! You naughty futa! Oh, Ava, pound my married cunt! I love your dick!"

My pussy grew hotter. Juicier. I thrust into her as my thoughts drifted to Eloise White. Ellie had stopped running and quivered at the other end of the building, her lusts swelling and swelling through her. They were consuming her.

This was perfect. Just what I wanted from her. My dick twitched and throbbed as I pumped away at her teacher's pussy. I couldn't wait to deflower that virgin. I would corrupt her. Transform her into such a wild and kinky slut.

It would be delicious.

"Ava!" Mrs. Jenkins moaned, her hands grabbing my ass. Fingernails bit into my rump. She pulled on me. "I want to cum on this cock again! I love this futa-dick!"

I grinned at her and pumped faster and harder into her pussy. Mrs. Jenkins's desk creaked. I lifted up from her body. My legs slid off the edge of the desk. I grabbed her hips, drawing her rump to the edge to keep her cunt buried around my cock.

I fucked her hard now. Standing up, I drove my clit-dick into her flesh. My breasts heaved while her large mounds jiggled. She squirmed. The married teacher, the sexy MILF, squeezed her twat around my futa-cock, massaging it with her hot flesh.

"Yes, yes, yes!" gasped the teacher, her moans echoing through the room. "That's so good. Oh, yes, yes, that's amazing."

"I knew you'd like that," I groaned, driving my clit-dick into her depths. "I'm going to make you cum so hard."

"Yes!" she whimpered, her face twisting with passion. The look on her face was pure delight to me. I savored every bit of it. I loved every second of driving into her cunt. I buried to the hilt in her again and again.

"Ooh, yes!" she whimpered. Her face twisted in delight. Her eyes squeezed shut. "That's... that's... Oh, that's delicious. That's amazing. I'm going to cum! I'm going to cum so hard on your clit-dick."

"Good," I moaned, driving my dick into her. "I want to feel that pussy spasming around my cock. Let me feel that cunt writhing."

"Yes!" she howled, her back arching.

I buried into her twat's depths. Her silky flesh built that ache at the tip of my dick. The pressure swelled in my ovaries. I drew back, her cunt squeezing around my cock. I savored the friction, feeling it feed my impending orgasm. Pussy juices dribbled down my thighs, reaching the tops of my stockings.

I slammed back into her depths. She gasped. Her lusts surged through her soul again. Then her pussy convulsed around my cock. Her twat writhed in orgasmic bliss. I savored that moment. I reveled in her cunt spasming with such friction around my dick. It was incredible to enjoy.

"Fuck!" I moaned, my head throwing back. "Oh, fuck, yes!"

My futa-cum erupted into her pussy. I fired my jizz into her. I pumped blast after blast of my cum into her cunt's depths. My snatch convulsed as I did. Cream gushed down my thighs as I basted her married pussy with my cum.

"Ava!" the teacher moaned, her body heaving. "Yes, yes, I love your girl-spunk! Flood me! Fill me with all your passion!"

"You're going to be dripping jizz through your lesson!" I gasped, savoring the pleasure of my orgasm.

It was so sweet here in this world of color.

Of freedom.

The bliss surged through my mind. The rapture blazed across my thoughts. This wonderful ecstasy slammed through my mind. I whimpered, spilling blast after blast of cum into her twat. My body trembled through the wild bliss.

"Yes, yes, yes!" I gasped as I unloaded that last spurt of cum into her pussy. "You're going to teach us while your pussy swims with my cum!"

"I will!" she moaned, her lusts feeding my soul what I craved. Her pussy rippled a final time around my cock.

I pulled out of her pussy and stumbled back. I admired my jizz leaking out into her black bush, matting her. I sank down naked on a student's desk, the polished surface cool against my rump. I smiled, my dick throbbing and aching.

My breasts rose and fell. I fanned my face, the heat swelling through me. This was wonderful. Just an absolute delight. I shuddered as I kept wafting cooling air over my blazing features. The heat brimmed throughout my body. My clit-dick throbbed and twitched. Then I shrunk my dick. My cock dwindled back into a little clit.

Fucking her was such a treat.

With a thought, I clothed myself while Mrs. Jenkins struggled to sit up. Her hair was still in her bun, but a few strands had escaped to dance down around her flushed cheeks. "Are you already dressed? Huh, I must have been really out of it."

"Mmm, and you should get dressed. Your first students will be arriving."

She gasped and then hopped off, those big tits jiggling. Some of my cum ran down her thighs. I shuddered as she searched around for her panties. I held them up, dangling the wispy, black pair from my pointer finger. Then I shoved them down the front of my belly shirt and between my breasts.

"You naughty futa," she moaned and then drew on her pencil skirt, her tits swaying.

"I left you your bra," I said with playful delight.

Mrs. Jenkins had barely managed to get dressed when the students started filtering in. The boys grinned at me. A few of them had no idea that I had already fucked their girlfriends or, at least, the girls they had the hots for. I felt that itch in me, savoring it. Jennifer and Scarlett burst in together, the pair wreathed in lesbian lust. They had spent the night together. I bet their lips were dewy with each other's cream.

They both took seats on either side of me and darted in to plant kisses on my mouth. The boys all groaned, salivating even more as

43

they realized two of the hottest girls had a thing for me. I preened, loving their attention even if I had *zero* interest in them.

I mean, boys didn't have boobs or pussies. Such a waste.

Eloise White slunk in last. The blonde girl dressed in clothes that didn't show off her body. Jeans that didn't hug her thighs and rump, a t-shirt at least one size too big for her, hiding any evidence of those small breasts of hers. Her glasses shifted on her nose, her blonde hair swaying about her shoulders. She didn't even look at me as she rushed over to her boyfriend.

She kissed him. I could feel how deliberate it was. Defiant. She was fighting the desires I stirred in her. She struggled against her own wants. That made this exquisite. The more she fought, the greater her surrender would be.

She couldn't resist me forever. Right?

Eloise glanced at me and then jerked her gaze away. She turned to her boyfriend, focusing on him, trying to find that lust for him. She had made a decision. She would go all the way with him. I frowned at that. I had to be careful. If she went to him for relief, she wouldn't be a virgin any longer.

And where was the fun in that?

~~*~~

Eloise "Ellie" White

"Your friends were kissing Ava before you walked in," Shane said to me. "What's up with that?"

"They've gone lesbian," I muttered. I glanced at him. "Not that I would. I'm your girl." I put my hands on his. "I can't wait for Friday and our date."

He grinned. "That's good to hear, babe." He studied me. "You okay?"

"Just been weird," I said. I felt Ava watching me. Somehow, she had set me up. She had *arranged* for me to walk in on her getting a titty job from our teacher. I couldn't believe Mrs. Jenkins would do that. She was married. A teacher. Not some eighteen-year-old coed. She should know better.

I darted in and kissed Shane on the mouth. His lips felt so strong and masculine. Here was the solution to the heat in my nethers. Friday night would be amazing. I just needed to do it. That was the key. Then I wouldn't think about her. Things would be right and proper.

As Mrs. Jenkins taught, walking back and forth in a tight cardigan she wore half-unbuttoned today, I couldn't help but remember those big boobs sliding up and down Ava's girl-cock. That had really happened. She did have a cock she hid beneath that skirt. A big one.

Fleshy and long and so big those large tits of Mrs. Jenkins couldn't cover all of it.

I squirmed through English and gave Shane one hot kiss before we parted. I left him grinning like a little boy. I had never done that before, but I was just so hot. My body brimmed with this heat that had to escape me. Somehow.

I was wondering if I should start bringing a maxi-pad pantyliner like I would wear during my period. By the end of my second class, my panties were soaked through and growing uncomfortable. I couldn't focus. Ava, Ava, Ava.

That annoying girl filled my mind.

I had lunch with Shane. Jennifer and Scarlett were having theirs with Ava. I couldn't help but glance at them as they laughed and giggled and shared french fries in a seductive manner before the trio stood up and headed to the bathroom.

I knew why.

"I still can't believe Jennifer went gay," Shane said as he watched the three heading to the little girls' room in such an obvious manner. It was clear what they were up to. "I mean, Scarlett, I get. I've heard rumors about her."

"Yeah," I nodded. "But not my best friend. I don't get it. This Ava girl..."

"I hear she's hitting on every girl in school." He shook his head. "She's like a lesbian Casanova or something."

I nodded.

He then pulled me onto his lap. I gasped and then smiled at him. Sitting on him was so different. His strong arms went around me. He kissed me. If he took me to the restroom or somewhere else, in that moment, I would let him go all the way with me. I was so hot. So on fire. So needing to be relieved as I kissed him. I felt his hardon beneath my rump.

But he didn't. Maybe he wasn't as bold as Ava. Maybe he thought I'd say no. I was too chicken to admit to acknowledging that I had these desires. I didn't want him to think I was a slut or anything.

"Love you," I told Shane when we broke for our afternoon classes.

"Love you, babe." His hands slid down. "Friday night. I'm going to rock your world."

I giggled. "I can't wait."

The moment I was away from him, Ava slammed back into my mind. Shane was a buffer. It should be him my thoughts lingered on, but that annoying redhead filled my imagination. My dreams echoed in my mind. My pussy grew wetter and wetter. I wished I brought a change of panties. I couldn't wait to get home.

Finally, my last class ended. I saw Shane for one last smooch with my hunky boyfriend then he was off to his job. He worked part-time at a bowling alley. Jennifer told me she was going home with Kimberly to "study."

I didn't know who Kimberly was, but it was clear from how they were holding hands, they didn't plan on doing much studying from the textbooks. As they walked away, I heard Kimberly mention Ava's name.

"Mmm, she was a good fuck," purred from behind me.

I gasped and whirled to see Ava lounging at the entrance to the school. "Kimberly, I mean. I left a nice load of cum in her pussy for Jennifer to enjoy."

"You're disgusting," I hissed, whirled, and marched away.

I heard her heels clicking behind me. There was no mistaking it. She even *sounded* like she strutted with a sensual sway. I didn't look behind me, my body bristling with anger. Ava was ruining everything about my school. Twisting every girl and woman. It was nasty. Sordid. I couldn't believe she would do something so foul. It made me want to screech.

I heard her catching up with me. So I walked faster, leaving the school grounds and heading towards my home. I shifted my purse and backpack, my feet taking long, quick strides. My heart beat faster. My breathing quickened from the increased exertion.

CLICK! CLICK! CLICK! CLICK!

The sounds of her heels followed me. Kept up with me.

I passed people on the street. The men were looking past me to stare at Ava. Her big tits must be bouncing just the way guys liked. Her nipples would be poking hard against her blouse. She exuded sensuality.

Then Ava was beside me. As fast as I walked, she kept up in those stiletto heels, her nylons whisking as her thighs rubbed past each other. I glared at her. She smiled back, her lips plump and crimson. Her green eyes smoldered.

"What do you want?" I demanded.

"I want you," she answered. "I thought I made that perfectly clear."

"Well, you can't have me."

"That's why I'm seducing you." She gave a throaty laugh. "Mmm, I can seduce any woman."

"No, you can't," I growled and turned onto the path that led through the park. A guy, jogging with his dog on a leash, passed us by.

"Sure I can." Ava swept her arms out at the park. "Choose a woman here, any woman, and I'll seduce her. I'll fuck her right here, right now."

"What?" I gasped, my cheeks burning. "I'm not going to do that."

"If you don't, I'll seduce your step-mother," the wicked thing said.

Anger boiled through me. "You're a filthy, disgusting worm! I can't believe you. My step-mother? She loves my father!"

"What does that have to do with her gasping and moaning on my big futa-dick?" she asked. "Choose a woman."

"I will not," I hissed.

Ahead, a blonde jogger approached. She wore a sports bra that cradled a pair of large tits. They bounced up and down, heaving as she ran. Flashes of Mrs. Jenkins's boobs working up and down Ava's cock flooded my mind. This heat sparked through me. I swallowed, watching the woman's breasts as she came closer and closer.

"Her, huh?" Ava purred. "You like the busty women, don't you? I wonder why."

"I am not picking anyone," I hissed. "I'm not playing your game. And I don't like big boobs."

"Liar." She bumped her hip into my mine. "You're practically drooling over the joggers. You want to see them. Don't worry. You will."

Ava marched ahead, heading straight for the jogger. She was a woman in her late twenties, her blonde hair pulled back into a ponytail. She planted her hands on her hips as she sucked in breaths, a gleam of sweat dripping down her cleavage and vanishing between those big boobs.

They were as large as my step-mom's. As Mrs. Jenkins's or Ava's. My cheeks burned.

Ava started talking to the jogger. She pressed up against her and whispered in her ear. The jogger shuddered. She said something back to Ava. What were they talking about? This strange, nervous writhe rippled through my stomach.

"Really?" the woman's lips seemed to say.

Ava nodded.

Then, to my shock, the blonde jogger pulled up her sports bra and flashed her big tits at me. They spilled out, soft and plump. I gaped at the creamy smoothness of her skin on display, nipples dusky-pink and fat, thrusting erect from wide areolas. Ava cupped those tits, hefting them. Then they headed off towards the bushes.

"No way," I groaned beneath my breath. I couldn't believe this was happening. I stood rooted in place as Ava led the stranger into the bushes by her nipples. She was pulling her along, twisting the woman's nubs. This was unreal.

I swallowed. They went deeper into the brush and vanished from my sight. I looked around, my face on fire. I should flee. Run away. I swallowed and couldn't help myself. My hot pussy drove me forward. I stepped off the grass and headed into the brush.

~~*~~

Ava Heart – The Futa-Succubus Shamshiel

"Let me see that cock," moaned the jogger as she fell to her knees. "I flashed her just like you asked."

I smiled. Eloise watched. I could feel her eyes as she pressed against a tree. She could see the jogger pushing up my tight skirt. I wore a pair of wispy, black panties. They were a little big for me, Mrs. Jenkins had a plumper ass, but then the jogger ripped them down.

"Where's your cock?" she moaned.

"Why, right here," I purred, knowing Eloise would see just how special I was. I could feel her confused lust. She was wondering the same thing.

My clit swelled. It grew thick and long. It thrust out from the folds of my pussy. The jogger moaned. Eloise gasped. Her lusts quivered as she witnessed me growing to my full prowess. My pussy clenched, and a naughty heat rushed through me.

Then the jogger engulfed the tip of my girl-dick before I'd even reached my full girth. She sucked with hunger. I seized her blonde ponytail and savored her hunger. I loved how she sucked hard on my cock as it grew larger in her mouth. Her tongue danced around the spongy crown.

She sucked with such hunger. She bobbed her head, working her mouth up and down my girl-dick. It was incredible. I shuddered, my pussy clenching. The heat swelled and swelled in me. My heart raced.

"That's it," I groaned. "Mmm, that's the girl-dick I promised you. Yummy, right?"

The jogger moaned around my cock.

"You're going to drink all my cum, aren't you?"

She groaned again, her blue eyes fluttering. I gripped her

blonde hair, savoring the virgin watching me. I felt Eloise's hot eyes on me. She wasn't running now. Oh, no, now she was watching it all. Her lusts were devouring her bit by bit.

The jogger made such obscene sounds as she sucked. She blew me with hunger. Her tongue danced around my girl-dick. She sucked with wild, aching need. Her flushed cheeks hollowed as she enjoyed my cock. She worked her mouth up and down my dick. She brought me closer and closer to erupting with every moment.

My pussy juices ran down my thighs. I grabbed my belly shirt and popped it off, revealing my bra. The black fabric cupped my breasts but left my nipples exposed. They thrust out hard and pink, fat and begging to be played with.

I grabbed the jogger's ponytail as she stared up at my tits. Her blue eyes smoldered with such excitement. She sucked with hunger, bobbing her head. She took me to the back of her throat and then sucked the entire way back up.

"Yes!" I groaned, her enthusiasm driving me to my orgasm fast. "You're making my ovaries quake. I have so much futa-cum to fire into your mouth."

She nursed harder. Her tongue danced around the crown. The ache swelled. That explosive itch built and built at the tip of my clit-dick. It had to burst out of me. I threw back my head as she sucked hard.

I erupted.

My cum fired hot and fast into her mouth. I pumped over and over into her. This incredible bliss shot through my body. I gasped, my pussy juices gushing down my thighs as I bathed her mouth with my spunk.

"Yes, yes, swallow it all!" I moaned, feeling the aching lust from Eloise. "Gulp down every drop. Don't waste any of my futa-cum. Empty rapture, yes!"

The jogger squealed and swallowed.

She sucked with hunger. She wasn't wasting a drop. Oh, no, she guzzled down my spunk flooding out of my futa-dick. The pleasure hammered my mind. It slammed into my thoughts and left them reeling from the pleasure. I savored it. My thoughts drank it in. Such wonderful ecstasy to enjoy.

"Yes, yes, yes!" I gasped as I pumped the last of it in her. She sucked a few more times, nursing to get the last drops of my cum. "Colorless passion, you naughty slut, that was good."

Her lips popped off my cock. "What are you?"

"A futa," I moaned. "A dickgirl futanari. Now stand up, turn around, and grab that tree. I am fucking you hard."

"Yes!" she moaned and did just that. She spun around, her naked tits bouncing together. She wore spandex jogging shorts that hugged her toned rump. She had such a gorgeous shape to it. Firm.

I thrust my thumbs into the waistband of her shorts, and caught her panties, too. I yanked both of them off her ass, her flesh paler than the rest of her body. My dick throbbed as I smelled her spicy juices. She groaned, grabbing the tree and bending over, pressing that rump at me.

"Fuck me!" she moaned.

Eloise quivered. I felt this envious lust flow through the virgin followed by a wash of shame. She had such a tight grip on her sexuality, frightened by it. She needed to let go. I would pry those fingers off her virginity and tear it away from her. Pluck her cherry with my cock.

I grabbed my dick and slid the tip down the jogger's firm rump. I loved Eloise's eyes watching me as my futa-dick moved down to nuzzle into the jogger's juicy bush. Her cream ran. I pressed up into her folds, found the woman's cuntlips.

Thrust.

"Fuck!" the jogger moaned as her pussy stretched and stretched to take my cock slamming into her depths. "You're fucking huge, Futa!"

My crotch smacked into her firm rump. My tits heaved in my bra. "And you're going to cum hard on my dick. Best cock ever, isn't it?"

"Yes!" she moaned. "Futa, yes, yes, fuck me!"

I slid my hands around her body and found those large and soft tits of hers. I kneaded them as I drew back my hips. Her cunt clenched around my futa-dick. The pleasure shot through me. My moans echoed through the grove.

Eloise whimpered.

I slammed back into the jogger's cunt. She gasped, her breasts jiggling in my hand. My big boobs bounced. I drove my cock over and over into the jogger, my crotch smacking into her rump. Her twat squeezed around me and held me tight.

It was so exciting being watched by the virgin as I pounded the stranger. Her hands gripped the tree. The slender birch swayed, branches rustling over our heads as I plowed hard into the woman. I fed on the jogger's lusts. I devoured them as I churned up her pussy.

Sucking my cock had already primed her cunt. Now my futa-dick drilling into her had her groaning. She clenched down around me. She held me tight as I drove hard and fast into her. I buried into her pussy's depths. I slammed to the hilt in her.

As I drew back, she gasped. Came.

"Oh, my fucking god!" howled the jogger as her pussy went wild about my retracting clit-dick. Her flesh massaged the tip. Pleasure shot through me. "This cock! Futa, your cock is the fucking best!"

"I know!" I groaned and slammed into her. "I told you!"

"You did!" she howled, her pussy writhing around my cock.

I savored the pleasure as I pumped away at her convulsing cunt. Eloise quivered, the words sending her reeling. She clutched her own tree with the same fierceness that the jogger gripped the birch. My pleasure swelled, my ovaries getting tight with another load of futa-cum to erupt.

I slammed hard into her twat, reveling in her flesh bringing me closer and closer to erupting. Pussy cream ran down my thighs. My cunt brimmed with orgasmic heat. Her snatch massaged me. Sucked at me.

"Cum in me!" she howled. "Flood me!"

"Yes!" I moaned, responding to her. I devoured her lust, feasting on her, and buried into the heaven of her twat.

My cum fired hot and hard into her pussy. My jizz pumped into her hot flesh. Her cunt spasmed harder. Another orgasm burst through her. She gasped, milking me. The tree creaked as she trembled through her bliss.

Pussy juices spilled down my thighs. The dual pleasure wreathed my mind. Ecstasy fired from my cock and rapture flooded from my cunt. Stars blazed across my mind. My head tossed back and forth. The ecstasy surged through me. That colorful bliss.

"Empty rapture!" I howled as I flooded her with my spunk.

I spurted the last jet of cum into the jogger's pussy. She milked me dry. I loved it. Juices ran down my thighs to the tops of my stockings. I quivered there, my futa-dick twitching in her delicious twat. My hands kneaded her tits.

"That was incredible!" the woman groaned.

I turned my head and glanced at the spying virgin for the first time. I winked at her.

She gasped and fled at a dead run. I laughed as she sought to flee her desires. But how could she outrun that wild itch in her pussy? She couldn't. She was fooling herself if she thought that was possible.

"What are you?" the jogger moaned.

"Hungry," I said, squeezing her tits. "Ever licked cum out of a girl's asshole before?"

She shook her head.

"Want to?"

She nodded.

I would let that naughty girl stew again. I still had a little time before her date with Shane. I could let her get so desperate for me that she would surrender. I couldn't wait to corrupt her utterly. I loved being a futa-succubus.

I would never return to the Black Earth. I would make this passionate world my home.

To be continued...

Tantalizing Ellie's Innocent Desires

Corrupted by the Futa Succubus 3

by

Reed James

Tantalizing Ellie's Innocent Desires

Eloise "Ellie" White

Ava Heart shuddered as she came in the jogger's pussy.

Then she glanced over at me, smiling with such triumph as her impossible clit-dick pumped jizz into the stranger's pussy. The busty redhead's green eyes sparkled in delight as they seemed to say, "You're next."

A wave of fiery heat washed out of my virgin pussy for her. For this insane girl who'd shown up at my college yesterday. She'd seduced my best friend, another friend, and my teacher. She kept promising I would beg for her futa-cock to take my cherry even though I liked guys.

I liked my boyfriend, Shane!

Everywhere I went, she showed up. She was obsessed with me. I didn't get it. How could her clit turn into a dick? How could she walk up to that busty jogger, whisper in the stranger's ear, and then the pair were heading off to have sex in the park. Sure, they were in some bushes, but they could be found by anyone. They hadn't exactly been quiet.

Now Ava arched an eyebrow in invitation.

I gasped and fled.

I had to get out of here before I joined them. Before that

disgusting and beautiful freak had me begging to suck her girl-dick and to take my cherry. I was giving that to Shane on Friday. On our date. I had to. I needed it. Ava was driving me insane with horniness.

I burst out of the bushes and broke into a full run, my schoolbag bouncing on my back. My purse swung off my arm. I raced down the path through the center of the park, my blonde hair streaming behind me. My glasses slipped down my face.

My pussy throbbed. My sodden panties clung to my pussy lips. They massaged me. Teased me. Heat washed through me. I whimpered as I ran faster and faster. I passed joggers and walkers. I burst out on the other side of the park and went left. I had to get home. Away from Ava Heart and her impossible girl-cock.

Her beautiful figure. Her perky and huge tits. Her perfect appearance. That naughty smile. The way girls melted about her and sang her praises. I kept running into her having sex. With my friend Scarlett. With my teacher, Mrs. Jenkins. Ava threatened to seduce my step-mother if I hadn't picked a random woman at the park to seduce.

I couldn't let her find my home.

I paused at the entrance to my street. I threw a look behind me, panting for breath. Sweat dripped down my face. I studied the empty sidewalk. No one followed me. No redheaded seductress, no gorgeous freak with a clit that turned into a cock. She was still with that jogger.

I darted across the street and ran down the middle of the cul-de-sac I lived on. Four houses down, I cut over to the fifth one on my left, skirting between two evergreen bushes before racing across the lawn to the porch. I leaped up the two stairs to the wooden decking and then hit the door. I scrambled to grab the handle. My step-mother stayed at home. It was unlocked. I burst inside and closed the door behind me.

I panted. Safe.

But those images of Ava fucking the jogger burned in my mind. My aching pussy clenched. My virgin flesh screamed for attention. I hadn't masturbated despite all the horniness Ava sparked in me. I'd been afraid of what I'd think about.

I had to now. I couldn't fight this any longer.

"Ellie, honey, that you?" my step-mom called.

"Yes!" I gasped and raced up the stairs.

"How was your day?"

"Uh..." I pounded up the steps. "Busy. I have homework."

"Okay. But you don't need to run in the house."

I reached the second floor and darted right. I crashed through my bedroom door and then flung it closed. I unslung my purse and bag, dropping them in the middle of my room. I ripped off my t-shirt, exposing my small breasts in my gray bra. I didn't undo the fastener, I just peeled it off over my head. I kicked off my shoes while attacking the fastener of my jeans. I ripped them down.

The tangy scent of my pussy filled the air. I groaned at the naughty aroma.

"How wet am I?" I panted, the scent stronger than I ever could recall.

I hooked my wet panties with my pointer fingers. I peeled them from my blonde bush. My juices had soaked up to the seat of my panties, my lower butt-cheeks feeling wet. The sodden cloth clung to my thighs, smearing pussy cream down my legs. I worked my underwear off and then held them up before me.

I couldn't believe how drenched they were. They were heavy with my excitement.

"What did you do to me, Ava?" I whimpered.

It wasn't natural. The way she seduced women. How she turned me on. I liked boys—Shane!—not girls. Not Ava, but her large breasts, so perky despite their size, filled my mind. Her fiery hair swayed about that sensual face. Lips plump. Kissable. Green eyes vibrant and seductive. Her legs long, her rump bubbly, and her stomach flat. She was perfect.

I threw myself on my bed and grabbed my pillow. I thrust it between my thighs, pushing it tight against my pussy. I shuddered as I squeezed my legs tight about it. I lay on my side, bit my lower lip, and humped against it.

I whimpered as the fabric rubbed on my virgin pussy lips.

I closed my eyes, my glasses shifting on my face, as I humped my pillow. My legs flexed and my hips thrust. I slid my virgin twat across the fabric, soaking it in my tangy passion. Pleasure rippled through my body. My clit throbbed, drinking in the friction. Sparks flared.

Ava filled my mind. I imagined her standing over my bed, her hand stroking her cock. She watched me with hunger. With need. Her clit-dick thrust from the shaved folds of her pussy, a gold ring gleaming on the tip. A piercing.

"*You know you want my girl-cock,*" she purred in my thoughts.

"No," I whimpered aloud, grinding my cunt against my pillow. My pussy clenched, aching deep in me to be filled. To have my cherry popped. "I don't."

"*Yes, you do,*" Ava cooed. "*You want it so badly. Look at you. Look what you're doing.*"

I squeezed my eyes shut tighter as if I could block out the image of the fiery redhead. My bed creaked as I frantically ground my twat against my pillow. My left hand squeezed my small tit. Firm. Barely a handful. I massaged it. My fingers dug into it, working against the flesh. I dug into it, groaning as I did.

I found my nipple, twisted it. I tweaked it and groaned. The pleasure surged through me. I shuddered, whimpering and moaning. I squirmed on the bed, panting. The heat swept through my body. I rubbed my face into my other pillow.

"*You want me so badly,*" Ava purred. In my fantasy, she stroked my cheek. Her futa-cock bobbed before me. "*Just open your mouth wide and suck.*"

I shook my head, whimpering. My pleasure rippled through my body.

"*If you don't, I'll seduce your step-mother,*" she taunted. Her finger reached my lip. "*Just open wide.*"

I did. I opened my mouth wide. I imagined her cock sliding past my lips. It would be so warm. What would it taste like? I thrust three of my fingers into my mouth. They had a salty flavor to them. I sucked on them, nursing with hunger as my orgasm grew and grew.

"*That's it,*" gasped Ava. "*You're going to get all my cum. You're going to drink it all down, aren't you?*"

I squealed about my fingers. I nursed with such hunger on

them. I shuddered, my tongue dancing around them. My thighs squeezed about the pillow. My virgin pussy felt so alive as I ground the silky fabric against my hot flesh. Feverish heat flowed through me. My orgasm built and built.

I sucked harder around my fingers. I made these sloppy, obscene sounds. I imagined it was Ava's cock. I swirled my tongue. I pleasured the redhead. She moaned above me. Her large tits heaving as I gave her pleasure.

"I'm going to cum!" she moaned.

I humped my pussy harder on my clit.

"I'm going to flood your mouth with my girl-jizz!"

I whimpered about my fingers.

"Yes!" she howled, and I imagined her cum pumping into my mouth. What would it taste like? I didn't know. But I sucked hard as my clit throbbed. Sparks flared.

I orgasmed.

I bucked on my bed. My virgin pussy spasmed. I felt my untouched flesh convulsing. Waves of bliss swept through my body. I gasped and whimpered, sucking and nursing on my fingers, swallowing the imaginary cum.

"That's it, Ellie! Swallow all my spunk, you dirty girl!"

I was a dirty girl for imagining this. My pussy convulsed harder. The pleasure drowned my mind. I squealed around my fingers. My bed creaked beneath me. I trembled, my juices gushing out and soaking my pillow. My thighs hugged it tight, pinning it against my climaxing pussy.

Ava laughed in my mind, mocking my surrender. She smiled down at me in triumph as I hit the peak of my pleasure. I quivered there and then I groaned into guilty bliss. I ripped my fingers from my mouth and opened my eyes.

No Ava.

I groaned and rolled over on my back, my thighs relaxing. The pillow felt so sticky. I hauled it out from between my legs and saw it stained in my pussy cream. I had soaked the maroon pillow casing. A large wet spot radiated out from where I pinned it to my hot flesh.

"What is wrong with me?" I panted, flinging it on the floor. I stared up at the ceiling, shame at the pleasure wreathing my body.

At how much I wanted to suck Ava's cock. To let her do even more things to me.

I couldn't get her out of my mind for the rest of the evening. I kept glancing at my step-mother through dinner. She sat by Dad, the pair chatting. She would never cheat on my father. They had a great relationship. There was no way Ava could seduce her. But flashes of it kept intruding in my mind.

I fled to my bedroom and spent a night of temptation. My wet pillow lay on the floor, begging me to grab it. I wasn't wearing panties, my pussy too wet. I would just soak them. I tossed and turned all night long.

I felt so exhausted the next morning. I put a maxi-pad liner on my panties the next morning to keep them from being a sodden mess. I packed away spare absorbent pads in my purse like it was that time of the month. I dressed in a baggy shirt and loose jeans. I didn't dress to show off my body.

Dread filled me the closer I came to school. I couldn't bring myself to cut through the park like I normally did. I was afraid I'd see the jogger or the place where they'd fucked, and it set me off in a fit of lust. Ava never left my thoughts. She was in them. Lurking. Stroking her pierced futa-cock. A naughty grin on her lips. Her green eyes sparkling.

The pit in my stomach churned and swelled. My feet dragged as I came closer and closer to the college. I spotted my best friend, Jennifer, walking into the school with her arm hooked around a Hispanic girl I didn't know. They looked close. Intimate.

Had Jennifer really become a lesbian? On Monday, she had boldly declared that girls did nothing for her then Ava had whispered in her ear and the pair had gone to the bathroom to fuck. Now Jennifer stared at me like she wanted to lick my pussy.

The weight grew and grew in my stomach the closer and closer I came to my English class. Ava would be in there. So would Mrs. Jenkins, Scarlett, and Jennifer. They were all Ava's lovers now. I couldn't face that.

I fled to the college's library in terror.

I had never, ever skipped out on a class in my life. I just couldn't face it. I buried my face in my math textbook and did the schoolwork I was supposed to do last night but couldn't focus on it. I struggled through the problems, Ava dancing in my mind.

I headed to my next two classes—I only had Ava in that first one—and then came lunch. I feared Ava could spring out at me at any moment. I found my boyfriend, Shane, and flew to him. I threw my arms around his chest. He grunted in surprise. I leaned up and kissed him.

It was the hungriest kiss I'd ever given him. I felt the strength of him. His rough stubble. His hard body. He was in great shape. There was nothing soft about him. Nothing feminine. He was the opposite of Ava. This was what I should be craving.

Not plump lips and big boobs and juicy pussy with a clit that turned into a big dick.

"Hello," Shane said, sounding half-dazed. "That was... unexpected."

"I'm just so excited for Friday," I said, holding tight to him. If I didn't let him go, he could be my anchor against Ava.

"Me, too," he said, grinning. His hands grabbed my lower back. "I didn't think you were here today. Missed you in English."

"I overslept," I lied. "Forgot to set my alarm."

"Not like you," he said. "You okay?"

"Fine."

I ate lunch with him. I spotted Ava flitting around the cafeteria, hitting on girls. They were all so excited around her. How did she do that? Why was she so attractive? I was glad I had that pantyliner in place because I was wet. I could feel it absorbing my juices.

Ava didn't come anywhere near me. She didn't even look at me. Was she ignoring me now? I kept glancing at her. Kept waiting for her to give me a look. A sultry smile. It never came, and I hated how that angered me. I felt... jealous of the attention she lavished on the other girls.

Where were her smoky looks and seductive smiles for me? Her breathy declarations that I would beg for her cock?

I couldn't believe I was getting jealous. This was insane. What had this girl done to me?

I threw myself into my class for the afternoon half of my day. If Ava was ignoring me, then I should be glad about it. I met up with

Shane once classes were done, and he gave me a ride home. We made out in his car. I kissed him with such hunger in the driveway, my tongue dancing with him. This feverish heat swept through me.

I would have done it with him if he asked. Instead, he broke the kiss and groaned, "I have to get to work."

I pouted. "Do you?"

"Sorry." He leaned back and looked frustrated himself. "You've changed, Ellie. I like it."

I blushed. I had just become so horny because of Ava. It was her my body wanted. Not Shane. It was so messed up. "I'm just... ready."

He grinned. "Good. Tomorrow night..."

I climbed out of his car and shivered. I headed up to my house and inside. My step-mom called a greeting. I shouted back on my rush upstairs. I had to masturbate again. I had to get naked and rub that pillow between my thighs.

The doorbell rang just as I reached the second floor. The chimes echoed through the house. I ignored it. I burst into my room and unslung my backpack and purse. I ripped off my t-shirt and reached behind me to undo the fastener of the white bra I wore.

"Ellie, honey, your friend's here," my step-mom called down.

Friend? Was it Jennifer? I groaned and then pulled my blouse back on. I wanted to masturbate so hard. I headed down the stairs, hearing talking in the living room. I hit the bottom of the stairs, rounded them, and entered the living room.

"Hey, Jen..." My words trailed off.

Ava Heart stood in my living room. Shock slammed into me. My step-mom smiled and then headed off, her blonde hair sweeping around her shoulders. She vanished into the kitchen, leaving me alone with just Ava. I blinked my eyes. This had to be a dream. A nightmare.

"What are you doing here?" I hissed, marching forward.

"Why, I'm here to seduce your step-mother," she answered, giving me a naughty smile.

"What?" I gasped. "I choose the jogger."

"No, you didn't," said Ava. "You looked at the jogger. You ogled her big breasts, but... What were your exact words? Yes, *I am not picking anyone. I'm not playing your game. And I don't like big boobs.'* See, you didn't play. I was just horny. But now you have to pay up."

"Here's that diet coke," my step-mom said, her voice a touch breathy. Her cheeks a touch pink. She handed the can to my friend then held out one for me. "Grabbed you one, too, Ellie."

I took it, numb. This couldn't be happening. Not my stepmother. There was no way she could succumb, but her green eyes were staring at Ava. The redhead wore her usual outfit, a tight miniskirt that barely covered her rump, her legs clad in thigh-high stockings. The waistband of a bright-red thong rode her hips. A tight belly shirt clung to her large breasts. They were thrusting out, lifted by her bra into jiggling perfection. The outline of her nipples was clear as day.

"You have such a daring style," said step-my mom. "I could never have worn something like that even when I was your age."

Ava laughed in a playful fashion. "Don't sell yourself short, Mrs. White. You look great. You exercise, right?"

"I have to stay fit," she said. "Can't let my body balloon."

"Mmm, and it's paying off," purred Ava.

My step-mom laughed like a college girl, her breasts jiggling in the faded t-shirt she wore. It went with the sweatpants she wore. Her "stay-at-home" comfortable clothes. "You're just being nice."

"No, no, you are looking great, Mrs. White. I bet you could wear this outfit and be sexy as fuck."

My step-mom's cheeks went bright red. "You think so."

I grabbed Ava's hand and shuddered at the heat bursting through me. I needed to drag her away from my mom. "We have to go. We're, uh, going to the mall for shopping."

My pussy clenched as I tugged her. My nipples throbbed. If I took her out of my house, if I led her away for my step-mom, Ava would do things to me. I knew it. But I couldn't let her seduce my step-mom. That wasn't right.

"Nonsense," Ava said, "we have some time."

"But..." I gave another tug. I had to save my step-mom from her.

"I bet beneath all those baggy sweatpants and that t-shirt, you have a rocking bod, Mrs. White."

My step-mother gave a pleased giggle while waving her hand as if that were ridiculous.

"No, no, you could be a model." Ava reached out and squeezed my step-mom's breasts right through her t-shirt. I gaped and then waited for my step-mom to object.

She didn't.

"See, you have great tits."

"Stop that!" I gasped and ripped Ava's hands away.

"Listen, your mom is hot," the redhead purred. "Like model hot."

"You really think I could be a model?" My step-mother's green eyes held a feverish heat. This couldn't be happening. I had to stop this nightmare.

"Why don't you put on some of that sexy lingerie I know you have in your panty drawer and show it off," Ava said. "Gives us a fashion show before we go shopping. Let's see that body! I bet you're gorgeous!"

"Okay!" My step-mom giggled. "This will be so much fun."

"Mom!" I gasped as she whirled around and darted for the stairs. "You can't do that."

"Oh, it's just some harmless modeling," she said. "Haven't you and your friends done that, Ellie?"

"Just harmless," Ava cooed, her eyes full of naughty hunger.

"What are you doing?" I groaned.

"Seducing your step-mother. I told you that." Ava licked her lips. "She's going to be so gorgeous. You're going to listen to her scream her head off as I fuck her with my big clit-dick. I hope you masturbate like you did when you got home yesterday."

How could she know that? "What are you?"

"Your future." She stroked my face. Heat blossomed across my cheek that jolted down to my pussy and electrified it. I stepped back, my nipples puckering hard. My absorbent pad soaked up more juices. I wanted to throw myself at her. I swallowed against this heat.

My step-mom burst into the living room wearing a purple, silk robe. It was open to show off a lacy bra that barely hid her nipples and a matching pair of wispy panties, her blonde bush bleeding through it. She stepped up before Ava.

"Oh, yes!" Ava whooped. She clapped her hands. "Let's see that bod, Mrs. White. You're looking hot. Doesn't she, Eloise?"

"Ellie," I muttered and glanced over at my step-mother.

She did look... attractive. This couldn't be happening. My step-mom struck a pose, hands on her hips, her robe fluttering around her. She had a naughty look on her face, green eyes smoldering. Did she look like this when she was alone with Dad?

I swallowed, struggling to find a way to stop this from happening. I had to think, but all this heat billowing out of my pussy made it so hard. Mom cocked her hips, shifted her thighs, her breasts jiggling in her bra. Then her robe slipped off in a fall of purple to puddle around her feet.

"Ooh, you got those big boobies!" Ava said, giving me a sly look. Yesterday, she implied I liked big breasts because I stared at that blonde jogger.

My step-mother's blonde hair swayed as she did more poses, her big breasts jiggling. She looked so happy as she showed off. Ava clapped her hands, her breasts jiggling in her belly shirt, her tight miniskirt clinging to her thighs.

"Now turn around and show off dat ass!" whooped Ava.

My step-mom did. She turned around and wiggled her hips. She was laughing in delight with a playfulness I had never seen in her. She looked over her shoulder, her green eyes flashing. I pushed up my glasses, shocked by this.

"Now thrust that booty out," moaned Ava. She fell to her knees, her red hair swaying. "Yes, yes, pop that ass."

My step-mom bent over and did a booty shake like she was in a rap video. I couldn't believe it. Her breasts heaved in her bra. How had Ava so effortlessly done this? Mom's wedding ring flashed on her left hand planted on her thigh as she shook her rump at the redhead.

"Oh, Ava," Mom groaned. "This is so much fun. You make me feel so young."

"And sexy?" Ava asked with a coquettish purr.

"Yes!"

"You are sexy, Mrs. White!" Ava's hands grabbed my mom's

panties and hauled them down. My jaw dropped as cloth spilled off my step-mother's rump and then exposing her pussy. My jaw dropped. Blonde curls peeked out between her thighs dripping in juices.

"Ava!" gasped my step-mom in shock.

The futa buried her face into my step-mother's pussy and licked. My jaw dropped as Mom just moaned. She shuddered there, grinding her twat into Ava's licking face. Shock struck me. I stumbled back a step. I couldn't believe this was happening right in front of me.

My mom arched her back. Her breasts jiggled in her bra. She groaned, her blonde hair sweeping about her face. Her hips wiggled. She humped her pussy into Ava's face. The redhead devoured her, licking, lapping, feasting.

"Ava! Ava!" my step-mom groaned.

"M-mom!" I gasped.

"Oh, your friend's tongue feels amazing!" Mom moaned. She glanced at me, her green eyes lidded. "Does she do this to you?"

"N-no!" I gasped.

"It's amazing!"

My step-mother threw back her head and cheated on my father. Right before me, she let Ava devour her. The redhead's hands gripped my mother's rump. She squeezed them as she licked and lapped at my mom's married cunt. I couldn't believe this was happening.

I wanted to ask her about Dad—how she could do this to him? —but no words wanted to rise out of my throat. It was strangled shut by shock. The heat rippled through me. My pussy drenched my absorbent pad. I shuddered, my heart pounding so fast. It pumped molten blood through my veins. My entire body shook.

Mom moaned.

Groaned.

Shuddered.

Ava feasted with hunger. I could hear her own moans and whimpers of delight. Her breasts jiggled in her top as she devoured my step-mother with hunger. Mom's face twisted with passion. Her groans echoed through the living room.

I stood rooted to the spot as my step-mother built to her orgasm. She would cum in front of me, not even caring that I was here. Utterly seduced by Ava. How was this possible? How could any of this be happening?

What was she?

"Oh, yes, yes, Mrs. White!" Ava moaned. "You have such a yummy-tasting twat."

"And you eat it so well!" groaned my step-mom. "I've never had a girl lick me. Ooh, that's good. You're tongue's amazing."

"Are you going to cum?"

"So hard!"

I swallowed. I was about to watch my step-mother cum on Ava's mouth. My hands rubbed at my stomach. My thighs squeezed tight. An aching itch blazed in my virgin pussy. I panted, my fingers wanting to creep lower and lower.

My step-mom's groans grew. Her entire body trembled. She threw back her hair and cried out. Her voice echoed through the living room. It resounded back and forth. I realized she was cumming on Ava's mouth. She trembled through her bliss.

"That's so good!" my step-mom groaned.

"Mmm, just let it all gush out!" purred Ava. "You taste so good."

"Yes!"

I swallowed at the naughty sight before me. The pleasure on my step-mother's face as she trembled through her orgasm, cuckolding my father with Ava. That sexy bitch who had turned my life upside-down.

My pussy clenched. Itched.

Ava pulled her mouth from my step-mother's pussy. Cream dripped down her chin and coated her cheeks. My mother had coated the redhead's face. Ava's tongue flicked out across her gleaming lips, lapping up the juices.

"Oh, Ava, I need to go down on you know!" my step-mom panted. "Need to return the favor." She grabbed Ava's hand and pulled her to the stairs.

"Mom!" I screeched. "What about Dad?"

Mom waved a hand. "Your friend's just being friendly. It would be rude of me *not* to eat her pussy."

"So rude," Ava said with malicious delight and winked at me.

I gasped as they vanished, leaving me trembling, my body on fire. I heard them climbing the stairs, moving across the hallway, opening the door to my parents' bedroom. It closed. The bed creaked. This couldn't be happening.

I attacked the fastener of my jeans, my virgin cunt on fire.

~~*~~

Ava Heart – The Futa-Succubus Shamshiel

I dropped my skirt and then sank down on the bed, my thighs spread wide. I shifted and peeled off my belly shirt. It revealed my breasts clad in a red push-up bra that didn't cover my nipples. Mrs. White groaned at the sight of me, the blonde MILF trembling. Her wedding ring flashed.

She had been so easy to seduce. A few compliments and she became vulnerable to my power. It slid past her fidelity and ignited her lusts. I loved it. My pussy clenched, soaking my thong. My pierced clit throbbed.

"I've never done this before," she moaned as she unhooked her bra. Her large breasts spilled out. They swayed before my face. They were such a delicious thing to look at. A hunger swept through my body.

"You'll be a natural," I said, winking.

She crawled onto the bed, her blonde hair swaying about her body. I felt Eloise masturbating downstairs, consumed by her lust. The virgin's resolve was breaking down by the second. The purity armored her against my direct influence, so I would have to corrupt her the fun way.

I shuddered as Mrs. White's hands slid down my black stockings to my pale flesh. Her wedding ring glinted on her left hand caressing my right thigh. I shuddered as her finger snagged my thong which barely covered anything. Her head leaned down, her green eyes brimming with lust for me. That wild desire to do naughty and kinky things to me.

She yanked my thong to the side, and her mouth nuzzled into my pussy. She licked my cunt. Her tongue fluttered up and down it. I groaned at how delicious that felt. I whimpered, savoring her caressing my pussy lips. I shuddered, my back arching and my breasts jiggling in my bra.

I closed my eyes and savored her tongue sliding up and down my pussy lips. Excitement flowed through the straight, married woman as she ate her first pussy. She licked up and down my twat. She caressed up to my pierced clit, flicking the bud. Pleasure flowed through me as the gold ring twisted through my clit. I groaned in delight, the heat sweeping through my body. I shuddered and squeezed my eyes shut.

"Mrs. White!" I moaned. "Empty rapture!"

"You taste so good," she groaned with feverish passion. "Just the best."

"Mmm, feast on me!"

She did. She fluttered her tongue up and down my pussy. She stimulated me. I grabbed my nipples, so glad to be free of the Black Earth. To dwell in a world of color and passion once more. I shivered, the heat building and building in me.

Her tongue thrust into my pussy. This sexy woman, the married step-mother to that gorgeous virgin rubbing her cunt downstairs, plundered my twat. Her tongue swirled around in my depths, stimulating me.

"Colorless passion, yes!" I moaned, my fingers twisting my nipples. Pleasure shot down to my cunt. I squeezed my pussy down around her tongue. "That's it, Mrs. White!"

"Such a yummy delight," moaned the married MILF. Her eyes stared up at me with feverish heat. She flicked her tongue up to my folds. Found my clit.

I gasped as she sucked on it. She nursed on my pierced clit. It throbbed and ached in her mouth. I arched my back, my large tits jiggling, shifting my nipples around in my grip. I pinched them hard. I tugged on them.

I reveled in them. The pleasure surged through me as she

nursed. Her tongue caressed my aching clit, twisting the piercing threaded through my bud. I bit my lip, trembling, the heat swelling and swelling in me. This was an amazing pleasure to be enjoyed.

"You like nursing on my clit, Mrs. White?" I asked.

She moaned and kept it up.

"Good," I groaned. "Because you're in for a treat. Empty rapture, you're going to love it!"

I let my clit-dick expand. My futa-cock blossomed into her sucking mouth. I shuddered as my bud grew thicker, longer. It expanded against her lips as it reached into her mouth. Her eyes widened as she realized something was happening. She felt it brushing the roof of her mouth. Her jaw had to open wider and wider.

"Yes, yes, that's my clit-dick blossoming!" I moaned, her marital bed creaking beneath me. "Mrs. White, you're going to get fucked by a real cock! A futa's cock!"

She stared at me in awe as she kept nursing. My cock reached the back of her throat, forcing her to lift her head. With every pounding beat of my heart, my futa-dick engorged thicker. Longer. Her lips sealed about it. Her tongue danced, exploring it, shifting the clit-piercing threaded through the spongy crown as it reached its full girth.

"Mrs. White!" I gasped. "Colorless passion, yes! Love my dick. Suck it! Then I'm going to pound your married cunt so hard. I'm going to fuck you like a slut!"

She sucked with hunger on my futa-dick. She nursed on it. My pussy clenched as she did. The heat swept through my body. My breasts jiggled. I twisted my nipples, savoring every moment she sucked on my cock.

The pressure swelled already. I would have such a huge orgasm from her blowjob. Just a detonation of bliss. Bright and colorful pleasure existed in this world. So many women to enjoy. I had been fucking coeds and teachers all week, sliding into so many different cunts and mouths and assholes while thinking about her.

Eloise White...

And now I had her step-mother sucking my dick. The woman who had raised and molded that sexy virgin, caring for Eloise as if she were the MILF's own daughter. It was so hot. So exciting. My futa-cock throbbed in Mrs. White's hungry mouth. Her blonde hair swayed about her face as she bobbed her head. Her green eyes stared up at me with such passion in them.

She worked her mouth up and down it, her hand grabbing the base. She stroked it, awe in her eyes as she pumped her hand up and down it. She groaned, sucking with such wild passion on my cock. It was intense to experience. My toes curled, the pleasure reaching towards the pinnacle of my bliss.

Towards my eruption.

That hungry mouth slid up and down my girl-dick. The MILF sucked with such passion. I groaned, my cunt clenching. I squirmed on her bed. Her tongue caressed around the crown of my cock. She stirred around my clit piercing, twisting it through my cock.

"Colorless passion, that's what I need!" I moaned. "I'm going to dump my cum down your mouth, Mrs. White."

She slid her lips up my cock. They caressed over my crown before she popped her mouth off my futa-dick. "Mmm, give it to me. I want to swallow every drop of your spunk."

"My futa-spunk!" I purred.

"Yes, yes!" she moaned and re-engulfed my cock.

My dick throbbed, her hand pumping up and down it. My pussy clenched. I felt her every suckle in the depths of my cunt. My ovaries responded, brimming with such a huge load of cum to fire into her mouth. I would baste her mouth with all my futa-jizz.

She would gulp it all down.

I squeezed my eyes shut and reveled in every second of her hungry mouth. She nursed on me with such feverish hunger. She sucked and slurped. Her tongue danced around me. It was incredible to feel. I reveled in every second of it. I squeezed my eyes shut, my pussy clenching. The heat swept through my body.

"Yes, yes, yes!" I groaned. "Mrs. White! Empty rapture, I'm going to flood your mouth if you keep sucking that hard."

She winked at me and kept sucking. Kept nursing.

The pressure soared to the tip of my futa-dick. My pussy clenched. Her tongue swept around my girl-dick, brushing my piercing. I gasped. My fingers twisted my nipples. I devoured her lust for my cum pouring out of her soul. It tasted delicious.

I erupted.

My futa-cum fired from my dick and basted her mouth. I pumped my jizz over and over into her. I groaned and bucked, the bliss surging through my body. Stars exploded across my vision. They danced and sparkled. They spilled over my mind. It was incredible.

I groaned, my pussy spasming. Juices gushed out of my twat. They soaked my thighs. The twin delights surged through me. She gulped down my cum while fisting my cock. She worked out every drop of jizz I had.

"Mrs. White, yes!" I moaned, feeling Eloise quivering downstairs.

She nursed the last of my cum out of my futa-dick. My orgasm hit that wonderful peak. I quivered there, eyes fluttering. She kept nursing on me, kept fisting my cock, to get out every drop of spunk I had. I shuddered from the delight of it.

Convinced I was empty, she slid her mouth off my cock, cum and drool running down her chin. "This... How?"

"I'm a futa," I purred. "Mmm, now you want my cock fucking that hot, married cunt, don't you?"

"Yes!" she moaned. "I want that so badly."

"Then kneel and beg for me to fuck you. Let your step-daughter hear you cry out!"

She crawled up onto her hands and knees, her large tits swaying beneath her. "Please, please, fuck my married cunt with your big cock! Your impossible clit-dick!"

A shiver ran through me. "Empty rapture, I love this world." I would never go back to the Black Earth. I would never let myself be banished again. I was here to stay. "That was so hot, Mrs. White."

"Good, because I need your cock in me! I need to be fucked. I'm so wet and hot. I've never needed anything more in my life."

Eloise climaxed downstairs. I felt her passion spilling over her as I moved down the bed to get in position to fuck her step-mother. I shuddered, my futa-dick throbbing before me, my large tits jiggling in my half-bra.

Once in position, I pressed the tip of my pierced cock into the

MILF's juicy pussy. I shuddered at the feel of her silky curls caressing my cock. The pleasure rippled over my shaft and down to my pussy. I groaned and pushed forward.

I entered her married pussy slowly. I savored the bliss of sliding into her flesh. My cock ring twisted. Pleasure shot up my futa-dick to my own cunt. The juices trickled down my thighs to the tops of my stockings, soaking my nylons as I sank deeper and deeper into her twat.

I groaned, my body trembling. This wicked delight swept through my flesh. I bit my lips, my clit-dick throbbing and aching in Mrs. White's pussy. She gasped and squeezed her cunt down on me. She gripped me with such tight passion.

"Oh, Ava, yes!" she moaned. "I love your dick! It's amazing!"

Eloise kept rubbing her pussy despite cumming. She could hear us. How long before she succumbed? I trembled, aching for her to fly up here and lick cum out of her step-mother's forbidden pussy. To revel in that taboo creampie.

It would be glorious.

I bottomed out in Mrs. White and then drew back, my clit-piercing shifting in her pussy. The pleasure shuddered down my cock while it rippled through her. I feasted on the MILF's passion. My succubal hungers devoured the pleasure coursing through her. I loved every moment of it.

I thrust away at her cunt. I pumped hard and fast. It was incredible. My breasts jiggled and heaved as I plundered her glorious cunt. I groaned, my cunt squeezing tight. Heat rippled through my body. I whimpered and moaned as I reveled in the pleasure of this moment.

"Yes, yes, yes!" she gasped as I thrust away at her married pussy. Her cunt squeezed about me. She gripped me with her feverish twat. "Ava! Ava! You're the best!"

"Better than your husband?" I groaned.

"So much better!" Her hips rotated. She threw a look over her shoulder, her face twisting in wild passion. "Yes, yes! Such an amazing girl-dick, Ava!"

"And your pussy is incredible," I moaned, slamming into her twat again and again.

My tits heaved in my bra. They bounced and jiggled while my snatch drank in the heat flowing down my girl-dick. My hands roamed her body. I stroked the MILF's silky skin. I caressed over her hot flesh. I loved every moment of touching her, caressing her.

I brushed her swinging tits. Then I grabbed them. They were so soft. Such wonderful tits belonging to such a sexy MILF. A rush of delight swept through me. I groaned, my cunt on fire. I pumped away harder. Faster. I thrust my girl-dick to the hilt in her cunt.

My orgasm built and built. In my ovaries, my futa-cum brimmed. The ache swelled up to the tip of my girl-cock slamming over and over into her pussy. I buried to the hilt in her again and again. I reveled in every thrust. Every plunge into her amazing cunt.

"Empty rapture, yes!" I howled. "You have such an amazing pussy, Mrs. White."

Eloise climaxed for a second time. Her virginal passion filled the house. I shuddered, wanting to experience that rush when I had fully corrupted her. I thrust hard into her step-mother's pussy, plowing the MILF while devouring both their passion.

Such lust brimmed in the house.

"Ava! Ava!" gasped Mrs. White. "I'm going to cum on this cock!"

"Don't hold back!" I groaned, pumping away at the MILF's twat. "Just let it explode out of you!"

"Yes!" she howled, her pussy clenching around my cock, twisting my cock ring around.

I slammed to the hilt in her. As I pulled back, her MILF pussy went wild about my girl-dick. Her hot flesh convulsed and spasmed. I groaned, savoring the ripping delight around my futa-cock. I slammed back into her, reveling in her heat.

"I'm cumming!" she moaned. "Ava! Ava! I'm cumming! Give me your jizz!"

"Yes!" I gasped. "Empty rapture, you're going to be filled with it!"

"I want that!" the MILF panted in feverish lust.

Her pussy sucked at my cock. Her hot cunt rippled and writhed around me. I shuddered and pumped into her depths, driving towards my orgasm. My tits heaved. My hands squeezed her jiggling breasts. I threw back my head.

Erupted.

"Yes, yes, yes, take my jizz, Mrs. White!" I howled.

Eloise came for a third time.

"You're pumping so much jizz in me!" the MILF squealed.

I drank in her orgasmic pleasure and Eloise's as my futa-cum pumped into married twat. My mind melted beneath the heat exploding from my girl-dick and rippling out of my convulsing twat. Juices gushed down my thighs, soaking my stockings.

My red hair danced about my shoulders. I shuddered through my bliss. My tits heaved. I squeezed Mrs. White's soft breasts as her hot pussy worked my cum out of me. She milked me, draining every drop of my futa-cum from my ovaries.

"Oh, god, yes!" panted the MILF. "That's amazing."

"And it's only going to get better," I purred, feeling Eloise hitting the peak of her third orgasm. I had to lure her upstairs. "I'm going to fuck your asshole next."

"Anal?" Mrs. White squealed as I pulled my futa-dick out of her pussy. I shifted it up and nuzzled it into her butt-cheeks. "Oh, yes, yes, I don't care. Just fuck me again, Ava!"

~~*~~

Eloise "Ellie" White

Masturbation did nothing to satisfy the fire in my pussy.

My step-mom's moans echoed from upstairs, begging Ava to take her again. Then I could hear them fucking again. Ava was pounding her hard with her clit-dick, just driving into my step-mother's pussy. I bit my lip as I rubbed at my virgin pussy, my jeans and panties around my ankles. I stood in my living room masturbating.

I had cum three times and it did nothing for me. Pussy juices dripped from my fingers. Ran down my thighs. My mom's gasps and moans resounded through the house. She was building towards another orgasm.

What was Ava doing to these women? To my mother. I swallowed.

What could she do to me?

Panic seized me. I couldn't let Ava get her hands on me. I needed Shane. I had to get to him right now. I yanked up my jeans and panties. I buttoned my pants with haste. I darted for the door and wrenched it open as my step-mother screamed out in ecstasy.

Shane would save me. He had to.

To be continued...

Claiming Ellie's Innocent Desires

Corrupted by the Futa Succubus 4

by

Reed James

Claiming Ellie's Innocent Desires

Ava Heart – The Futa-Succubus Shamshiel

I rammed my pierced futa-cock into Mrs. White's asshole.

This wicked thrill ran through me to seduce and fucked the mother of Eloise White. I could feel her cumming a third time downstairs, masturbating as she listened to me turning her mother into my whore. It was such a wicked thrill. My lusts throbbed. My futa-dick throbbed as Mrs. White's asshole surrendered to my cock's tip.

That wonderful anal ring parted around my crown, brushing my gold piercing. The velvety delight of penetrating the married woman's bowels shuddered through me. She moaned, her head throwing back. Her blonde hair tossed back and forth as she groaned out her pleasures.

"Ava!" she moaned, voice thick with the strain of having her virgin asshole broken in.

I couldn't wait to break in a truly cherry hole. Eloise's cunt. It would be magnificent to enjoy the virgin. To complete her corruption. My large breasts heaved as more and more of my futa-dick vanished into the warm, velvety embrace of Mrs. White's asshole.

"Empty rapture!" I moaned, my red hair swaying. I loved being a futa-succubus and free of the Black Earth. I would never go back to that colorless, passionless realm. I was here to stay. "You love it, don't you, Mrs. White! You love being my anal slut!"

"Yes, yes, yes!" she moaned as my futa-dick bottomed out in her. My shaved pussy lips pressed into her bubbly rump. Her asshole clenched about my dick. Her hips wiggled from side to side. She pressed her face into one of her pillows, trembling on her marital bed.

I had seduced her with ease, proving to Eloise that I could have any woman, she included. Only her virginity kept my powers from working on her. I had to corrupt her into uninhibited passion. I had to get her so horny she didn't care about the depraved acts she committed.

Eloise White would become my delicious whore.

Something changed in Eloise's emotions. As she descended down from her third orgasm, masturbating to me fucking her mother in her parents' bedroom, the college girl panicked. Fear surged through her at her lust. Flight entered her mind.

Shane blazed in her thoughts.

I could just hear her drawing up her jeans and panties. She was fleeing to her boyfriend. If she gave him her virginity, she'd lose the protection against me. I could make her my whore with ease. Where was the fun in that? The challenge?

The transformation?

I couldn't have that. As Eloise rushed for the door to flee the house, I drew back my hips and snarled to Mrs. White, "Is this the best cock you've ever had?"

"Yes," the MILF moaned, her bowels clinging to my dick as I drew back my hips further and further.

"Yes!" she moaned as I slammed back into her velvety heaven. The pleasure spilled up my pierced clit-dick to my pussy. It radiated out through me. My breasts heaved as I buried to the hilt in her, smacking her rump.

"Then scream it out," I moaned, my hands stroking down her sides. "Let the world know, Mrs. White."

"This cock is better than my husband's dick!" she screamed at the top of her lungs.

Eloise "Ellie" White

I froze at the door, my hand gripping the doorknob. My glasses slipped on my face. I panted, blonde hair swaying about my face. The scent of my sweet pussy juices filled the air, my fingers gripping the brass knob wet with them from my shameful self-pleasure.

"Ava's cock is better than Dad's?" I whispered.

I stood there frozen. I should flee. Get to Shane. Beg him to fuck me. To take my cherry and free me from these aching lusts. I swallowed, aching for my hand to turn the doorknob. My heart screamed in my chest. This was my chance. If I didn't flee...

I threw a look at the stairs, at the sounds of passion drifting from upstairs. What did Ava do to women to make them into sluts? My friends at college, my married English professor, the jogger in the park, and now my mother.

Better cock than my father...?

My hand relaxed on the doorknob. I let out a whimper as a tide of heat rose out of my pussy. That itch building and building. The one that masturbation couldn't touch. The one that nothing I did could relieve.

"Damn you, Ava Heart," I cursed as I crept towards the stairs.

~~*~~

Ava Heart – The Futa-Succubus Shamshiel

I shuddered as I felt the war in Eloise's heart. Curiosity and lust won out.

I threw back my head and moaned out my triumph as I fucked into her mother's asshole hard. I plowed into Mrs. White's bowels, my tits heaving. My pussy drank in the heat spilling down my cock. That velvety friction bathed my clit-dick

That wonderful heat. It was incredible. I grunted and groaned as I plowed away. I fucked the MILF hard and fast. I buried into her over and over again. I ravished her. I fucked her hard. I buried to the hilt in her again and again. I filled her to the hilt with my futa-dick.

She whimpered and shuddered, her hips wiggling from side to side. She gasped and moaned, squeezing her cunt around my dick. She held me tight. She gripped me with that wonderful embrace. That velvety grip that would have me exploding in passion.

I pumped away hard and fast at her. I fucked her with passion. I plowed to the hilt in her again and again. My breasts heaved as Eloise crept up the stairs. She came closer and closer to witnessing her mother's surrender to my depravity.

"Ava! Ava! I love this cock!" moaned Mrs. White. "I love your dick fucking my asshole while your cum leaks out of my pussy!"

"Mmm, you're such a naughty wife!" I gasped.

"I am!" she gasped.

"A wicked mother."

"So fucking wicked!" she howled, her bowels squeezing around my futa-dick, massaging the tip of my girl-dick. The heat swelled in my ovaries. That wonderful explosion that would have me erupting in spurt after wild spurt of jizz.

I thrust hard and fast into the married MILF's bowels. I drove my dick into her again and again. I buried to the hilt in her over and over again. It was incredible. Her hot flesh squeezed about me. The velvety grip of her bowels about my dick would have me spurting my jizz fast. My cum would erupt over and over again.

I threw back my head and groaned. My hair danced around my head. I pumped away at her. I plowed into her hard and fast, building and building her orgasm while her daughter crept down the hallway.

She reached the open door.

I felt Eloise watching us. Heard the intact of her breath. The growing heat between the virgin's thighs as she witnessed her mother taking my futa-dick. I thrust hard into the woman's bowels. I pounded her, enjoying the velvety delight.

"Ava! Ava! I'm going to cum so hard on your amazing girl-cock!" moaned Mrs. White. "I love your dick. I love it so much!"

Eloise trembled. Swallowed. Her eyes were locked on us. Her hips wiggling. I heard the rasp of her jeans as her thighs pressed tight. Her clit throbbed. I fed on her virginal lusts while I devoured the MILF's passions.

This world was so rich with food.

I thrust as hard as I could into Mrs. White's bowels. My big tits heaved before me, my red hair dancing around my head. The married woman's asshole massaged my futa-dick. That velvety hole gripped me tight, stimulating my cock's crown.

"I'm going to dump my cum into your asshole, Mrs. White!" I moaned. "Flood your bowels like I flooded your cunt!"

"Oh, yes, yes!" she moaned. "You dumped so much jizz into my pussy! I want it in my asshole. I want your cum in me, Ava!"

Eloise shuddered.

My orgasm built and built just like Mrs. White's grew. My hands stroking her sides reached her breasts. I squeezed the MILF's pillowy mounds. They were softer than mine. Not as firm and perky though we had the same size tits. I kneaded them as I plowed into her asshole. I breathed in the musk of sex. Salty sweat and jizz mixed with our pussy cream: my spicy, Mrs. White's tangy, and just a whiff of cherry sweetness.

My ovaries brimmed with cum. I hovered on the edge of my orgasm. Mrs. White climbed towards hers. My fingers squeezing her tits slid up them, almost milking them like udders. I found her nipples. Fat and hard, begging to be played with.

I pinched them. Twisted them.

"Ava!" squealed Mrs. White. "Yes!"

She came before her daughter.

Hot bowels writhed and spasmed around my futa-dick. I groaned as I pumped away at her. The delicious friction melted straight to my bowels. It wreathed my naughty hole. The heat swelled and swelled in me. I groaned, pussy juices spilling down my thighs.

"Ava! I'm cumming!"

"Yes, yes, yes!" I groaned. "Empty rapture, you love my futa-dick, Mrs. White!"

"I do! It's the fucking best! Cum in me!"

I felt Eloise's lust quiver. She trembled as she watched me drive into her mother's asshole. I threw back my head, my tits heaving, and dumped my cum into Mrs. White's asshole. Spurt after spurt of my jizz pumped out of my ovaries and into the woman's spasming anal sheath.

The pleasure surged through me. It rushed through my body and struck my mind. I groaned as my futa-spunk fired out of me over and over. My pussy convulsed, juices gushing down my thighs to my stockings. I shuddered, my big boobs heaving as the pleasure surged through my body.

"I love dumping my cum in your asshole, Mrs. White!" I howled, drinking in the wonderful pleasure. "Colorless passion, I love spurting my futa-jizz in your holes!"

"Yes!" she howled, her asshole milking my cock.

I twisted her nipples. I tugged on them as I rode my orgasm, spurting my futa-cum into her bowels. The pleasure rushed through me, that wonderful ecstasy sweeping through my body. It was ecstatic. I savored every spurt of cum that burst from my ovaries.

I hit that pinnacle of rapture, my big tits quivering. Mrs. White's asshole wrung out the last of this load of cum from my ovaries. The final spurt of my girl-spunk fired into her bowels. I panted, savoring the pleasure for one moment.

But I had a virgin to corrupt.

I ripped out of the mother's bowels and moved around the bed, turning not to the door, but the wall. However, I could see Eloise lurking in the shadows, her flushed face watching, blue eyes wide behind her glasses. A slender girl of eighteen, her blonde hair pale around her scarlet cheeks. Her nipples hard beneath blouse and bra. Her panties soaked with her virgin passion.

"Now suck my dick clean of your asshole, Mrs. White," I purred, shaking my dick at her. Not looking at Eloise. I couldn't spook her. "You got it dirty."

"Oh, no," panted the MILF. She turned her body, aiming her ass right at the door now as she leaned her head down. "Let me lick you clean, Ava."

"*Lick her clean,*" mouthed Eloise. The shock from the girl almost had me erupting again. She couldn't believe anyone would

85

do something that filthy. She could see her mother's asshole gaping open from my big dick, the cum bubbling out. More leaked down the MILF's thighs, proof that I had utterly enjoyed the married woman.

That I had cuckolded Eloise's father.

Mrs. White's tongue licked at my dirty cock. The sour musk rose up to my nose, filling it. I shuddered at the delight of the MILF licking and lapping at my cock, her tongue caressing over it. The hunger she had as she moaned in delight had me smiling.

And Eloise trembling.

~~*~~

Eloise "Ellie" White

I licked my lips as Mom licked Ava's dirty cock.

I couldn't see Mom doing it, her rump facing me. Cum leaked out of her pussy and bubbled out of her asshole. This was insane. I shuddered as the heat surged through me from my pussy. That creamy, pearly cum leaked out of my mother.

She had succumbed to Ava. The best cock ever...

The only cock that could satisfy this heat in me.

I stared at the jizz leaking out of my mother's pussy. It ran thick down her thigh. She sucked now, buffing clean Ava's cock. The futa-temptress moaned her delight. She had utterly corrupted my mother. Turned her into a whore that loved that cock.

Loved Ava's cum.

That pearly cum. So thick. So beautiful. It looked so delicious. My tongue swept over my lips. The feverish heat blazing in my pussy overwhelmed me. I pushed up my glasses then stumbled forward. I couldn't stop myself.

Ava's green eyes met mine. They glowed with such delight. A perverted smile of triumph spread over her lips. She knew she had won. That I was hers. I couldn't resist this any longer. My friends all sang their praises. Jennifer, my BFF, told me I needed to try this.

Shane faded from my mind. I liked guys, but...

I reached my parents' rumpled bed. The thick musk of sex filled the air. Salty sweat and this hot scent of pussy. Not my own sweet musk, but a spicy aroma and a tangy one. I groaned as I fell on my knees onto the bed. The mattress springs creaked.

Mom didn't even stop suckling. She just kept it up. Her mouth nursed with hunger on the futa's cock. It was insane. I shuddered, my heart thundering in my chest. I stared at my mother's blonde-furred muff. Jizz coated her strands.

My tongue caressed over my lips. I leaned over, breathing in that salty, tangy musk coming from my mother. My head came closer and closer. I couldn't fight this. I could tell Ava wanted me to do this. She would be happy.

I licked at the cum adorning my mother's inner thigh. This salty flavor blazed across my tongue. Jizz was so thick and creamy. It tasted so good. I couldn't believe it. The flavor burst to life on my tongue.

"That's it," Ava cooed. "Mmm, just like that Eloise."

"Ellie," I whimpered. I hated being called Eloise, but... What did it matter? I was licking girl-jizz off my mother's thigh.

I stared up at the pussy that birthed me. The incestuous nature of this propelled me. My tongue climbed higher and higher, gathering more and more of the jizz. The tangy scent grew stronger. My mother's cunt...

I was about to eat my mother's cunt.

My fingers dug into her fingers as my tongue lapped up more of Ava's futa-cum. I savored it spilling over my tongue. My taste buds. The flavor was incredible. My hips wiggled, my pussy on fire. I couldn't stop myself from this forbidden act.

I licked to my mother's pussy.

She moaned as she sucked on Ava's dirty cock. Mom didn't care at all that I was licking at her cunt. That we were committing incest. And were cheating on Dad. My tongue slid through her folds. I lapped at her tangy folds bubbling with Ava's spunk. Wet pubic hair rubbed at my cheeks and nose.

I liked it. Loved it.

The taste of my mother's pussy, that tangy flavor, mixed with the salty delight of futa-cum. The feel of the hot folds on my tongue that had birthed me sent such a wicked thrill through me. My tongue fluttered up and down, lapping at her, gathering the cum flowing out of her.

My virgin cunt clenched in my jeans. I wiggled my hips back and forth, the heat surging through me. I closed my eyes and feasted on my mother's cunt. I reveled in the incestuous delight. I devoured her, my tongue fluttering up and down her slit.

"Yes, yes, that's it!" Ava moaned. "Oh, Eloise, eat your mother's pussy. Devour her. She loves it. She's sucking so hard on my dick. Empty rapture, she's loving my cock."

"Good," I moaned and licked again.

"You love the taste of your mother's pussy, don't you?" the redhead seductress purred.

"I do!"

Mom sucked with noisier hunger on Ava's girl-dick. The obscene, wet sounds echoed through the world as my tongue thrust into her depths. I scooped out the jizz, reveling in the depraved delights. This was so wrong.

That made me lick harder. Feast with more hunger.

I sealed my lips over my mother's pussy and sucked the cheating spunk out of her cum. The proof that she had cuckolded my father. Tangy cream and salty futa-jizz flowed into my mouth. I gulped it down. More ran down my chin.

Mom wiggled her hips. She rubbed her hot cuntlips and silky bush against my face. My tongue thrust into her depths over and over again. I stroked up and down her cunt with wild abandon. Incestuous lusts and forbidden passions consumed me.

My glasses slipped on my nose as I devoured my mother's cunt. My tongue licked from her clit to her taint. Over and over again. More cum bubbled out of her asshole and ran down to her cunt, adding more salty delight to lick up.

This seed was seasoned by her sour musk.

The same sour, earth taste she sucked off Ava's cock. My virgin cunt clenched, feverish heat rushing through me. My hips wiggled, jeans rasping as I attacked my mother's cunt with such hunger. I attacked her with all the passion I could muster.

"Your mother's about to cum on your licking mouth, Eloise!" moaned Ava. Her big boobs heaved above me. Her green eyes stared down. "Oh, yes, yes, you're going to make your mother cum hard. What a nasty thing you are. Such a depraved, little slut."

My cunt clenched.

My mom moaned.

Tangy pussy cream gushed out of her pussy. A flood of juices that splashed on my face, soaking my cheeks and chin. I gasped and opened my mouth wide. I drank down my mother's orgasmic delight. Her muffled squeals echoed through the bedroom.

"Colorless passion, that's it!" howled Ava. "Swallow all my cum. Yes!"

I heard my mother swallowing now. She gulped down that impossible futa-jizz I'd just lapped out of her cunt. I kept licking up the tangy cream flooding out of my mother's cunt. I feasted on her, my body feverish with heat. The incestuous depravity consumed me.

I made my mother cum *and* loved it. I was a slut.

"Mmm, Mrs. White, your daughter was such a naughty thing, wasn't she," Ava cooed.

I heard my mother pulling her mouth off of Ava's cock. A wet plop and then heavy panting. "Yes... she is... She made me... cum so... hard."

"Let's strip her naked and make her explode, Mrs. White," Ava cooed. "Let's make your daughter erupt in passion."

"Yes!" Mom whirled around, her green eyes blazing with lust for me. Taboo, motherly desire.

The futa's dick bobbed before her, moving with her large breasts, as she pounced on me from my right. My mother came from my left. I gasped as they were ripping at my clothes. I shuddered as lips kissed at my face. My mom's. Ava's. They lapped at my cheeks and chin.

They were cleaning off the pussy juices.

Mom moaned as her tongue fluttered over my cheeks, lapping up her own pussy cream. Her hands were busy attacking my jeans. I turned my head and then I was kissing her. Our tongues danced together. I shuddered, kissing her with hunger while Ava pulled up my top.

"Mmm, that's some hot, mother/daughter incest," the dickgirl purred.

She yanked my shirt up higher, forcing me to break my kiss with my mother. I panted as it spilled over my head, jostling my glasses. I adjusted them as Mom shoved her hands into my open fly. I gasped as she stroked along my panties, cupping them. She rubbed my hot lips into my snatch, stroking up and down me.

"Mmm, you ate my pussy, Ellie," she purred. "That was so hot. You made me cum while I was sucking Ava."

"I did, Mom," I moaned, whimpering at her taboo touch. She pressed my panties into my crotch. She stroked me. Made me shiver. "Mom. This is..."

"I know, and I don't care." She leaned in. "It makes Ava happy." My mother kissed me hard.

Happy...

"Yes, it does," Ava purred, her fingers unhooking my bra. She peeled it off while my tongue danced with my mother's.

I kissed Mom with hunger. Our lips moved together. They were so soft and sensual. Different from kissing Shane. I shivered, my nipples throbbing, exposed to the air. My mother's swaying breasts brushed my tits, her fatter nubs sliding across my flesh.

This was so wrong.

I couldn't stop.

Ava had unbottled all my lusts, they spilled out of me. Contained. I groaned, my pussy aching. I was so wet, soaking through my panties. My cream must be coating my mother's fingers rubbing up and down my flesh and sending such naughty sensations through my body. I whimpered into the kiss, groaning.

Mom broke the kiss and purred, "Mmm, you're loving that, aren't you?"

"Yes, Mom!" I moaned.

"Let's get those jeans off," she moaned and then ducked her head down. She kissed at my breastbone as she worked at my jeans, pulling them down. Then my mother's mouth kissed up my breast.

She reached my nipple.

"Mom!"

She sucked hard on my nub. It throbbed in her wet mouth. I

gasped at how incredible it felt. The wet pressure on my nipple was like nothing I had imagined. It was this insane rush of heat that swept through me. I groaned, wiggling my hips from side to side, my pussy growing so hot and juicy. I whimpered, squirming. This heat rushed through my body.

"Mom!" I groaned, my entire body shuddering. "This... I... Mom!"

"I know," she purred, her lips sliding off of me. "You want me to lick your pussy?"

"Yes!" I blurted out before I could stop myself.

Ava giggled. "Mmm, Eloise, you're going to have such a huge orgasm."

"Ellie," I moaned as she pulled me down onto my back while my mother kissed at my stomach. She tugged my jeans down my legs now, able to pull them off since I wasn't kneeling on them any longer. My legs straightened. "My name's Ellie."

"Ellie is a girl's name. You're becoming a woman, Eloise." Ava stroked my cheek. "Mmm, you're going to blossom."

She leaned down, her red hair spilling around me, and kissed me on the lips. An upside-down kiss. I groaned at the feel of the dickgirl's mouth on mine. She had changed everything at my college. She had turned all my friends into lesbians.

Now me, too.

I kissed her with hunger, my mom pulling my jeans off my feet. I shuddered, my tongue dancing with Ava's. The redhead kissed me with such passion. She smelled so good. The spicy musk of her pussy mixing with a flowery perfume. An intoxicating scent. My blood boiled.

"What cute ankle socks," Mom cooed. She peeled off the left one, exposing my foot. "And such dainty, kissable toes."

She licked my toes. I gasped as she swirled her tongue between them while I kissed Ava harder. I savored the futa's mouth on mine while my mother sucked at my big toe. My pussy clenched at the heat. The depravity of this. Incestuous sensations rippled through my body.

"Mmm, cute feet. Delicious feet. My daughter is so sexy."

My mom ripped off my other sock and then licked the sole of

my right foot all the way up to the pinnacle. I groaned, my body shuddering. My cunt clenched, the heat rippling through my body.

Ava broke the kiss with me. Her finger stroked my cheek while I panted. Mom sucked at my other big toe. She nursed on it, tingles racing up my leg to my pussy. My body squirmed on the bed. This feverish heat swept through me. This was all so incredible.

"Now let's get your panties off," Ava said.

Mom's mouth popped off my big toe. "Yes!"

She shot her hand to my panties. She grabbed the waistband and tugged them down. I lifted my rump off the bed, panting as she exposed my blonde bush soaked in my virgin cream. The sweet scent filled the air, free of my panties. Mom rolled the sodden cloth down my thighs and past my knees. My toes flexed and curled.

She peeled them off and pressed them into her mouth. Her large breasts jiggled as she sniffed my panties. She rubbed them across her face. She groaned as she did it. It was so depraved. So wrong. My mother licked at the crotch of them, lost to her feverish heat.

"What are you, Ava?" I groaned.

"A futa," she purred, rolling me onto my side. She was behind me, her futa-cock nuzzling into my rump. "A futa who's going to give you such rapture. You're going to know a life of bliss and wanton ecstasy because of me."

"I... I..." Conflict arose in me. Shane flew through my mind, but then was swallowed up by the tide of lust rising out of my aching pussy. I don't care about anything any longer but cumming. I just wanted to be fucked so hard. "Fuck me, Ava! Please, please, fuck me! I want your cock in me! I want that itch satiated."

She hugged me from behind, her large breasts pressing into my back. They were firm and soft at the same time. Her nipples hard points that rubbed across my fiery skin. A feverish heat swept through me from the contact. She nuzzled into my ear; licked my lobe.

"I told you," she purred. "I told you that you'd beg for my futa-cock, didn't I?"

"Yes!" I howled, trembling against her.

"Now lift your thigh. Your mother deserves to eat that pussy while I fuck your asshole," cooed Ava.

"W-what?" I gasped. "Not my pussy. I need *you* in my pussy."

"We'll get there." She licked my ear again, sending another shiver through my body. Her arms held me tight, her futa-dick rubbing into my rump. "Let's not spoil the feast with that sweet dessert. Mmm, there's still so much pleasure to enjoy before we cross that line."

"Yes!" I moaned, not caring. I humped my rump back into her while my mother stared at me over my panties pressed to her mouth and nose.

"Now lift that leg and flash that twat at your naughty mommy," the futa whispered into my ear. "She wants to eat you out. She's hungering for that yummy, virgin pussy. She's going to devour you and make you explode while I fuck your asshole."

"Yes, yes, yes!"

I lifted my leg.

"Mom, eat my pussy!" I moaned, flashing my twat at her.

My mom dropped my panties. The wet pair landed on her right breast. It slid over her tit and fell to her lap, leaving a gleaming streak behind on her swaying mound. She licked her lips, motherly hunger rising in her eyes. Forbidden lust for the daughter she'd created.

She crawled to me, wedding ring flashing on her left hand. Her blonde hair fell around her hungry face. Her large breasts swayed. She fell onto her own side, her face staring right at my pussy. Her breath washed through my drenched bush, caressing my aching lips.

I trembled there, my heart pounding so fast. My mother nuzzled her lips into my bush. I felt the hairs shifting about. Then her lips kissed my feverish flesh. I shuddered at the incestuous contact of her mouth on my nethers.

On my virgin pussy.

"Mom!" I gasped.

"Mmm, Ellie, honey," she moaned. "You taste so good."

Her tongue licked out. I shuddered in the futa's embrace, my rump pressing back into her futa-cock. My mother's tongue stroked through my pussy folds. She caressed my labia and brushed my clit. I gasped at the wonderful pleasure.

93

It was so much better than touching myself. Than caressing myself. It was incredible. I groaned, savoring the heat of her tongue stroking across my flesh. She licked again and again, digging deeper, caressing over my hymen, moaning as she crossed that forbidden line.

My mother made love to my pussy.

"Mom!" I whimpered.

"You're so delicious," she groaned.

"Mmm, this is perfect," Ava moaned. "Colorless passion, this is better than I could imagine. Eloise, the things we're going to do together."

I shuddered as she drew back her hips. She slid her cock through my crack. Then I felt her tip nuzzling in. She was really going to ass-fuck me with a dick soaked in my mother's saliva. I would lose my anal cherry before my real one.

This was insane.

"Yes, yes, fuck my ass!" I moaned, the depraved words spilling out of me. I couldn't contain them. Ava had corrupted me. I ached to be soiled now. Violated. My mother's tongue caressed my pussy as Ava's dick nuzzled into my sphincter. I felt her cock ring rubbing on my hot flesh. "Take me, Ava! Fuck me so hard. I want it!"

"Empty rapture, yes!"

Ava pressed her dick forward. She pressed on my asshole. I groaned, the heat building and building in me. This amazing heat was incredible. This pleasure was intense. Insane. I groaned, my heart pounding in my chest as my anal ring stretched and stretched to swallow the tip of her pierced cock.

Heat melted down to my pussy being feasted on by my hungry mother. My cunt clenched deep inside of me. I groaned, trembling on my side. Ava's big boobs rubbed across my back as her cock pushed harder at my virgin asshole.

"Oh, yes!" I gasped as my sphincter widened more. "You're going to pop inside."

"You're going to love it, Ellie," Mom moaned and then licked my pussy up to my clit.

She danced around my bud. The surge of pleasure relaxed my asshole. Ava popped into my bowels. Her pierced futa-dick slid into my anal depths. I gasped and trembled at the velvety heat that blazed around her cock, her ring massaging me. She pushed deeper and deeper into my virgin body.

My toes curled as that big dick filled me up. She rubbed against my hot flesh. I groaned, squirming. My fingers flexed and my toes curled. It felt incredible. More and more and more of her entered me. I loved how her piercing caressed my velvety flesh.

"Oh, god!" I gasped.

"Empty rapture!" groaned Ava. Her pussy lips rubbed into my rump. She was all the way in me. I could feel her so deep. She had reached to the limits of my bowels. "I have you. You're mine, Eloise."

"Yours!" I cried out, not caring with my mother's tongue fluttering against my clit and that massive futa-dick in my bowels.

Ava drew back. Just when I thought I had found the height of pleasure, it became even better. My bowels clenched around on her writhing dick. I shuddered, my clit throbbing against my mother's licking tongue. She fluttered against me, caressing me, sending such bliss surging through me. I loved it.

The velvety friction melted to my virgin pussy. My orgasm grew and grew. Ava slammed back into me. She buried her pierced cock to the hilt in my bowels. I groaned, savoring her large futa-cock filling me up again. The velvety stimulation was incredible. Insane. I groaned, my eyes squeezing tight as I reveled in every moment of her pumping away at me.

She thrust it deep and hard into my bowels. Her pussy lips smacked into my rump with her every thrust. I shuddered, my clit throbbing against my mother's hungry mouth. I trembled as they pleasured me.

"Mom! Ava!" I moaned as my orgasm built and built.

"Yes, yes!" gasped the futa as she drove her futa-dick into the depths of my bowels again and again. She plumbed my assholes limits, her hard piercing massaging my aching sheath. "Eloise! You're going to make me cum!"

"You think you're going to cum?" I howled, my orgasm building. "I have my mother sucking my clit."

"Mmm," purrs my mother as she sucked hard on my clit.

Her tongue fluttered against my bud. She caressed me. Teased me. The pleasure shot through my body. I groaned, trembling. The heat swept through my body. I squirmed and bucked as she slammed her shaft into my anal depths.

She fucked me hard and fast. She buried into me again and again. She slammed that big dick to the hilt in me while my mom nursed on my clit. She sucked so hard on it. My virgin depths clenched tight. I bucked.

Climaxed.

I had my first orgasm at the hands of another. My bowels writhed and spasmed around Ava's thrusting cock. Wordless pleasure burst from my lips. My pussy convulsed. Juices gushed out. My mom lapped them up with hunger.

"Oh, Ellie, honey, yes!" she moaned as I bathed her face in my pleasure.

"You sweet virgin!" gasped Ava, her voice hungry. She pumped her pierced futa-cock in and out of my asshole, her hands massaging my little titties. She gripped them hard as her own big boobies rubbed into my back.

I thrashed in her embrace, my asshole convulsing around her cock. Waves of heat billowed through my body. They swept out of my writhing twat and swept through my thoughts. My mind smoldered with ecstasy.

"Empty rapture!" the futa howled and buried her cock to the hilt in me.

Hot futa-cum jetted into my writhing bowels. She fired her spunk into me. I gasped in delight, my asshole convulsing about her hot shaft and hard ring. I shuddered, my toes curling. The heat surged to the pinnacle in me. It hit this wonderful burst of rapture.

I hung there, groaning and shuddering while more and more of her cum pumped into me. Mom lapped at my cunt with feverish, incestuous hunger. She drank the cunt cream gushing out of me as I trembled through my bliss.

"Oh, Eloise, yes!" Ava moaned and no more of her futa-cum pumped into my body. "You're ready! You're so ready!"

"I am!" I moaned in understanding. "Take my virginity. Pop my cherry. Ram that dirty futa-dick into my pussy! Corrupt me!"

"Yes!" Such joy resounded in Ava's voice. Such triumph. She had done it.

Ava Heart had turned me into her whore just like shad had to all the others. Just like she'd done to my mother lapping at my cunt.

I shuddered as Ava pulled her pierced futa-dick out of my asshole. I trembled at the velvety friction. Heat washed through me, almost like a mini-orgasm. I quivered beneath her, my heart pounding hard. Inch after inch of her cock slid out of me.

PLOP!

Her dick popped out. My asshole squeezed shut. I felt her cum brimming inside of me. I groaned, my pussy on fire. Mom kept licking at it, flicking her tongue up and down it, teasing me and having me shiver.

Then I rolled onto my back. My mom lifted her head. Her green eyes, glossy with lust, stared at me. My pussy cream dripped down her chin. Coated her lips. She licked them and shuddered, her large tits swaying.

She crawled up beside me and lowered her lips to mine. My mother kissed me coated in my sweet cream. I groaned at the taste of my virgin pussy. I kissed her back with enthusiasm, my tongue dancing with hers. Heat swept through my body, a preview for my next orgasm.

The one I'd have on Ava's big futa-dick.

I kissed my mother with greedy hunger. My tongue danced with hers. I shuddered on my back, the rumpled sheets so cool against my feverish flesh. I squeezed my eyes shut, my glasses shifting on my nose as I loved my mother. I knew it was wrong. Forbidden.

I loved it.

Ava had twisted me into something new.

"Mmm, that is so sexy," the futa groaned. "Empty rapture, I'm going to enjoy this."

She moved between my thighs. I lifted my left leg up, exposing myself, so open and inviting, just wanting the futa to thrust her girl-dick into my pussy. To take my cherry and make me cum so hard.

I wanted that itch scratched.

I kissed my mother with such wild hunger. Complete abandon.

My pussy clenched as I felt Ava's cock coming closer and closer to me. Then the first nuzzle of her dick into my wet bush. The shifting of curly hairs.

The sizzling contact of her futa-dick on my virgin pussy lips.

I broke the kiss with Mom to gasp, "Fuck me! Deflower me."

"Yes, yes, deflower my baby girl," cooed Mom as she straightened. She grabbed my panties and shoved them between her thighs. She rubbed them on her pussy and watched my deflowering.

Ava thrust.

My hymen stretched.

Groaning, I stared up at the futa, her green eyes brimming with hunger. She desired this. My maidenhead resisted with elastic stubbornness. I groaned, my toes curling. She kept pushing, driving her cock towards my virgin depths.

A flare of pain. My cherry popped.

"Ava!" I howled as her dirty futa-cock rammed into my pristine pussy.

Fresh from my asshole, her filthy dick slid into my deflowered twat, the hard piercing massaging my untouched flesh. I gasped, the rush of pleasure shooting through me. A wave of orgasmic delight. My eyes widened as I realized I was already cumming. My pleasure already spilling through me.

"Ava, yes!" I howled as my pussy convulsed around her dirty dick, buffing my asshole off her thick futa-cock. "You're in me! Oh, yes, yes, you're in me!"

"In the nastiest way possible," groaned the futa, her large breasts swaying.

"Yes!" I hissed. I thrust my hands up and grabbed her big boobs. I kneaded them, reveling in their firm softness. The contradiction made me shudder. They were so different from my small tits. I kneaded her boobs and moaned, my pussy clenching around her cock. "Fuck me! Cum in me!"

Pleasure rippled out of my cunt, waves of orgasmic delight. My flesh spasmed around her twat and that small, hard ring at the tip of her dick. I wiggled my hips, squirming on my bed. My small breasts jiggled while my fingers dug into her tits. I gripped her, my cunt writhing around her shaft.

She drew back her cock and another orgasm burst through me. I gasped, my body bucking. My glasses shifted on my nose while my pussy worshiped her dirty dick. She thrust back into my frothy depths. My cunt washed her futa-cock in my excitement while the pleasure surged through me.

"Oh, Ellie, honey, you look so sexy," my masturbating mother moaned, rubbing my panties into her married cunt. "You took that big girl-dick!"

"Empty rapture, she did!" groaned Ava. Her back arched. Her large breast jiggled in my grip. She plunged her futa-dick and cock ring in and out of my virgin twat. "Mmm, she's polishing my dick clean, the little slut."

"I am a little slut!" I moaned, more pleasure bursting through me. "Oh, I keep cumming. Your dick is amazing!"

"So is your pussy!" Ava face twisted in rapture. "Finally! I have you! You're mine, Eloise White!"

"Yours!" I gasped, my pussy convulsing with wild abandon.

I bucked on my back, my fingers digging into her back. My orgasms spilled from one to the next. There was no pause between them. Wave after wave swept from my twat convulsing around her futa-dick ramming into me. Tidal waves, mighty tsunamis of rapture, crashed into my mind.

Stars danced before my eyes as the pleasure never ended. I gripped her big boobs and squirmed on my back as she slammed into me. She pumped hard and fast. She plunged that huge cock into my cleansing depths.

She soiled me with her dirty dick. I loved it.

"Fuck me harder!" I hissed, my lusts on fire. "Pound me. Keep me cumming! Then dump your seed in me!"

"Flood my baby girl with your cum!" Mom moaned, her body quivering beside me. She rubbed her cunt with my panties. "Just pump her full of all that spunk. Bathe her. Coat her in jizz. It'll be incredible."

"Yes!" I moaned, my body bucking, the pleasure spilling through me. "Please, please, Ava. Give me your cum!"

"Empty rapture, I'm getting there!" the redhead moaned, her hair dancing like silken fire around her face. Her green eyes sparkled.

"Your cunt is sucking at me. You're pulling at my ovaries. I'm going to dump so much futa-cum in you!"

"Yes!" I squealed and another orgasm burst through me.

I spasmed on my back. I squirmed, rubbing my shoulder blades into the sheets. The bedsprings creaked. My pussy writhed around that thrusting cock. My hands fell from her tits as the pleasure intensified.

It drowned me.

The rapturous tide washed away my thoughts. So much bliss flooded through my body. I gasped and moaned, stars blazed hot through me. I groaned, my pussy convulsing and writhing around her cock, hungry for her cum.

"Flood me!" I begged as I spasmed through another orgasm.

"Flood my daughter!" howled Mom. She bucked beside me, cumming, too. Soaking my panties in her married cream. "Pump my daughter's pussy full of your cum, Ava!"

"Colorless passion!" the futa howled. She buried to the hilt in me and erupted.

Hot cum fired into my pussy. She utterly soiled me now. I gasped, bucking and quivering. My cunt convulsed harder. My orgasm burst with rapture. A tsunami of ecstasy rushed out of me and crashed into my mind.

Waves of darkness devoured my vision as I bucked on my back. My pussy milked her cock, wringing spurt after spurt of her futa-cum to fire hot into my deflowered depths. All three of our feminine delights echoed through my parents' bedroom.

"Ava! Ava!" I moaned.

"My Eloise!" she groaned. "Yes!"

Ava fired that last blast of her cum into me. I gasped, my orgasms finally surging towards that pinnacle. I hit it. I floated there at the utter peak of pleasure. Ecstasy saturated every bit of my body. I brimmed in bliss.

Loved it.

I quivered as my orgasm died down. My body squirmed on the sheets. I panted, buzzing with rapture. My pussy clenched on the dickgirl's shaft as I glanced at her. Her green eyes sparkled. Her red lips pursed together while her breasts swayed back and forth.

"You have to seduce Shane's mother to complete your corruption," the futa said, her clit-dick throbbing in my deflowered cunt. I swam with her cum.

"Yes!" I gasped, agreeing without hesitation. I would do *anything* for Ava.

She grinned at me, her emerald eyes brimming with inhuman hungers.

To be continued...

Unleashing Ellie's Innocent Desires

Corrupted by the Futa Succubus 5

by

Reed James

Unleashing Ellie's Innocent Desires

Ava Heart – The Futa-Succubus Shamshiel

My corruption of Eloise had begun. Her virginity was mine. She had fallen into the depravity of incestuous sex with her mother. But more had to be done. She had to be far, far more active in her own passion for what I craved.

She had to seduce her first woman.

"You can do this," I said as we stood outside the home of her boyfriend, Shane. I rubbed her shoulders. She wore a light sundress, the sexiest garment she owned, the skirt short enough to show a good deal of leg, sleeveless and fitting tight enough in the chest to show off her small breasts. She looked adorable with her blonde hair framing her cute face, her glasses perched on her dainty nose. "You can seduce her."

"How?" she asked, a tremble in her voice. Not fear in her desires. Oh, no, she wasn't running away from this any longer. This was doubt in her own abilities.

"Just be bold," I told her as I shoved my hand beneath her skirt. I slid up to her pussy. I brushed her bush soaked in her cum and juices. She shuddered at the touch of my fingers on her pussy lips. I slid them through her folds and gathered cum and pussy juices on my fingers.

Then I smeared them on her mouth, painting it on her like a frothy lipstick. The tangy scent of her pussy and my salty futa-cum filled my nose. A shiver ran through my body, starting at my clit yearning to be a dick.

I loved this world. I would never go back to the colorless, passionless Black Earth where I had been trapped for eons.

"Have fun," I told her and winked.

Eloise shuddered, her tongue flicking across the mix of juices. Then she nodded. Oh, yes, her corruption was almost complete.

~~*~~

Eloise "Ellie" White

I rang the doorbell as Ava retreated to wait in the car. I couldn't believe I was here to seduce my boyfriend's mother into lesbian sex. After my threesome with Ava and my mother, I was eager for this betrayal of my boyfriend's trust. I had found something better than Shane. I understood why all the women who let Ava fuck her sang her praise.

She and her futa-dick were amazing.

The door opened and Mrs. Thompson appeared. Shane's mother had wavy, dark-brown hair spilling about her mature and lovely face. She wore a simple tank top and white shorts, the outfit showing off her ample tits. She had those big breasts that I was realizing I loved.

My mother's tits. Ava's. That jogger's in the park.

"It's Ellie, right?" asked Shane's mother. She blinked. "This is a surprise. You know that Shane's at work."

"I just wanted to talk to you," I said, squirming. "I hope that's all right."

"Sure, sure," she said, sounding a little shocked. We had met only briefly. "I'm happy to get to know my son's girlfriend."

I smiled and then hugged her. I ducked in and gave her a quick kiss on the lips before I broke the embrace. She blinked at that, her tongue absently swiping over her lips. I shivered, knowing what still lingered on mine.

"You're, eh, friendly," Mrs. Thompson said as she stepped aside to let me enter.

"I come from a friendly family," I told her. "That's how I greet my mother, too."

She closed the door behind her and asked, "So, eh, why are you here?"

I shivered and turned to face her. I couldn't have any fear. Ava wanted me to do this. *I* wanted to do this. It was so hot licking my mother's pussy and having her lick me out was amazing. Women were such a delight. Even if Ava didn't have a cock, I'd be addicted to it. I wanted more. It was like I had all these desires stuffed inside of me, all held back by my hymen.

Once Ava popped my cherry, those desires were unstoppered. My lusts flowed freely through me.

"It's just..." I squirmed, my skirt swaying. My asshole and pussy both brimmed with all the cum Ava had fired in me. "I just am afraid I'm not beautiful enough for your son."

"Oh, Ellie," she said as she rushed over to me. She cupped my face. "Don't do that to yourself. You're gorgeous."

"Really?" I looked up at her, my glasses shifting on my face. "I mean... I'm so plain. I have glasses, and look at how flat I am."

She glanced down at my top. "Well, you have *something*, honey. And, trust me, something is really all guys want. More than a handful's a waste."

"Easy to say when you're so blessed," I said, staring down at her breasts. "Look at you, Mrs. Thompson. You're gorgeous. This is what your son expects from his girlfriend, and then look at me."

"Gorgeous?" she asked. "I'm old."

"You're not old. You're mature." I looked her up and down. "You're hot. A MILF."

Mrs. Thompson blushed. "That's nice of you to say that. But it's not like Shane wants to date me."

"Don't guys always want to marry their mothers?" I asked. "I mean, they marry girls *like* their mothers."

"Marriage? Haven't you two barely been dating? It's a little early to be worried about that."

"I just don't want to disappoint him," I said. I slid my hands up my body and cupped my breasts. I squeezed them. "There's barely anything there. I'm an A-cup. You must be, what Double D's. Even an F-Cup."

"F," she said, shifting. "But that's fine. My breasts weren't this big when I met his father. Yours are fine. They're young and firm and perky. That goes a long way. They're not like these breasts."

"Your breasts are perfect," I said. "How can you think that?"

"They're not as firm as they were."

I scoffed and shot my hands out. I squeezed her through her sports bra. I kneaded her while she gasped. Her eyes widened as I felt them. They were soft and pillowy. They were just like my mother's tits.

"Ellie!" she gasped. "What are you doing?"

"Showing you that you have great tits," I said and then grabbed her tank top. I had to be bold.

She gasped as I ripped it up her body. Her hands went to stop me, but I shoved it up and over her tits, revealing them in a flesh-colored bra with little rosebuds worked into the fabric of the cups. Her breasts jiggled.

"You shouldn't be doing that!" she gasped, her cheeks going red.

I shoved up her cups and her breasts popped out into my hands. I cradled them. They were heavy and soft, not as firm as Ava's equally big boobs, but these were a MILF's tits. They were still so gorgeous. They didn't have much sag and still possessed a lovely, plump shape. Her nipples were dark red and soft, surrounded by oval areolas.

"See, these are gorgeous," I said, squeezing them. "If I had breasts like these, I wouldn't be worried about Shane."

"Okay, okay," said Mrs. Thompson. "You can stop fondling them."

My thumbs swept over her breasts. I brushed her areolas and then rubbed at her nipples. She gasped as they puckered up erect. They were fat and short; squat nipples that just begged to be sucked on. She shivered.

"Ellie!" she groaned, her wavy hair swaying about her face. "That's... You're..."

"They're just gorgeous breasts, Mrs. Thompson. I darted my head down and sucked on her right nipple.

"Oh, my god!" she gasped in shock.

I squeezed her breasts and nursed on her nipple. I loved the feel of that fat nub in my mouth. There was something so comforting about having my lips wrapped around a MILF's nipple. It felt so wicked and naughty. And this was my boyfriend's mother. This was extra wrong.

I reveled in it.

"Ellie, you have to stop!" she moaned even as she trembled. She tried to shove down her bra cups, but the fabric just rubbed into my face.

I sucked harder. She gasped. Her body bucked. I gave her left tit a final squeeze then shoved my right hand down her bare stomach. She was in great shape, flat and toned. My pussy clenched, juices and cum leaking out of my twat's depths. More dribbled out of my butthole, my ass-crack a mess of girl-jizz.

I nibbled with my lips on her nipple. I loved her nub as my right hand drifted down her stomach to the waistband of her shorts. I found her fly and unsnapped it. She gasped again, her face contorting as she felt this bliss.

"Ellie! You have to stop! You're dating my son and... No, no, don't do that!"

I shoved my hand into her shorts. Her zipper rasped down. My fingers found the waistband of her panties. I pushed into it. It was so exciting to slide my hand into the MILF's panties. I was seducing a married woman, my boyfriend's mother. I nursed with hunger while my digits pressed through her bush. She grew warmer. Wetter.

I brushed the folds of her pussy, her clit already hardening and jutting out of her thick pussy lips. She shuddered again, her boobs jiggling. I sucked with all my might, drawing in half her areola into my mouth. At the same time, my fingers slid through her labia, getting soaked by her married juices.

"This can't be happening," she moaned, her face contorting.

I popped my mouth off her nipple. "Mmm, it is. You're just so sexy, Mrs. Thompson. I can't resist. I love busty MILFs."

I darted my head over and sucked her other nipple into my mouth. I nursed on it with all my passion as I ran my fingers up and down her juicy pussy. Her cream soaked my digits and my palm. I pressed the heel of my hand against her clit.

She gasped and bucked.

I jammed two digits into her cunt's depths.

The MILF whimpered, her hot sheath squeezing down my fingers. I pressed my digits deeper and deeper into her married sheath. I massaged her clit, my own bud throbbing. Jizz and cream ran down my thighs. My skirts swirled about my legs while my glasses shifted on my nose.

I worshiped her nipple and fingered her twat. The MILF made such wonderful sounds. Her cream soaked my right hand. Her silky pubic hairs caressed my palm as I ground the heel of my hand into her clit. I massaged her bud in circles, her cunt squeezing and relaxing on my digits.

"Oh, my god, this can't be happening," she moaned.

I popped my mouth off her nub to purr, "It is, Mrs. Thompson. You're just that hot."

I kissed her hard and drove her back. She hit the entertainment system. It rattled and groaned as I pressed her against it, my tongue thrusting into her mouth. She kissed me back, tasting the cum and pussy juices smeared on my mouth by the naughty Ava.

The futa had changed my life, and I loved it.

I made out with the MILF. Our tongues dueled as I thrust a third finger into her pussy. Her hot sheath squeezed my three digits together. She shuddered and whimpered. I thrust them into her faster and faster, savoring her married depth's silky delight.

My left hand squeezed her boob until I found her nipple wet with my saliva. I twisted it. She shuddered, the shelf rattling behind her. Her hands grabbed my hips. She held me tight as we made out with furious passion.

I broke the kiss and pressed my forehead against hers. "You're going to cum for me, aren't you, Mrs. Thompson?"

"Yes!" she moaned. "What are you doing to me, Ellie?"

"Loving your sexy body!" I jammed my fingers deep into her

cunt and rubbed hard on her clit with the heel of my hand. "Mmm, you're just gorgeous. I love how hot you are. Such a MILF!"

She groaned and then kissed me. Her tongue thrust into my mouth. Her pussy clenched on me. Her hands clutched my hips and then her cunt went wild. Her sheath writhed around me, hot cream gushing out. A spicy musk spilled through the air as we moaned into each other's lips. I squeezed her nipple as I savored making her cum.

I broke the kiss and hissed, "That's it, you sexy mother. Mmm, you deserve that."

"Oh, god, it's been so long!" she moaned. "So long since I really came! Yes, yes! Ellie!"

She bucked, rattling the shelf. I loved it. My pussy blazed. My clit throbbed. I had to enjoy her next. I churned up her writhing pussy, thrusting my fingers into her depths over and over. I loved the way her face twisted with her bliss. Her eyes squeezed shut, cheeks twitching.

"Oh, yes, yes!" she moaned.

I ripped my fingers out of her cunt and stepped back. I shoved them into my mouth, pushing all three at once. I sucked her married juices off my digits, loving the spicy flavor. I shuddered, my left hand grabbing my skirt and hiking it.

She stood there, her bra and tank top shoved up and over her tits. Her shorts were undone and half-hanging on her hips. Her panties were gray and plain, peeking out through her open fly. She stared at me with dark eyes, her breasts jiggling as she panted.

I popped my fingers out and moaned, "I need you to eat me. Please, please, Mrs. Thompson, eat my pussy."

"I've never..." She stared at me. "Is that cum on your thighs."

"It's not your son's," I purred. "It's a girl's. You'll love it." I exposed my pussy, my blonde bush feeling so sticky. Eat me out, Mrs. Thompson."

With a groan, the MILF fell to her knees. She grabbed my hips again, this time with no dress in the way. I kept pulling it up, peeling it over my stomach and then exposing my small breasts. I took it off, my blond hair flying.

She licked at the cum leaking down my thigh, following it up and up to my pussy.

~~*~~

Ava Heart – The Futa-Succubus Shamshiel

I stroked my cock as I waited in the car, feeling the passion in the house. I smiled as I felt Mrs. Thompson's orgasm. The power of a woman who'd gone years without properly being satiated. I feasted on it, my dick throbbing. And through it all, Eloise was becoming more and more corrupt.

She was on the verge of it. I shivered, stroking my cock as I felt it building.

"You're going to love it, Eloise!" I moaned as Mrs. Thompson's lust for Eloise's cum-filled pussy exploded out of the house. I felt the MILF falling to her knees. She licked up my spunk. "You're going to explode, Eloise!"

~~*~~

Eloise "Ellie" White

Mrs. Thompson's tongue licked into my bush. She moaned as she stroked through my silky curls to caress my pussy lips. I gasped as she licked the jizz leaking out of my depths. My small breasts jiggled. I pushed up my glasses with my middle finger, trembling at the bliss rushing through me.

I had my boyfriend's mother lapping at my cunt.

Her tongue took another lick while she let out a feverish moan. She stroked my labia. She brushed my clit. It burst with pleasure, throbbing and aching like never before. I threw back my head, squeezing my eyes shut. I could feel Mrs. Thompson's desire. The feverish lust she had for my pussy.

She licked my pussy with such hunger. She fluttered her tongue up and down, lapping out the cum that leaked out of my depths. My cunt clenched, forcing more out into her mouth. She moaned with wild abandon.

"So good!" She took another lick, stroking my labia and brushing my clit. "You taste so good, Ellie."

"Mmm, just lick all that futa-cum out of my pussy," I moaned, my clit throbbing. It needed to be played with.

"Yes, yes!" gasped Mrs. Thompson, her dark eyes glossy with passion.

She thrust her tongue into my pussy. She buried it in deep and then scooped out the cum in me. I gasped at that. The heat swept through my body. I groaned, squeezing my eyes shut as the pleasure rushed through my nerves to my mind. My hips wiggled back and forth, grinding my pussy on her mouth. It was incredible. The pleasure was incredible.

"Yes, yes, yes!" I moaned. "Oh, that's it. That's what I need. Lick that cum out, Mrs. Thompson."

My pussy clenched around her tongue as it darted in to scoop out Ava's girl-cum. The MILF sent pleasure through me. She groaned as she did. I loved it. My clit throbbed and pulsed. I needed her to nurse on it.

I squeezed my little titties. I kneaded them, my nipples throbbing. My fingers slid up my firm mounds and found my nubs. I twisted the buttons. I gasped at the jolts of electricity shooting down to my pussy. To my clit.

"Mrs. Thompson!" I moaned.

"I love this cum in you!" she panted. "This pussy." Her tongue thrust deep into me, swirling around and stroking all my naughty bits.

"Please, please, suck on my clit!"

She fluttered her tongue to my bud. She stroked it and then latched on. The MILF sucked. I gasped at the nursing pressure on my clit. It was incredible. I moaned in relief. My bud felt so swollen. As she nursed, it pulsed and throbbed, growing more and more sensitive. Her warmth squeezed around her. Her lips were so tight about me. Her tongue stroked around it and... and...

Was my clit growing bigger?

I stared down at her as she nursed. I could feel more of her tongue on my clit. I gasped as she slid her mouth back, her eyes widening. The MILF had her lips wrapped around a growing shaft. It had the same beige as my skin as it thrust out of my pussy.

"No way," I gasped as my clit brushed the back of her throat. She pulled back farther, sucking and moaning.

I had a blossoming girl-cock. My shaft was growing so thick, as wide as Ava's. She kept pulling her head back as fast as I was growing, her lips sliding up my shaft. Then I stopped. I was hung, like Ava. Mrs. Thompson ripped her mouth off of me.

"Ellie!" she gasped in shock, her eyes were wild. "What? This? You have a cock!"

"I know," I hissed, my pussy clenching. I had a cock. I was a futa. None of the other girls Ava fucked became futas. My mother hadn't.

Why me?

Then Mrs. Thompson licked my dick. She groaned, grabbing it, fisting it. I shuddered as she licked it. Her eyes stared at me with such a feverish heat. I could feel it building between us. This wild lust. I had to fuck her.

"On your hands and knees!" I moaned, not hesitating. "I'm going to pound you so hard, Mrs. Thompson."

"Yes!" she hissed and spun around, aiming her ass at me.

I fell to my knees and ripped down her shorts barely hanging onto her rump. Then I hooked those gray panties hugging her bubbly butt. I yanked those down, exposing her dark-brown bush peeking through her thighs. Juices dripped from her. The spicy musk of her cunt mixed with the tangy scent from my own pussy.

I grabbed my futa-dick. Instinct guided me. I aimed it at her pussy, so eager to use my new appendage. Fingering her pussy had felt amazing. Now I needed the real delight of being in her married cunt with my girl-cock. The tip nuzzled through her silky bush. A heartbeat later, I found the wet folds of her cunt. Her thick labia spread around the crown of my dick.

I rammed into the MILF's depths.

Her head threw back. Her wavy hair fenced as she gasped out in delight. Her living room echoed with her passion. I added my own voice. It was incredible. A heady sensation that was almost indescribable. Her silky walls squeezed around my thick shaft. The tip was extra sensitive, drinking in the wet slide into her cunt.

"Oh, my god, yes!" I moaned. "Mrs. Thompson!"

Then I drew back. My cock throbbed in her pussy. This wild pleasure surged through me. I gasped at the silky grip of her twat around my new clit-dick. It was outstanding. My head threw back, glasses shifting on my nose. My blonde hair danced around my shoulders. Heat flowed down my shaft and diffused through my own twat.

It reached these points in me. Hard and throbbing. They were full of something that had to escape. My cum. I had to spurt my seed into Mrs. Thompson's pussy. This wild need to erupt seized me, and I thrust forward.

I buried to the hilt in Mrs. Thompson. I slammed hard into her. Her bubbly butt-cheeks jiggled. My small breasts quivered. The heat surged through me. I groaned, loving every moment of it. This amazing heat swept through my body. I shuddered, squeezed my eyes shut as I loved every last moment of pumping away at her hot snatch.

"Yes, yes, yes!" I moaned. "Mrs. Thompson! Your pussy!"

"Your cock!" she squealed, her wavy hair swaying as she shuddered. "Oh, my god! Your cock is amazing! How?"

"I don't know!" I pumped away at her, driving my girl-dick into her pussy over and over again. It was incredible. "Does 'how' matter right now?"

Her pussy squeezed about my dick. It was incredible to feel. To experience this wonderful passion. I thrust away hard and fast at her pussy. Her married twat gripped me. She massaged me, building and building that orgasm at the tip of my cock.

I would erupt in her. I would fire so much cum into her twat. I shuddered, plunging hard and fast into her pussy. I savored her hot flesh squeezing about me. That wonderful passion brought me closer and closer to erupting.

I wanted to cum. To explode in her. The feverish need gripped me.

My hands swept up her sides to grab her large breasts. I squeezed her soft mounds. I held them as I buried into her MILF pussy again and again. Her silky, hot sheath gripped me. Massaged me. I drank in the friction as I slammed into her hard and fast.

Her moans echoed through her living room. "Yes, yes, yes! Fuck me with this impossible cock, Ellie! Ram that dick into me!"

"You're going to cum so hard on me!" I moaned. "And then I'm going to flood you. I'm going to fill you with so much jizz!"

"Yes!" she moaned, her pussy squeezing around me.

The heady rush of her pussy gripping me was so wonderful. It was such a treat. I savored it, my heart pounding in my chest. The pleasure swept through me as I plunged into her cunt again and again. I gasped, burying hard into her. I slammed to the hilt in her cunt. I loved the heat of her twat gripping me.

It was outstanding. I shuddered, loving her snatch squeezing about me. She gripped me tight. She held me with that wonderful cunt. I groaned, thrusting into her again and again. My fingers dug into her tits as her pussy brought me closer and closer to my first futa-climax.

I wanted it. Ached for it.

"Mrs. Thompson!" I moaned, driving into her silky depths. "Oh, Mrs. Thompson!"

"I know!" she moaned. "Oh, my god, I know! This cock... Holy shit, this cock! You're huge. You're impossibly huge! I'm going to explode on you!"

"Do it!" I moaned, driving to the hilt in her again and again.

I slammed to the hilt in her. I buried with all my might into her cunt. I slammed in, my titties jiggling. My hair danced around my shoulders. The pleasure rippled through my body. I gasped as the ache in the depths of my body swelled. The pressure built and built.

My cum had to escape.

It had to spurt into her pussy.

I couldn't stop fucking her if I wanted to. This feverish heat gripped me. Her pussy felt so amazing. She massaged me, bringing me closer and closer to that wild moment of my eruption. I would explode in her. I would fire so much cum into her pussy. Spurt after spurt of my spunk. It would be incredible.

I reveled in it as I plunged into her again and again. I buried hard and fast into her. I plunged to the hilt in her over and over again. It was incredible. I loved it. Savored every last moment of burying into her twat. I loved it. My body shuddered, the rapture swelling and swelling in me. I climbed towards that wonderful explosion.

I slammed into her.

"Ellie!" she gasped. "Yes!"

Her pussy went wild about my clit-dick. She spasmed and writhed. She felt incredible. I groaned, savoring her flesh writhing around my girl-cock. It was stupendous to feel. To experience that wonderful passion rippling around my clit-dick. I would have such a huge explosion of rapture. I would fire all my cum into her.

I would hose her married pussy down. It would be incredible.

"Mrs. Thompson!"

"Cum in me!" she moaned as her twat sucked at my dick.

I thrust into her writhing depths, the pleasure surging to the tip of my cock. I threw back my head and gasped. My hands squeezed her tits as my first futa-climax burst inside of me. The cum rushed out of my cock and fired into the MILF's pussy.

I spurted into her pussy. I groaned, my heart beating so fast as I unloaded my cum into my boyfriend's mother. Intense ecstasy erupted from my clit-dick that met the heat sweeping through my body from my writhing twat. I swayed there, dizzy from the dual raptures that filled my body.

I groaned, pussy juices gushing down my thighs. I pumped more and more spunk into her pussy. Her flesh sucked at my cock. She rippled and writhed around me, working out the jizz from my spurting clit-dick.

It was incredible.

"Yes, yes, yes!" I moaned. "Oh, my god, that's good. That's awesome! I love it!"

"You're flooding me!" she gasped. "Oh, yes, yes! That's so amazing!"

My cum fired over and over into her pussy. I unloaded spurt after spurt of passion into her. I couldn't stop. My pussy writhed as I bucked through my bliss. The dual pleasures blazed through my mind. ecstasy consumed my thoughts. I groaned and gasped.

Fired the last of my spunk into her pussy.

"Oh, my god!" she panted as her pussy's spasms slowed. "Oh,

Ellie, that was incredible. I can't believe that just happened."

"I know," I moaned, shuddering in bliss.

Then the door flew open and Ava Heart entered. The redheaded dickgirl was naked, her large breasts bouncing. Her futa-cock thrust from the shaved folds of her pussy. Her green eyes smoldered. She was an eighteen-year-old goddess. I shuddered at the sight of her.

"My turn," she purred.

~~*~~

Ava Heart – The Futa-Succubus Shamshiel

Eloise's corruption was almost complete. She had just one more step to follow. That would have to wait for tomorrow. For now, I had to enjoy that girl-dick. I shuddered as she pulled her cock out of Mrs. Thompson's pussy. A flood of pearly spunk matted the panting hot wife's bush.

I had fed on both their lusts. It had been delicious.

I licked my lips, my anticipation sweeping heat through my body. I shuddered, my hips wiggling from side to side. This would be such a wicked delight to enjoy. I couldn't wait to experience every moment of it. I would revel in it.

"On your back," I moaned. "I'm riding that cock."

"Another one!" gasped Mrs. Thompson, staring at me, her large tits swaying beneath her. She licked her lips as she stared at my perfect, succubal flesh. She shuddered, her eyes wide as they drank in the curves of my body. "Oh, my god, where do you come from?"

"Far, far away," I moaned. "Empty rapture, I need that cock in me, Eloise."

"Yes, yes," the once-pure girl moaned. The corrupted futa sank back onto her back, her dick soaked in MILF pussy cream. She held it up before her, the shaft gleaming.

The scent of salty cum, spicy cunt, and tangy twat filled my nose. I breathed it in as I straddled Eloise. Her little titties quivered. Her blue eyes stared up at me with a feverish light through her glasses. I smiled at her as I grabbed her dick.

"Mmm, enjoy it?" I asked even though I had felt her passion out in the car.

"Yes!" she moaned as I lowered myself to her dick.

My pussy lips touched the tip of her cock.

She gasped in delight. "Ava!"

"Colorless passion!" I moaned as my labia spread over her futa-dick. I shuddered as I sank down her. It was such a treat to feel her nuzzling apart my pussy lips.

I sank down the corrupted virgin's cock. I shuddered, squeezing about her. She gasped, her face contorting in delight. She was gorgeous. Perfect. I had so much fun bringing her to this uninhibited state. My hands slid up to her breasts. I grabbed her little titties as I swallowed more and more of her girl-dick.

It was a huge shaft. A proper cock. Not like those little things Shane and the other guys at the college had. This was a dick. A futa's dick. I threw back my head, my large tits jiggling. I sank down the last few inches of her shaft, my dick resting on her belly.

"This is so hot," Mrs. Thompson moaned, convulsed by lust, not caring about betraying her husband or son. "You both are so sexy."

She ripped off her top and bra and then knelt by us, staring at my cock as I slid up Eloise's amazing futa-dick. My cunt gripped her. I held her tight as I climbed higher and higher up her shaft. I groaned, squeezing about her. She was incredible.

I reached the pinnacle of Eloise's futa-cock. I hovered there, my hips wiggling from side to side, and then I impaled myself back down her girl-dick. My cock smacked into her stomach. I groaned at the thudding impact. It echoed through the room. I shuddered, trembling as the heat flowed through me.

My pussy gripped her dick, my own shaft bobbing before me as I rode her. Eloise's face twisted in delight. Pleasure rippled across her expression while the friction sent such stimulation through me. I drank it in, my large tits swaying.

"Oh, yes!" Eloise moaned. "Ava! Ava! This cock is incredible!"

I winked at her.

She grinned and winked back.

She was blossoming into her sexuality now, no longer repressing it. She was free to enjoy herself. I shuddered as I slammed down her again, my dick smacking into her belly. Precum flicked out and splattered her little titties.

They gleamed with my cream on them. They looked so cute decorated in the clear precum. I grabbed them, massaging my juices into her firm titties. I smeared it across her pink nipples. She moaned, her back arching as I rose up her cock.

Lust surged from Mrs. Thompson. I devoured it as she ducked her head down and, gasping out, "I need this!" engulfed my futa-dick.

She sucked it hard into her mouth. She nursed on it. My pussy clenched around Eloise's cock. I groaned and slammed down her shaft. I took her futa-dick to the hilt in me. I reveled in it. My back arched, my tits jiggling.

It was incredible to feel Eloise's shaft in me. That wonderful shaft stretched out my pussy. I groaned, squeezing my cunt around her girl-dick. I rose up her as the MILF nursed on me, sending all that pleasure down my shaft to my twat gripping hard cock.

"Oh, that's hot!" moaned Eloise. "Mrs. Thompson, suck that girl-dick!"

"Mmm, just drink down all my cum when I erupt!" I moaned. "You naughty wife. I bet you don't do this for your husband."

She moaned around my cock and sucked harder. I could feel the truth of it as I ate her lust. I feasted on both their pleasure, devouring it as I worked my pussy up and down Eloise's cock. I shuddered, slamming down her, my orgasm building.

So was hers.

"Empty rapture!" I moaned, my tits heaving when I hit the pinnacle of her dick. Then I slammed down her.

"Yes, yes, Ava!" she moaned, trembling. "I love having a futa-cock!"

"I know!" I moaned. "It's amazing!"

She nodded.

Mrs. Thompson nursed on my futa-dick. Her tongue danced around my tip. She caressed it. Stroked it. She sent such bliss flowing down my cock. My cunt clenched around Eloise's thick shaft. The friction increased.

My pleasure built.

It was a feedback loop. The more Mrs. Thompson sucked on my dick, the better Eloise's cock felt in my cunt. The better her cock felt in my cunt, the more my dick ached in Mrs. Thompson's mouth. The loop built and built my ecstasy, driving me towards my explosion.

I groaned, not holding back. This was such a magical moment. It was amazing. I trembled, my cunt squeezing down on Eloise's thick girl-dick. The friction sent pleasure shooting up to the aching tip of my girl-dick. My ovaries brimmed with my huge load of cum.

I would fire so much into the hot wife's mouth.

"Empty rapture, don't stop sucking!" I moaned, my pussy squeezing about Eloise's big dick as I impaled myself down her girth.

"Are you going to cum on me?" gasped the cute Eloise.

"Yes!" I howled as it happened. I climaxed. "Colorless passion!"

My pussy convulsed around Eloise's futa-dick. Hot cum jetted out of my girl-cock and into Mrs. Thompson's hungry mouth. The MILF moaned, her lusts going wild as she drank down more of my salty cum, recognizing the flavor from Eloise's cunt.

The dual pleasure rushed through my body. The delight of cumming with a pussy and a cock swept through me. My cunt writhed and spasmed around Eloise's girl-dick, sucking at her. Waves of ecstasy washed from my twat. Jolts of rapture fired from my shaft.

"Empty rapture, I love this world!" I howled.

"Ava! Ava!" squeaked Eloise, her pleasure surging through her. It hit the pinnacle of her cock.

Hot cum jetted into my pussy. I shuddered, reveling in the wild thrill of having futa-cum firing into my pussy once more. It was wonderful. Amazing. I loved every moment of it. My body trembled and bucked, the rapture surging through me.

My pussy spasmed wildly. Mrs. Thompson sucked out my futa-cum while my cunt milked the girl-seed from Eloise's dick. I shuddered through the pleasure. I moaned and gasped, my big boobs heaving.

"Colorless passion!" I gasped, hitting the peak.

"So good!" whimpered Eloise. "It's so good."

"It is!" I moaned and glanced over at the MILF. "On your knees. I want to lick that pussy clean. Eloise needs to enjoy my asshole!"

The girl, spurting the last of her cum into my pussy, gasped, "Yes!"

The MILF spun around and bent over. Her bush held much of Eloise's delicious cum. I breathed in that mix of spice and salt. I groaned and slid my pussy off of the blonde cutie's big dick. Pleasure shot through my body. I groaned.

Her cum rushed out of me the moment I popped off. Her jizz spilled down my thighs. I moaned, feeling so naughty as I turned to Mrs. Thompson. I bent over, grabbing her plump butt-cheeks and nuzzling my face towards her sloppy cunt.

I licked at the cum coating her bush, savoring that mix of salty and spicy cream. I shuddered. Another futa's seed. It had been so long since I had the pleasures a *real* cock provided. More of Eloise's jizz ran down my thighs, that wonderful, ticklish sensation of sending a shiver through me.

I groaned and wiggled my hips, feeling the effect my teasing had on Eloise.

"Mmm, you want me to fuck your asshole with my cock," she said with such confidence. "You want me to ram my futa-dick into your naughty bowels." She smacked her wet cock against my right ass-cheek.

"Yes!" I moaned and then licked up more cum from Mrs. Thompson's silky bush. "So hard. Empty rapture, I want you to fuck my slutty asshole."

Eloise purred in delight and smacked my other butt-cheek with her cock, leaving more of my juices coating my flesh. This was so delicious. My large boobs swayed beneath me as I quivered. She had metamorphosized into something beautiful.

Tears almost came to my eyes.

I nuzzled deeper into Mrs. Thompson's dark-brown bush to find the thick folds of her pussy. I stroked her labia, gathering up salty cum flavored by her spicy delight. My fingers dug into her rump. I kneaded the MILF ass while I licked and lapped.

As I did, Eloise's cock slid down into my crack. I shuddered as her wet tip probed between my butt-cheeks. She slid lower and lower. I trembled, my futa-dick throbbing beneath me as she neared my naughty asshole.

I had to be fucked so hard by her. I needed that thick dick ramming into me. It would be incredible. I would cum so hard on her. I gasped into Mrs. Thompson's pussy as that thick dick nuzzled into my backdoor.

"I'm going to pound your asshole, Ava Heart!" Eloise moaned and thrust.

The tip of her girl-dick pushed on my sphincter. I groaned into Mrs. Thompson's pussy. My asshole stretched and stretched, my anal ring surrendering to Eloise's passion. Her confident lust surged through the air, feeding my succubal hungers even as her futa-cock fed my carnal desires.

My tongue thrust deep into Mrs. Thompson's married pussy. I fluttered around in her, stirring cum and pussy cream into a delicious froth. At the same moment, my asshole stretched to its limits. Eloise's futa-cock popped into my bowels.

"Oh, my god, yes!" the girl moaned as she savored her first taste of receiving anal delights. "Yes, yes, yes! You're so hot! So tight!"

"Ooh, sodomize her, Ellie!" the MILF moaned. "She's got her tongue so deep in my pussy. She's stirring me up."

"Mmm, I am," I moaned as more and more of Eloise's cock penetrated my bowels. I sucked at Mrs. Thompson's pussy and drew out that frothy mix of cream.

I shuddered, the heat swirling through my body. It was incredible to enjoy. The pleasure was intense. Fantastic. I savored the cum and pussy cream I sucked out of the MILF's pussy as the heat from my bowels washed through my cunt.

My pussy drank it in. Hot cream and futa-jizz dripped down my throbbing shaft as more and more of Eloise's girl-dick invaded my bowels. I clenched down on her, loving the spike of pleasure that shot through her body.

Then she bottomed out on me.

"Mmm, that's what you want!" she moaned, her hands sliding around my waist. Her left hand found my boob, squeezing it. Her right found my cock dripping in cum and cream. She smeared the sexual fluids up and down my shaft as she stroked me. "Isn't it?"

"Yes!" I hissed, squeezing my bowels down around her, pleasure flowing up my shaft to my pussy, meeting the heat melting from my asshole.

She drew back.

I moaned into Mrs. Thompson's pussy. I squeezed and kneaded her asshole as I feasted on her spicy cunt. I had sucked out all of Eloise's cum, leaving just delicious cream to drink. I feasted on it as the new futa rammed her clit-dick into my bowels.

Her silky bush rubbed into my rump when she bottomed out on me. Her right hand flew up and down my girl-cock, stroking me twice for every once she slammed her futa-dick to the hilt in my bowels. I groaned, reveling in it. This wonderful heat swept through my body.

I whimpered and moaned, wiggling my hips back and forth. I stirred that amazing cock around inside my bowels as she sodomized me hard. I devoured their pleasure, both of them gasping and moaning as they enjoyed my body in different ways.

"Oh, god, Ava!" moaned Mrs. Thompson. "That tongue. That sweet tongue!"

"Ava! Ava! Your asshole!" squeaked Eloise, her dick thrusting harder and faster into my bowels. Her hand fisted my dick.

The dual pleasure swirled through my dripping cunt. The heat fed the pressure in my ovaries. Another explosion would consume me. Another burst of ecstasy. I wanted it. Craved it. I clenched my bowels around her thrusting cock.

She gasped in delight at the increased friction. She fucked me as fast as she stroked my clit-dick now. Her girl-cock buried into my asshole again and again. I felt her pleasure rising as she built my own. I licked at Mrs. Thompson's pussy, drinking her cream and passion.

Then I sucked on her clit.

"Oh, god, yes!" the MILF groaned. "Ava! You naughty dickgirl!"

"She's so naughty!" Eloise moaned, driving her girl-cock to the hilt in me. "She's a wicked, naughty succubus!"

"Mmm, I am," I moaned, squeezing my pussy around her clit-dick. The wild passion surged through me. It was amazing.

Eloise rammed her girl-dick in me and came.

"Ava!"

Her cum fired hot into my bowels. Her hand pumped wildly up and down my clit-dick as she unloaded spurt after spurt of her spunk into me. I shuddered, savoring that delight flooding into me. It was amazing. I moaned on Mrs. Thompson's clit.

Then her orgasm burst through her. "Ava! You naughty dickgirl-slut, yes!"

Her spicy cream bathed my face. Her MILF pussy gushed so much juices. I opened wide and gulped them down as more and more of Eloise's jizz fired into my bowels. The heady rush swept over me. I feasted on both their orgasms.

Eloise's hand stroked to the pinnacle of my cock.

I joined them.

"Empty rapture!" I howled into the hot wife's cunt.

My futa-dick erupted. Hot cum fired from my cock and hit the carpet. My body bucked. My asshole writhed around Eloise's unloading shaft. Her futa-seed pumped into my spasming bowels while my spunk splashed the floor.

Pussy juices gushed out of my cunt. Hot cream flooded down my thighs and my shaft held in her stroking hand. She pumped up and down my erupting shaft, milking my clit-dick just like my asshole wrung dry her girl-cock.

"I love being a futa, Ava!" howled Eloise. "I'm so glad you seduced me. Yes, yes, yes!"

I shuddered, savoring the passion bursting through her. It drowned me as I trembled through my orgasm. I licked up Mrs. Thompson's pussy cream and savored the corruption of the once-innocent and virginal Eloise.

I loved being a futa-succubus.

As my asshole milked out the last of her cum and my dick fired the last spurt of my girl-seed, I knew that her corruption was almost complete. I couldn't wait for that moment. It would be stupendous. I loved this world. All the vibrancy. All the passion.

All the sexy women to enjoy.

~~*~~

Eloise "Ellie" White

I panted as Ava and I left Mrs. Thompson to clean up. My clit felt so strange now. I could grow it into a cock. I shuddered as I glanced at Ava. The redheaded futa glanced back at me, dressed again. Her belly shirt held those lovely tits.

"What are you thinking?" she asked me, her lips smeared in Mrs. Thompson's yummy cream.

"I'm wondering what other naughty fun we can get up to?"

I smiled. "There is one last thing, but it has to wait for tomorrow on your date with Shane."

I blinked at that. "I shouldn't break up with him?"

"Oh, no," she said and grinned. "Trust me. Go on the date. It'll be memorable."

To be continued...

Transforming Ellie's Innocent Desires

Corrupted by the Futa Succubus 6

by

Reed James

Transforming Ellie's Innocent Desires

Ava Heart – The Futa-Succubus Shamshiel

A shiver of excitement rippled through me. I stood on the second floor of Eloise's house, her mother's mouth wrapped around my girl-dick and sucking it. I was so excited about what was to happen. The final steps in Eloise's corruption.

I watched her through the bedroom window as her boyfriend Shane picked her up for their Friday night date. He had no idea the girl in the pink dress had a big surprise beneath her skirt. I shuddered, as Mrs. White sucked hungrily on my girl-dick.

Mr. White whimpered in the background, getting off on me using his wife as my whore.

"Mmm, drink all my cum, and then I'll have time to fuck you maybe three times before I have to go," I told Mrs. White.

The sexy MILF moaned and sucked harder, bobbing her head. Her husband groaned in the background and masturbated his cock faster, corrupted by my lusts just like his busty wife. I smiled, so eager for Eloise to take that final plunge.

~~*~~

Eloise "Ellie" White

I still couldn't believe that Ava wanted me to go on my date with Shane. I think she wanted me to make a cuckold out of him like she had my father. He had spent last night watching Ava and I fuck my mother while he begged us to use her.

"I'm just a small-dick cuck," he had groaned. *"Fuck my wife with real cocks! Give her pleasure."*

It had been so kinky.

"God, you look gorgeous," Shane said as he pulled away from my house. "Just radiant. You've looked this way all day. You've changed, Ellie."

"Mmm, I've matured," I said, my clit throbbing. It wanted to be a dick. I wanted to fuck so many girls. I had enjoyed fucking my friends at school. My best friend, Jenifer, had squealed on my dick. Scarlett had loved every second of it. I was so glad I was a futa now. I loved women. Ava had corrupted me with her girl-cock.

And she would be waiting for us. The last stage of the date.

"This is going to be a special night," he said.

"Yes, it is," I said, my pussy on fire. It took all my self-control not to grow my girl-dick.

"You can't unleash it until I tell you," Ava had said. *"Not once Shane picks you up. If you can control yourself, you'll get something amazing."*

I wanted that amazing delight. I pushed my glasses up my nose, my body trembling in the sleek, pink dress I wore. My blonde hair fell around my face in a mass of curls. I wasn't wearing panties or a bra, my nipples poking at the dress.

Shane noticed. He kept glancing at me. I enjoyed the attention. It was a shame he wasn't attractive to me any longer. I liked Shane; he had been a great boyfriend. I really thought he would get my virginity, that our relationship might last, but now...

I had fucked his mother. She had guzzled down my girl-cum.

We reached the restaurant. It wasn't that fancy, he was a college student after all, but it also wasn't Olive Garden. It was fun going in and having dinner, even if the waitress had my interest more than him. God, she was sexy in these tight, black pants that hugged her ass. I just wanted to bend her over, grow my cock, and fuck her right there at the table. Just pound her hard.

After having all my lusts uncorked by Ava yesterday when she fucked my mother, it was hard not to just indulge when I felt the itch. My toes curled in my shoes, my pussy all hot and juicy. And my clit...

God, did my clit throb and ache. It wanted to burst out and play with that sexy waitress. Alicia... What a yummy name. I wanted to be screaming it out as I fired my cum into her asshole while the rest of the diners watched and envied my big girl-cock.

Eloise White, I thought to myself, *you are becoming as big a pervert as Ava.*

I smiled at that.

"You really are different," Shane said as he sat across from me.

"Aren't we all different from who we were the previous day?" I asked, a toying smile on my lips. "New experiences. New thoughts. New atoms making up our body. Cells die every day in our bodies and new ones grow to replace them. We're reborn in a thousand ways every minute."

"Huh," he said. "That's kind of deep." He smiled. "Your confidence is sexy, Ellie. You know that?"

I winked at him. "You're going to love tonight."

He grinned.

Dinner was delicious. I was told to order whatever I wanted, money wasn't a consideration, but I didn't see the need to order the most expensive thing on the menu. They had a salmon dish that sounded delightful. It came with a spicy, squash sauce. Shane got the steak. He drooled at it when it came with fried onions on it.

We chatted, the waitress coming by attracting both our attention. For a moment, I realized we were both checking out her ass. That was something I certainly hadn't expected. I squeezed my thighs tight against my clit.

For dessert, we shared a slice of chocolate lava cake that was delicious, and then we were off to the movie. I thought we were going to the local cinema, but instead he took me to the drive-in. In a move that utterly shocked me about Shane, we were here to watch a pair of Forties-era romances. Those old-fashioned ones where the men were dashing and the women elegant.

It was great. And when Shane put his move on me, I found I didn't mind kissing him. I was excited. This was important. I had to get him in the right mood. Ava was quite clear on that. So I kissed him, his lips strong and rough. Despite shaving, I felt a hint of stubble, not soft like Ava's or my mother's or even his mother's lips.

"Do you love me?" I asked in between kisses.

"I do," he groaned, his hand on my thigh. "God, Ellie, I do. You're radiant. Never had a girl who made me, you know, work for it."

"Who didn't put out at the drop of the hat?" I asked.

"Yeah," he groaned. "It's exciting. You stand out. You're perfect." He kissed me again, and I shivered.

I felt his love. I shuddered, my pussy growing hotter and hotter. It was getting closer and closer to the time. I broke the kiss with him, both of us panting. Despite my attraction being for the same sex now, I was getting turned on.

"I have a hotel room," I said. "I want this to be a special night."

"Damn," he said, leaning back, looking stunned. "A hotel room?"

"There's no privacy at my place, and you still live with your parents, too."

"Yeah," he groaned. "Backseat's not that special, is it?"

I giggled. "Surprisingly, it's not."

He grinned at me and then kissed me again. I closed my eyes. If Ava hadn't come into my life, I would have really enjoyed this. I would have let Shane take me into the backseat and take my virginity. I could feel that now.

But Ava and her futa-cock and *had* thrust into my life and changed me. A moment of sadness swept over me for the Ellie I used to be. But that was the past. I had been transformed. And there was something naughty waiting.

When the second movie ended happily ever after, which made me smile, Shane looked eager for more. I told him about the hotel, and he drove there was a reckless enthusiasm. My excitement mounted, aching to be there. I couldn't wait for the fun to begin. The big and wicked surprise.

131

I put my hand on his thigh, squeezing him through his slacks. He glanced at me, his handsome face blazing with passion. He had that square-cut chin that made girls—girls who hadn't gained clit-dicks—swoon. I had always been surprised he dated me. I couldn't wait for him to become my little cuckold. That had to be Ava's plan.

She would make him like we made my father.

My pussy soaked my panties. My clit pulsed and throbbed. We approached the hotel. Then we were pulling up before the front doors. The valet was there, waiting for us. He didn't seem that surprised that we had no luggage with us. He saw us dressed for date night. He must have known.

Shane escorted me in. He kept caressing me as we checked in, amorous and ready for the fun to come. The concierge, a tall woman with her brown hair in a bun and a nice rack that her buttoned-up uniform couldn't hide, had a smile on her lips as she finished checking us in and handed over our keycards.

"Enjoy your stay," she said. I wanted to enjoy her. Pull those hairpins, let her hair down, and then fuck her mouth. She had such plump lips.

Shane took the short elevator ride to pin me against the wall and kiss me. I groaned, my body so ready for the fun. I was on fire. My heart pounded in my chest. The heat swept through me as Shane's passion filled me.

He wanted me bad. I could feel it. This was so naughty.

Then we were heading down the hallway. It was incredible. My heart pounded in my chest, pumping the exciting heat through my veins. My clit pulsed and throbbed as we counted rooms. I was giggling as we came closer and closer.

"623!" I shouted, clinging to him.

He thrust the keycard in. The door opened. He kissed me again before I could stop him. He pushed me back, his tongue in my mouth. I shuddered as a feminine voice cleared her throat to get our attention.

Ava Heart lay stretched out naked on the king-sized bed in the middle of the room. I had no idea how she had gotten in here. She had told me not to worry about that issue. She would be waiting for me. I shuddered and broke the kiss.

"What?" Shane gasped. "Ava? What are you...?"

"If you love me," I said, breaking from Shane, "I want you to watch. Just sit there and witness my pleasure. Will you do that for me."

"Jesus, Ava got you, too?" he groaned even as his hand went down to his pants.

Ava hugged me from behind, her large breasts pillowing into me. She had perfect tits. Nice and big the way I loved them. Everything about her was perfection. Her red hair falling about her youthful and vampish face, the glint of her green eyes, the curve of her hips, the shaved perfection of her vulva, and that big clit-dick she could grow.

"You do love me, right?" I moaned as Ava swept aside my blonde hair to kiss at the inner slope of my neck.

"Yes," groaned Shane, watching me, his hand massaging his dick. "You're going to let her do things to you?"

"Mmm, yes," I moaned. "I told you, I want this to be special."

Then I turned in Ava's arms. I came face to face with my seductress. She had a big grin on her face, delight in her green eyes. She kissed me on the mouth with hunger. Her lips felt so soft and silky. No whiskers brushed me.

It felt so right.

I melted into it, kissing her back with passion. Shane groaned as he watched us make out. Ava's hands grabbed my rump. She gripped my ass hard. She dug her fingers into my rump, kneading me as I trembled in her arms. It was delightful. I shuddered my tongue dancing with hers. They played together as our bodies trembled.

My pussy clenched, juices soaking through my bush to dribble down my thighs. Ava's tongue plundered my mouth and danced with mine. She tasted so sweet. Her spicy musk filled the air, mixing with my own tangy delight. My glasses shifted as we made out.

Then she turned me. She pushed me back onto the bed. I gasped as I fell backward. Our lips broke apart. I felt like I floated for a moment and then I was bouncing on the soft mattress. My skirts flared up my thighs. Ava licked her lips.

"Mmm, just watch me love your girlfriend," Ava purred, staring down at me.

"God, yes," groaned Shane, still groping himself.

"You do love me," I moaned in delight, savoring this thrill. Did my mom feel this last night when we fucked her in front of my dad? This wonderful joy of being watched by someone who loved you while you enjoyed futa-passion.

Ava was on me, her large breasts swaying. I grabbed them, squeezing those big boobs in my greedy hands as her fingers grabbed the top of my dress. She tugged the sleek material down. It slid over my breasts. My small titties popped out, both quivering for a moment.

"Mmm, is this your first time seeing these breasts, Shane?" Ava asked as her hands squeezed my tits.

"Yes," he groaned.

She massaged mine, her thumbs working in slow circles. "Is it hot watching me play with them instead?"

He let out a strangled, "It is."

Ava shuddered. "Empty rapture, I love this."

She ducked her head down and sucked my nipple into her mouth. I gasped at the warmth of her lips slipping around my nub. She sucked hard. The pleasure shot through me. My cunt clenched. A wild heat rippled through my body. I groaned, my heart bursting with passion. This was so insane. I couldn't believe this was happening.

And yet here she was sucking my nipple while Shane watched. He became my cuckold as Ava's tongue danced around my nub. I groaned in delight, my cunt on fire. Her every suck sent pleasure shooting down to my twat. This night would be so wild. So magical.

Then her mouth popped off. She smiled at me. "Mmm, her nipples taste so sweet. Your girlfriend is such a sexy thing, Shane."

"She is," he groaned. "God, you're hot, Ellie. This is so hot."

"Shane," I moaned, smiling at him.

Then I gasped as Ava engulfed my other nub in her mouth. She sucked hard. Her lips sealed about it. The pleasure shot through me. I groaned, my cunt clenching. Wild heat swept through my body. I savored it. My cunt squeezed tight.

She nursed on me with hunger. Her hunger swept through me.

I groaned as my nipple throbbed in her mouth. My thighs rubbed together. My pussy grew juicier and juicier, soaking my bush. I groaned and trembled, blonde tresses spilling about my cheeks, my glasses shifting on my nose.

"Oh, yes, Shane!" I gasped. "You're going to watch Ava fuck me because you love me!"

"I will!" he panted, his face flushed. His dark eyes were glossy. Then he started unbuttoning his shirt, exposing his muscular chest, a dark patch of curly hair across his pecs and breastbone.

Ava popped her mouth off and moaned, "If you haven't seen her tits, then you haven't seen her pussy yet, have you?"

"No," he croaked as Ava crawled down my body. She rubbed her cheek into my stomach covered by my dress. Her hands grabbed my skirt and pushed it up.

I lifted my rump, letting her bunch my skirt around my belly, exposing almost all of me. She rubbed a finger through my blonde bush, sliding it down to my hot folds. She brushed my clit. I gasped, aching to transform.

But she hadn't told me to do it. I wanted that special reward. I could control myself. For a little while longer. She massaged my bud and then threw a look over at Shane now shoving down his pants, his cock tenting his boxers.

"Look at this," she said, her fingers parting my pussy lips. "Mmm, can you see down into her pink." She shifted out of the way. "That's her pussy. She doesn't have her cherry any longer. I took it from her yesterday."

"Oh, god," groaned Shane. "With a strap-on? Your fingers."

"Wouldn't you like to know," Ava said. "I got to touch this pussy before you. Mmm, your girlfriend gave me what she wouldn't give you. And you're still here. Still watching me do this."

Shane groaned as Ava darted her head down. She pressed her mouth against my pussy. She kissed at my vulva and then she thrust her tongue right into my twat. I gasped and shuddered, my clit wanting to turn into a dick. But I didn't let it.

I controlled myself.

Shane stroked himself as he watched Ava feasting on me. The naughty redheaded futa had her tongue thrust into me. She fluttered it around in me, stirring me up. Her fingers still held my cunt lips open. My labia rubbed into her lips.

I gasped, the pleasure rippling through my body. It was intense. Delicious. I enjoyed every bit of it. The heat built and built in my juicy depths. Her every lick drove me towards my orgasm. It wouldn't take much.

I had been simmering all night.

I grabbed the sheets, clutching tight to them as Ava fluttered her tongue around in me. Then she attacked my clit. I gasped, my bud wanting to sprout, but I held it off. I whimpered, my breasts jiggling. Shane watched me, his hand sliding up and down his little cock.

He was small, like my dad. He didn't have that huge dick that Ava did. My pussy clenched, aching to be penetrated as she nursed on my clit. My moans gasped through the room. She groaned, staring at me with such hunger.

"Ellie, damn," he groaned. "That's so hot."

"Yes!" I moaned. "I'm going to cum on her mouth, Shane. And you still love me?"

"I do," he groaned. "I love you, Ellie. Cum on her face. Oh, god, do that!"

"Yes!" I gasped and that did it.

I came.

My pussy convulsed. My clit throbbed in Ava's mouth. I almost lost all control. I almost let my futa-dick explode as the waves of rapture swept through me. Luckily, Ava abandoned it. The redhead lapped at the flood gushing out of me. She licked up the cream pouring out of me. It was such a delicious thing to feel. I loved every moment of it.

My body trembled, the heat surging through me. I loved every second of her licking and lapping and nursing at me. The pleasure surged through me. It was outstanding. I shuddered on the bed, whimpering, moaning.

"I'm cumming so hard, Shane!" I moaned. "I'm drowning her."

"I can see that," he groaned. "Damn."

"Mmm, colorless passion," purred Ava. She rose, her face drenched in my juices. "Do you want to see how I took her virginity,

Shane?"

"Yes!" he groaned.

"With this!"

From her shaved pussy folds, her clit blossomed. It thrust out, pink at first, pulsing with her heartbeat. Shane's hand stopped stroking his cock as his jaw dropped. He watched her futa-dick grow thicker. Longer. It swelled and swelled, the shaft fading to her pale beige. All except that gorgeous tip. I licked my lips, staring at the crown gaining its slit.

Beading with precum.

"This is what I took your girlfriend's cherry with!" Ava moaned. "My big futa-dick. It's so much bigger than yours!"

"Yes, it is!" I moaned. "And she's going to fuck me with it, Shane!"

"Damn," he groaned and resumed stroking his cock.

~~*~~

Ava Heart – The Futa-Succubus Shamshiel

As I moved over the trembling Eloise, I felt the love and lust from Shane. That perfect mix of attraction and desire that made a cuckold such a treat. He was watching me fuck his girlfriend. He hadn't even done anything with her. I had stolen every bit of her away.

Perfect.

Eloise's blue eyes stared up at me from behind her glasses. Her small titties quivered as her arms thrust out towards me. her pink nipples gleamed with my saliva. Her tangy juices lingered on my mouth. I savored it as her hands seized my big dick. She guided me to her pussy with such hunger.

I could feel the battle of lusts in her. That desire to grow her own futa-dick. She wanted it, but she was holding off. That was important. She had to be a master of her lusts now. In control. I quivered as I let her guide me to her pussy.

She pressed me into her soft, silky bush. Her blonde curls slid around the tip of my girl-dick. Then I was rubbing at her pussy directly. I moaned at that wonderful contact. It was the best. I groaned as she worked me up and down, caressing me, teasing me.

Then I was penetrating into her. I slid to the hilt in her pussy. I groaned, my back arching as inch after inch of my dick slid into her twat. She groaned, squeezing her snatch down around me. Her hot flesh gripped me. I went deeper and deeper into her pussy, savoring her flesh spilling around me.

"Empty rapture!" I moaned.

"Oh, Shane," she groaned, glancing at him as my shaved pussy lips rubbed into her bush. I had penetrated every inch into her. "She's so huge. She's stretching out my pussy!"

"She is," he groaned, his lust spilling through the room.

She liked that he watched her. It excited her. She stared at Shane, not me, as she grabbed my tits. She kneaded them and squeezed her pussy around my cock. She whimpered, her thighs gripping my hips. She stirred her twat around my clit-dick.

"Oh, Shane, Shane!" she gasped. "Watch her fuck me hard. I'm going to cum on this big futa-cock!"

"I'm watching," he panted. "Shit, she grew a cock. That really happened."

"Oh, it did!" Eloise squeezed her pussy tight around my futa-dick. "And she's in me. Every last inch."

"Mmm, I am," I purred and drew back. "Colorless passion."

It felt so wonderful enjoying Eloise's pussy. Her twat gripped me. So tight. She gasped, her small breasts quivering. Her fingers kneaded my tits. I slammed into her, feeling her pleasure rippling through her body while I savored the silky friction of her juicy pussy gripping me.

Shane fisted his cock faster as he watched me ream his girlfriend. My big tits jiggled in her massaging hands. I pumped away at her. I thrust in and pulled out. Her pussy clung to me. Massaged me. My ovaries swelled with that load of girl-cum that I would fire in her.

I would flood her with so much spunk.

She would be dripping with it. This would be such a delicious treat. She would gasp and moan and cum so hard on my futa-dick.

It turned me on so much. My clit-dick throbbed and ached as I fucked into her. I pounded her hard. Fast. I buried to the hilt in her juicy twat. She groaned, her pussy clenching down on me.

"Yes, yes, yes!" she moaned. "Shane! Shane! She's reaming my cunt! She's going to make me cum on her big dick!"

"Cum on her!" he groaned, his lusts surging. He fapped his little cock.

"Mmm, your dick's so cute compared to others!" whimpered Eloise. "She's stretching me out so much. I love it!"

"Yes, you do," I groaned, pumping away. "How hard are you going to cum on my girl-dick?"

"So hard!" she moaned, head turning. She stared up at me. "Mmm, it's going to be awesome. My clit... My clit is going mad!"

"Yes!" I gasped, feeling that war, but she was holding back. Not growing her futa-dick. She just had to last a little bit longer.

Her hands kneaded my tits. Mine slid up her stomach and found her small breasts. I squeezed them as the hotel bed creaked. I fucked her hard and fast. I buried to the hilt in her. I plunged every inch of my dick into her pussy. I reveled in her hot twat squeezing about me, massaging my clit-dick.

My ovaries brimmed with all that wonderful jizz I would pump into her. I shuddered, drinking in all the lust in the room. I fed on them both. I devoured his cuckold's passion and her wild lust. Eloise moaned, her blue eyes squeezing shut.

"Oh, god, this dick, Shane!" she moaned. "I love this futa-dick fucking me! I'm going to cum!"

"Don't hold back!" I moaned, driving my girl-dick into her over and over again. I fucked her so hard. I pounded that juicy twat.

"Yes, yes, yes!" she gasped, her snatch squeezing about me. "Oh, Ava, yes! That's incredible. That's so amazing."

"Enjoy it!" I panted, driving into her. I buried to the hilt in her. I fucked her hard and fast. "Oh, yes, yes, enjoy it!"

"I will!" she moaned. Her pussy clenched around my girl-dick. She massaged me. It was amazing. My big dick throbbed in her cunt, ached. It felt so wonderful.

"Ellie!" Shane panted, his orgasm swelling in him. "Oh, god, she's pounding you hard."

"She is!" Eloise moaned. Her pussy clenched around me. "Oh, yes, yes! I'm cumming!"

Hot cunt writhed around my thrusting girl-dick. Her body thrashed. Her little titties jiggled in my squeezing grip. Blonde hair flew and her glasses shifted on her dainty nose. I pumped my futa-dick in and out of her convulsing twat. Her hot flesh sucked at me.

Greedy for my futa-cum.

The ache swelled up to the tip of my girl-dick. Her fingers dug into my tits. She held me tight. She massaged me while her pussy brought me closer and closer to exploding. I would fire so much cum into her twat. I would flood her with all my spunk.

A dizzying rush swept through me. A wild heat. I groaned, my pussy clenching. I slammed hard into her pussy's depths. Eloise's cunt sucked at me. That wonderful, hot, silky heaven hurtled me towards my orgasm.

"Empty rapture!" I howled and came.

My cum flooded into her pussy. I pumped Eloise's pussy full of futa-spunk while her boyfriend groaned behind me. He shuddered, his jizz spurting out over and over again. I heard it firing from him. The sound was so wicked.

It had me shivering and shuddering. I swayed, drinking in the sounds of him groaning through his orgasm. Pussy juices gushed out of my spasming twat. They flooded down my thighs as my jizz basted Eloise's pussy.

"So much girl-spunk!" moaned the blonde cutie. "Oh, Shane's, she's basting my cunt with her cum. She's giving it to me."

"Yes, yes, yes!" he groaned.

"I love her futa-dick!" she howled.

I smiled at her, seeing the desire blazing in her eyes. I fired the last of my cum into her, knowing she was ready. This was it. I savored being in her pussy for one more heartbeat, her flesh rippling around me, and then I ripped out of her.

"She's all yours," I moaned to Shane, cum dripping down over his hand. "Fuck her."

~~*~~

Eloise "Ellie" White

Right now, I was so aching with lust, so swamped with passion, I didn't care that Shane was a guy with a little dick. "Fuck me!"

I wanted him to be in me. This hunger swelled in me. My pussy dripped with cum. My clit throbbed and ached. He stared at me with all that love and lust. I felt it pouring off of him. I wanted him in me. I wanted to devour me.

"Fuck me, Shane!" I moaned. "Give me your love!"

Shane flew at me. His strong, masculine from was on me. He had no big boobs but a hairy, brawny chest. His brown eyes blazed with lust as he slid his cock into my sloppy depths. I hardly felt him after Ava.

My legs wrapped around him. I pulled him in my depths and squeezed my pussy on him. I felt that love and lust in him. I sucked at it. My pussy clenched and rippled around him as energy poured into me. I gasped, feeling this virile passion flowing out of Shane.

My pussy swallowed it.

My soul devoured it.

I gasped as I took more and more of it. Shane gasped, his face twisting in shock. Then his features began changing. I gasped as the square jaw blunted. His Adam's apple dwindled. Cheekbones softened. The shadow of his stubble vanished as lips grew plump and soft.

"Ellie?" he gasped, his voice sounding so much higher pitch.

I kept feeding on that virile energy. Body hair vanished from his chest. I watched in awe as his shoulders narrowed and then mounds formed. Round protrusions thrust from his chest forming into...

"Boobs," I said in awe, watching my boyfriend becoming a woman.

"What?" he—she?—gasped. Shane grabbed her growing breasts. She gripped them, her eyes widening as they became so large and ripe, just the way I liked them. "What's going on?"

"You're being reborn, *Shawna,*" moaned Ava. "Eloise is taking her first meal. Mmm, she's becoming like me. A futa-succubus."

I gasped as I kept feeding on Shane's virility, taking it in me. It was changing me, too. Not making me into a man, but giving me lusts. Powers. This was how Ava turned on girls. She had taken a man's virility and now used it to turn on girls so she could fuck them with her futa-dicks.

Shane's hair grew long, spilling down around her feminine face. She squeezed her tits, her thighs growing sleek, her hips curving, waist narrowing. Nothing masculine remained but that cock. And I stole the last of its manhood. I devoured it.

Her cock dwindled, pulled out of me. Shriveled away.

"I'm growing a pussy," moaned Shane. No, no, that wasn't the right name.

"Shawna!" I gasped. "You're a woman, Shawna."

"Oh, god," Shawna moaned, her voice so throaty.

I could feel her lusts. I could feel them brimming in her, and that love. I had taken both into me. I shuddered and then I let my futa-dick grow. It thrust out from my crotch, a big and thick shaft swelling longer and longer. It reared up between us, rubbing against her stomach. Her eyes widened as she released her breasts.

She stared down past her big tits to see my cock thrusting out of my blonde bush. "Ellie?"

"I'm a futa, too," I moaned, and I felt her lusts from her. That virginal desire. She was a virgin. That was so delicious. I had to take her cherry. "I'm going to fuck you with my cock. Isn't that amazing?"

"What?" Shawna asked.

Ava giggled beside us, loving it. The redhead felt different from Shawna. I couldn't feed on her lusts. I couldn't even feel them. She was nothing. Like a rock. But there were others in the hotel I could feel. Women who needed my cock.

But this new woman needed it the most.

"Don't you love me, Shawna," I purred, hooked the back of her neck and pulling her down to me.

"I do," she said, sounding so confused.

"Mmm, well, then let's love each other."

I pulled her lips down to mine. Our mouths met in a hungry kiss. I shuddered as her mouth glued on mine. This wonderful heat swept through me. My lips kissed hers with hunger. My gender-swapped girlfriend's boobs pressed into my little titties. My futa-cock poked up into her stomach.

Ava giggled in delight beside us.

I kissed my Shawna with hunger. I rolled us over. I ended up on top of her, my small tits rubbing into her big boobs. She trembled beneath me. I was so horny for her, and I could feel her lust for me. Her desire for my big futa-cock.

We were linked. Connected. Her love was in me. I felt the depths of her emotions. It was incredible. I kissed her back with such hunger, devouring that sweetness coming from her while my futa-cock ached to get to know her even more intimately.

I broke the kiss and purred, "I'm going to make such love to you, Shawna."

"Oh, god," she moaned.

"Mmm, someone's losing her cherry tonight," I cooed. "Just not who you thought, huh, cutie?"

"No," she groaned. "Oh, damn, Ellie, I'm so wet. Do girls get this wet?"

"They do when they have a cute futa-succubus on them," I purred. "I am cute, right?"

"Fucking adorable."

I kissed her again, my futa-dick throbbing against her naked stomach. My dress was bunched around my waist. It was in the way. I just... removed it. Suddenly, I was naked. What else could I do with these new powers?

Besides drive women into being sluts for me.

The more I kissed Shawna, the more my excitement grew. She just felt so wonderfully feminine beneath me. I had changed her, remade her into perfection. I shuddered, her hands sliding up and down my back. She grabbed my rump.

My pussy clenched. Ava's jizz leaked out of me. That wonderful heat swept out of me. I kissed her with such passion, savoring this moment. My futa-cock throbbed between us, just dying to be in my sweet Shawna's pussy. My nipples caressed over hers. Sparks flared.

She moaned.

I broke the kiss. "I want to eat you out, but I also want to be in you."

"I know," she moaned. "I... I... want you in me, too. She bit her lip. You've really made me into a woman, and you're already so cute and sexy... Just... I mean... Fuck it! I want you to fuck me! Make love to me, Ellie."

I smiled at her and kissed her again. Our tongues danced and played. Her soft lips worked on mine. She tasted so sweet. I groaned and shifted on the bed. I settled my legs between hers and pushed up on my knees. I thrust a hand between us.

So did she.

We grabbed my throbbing futa-cock at nearly the same moment. It was amazing to feel her hands wrapped around my girth. She gripped me. Stroked me. I shuddered at that heat. Then I groaned as she pressed me down between her thighs.

I slid through her silky bush. Her juices coated the tip of my cock. Then I found her hot, virgin folds. She had a tight slit. She kissed me with even more hunger as we guided my dick's tip lower and lower until...

I felt her hymen.

That wonderful barrier.

I broke the kiss with Shawna. "Ready?"

"Yes," she moaned, her body trembling beneath me. Her breasts rubbed against me. "Take me, Ellie. I want you. God, I've wanted you for weeks. I'll take you any way I can."

I felt her love swelling in her. I didn't need this emotion from anyone else. Lust I could get from women like my mother, my friends, or Mrs. Jenkins. This golden passion from Shawna was special. I had taken it in me and tied it about my soul. We were spiritually linked.

Now we would be united physically.

I pushed forward with my girl-cock. She gasped and shuddered. I loved how she whimpered in delight. Her boobs jiggled beneath mine. Our nipples brushed again. I loved the feel of her fat nubs against my little buds.

"Ellie!" she moaned. "I love you!"

"I love you, Shawna!" I groaned and thrust harder.

I popped my gender-swapped girlfriend's cherry.

She gasped as I slid into her. Inch after inch of my girl-dick penetrated into her pussy's depths. She gasped and groaned, her cunt squeezing around me. She clenched tight, holding onto me as I went into her. It was incredible to experience.

The pleasure swept through me. I groaned, savoring that wonderful passion as I went deeper and deeper into her pussy. I penetrated her with my cock. It was incredible to feel. That wonderful majesty engulfed my futa-cock.

She was so much tighter than her mother, my mother, my friends, Mrs. Jenkins, and even Ava. Shawna's pussy felt special around me. I stared into her dark eyes, my glasses shifting on my face. Her hands grabbed my rump, pulling on me. Our boobs rubbed together.

"Yes!" she moaned. "Ellie! You're in me, Ellie!"

"I am," I purred as I bottomed out in her. "Mmm, do you love my futa-dick stretching out your naughty, little cunny, Shawna?"

"Yes, yes, yes!" she moaned, her body trembling. "Oh, Ellie! I do. I love you being in me. I want to cum on your girl-dick. I want your... your jizz to fire in me."

I kissed her with hunger and drew back my hips.

We both moaned and shuddered as we moved together. It was amazing. A delicious treat. I pumped my hips forward. I thrust into her again and again, reveling in the silky passion of her pussy squeezing about me. That wonderful delight rippled about my futa-cock. Our nipples brushed, kissing.

Sparks flared.

They fed that wonderful ache in the depths of my cunt.

My ovaries brimmed with the first load of my futa-cum Shawna would take. But it wouldn't be the last. Oh, no, we would have so much fun together. I could feel it. We would do so many wicked and naughty things together.

I couldn't wait to see her lick my cum out of my mother's pussy, to feast on that incestuous creampie. I would fuck her mother, too, and watch as they writhed in lesbian incest. No girl or woman would be safe from us. We would enjoy them.

And they would enjoy us.

We would spread passion together. Inspire lust. We would be a team, feasting on feminine passion.

I broke the kiss and moaned, "Shawna! Shawna!"

"Ellie!" she groaned. "God, I know. You're incredible."

"So are you." I stared in her eyes. She truly was the one. I grinned at her, pumping away, my girl-dick plundering away at her. "We're going to have such an incredible life together, aren't we?"

"We are," she moaned, her cunt clenching around me. "Ooh, this dick... Yes, yes, your clit-dick is stirring me up."

"Don't hold back!" I told her, thrusting away. "I want to feel that pussy cumming."

I could feel her orgasm building just like mine was. I felt her emotions and nibbled on her lust. Her passion tasted so sweet. I groaned, realizing just how different I was. I wouldn't need food or water, just feminine desire. The passion from women gasping in my futa-dick.

And I wanted Shawna to gasp.

My hands slid up and squeezed the sides of her boobs as I thrust into her. She had sensitive tits. She gasped as that added pleasure rushed through her body. It spilled down to her pussy squeezing around me.

Her face scrunched up. Her orgasm built and built in her. I loved it. I gave it a nudge, flaring her pleasure as I slammed to the hilt in her. She gasped, her eyes widening. Her cunt clamped down on my dick, drinking in the friction.

Then she gasped and exploded.

"Ellie!" she moaned as her first feminine orgasm burst through her.

I groaned, savoring that hot flesh convulsing beneath me. It was outstanding to feel. To experience. I reveled in her cunt writhing about me. That hot passion spilled through my body. I gasped and moaned, bucking atop her as her cunt writhed around my girl-dick.

My pussy clenched, the heat swelling in me. I shuddered, thrusting harder and harder in her. I savored her pussy convulsing around me. That hot twat rippling and writhing about my cock brought me closer and closer to my climax.

"Ellie!" she moaned. "Please, please, fire your cum in me! I want it!"

I felt that need. That ache. It pulled at me.

I kissed my gender-swapped lover and buried to the hilt in her spasming pussy. Her silky flesh sucked at my cock. The pleasure shot up to my twat dripping with Ava's girl-cum. The heat reached my ovaries. They quivered.

Exploded.

My climax burst inside of me. My futa-cock erupted. Spurt after spurt of hot cum fired out of me. I groaned atop my lover and basted her new pussy in my girl-spunk. My seed pumped into her while her lusts drowned me.

I feasted on them, her cunt spasming and convulsing around me. I shuddered, reveling in this magical moment. Our tongues danced as we kissed each other. My pleasure carried me to such heights of rapture.

My cock erupted.

My pussy convulsed.

The two delights spilled through my succubal flesh. I squirmed on her as she milked my ovaries dry. She worked out every drop of futa-spunk in me. I loved it. I kissed her passionately. My tongue danced with hers. They stroked each other. They kissed, sharing this wonderful passion.

She stroked my back, whimpering beneath me. I spilled the last of my futa-seed in her. Our passion died down with our dwindling orgasms. But not her love. That stayed so strong. I bathed in it. Luxuriated in it.

My gender-swapped lover held me so tight.

~~*~~

Ava Heart – The Futa-Succubus Shamshiel

Shawna panted as she lay on her back, cum leaking out of her pussy as Eloise rolled off of her. It was ten minutes after they had cum together, and they were finally breaking apart. Eloise stretched out on her back, her little titties quivering. She looked so full. I couldn't feel her emotions any longer. She felt like nothing to me. Empty. But she was also like me. I had corrupted her. Made her into a futa-succubus.

What a delicious treat.

"Mmm, that was a yummy meal," Eloise moaned. She glanced at me as if forgetting I was there. She blinked and then smiled. "Thanks."

I leaned in and stroked her face, adjusting her glasses. "Mmm, you're going to have so much fun. You might even find your own virgin to corrupt."

"How wicked," Eloise said, a kinky gleam in her blue eyes. That innocent girl was utterly washed away.

"Shawna's your anchor," I told her. "As long as she loves you, you can't ever be thrown into the Black Earth."

"Black Earth?"

"A terrible place." I shuddered, remembering the empty place. No rapture. No color. No passion. "Trust me, you don't want to go there. I'm free of that place, and I don't ever plan on going back."

"Did yours stop loving you."

A long-forgotten pain rose in my heart. "Doesn't matter. I'm free again. I have other virgins to corrupt."

Eloise smiled, radiant and naughty.

I kissed my fellow futa-succubus. I savored the taste of her lips. And then I closed my eyes and faded away. I had other places to be. Other virgins to corrupt. I would enjoy my freedom immensely. I would have so much fun.

Hopefully, Eloise wouldn't make my mistake. She and Shawna would have their fun. They had so many women to play with. Humming, I let myself drift until I caught such a sweet scent. A virgin. I followed the trail.

Eager to corrupt again. I loved being a futa-succubus. Eloise would love it, too.

~~*~~

Eloise "Ellie" White – The Futa-Succubus

Monday came.

I strode onto the school with Shawna at my side. My gender-swapped girlfriend had a new wardrobe curtsy of a sexy salesgirl. She had been more than happy to hook us up with a discount after we fucked her hard in the changing room, my dick in her pussy and Shawna's pussy on her mouth.

"Who should we play with?" Shawna asked me, her arm around my waist.

"Ellie!" my best friend called. Jennifer rushed up.

I smiled. It was going to be a great day. I had my lover at my side, her passion for me my anchor to this world. It was exciting sharing women with her. We were having so much fun. And we would continue to play.

"Hey, Jennifer," I said, my clit throbbing, her lusts piling out of her like a tidal wave. I was ready to drown in it.

The End

Pandora's Naughty Gifts

Pandora's Naughty Futa Box 1

by

Reed James

Pandora's Naughty Gifts

Hephaestus, God of Crafting, set down his tools. He had finished his greatest creation. His newest human.

Not man. Not woman. But something different. Unique. Man and woman combined.

Futanari.

She lay on his workbench in the bowels of Mount Etna, her breasts rising and falling with her new life. Her eyes were closed. She slept. At peace. A slender body. Petite. Round breasts. Fair face. Black hair. And there, thrusting out of the folds of her pussy where her clit would be was her cock.

Her rich, brown eyes opened.

"Good morning, Pandora," rumbled the hunchbacked, clubfooted god.

* * *

Pandora

My stomach roiled as I followed my father, Hephaestus, up the stairs to the great palace atop Mount Olympus. We were far, far above the clouds. The world stretched out around the mountain, the entirety of it visible. The humans were like little ants in their villages, towns, and cities. It was dizzying to look below me at the sight.

So I stared at my limping father.

Hephaestus limped up the stairs, his left foot twisted. He was bent and gnarled, his brown toga clinging to his muscular physique. He grunted with each step, laboring. I swallowed, my sandaled feet whisking on the marble steps.

We passed other palaces. The perfect geometry of Athena's. The lush gardens surrounding Demeter's. Grapevines grew over Dionysus's. The gold of Apollo's palace shone like the sun while the silver of Artemis reflected back her brother's brilliance. And above all, Zeus's white palace. Like clouds solidified into stone.

I could feel the other Olympians in there. The eleven others, beside Hephaestus, who ruled the heavens. My hands rubbed at my green toga. What if they hated me? Rejected me? I was different. Unlike any other who had been born. Hephaestus had created something different in me. He was proud of what he had done.

Would the others be?

He reached the doors, a double set that was as golden as a lightning bolt. The air crackled with energy. He planted both his hands on the doors and pushed. Power sizzled around us. The hairs on my arms rose as he pressed open the doors. They creaked open onto a hall. At the far end, two figures sat on thrones.

Zeus loomed over all upon his seat of power. The god wore a toga of sky-blue. His beard and hair were snowy white, but he didn't look old or infirm. His body was strong and fit. Beside him sat his wife, Hera. The Queen of the Gods, looked regal in her purple toga. Her black hair was gathered up in an elaborate mass of curls, leaving her neck bare.

The other gods stood in two lines on either side of the center aisle. Their conversation broke off as they all stared at us. I swallowed, feeling their scrutiny on me. Mighty Poseidon, wearing only a kilt wrapped around his waist that fell to his knees, crossed his broad arms. He gleamed like the sea reflecting sunlight. Across from him, Demeter stood in a toga of spring green, her body lush and ripe. Fierce Ares had an oily grin while Aphrodite, my father's wife, wore a toga of such thin cloth that glimpses of her busty figure bled through the diaphanous fabric. Her black hair fell in curls around her pale face, her lips a bright and exciting crimson. Dionysus sipped at a flagon of wine, his cheeks rosy. Apollo stood radiant in his golden toga, laurels on his head that gleamed like rays of the sun. His twin sister stood opposite him. Slender Artemis in the silver toga of a boy, her lithe legs left bare. She had a predator's look, hungry. Wild. Hermes's winged sandals fluttered as he yawned. Athena stood tall, a studious look on her youthful face. I felt her scrutinizing me. Judging me.

"Ho, father," Hephaestus said as he finished limping up to the throne. The gods closed in behind us, forming a semi-circle around us. I swallowed, coming up beside him. "I present my latest creation."

"A woman?" Zeus asked, disdain in his expression. A slight curl of disgust at the corners of his lips.

I flushed and squirmed.

"There are thousands of them down on the ground. Of what import is one more woman, my son." The King of the Gods, the Lord of the Heavens, scowled.

"I present Pandora, the All-Endowed," growled Hephaestus. That was what my name meant. All-Endowed. I possessed everything. "My gift to the world. Show them, daughter."

"Yes, Father," I said. He wasn't my father. Not really. He was my creator. Father and daughter were convenient terms, though.

I unwound my toga. My nervousness increased as I exposed my round breasts. I felt the gods' eyes on me, especially Zeus. He leaned forward as he stared at the plumpness of my breasts swaying as I unwound more of the toga.

My stomach exposed and then the cloth fell away to reveal my cock thrusting out of the bare folds of my pussy. My father had me pluck all my pubic hair so my vulva and dick could be seen. The gods' scrutiny throbbed up my shaft.

Zeus recoiled in shock and horror, the lust vanishing in his eyes.

"Oh, my," Hera said, leaning forward. The queen of the gods stared at me with such intensity. Her blue eyes something delightful.

"What a wonderful creation you have made, husband," Aphrodite said. She stood by her suspected lover, Ares.

"Impressive," said Athena.

"It is something," said Poseidon, staring impassively.

"Why would you make *that?*" asked Artemis. She shivered, her eyes looked on it, her maidenly cheeks blushing bright.

"Yes, my son, why?" Zeus asked.

"Because the greatest flaw humans have is their divided sex," said Hephaestus. I have corrected that in Pandora. I have perfected them. She is the start of something better. I asked, my fellow Olympians, that you bless her and send her on her way. I have already given her the greatest gift I can: existence."

I smiled, glad that my father had created me. That he had forged me and breathed life into my nostrils. Even though Zeus had recoiled. I felt the scrutiny of the others. Athena licked her lips as she studied my cock.

"Plants can be hermaphroditic," Demeter said. "Why not humans."

"Why not indeed," muttered Zeus.

"Hephaestus has wrought something new," Poseidon said. "Let her loose upon the world. Let us see how the humans will react."

"Why not?" Dionysus said, wine spilling from the end of his goblet. It seemed full despite how much he'd already drunk.

"She'll cause problems," Ares said, his smile growing delighted. "Let her go. It'll stir up the mortals. They are getting complacent."

"Oh, yes, let my husband's creation flourish," said Aphrodite, her voice throaty honey.

"She is remarkable, Father," Athena said. The goddess had no mother. She had been birthed as an idea from Zeus's mind, almost as if she willed her own existence out of his thoughts. "Let us think and then bestow our blessings on her."

Zeus glanced around at his court, then at his son. His face tightened. "Always do you vex me, Hephaestus. Always. Since your foul birth when you wriggled deformed from your mother's womb."

Anger rippled through me for a moment at the king of the gods. But I swallowed it.

"Fine, fine, let her take a room in your palace here on Olympus, my son, while we decide upon the gifts to place upon her."

"Thank you, Father," said Hephaestus. "She shall remake the mortals."

Zeus did not look happy about that. Not one bit. Then a sly gleam entered his eyes. I shivered and gathered my toga, then dressed myself before I followed my father out of the palace of Zeus. I trembled.

* * *

An hour later, I sat on the bed in my room. I had a soft mattress and pleasant sheets. To my left lay a balcony that looked out onto the world from a dizzying height. Everything in the palace was superbly crafted, all built by my father.

His touch was everywhere.

I supped on the provided refreshment. Not Ambrosia, that was for the gods alone. My mortal flesh would die from the intensity of that elixir. I drank sweet water and nibbled on lemonbread. I wondered what would happen once the gods had blessed me. What it would be like down in the world of men?

The door opened, and Ares swaggered in. The god, in his red toga, moved with darkness. It wreathed around him, almost spilling over him and sweeping into me. I shuddered as he reached the foot of the bed and stared at me.

"Pandora, the All-Endowed," he said. "You have made my father taste fear. The dread that all the women he loves will one day have a cock to rival his. But do you have his endurance? His stamina?" Ares smiled. "I gift you, Pandora, with Endurance. You shall have the strength to run all day and fuck all night."

A shiver ran through me as he spoke those words. A wash of heat ran through my skin. I gasped as I felt it settling into my muscles, strengthening them. My cock swelled hard beneath my toga, a sudden surge of throbbing lust. I bit my lip, whimpering at the intensity of the sensation.

With a mocking bow, he left.

Zeus would be jealous of me? That did not forebode well for me. I swallowed, my hands rubbing at my thigh. I struggled to ignore the throbbing ache of my cock and the growing itch in my virgin depths. I squirmed.

Soon, the next god entered. Apollo burst into my room like the sun rising over the horizon. He had a fair and handsome face that was hard to see over the radiance of his golden toga. It spilled light around me as he moved before me, a lyre clutched in the crook of his arm.

"You are unique," said Apollo. "And all who are unique should have a charm about them. Pandora, I give you the gift of song. The perfect pitch of voice and intonation of poetry. Let your words sing upon the wind."

Another wave of heat washed through me. A burst of trilling notes rose from my lips, almost like songbirds. I shuddered as the god bowed to me and then he swept out of the room. I found myself unable to stop the song that poured from my lips.

It was a thrill to sing. It helped take my thoughts off the fact my cock was aching and hard. That it pressed at my toga. I shuddered at the hot itch in my pussy. I lay back on my bed, the words trilling from my lips. There was a freedom in song. The notes echoed off the room.

The door opened. Aphrodite entered. I shuddered as her presence washed over me. I sat up and bit my lower lip at the sight of her beauty. Her pink robes did nothing to hide the lush form beneath. Her large breasts held a perky sway as she sauntered towards me. Her dark eyes burned with hunger. They fell on my cock.

Her toga dissolved off of her in motes of pink lights. I gasped at the beauty of my father's wife. The Goddess of Love and Beauty had my dick throbbing harder and my virgin pussy clenching in such wild delight.

"I'm here to give you the gift of beauty," said Aphrodite, her voice as smooth as honey. She reached out and took my hands.

I didn't resist her as she drew me to my feet, my dick throbbing as I slipped off the bed. It bulged the front of my toga. The goddess licked her ruby lips. They were so red. So kissable. I groaned, aching for her. She grabbed my toga and began unwinding the cloth off my body with such deft skill.

My breasts came free, and her hands found them. She ducked her head down and nuzzled her face between my tits. I gasped at the goddess's black hair spilled over my boobs and rubbed at my

157

nipples. The heat throbbed up my futa-dick. My virgin pussy clenched.

"Mmm, my husband has made something special in you," she moaned then her lips kissed at the inner slope of my breast.

I knew I shouldn't let this happen. She was my father's wife. This would be cuckolding my creator, but the heat in my pussy and the ache at the tip of my cock couldn't be denied. Not after Ares's blessing. I groaned as she kissed and nibbled on my breast, working up it. Her lips smooched higher and higher, reaching towards the pinnacle of my breast.

She latched right onto my nipple. She sucked it into her mouth. I gasped at the pressure. My pussy clenched against it. This heat rushed through my body. It was such a treat to feel. The heat was exciting.

I moaned, my pussy clenching. I swayed my hips from side to side, loving every moment of her sucking on my tit. The pleasure rushed through my body as her plump lips nibbled on my nub. Her tongue danced around it.

"Aphrodite," I moaned, my futa-cock pressing against the cloth. "You're... This..."

"Mmm," she cooed and sucked harder.

My pussy clenched. I felt juices dripping down my thighs. I couldn't believe how turned on I was. How aroused. Ares's gift of endurance and stamina had changed something in me. I groaned, my hair swaying about my naked shoulders. Aphrodite's fingers kneaded my tits. She groped them and massaged them. The pleasure she gave me was intense. Delicious.

She popped her mouth off, her eyes glossy with delight. Then she pulled the last of my clothing away. My cock popped out. It thrust out before me. She grabbed me. I gasped at the silkiness of her hand on me. None had ever touched my futa-dick before.

"Lady Aphrodite," I whimpered as she stroked me.

"This cock..." she moaned. "My husband has a gift for making works of beauty and majesty, but this..." She fell to her knees.

"We should not do this," I moaned. "You are his wife and—"

She sucked my cock into her mouth.

"Lady Aphrodite!" I gasped at that warm, wet delight

surrounding the tip of my cock. She nursed on it. My virgin pussy clenched. My body bucked from the intensity of it. More juices ran down my thighs. "This... I... Lady Aphrodite!"

She sucked at my cock with her hungry mouth. My round breasts jiggled from my body shaking. My pussy clenched. My rump clenched tight. The suction she created radiated down my cock into my virgin twat to something deep inside of me. Two somethings. My ovaries brimming with my seed.

"Oh, no, no," I moaned, my cock throbbing and aching in her mouth. "That's... Lady Aphrodite, that's incredible. But this is wrong. You are married. Your husband..."

She winked at me. Then her right hand grabbed the base of my cock and stroked it while her left hand slid up my thigh to my pussy. I groaned as her delicate touch stroked my petals. She nursed on my clit-dick, the ache building and building at the tip. I whimpered, my face scrunching up. This was incredible.

Amazing.

Her touch slid up and down my slit. She parted my folds and reached in to rub at my hymen. She caressed over it. I groaned at her naughty touch. My heart pounded faster and faster. My pussy grew juicier and juicier as she stroked me. She brushed my hymen while she nursed on my cock.

"Aphrodite," I groaned, the pressure rising. My seed wanted to rush out of me. "Please, please, Aphrodite, if you keep sucking..."

She nursed harder. She moaned, her passion vibrating around the crown of my cock. I gasped, my cunt clenching in my depths. My ovaries throbbed and swelled. They drank in the pleasure her mouth and fingers gave me. My cock pulsed.

I whimpered, unable to stop it from happening. I squeezed my eyes shut, groaning. My futa-cock throbbed in her mouth. Her tongue caressed over the tip of it. My head swayed from side to side. My hands balled into fists.

I erupted.

"Aphrodite!" I gasped and came into the mouth of my creator's wife.

I spurted blast after blast of my seed. Each one sent a surge of ecstasy through my body. A rush of euphoria. With it, came the waves of rapture washing out of my virgin pussy. My cunt convulsed and writhed, juices spilling down my thighs.

Stars exploded across my vision. I groaned as I fired more and more of my futa-cum into her mouth. Aphrodite gulped it down with hunger. She sucked out more and more. I whimpered, hitting such a wild plateau of pleasure.

"Oh, Aphrodite!" I groaned, swaying there from the dizzying rapture.

She swallowed the last of my cum and then slid her mouth off my cock. With a wet plop, her lips popped off. She smacked them, cum beading on them. "Mmm, yes, yes, my husband made something special in you and..." Her hand squeezed my cock. "Not even going soft." She sniffed the air. "Oh, I see, Ares's gift. Stamina. How delicious of him."

"Lady Aphrodite?" I whimpered.

She rose, her dark eyes swimming with passion. Still holding my cock with her right hand, her left arm hooked around my neck. She pulled me to her. I gasped as her large breasts pressed into my smaller boobs. Then our lips met.

I tasted my salty girl-seed on her lips. I groaned at that. Her tongue thrust into my mouth. She swirled it around in me. I whimpered, shocked by what she was doing. This heat rushed through me. My breasts pressed against hers.

She moaned, kissing me with hunger. I quivered against her, my nipples rubbing into her breasts, my dick throbbing in her hand. The tip rubbed against her stomach. I was still hard. Still throbbing in delight.

She pushed me back. I groaned as my legs hit the edge of the bed. She pushed me down.

Our lips broke apart as I landed on my rump and then stretched out onto my back. She followed me down, straddling me. Her large breasts heaved over my head as she gripped my cock still. She guided me to her thick, black bush. Her juices dripped on this.

"I have to experience this cock," she moaned and then slammed her cunt down on my dick. My eyes bulged at the heat of her pussy sliding over my shaft. "Lady Aphrodite!"

"Oh, yes!" Aphrodite, moaned, her back arching, thrusting her bountiful tits forward. Her pussy swallowed every inch of my cock. "This is a delicious treat. A woman with a big dick. Husband, you have outdone yourself!"

Her pussy clenched down around my futa-dick. The heat melted down to my virgin twat. Her hands grabbed my breasts. She squeezed them. Kneaded them. I whimpered as her fingers dug into my breasts and massaged them. This heat rushed through my body.

She clenched her twat around my dick and slid up me. My toes curled. I groaned, squirming on my back at the rapture of this oral delight. Her pussy felt so wet and silky. The heat of it melted through my body. My toes curled.

"Lady Aphrodite!" I moaned, shocked by how much I liked this. How amazing this felt. I groaned as she slammed her pussy back down my cock. This amazing heat engulfed me. It was this fabulous delight. This wonderful passion that would deliver upon me such intense delight.

I groaned, my face twisting in rapture. An amazing heat rushed through my body. This fantastic delight that would have me bursting with passion. I groaned, my toes curling. I shuddered as she worked her pussy up and down my cock. Her breasts heaved as I squirmed on the bed.

Her tongue flicked over her ruby lips. Her black hair swayed about her fair face. She arched her back, her tits bouncing. They smacked together in such a hypnotic way. I groaned and slid my hands up her body.

I groped her big boobs.

I squeezed them. Kneaded them. They were so soft and wonderful. My own breasts jiggled, mounds quivering at the bottom of my vision. I groaned, my toes curling. My virgin pussy drank in the heat of her juicy passion working up and down my cock.

"Oh, yes, yes," I whimpered, my face scrunching up as the pleasure rushed through me. "Lady Aphrodite."

"Mmm, that's it," she purred, her hands squeezing my tits. She returned the favor.

Our fingers kneaded the other's boobs. We groped each other as her pussy slid up my cock and then slammed back down it. Her hot and silky flesh built and built this amazing ache in the depths of my cunt. My ovaries brimmed with more futa-cum to fire into her. My dick's tip rejoiced, drinking in the silky friction of her hot flesh and converting it into bliss.

"Oh, Lady Aphrodite," I groaned, her thumbs massaging up my breasts to my nipples. She brushed them. My cock twitched in her pussy. "Yes!"

She smiled at me as she worked her cunt up and down my dick. She slammed her pussy down my cock again and again as she pushed her thumbs down on my nipples. Delight shot down to my cunt. The heat swelled in them.

My kneading fingers worked up her bountiful breasts and found her nipples. I squeezed them. Pinched them. I worked at them as she clamped down that naughty pussy on my dick. My cock throbbed in her cunt's grip. The heat rushed through me. I groaned, loving every second of the bliss she created in me. I bit my lip, squealing in delight. The heat rushed through my body.

"Oh, yes, yes, that's amazing," I gasped. "Your pussy..."

"Your cock!" she moaned, slamming her twat down my shaft. Her bush rubbed into my vulva, caressing my pussy lips with ticklish delight. "Yes!"

Her cunt squeezed down tight as she rose up my cock. I gasped, the pressure building and building at the tip. I pinched her fat nipples harder. I twisted them as she rode me. Her black hair swept around her shoulders as she worked her cunt up and down my futa-dick. The juicy heat brought me closer and closer to another climax.

I ached for it. I wanted to cum in her pussy. The wife of my creator rode me. I cuckolded Hephaestus with Aphrodite's twat. I whimpered, the pressure in my balls swelling and swelling. I would have such a huge orgasm. I would fire all my jizz into her cunt.

"Oh, yes, yes!" I moaned. "Lady Aphrodite!"

"Cum in me!" she moaned. "Oh, yes, yes, cum in me, Pandora! Fill my jar with your cum!"

She slammed her cunt down my cock. Her pussy took me to the hilt. Her cunt clenched around me as she slid back up. The suction was incredible. My clit-dick throbbed. My virgin twat drank it in, growing hotter and hotter.

The pressure at the tip of my dick burst.

My futa-cum fired into the goddess's pussy.

"Yes!" I howled as my pussy convulsed. My body bucked. The two delights rushed through me, firing from my cock and flooding out of my cunt. I bucked on the bed, my dick unloading blast after blast of cum into her pussy. "Lady Aphrodite!"

"Delicious Pandora!" moaned the goddess. Her pussy went wild around my cock. "Yes, yes, that's such a better dick than my husband. Amazing futa-cock!"

Her pussy writhed around my dick. Her flesh sucked at me. It was incredible. It made the blowjob pale in comparison to this ecstasy. The pleasure intensified as I pumped spurt after spurt of jizz into her twat. I bucked on the bed. It creaked beneath me as I unloaded every bit of cum I had into her pussy. I groaned at how amazing it felt.

"Oh, yes, yes!" I groaned. "Oh, that's amazing. That's wonderful. Oh, my goddess, that's awesome. Yes!"

"Mmm, that's it," she purred, working out my futa-cum. She emptied my ovaries with her convulsing pussy. "Oh, Pandora."

I fired the last of my spunk into her. I shuddered at that final spurt. I quivered as her pussy kept rippling around my cock. Kept spasming. I shuddered as she moaned. She stared down at me, her hands squeezing my tits.

"I give you the gift of beauty," she said, heat rippling through me. I felt... perfected. "You will be the envy of all and the desire of maidens and matrons alike. What you have must be shared, Pandora."

She tweaked my nipples. She tugged on them. A burst of delight washed through my cunt.

Then she slid her pussy off my dick. I lay there panting as she turned and marched away. My cum trickled down her thighs, her curvy ass swaying. In a shimmer of pink, her diaphanous toga reappeared around her.

She reached for the door, but it opened before she touched it. A girl gasped. Aphrodite laughed and strode out. A moment later, Artemis entered. The virgin goddess froze at the sight of me naked on the bed, my futa-cock thrusting up in the air, soaked in pussy cream. I blushed at the feeling of the Goddess of the Moon and the

Hunt staring at me.

She licked her lips, her cheeks growing redder and redder. Her boyish, silver toga rustled as she approached. She wore sandals with the lacing reaching up her calves to her knees and moved with a feral grace. A wolf in maiden form.

"You're... you..." She swallowed, staring at my cock. I was still hard. Still aching with that need to cum. She froze before she got closer. I sat up and she took a step back, raising a warding hand. "My maidenhead is not for you. It's not for anyone!"

"I... Of course." I blushed. Just knowing she was a virgin made me want to pounce on her and fuck her hard. To ram my clit-dick into her cherry and feel her cumming on my futa-cock. I shivered, feeling so naked.

"I'm here to give you the gift of stealth," Artemis said. "Your prey shall never hear your approach. You shall always be vulnerable and non-threatening in their eyes. They will see not the wolf but the innocent lamb."

Then she turned and fled the room, slamming the door hard behind her.

I swallowed, my dick so hard. Aphrodite's cream slowly dried on my cock as I padded to my discarded toga. I picked it up, aching so badly. I went to draw on my toga when I heard my door open and then shut.

I looked up to see Athena sweeping to me. She had a face that was both serene with wisdom and youthful with girlish curiosity. She stared at my erect and gleaming cock, a smile forming on her lips. Her white toga melted from her body. She had a figure much like mine. Round breasts and slender hips. A thick, brown bush, matching the curls of her hair, grew between her thighs.

The first drops of dew appeared on them.

"My, oh, my," she said, this eager grin on her face. She slid onto the bed, reclining back. "I have had maidens devour my pussy before, but you are not quite one of those. You are a futanari. Mmm, let me see your skill. If you please me, I shall gift you with my knowledge of engineering."

I stared at her bush. I could see the folds of her pussy peeking through her curls. My futa-cock throbbed. The lust in her eyes was obvious. Her pink nipples thrust up from her breasts. They quivered. I bit my lip and then I slid onto the bed, dropping my toga.

My round breasts and hard cock swayed beneath me as I crawled across the bed to her pussy. A tangy musk filled the air, so different from Aphrodite's sweet delight. My pussy clenched, forcing out juices to spilled own my swinging cock. I hungered for her.

"Yes, yes, let's see what skills you have," moaned Athena. "Mmm, don't be afraid. Just nuzzle in and lick. Light ones at first, but then grow bold. Make me cum."

"Yes, Lady Athena," I moaned and grabbed her thighs. I leaned my head down, her tangy scent drawing me closer and closer to her pussy.

I nuzzled my face into her bush. I pressed my face into those silky curls. They caressed my cheek and nose. A moment later, my lips found the wet folds of her pussy. I shuddered at that contact. My tongue flicked out and slid up her slit, parting her folds.

Her tangy cream melted across my taste buds. This growl of delight rose from my throat. My tongue darted up through her folds again. And again. My fingers grabbed her rump as my hunger increased.

I devoured her with a feverish heat. My tongue ran up and down her folds, caressing her silky lips. She groaned, her body shifting as I lapped at her. I loved the feel of her. My tongue ran over her hymen. She was a maiden, like me.

My fingers squeezed at her rump as I licked and lapped at her. Athena moaned, her hands squeezing her breasts. She kneaded those round tits as my tongue laved up and down her pussy, her tangy juices coating my taste buds.

"Oh, that's delicious," she moaned. "Pandora, yes! You have real skill. You are delicious. Loving women... Oh, it is such a delight."

I understood now why she had defied Ares's advances. Athena cared not for him. It was intoxicating. I loved her pussy. My tongue fluttered up and down her cunt. My fingers dug into her ass as I flicked faster and faster, pushing on her hymen before sliding up to this little nub.

That must be her clitoris. Her clit. Hephaestus had shaped my clit into the mighty cock swinging between my thighs. But Athena just had this little nub. I sucked on it. She gasped. Her entire body bucked, her breasts jiggling in her hands.

"Yes, yes, that's it!" she moaned. "Oh, Pandora, yes, yes, that's it. Just do that. Lick my clit. Suck on it. Ooh, yes, yes, you know what I crave. What I need. Oh, that's it."

I nursed on her clit. I sucked on her bud with such hunger. It was a delight to enjoy. I swirled my tongue around her little nub. She groaned, her thighs squeezing tight about my face. She held me to her cunt as she humped against me.

My futa-cock grew harder. The ache at the tip swelled and swelled. Athena's tangy juices soaked my lips. The delight spilled past them. I groaned, my tongue licking and lapping at her twat. I caressed her folds. I fluttered against her clit.

"Oh, Pandora!" she moaned, her finger clenching tight. "Yes!"

Her virgin juices gushed out and anointed my lips and cheeks. I opened my mouth wide and drank them down. I savored them. They tasted so delicious. I shuddered, my futa-cock swaying back and forth between my thighs as I drank her tangy cream.

"That's amazing!" she moaned. "Oh, Pandora, you have such skill. Oh, yes, yes, I declare you to be a lesbian of extraordinary skill. And you have a cock. A lesbian with a dick. A futa-dick. Oh, I must try it!"

A quiver of excitement rushed through me as I slid my tongue across her hymen. My own virgin twat clenched. She pulled away from me and then rolled over onto her hands and knees. I came face to face with her plump rump, her bush soaked in her juices now. More dripped off my own chin.

She wiggled her rump at me. She whimpered and moaned, her passion undeniable. My cock needed satisfaction. I rose, my breasts jiggling. I grabbed my clit-dick, so eager to enjoy my second pussy ever. Another goddess cunt. I aimed my cock at her bush and pressed it right into her silky curls.

"No, no!" she gasped. "I must remain a virgin! My jar must never be unsealed, but my asshole... Fuck my asshole! Ooh, there is more than one way for women to love each other. You don't need a dildo when you have a girl-cock!"

A shiver ran through me. I suddenly became aware of my own asshole. My puckered hole clenched. I noticed hers just peeking out from between her butt-cheeks. I quivered and then I slid my cock up through her bush and into her crack. I found it.

Her asshole felt so naughty against my cock. I whimpered and then I thrust my dick against her sphincter. She gasped and groaned as her anal ring parted for my wet cock. Aphrodite's juices still lubed it along with my own cream that had run down my shaft as I ate her out.

"Oh, Pandora, yes!" Athena moaned, her goddess's brown hair swaying about her head. "Ram that cock into me!"

I thrust harder. Her asshole widened more and then slid over the spongy crown of my cock. The velvety friction melted down my dick to my cunt. I groaned as I slid into her bowels. Her tight sheath squeezed about me.

I whimpered as I slid deeper and deeper into her. She squeezed about me. She held me tight as I ventured into her bowels. I groaned, the heat rushing through my body. My cunt drank it in. My ovaries readied another load of futa-cum.

I bottomed out in her. My bare pussy lips rubbed into her rump. I licked my lips, savoring the tangy flavor of her cunt on them. I groaned as her bowels clenched around me. Then I drew back. I pulled out of her, loving the friction.

"Pandora!" she moaned.

"Oh, Lady Athena!" I whimpered. Her asshole felt so different from Aphrodite's pussy. This was a tighter, hotter pleasure. Almost rougher. It was exciting. Exhilarating.

I slammed back into her bowels, my breasts jiggling. I gripped her hips, clutching onto her as I reveled in the thrill of fucking her. I pounded her hard and fast. I rammed to the hilt in her again and again. I slammed deep into her body. It was an incredible delight. A wonderful sensation to bury into her asshole.

The pleasure rushed down my cock to my cunt. I moaned, loving this active role. This time, I did the fucking. I didn't just lie there. I reveled in this, my black hair dancing around my shoulders. I whimpered and groaned, pumping away at her bowels with hard strokes.

It was incredible to experience. It was an amazing delight. I groaned, loving the pleasure of this moment. I savored every moment of plowing into her. I groaned, her asshole squeezing tight about my clit-dick.

"Oh, yes, yes, that's it!" Athena moaned. "Oh, Pandora, that's how you use your clit-dick on a woman. Do you hear the sounds I'm making?"

"Uh-huh," I groaned, my hands clenching about her hips. I held on tight as I drove into her bowels. I fucked her with hard strokes.

My dick slammed to the hilt in her as the room grew darker and darker. Night descended. Twilight spilled around us as I slammed my futa-cock into her bowels. She moaned and gasped, the sounds sending such a heady rush through me.

I loved it.

My pussy clenched. My virgin twat ached while the pressure grew and grew at the tip of my cock. I shuddered, loving every moment of plowing into her bowels. The ache at the tip of my dick swelled with each thrust.

I would have such a huge orgasm. I would pump her full of all that wonderful spunk brimming in my ovaries. I groaned, savoring every bit of this. I shuddered, slamming hard into her bowels. I buried to the hilt in her.

"Yes!" squealed the virgin goddess. "Pandora! You're amazing! I love your futa-dick!"

Her asshole writhed and spasmed around my cock. I gasped as I felt her orgasm. Her juices gushed out and bathed my thighs. The tangy aroma swelled through the air. Her velvety flesh sucked at my girl-dick, and I pulled back.

My ovaries burst into frothy passion. I slammed into her and erupted. "Lady Athena!"

"You can fire cum!" she gasped, her asshole spasming harder. More juices gushed out of her pussy and bathed my thighs. "Oh, Pandora. Sweet, sweet Pandora, this is amazing. This is incredible."

I loved it. My cunt savoring the heat rushing out of her pussy. My dick throbbed and ached. The bliss out of my snatch. It was incredible to enjoy. I groaned, my cock spurting over and over again.

My head swayed, my pussy convulsing. Juices gushed down my thighs.

"Oh, that's incredible. That's wonderful." I bit my lip. The pleasure washed out of my cunt. Juices spilled down my thighs. "Oh, my god, that's amazing. Yes, yes!"

My futa-cock pumped her asshole full of my cum. It was such a heady rush. I whimpered and swayed. I felt dizzy from it. Athena groaned, her bowels milking my cock. I gripped her hips and fired a last spurt of jizz into her. A final blast of rapture shot into my mind.

"I give you the gift of knowledge!" Athena moaned. "Of engineering and geometry!"

I gasped as the heat spilled over my thoughts. Her gift settled into my mind. Ideas like pulleys. Ropes. Levers. Fulcrums. Right angles. The Golden Ratio and more. I swayed and fell backward, my cock popping out of her bowels. I lay on my bed, panting.

"Mmm, that was wonderful, Pandora," Athena said. "Futanari... What a delight Hephaestus has created."

I just nodded, panting. Darkness engulfed my room now. I felt sleep calling. I drifted into it as the goddess crawled off my bed and padded out of my room. My eyes closed. I fell into peace for a time. I don't know for how long.

Then I felt someone slip into my bed. A busty figure pressed against my side, breasts large. A thigh slid over my stomach. A hand slid up and cupped my breast. I groaned as lips kissed at my mouth. They were hungry.

Aggressive.

I moaned as I came awake into the dark. The goddess thrust her tongue into my mouth. My futa-cock throbbed and ached as she kissed me with hunger. She slid over me now, her wiry bush rubbing against my futa-cock, tickling my shaft. Her large breasts pillowed into my round tits as she kissed me with hunger.

Who was it? Aphrodite again? No, it didn't feel quite like her. Demeter? She had a curvy figure. The Goddess of Cultivation was a fertile entity. Maybe she craved me. I groaned, kissing her harder, my futa-cock throbbing.

The goddess rolled us over. I settled on her, our bodies pressed tight. I moved out of instinct, sliding my cock down and down her bush. Her silky hairs caressed over my cock's tip. Then it ducked down to nuzzle at her folds.

I thrust forward, aching to be in another goddess's pussy.

My cock slid upward, brushing her clit. She moaned into the kiss as I popped up between our stomachs, missing the entrance of her jar. I groaned, aching to be in her. She had turned me on so fast sneaking into my bed. I drew back and tried again. My cock slid against her folds. I loved the feel of them.

I thrust.

Popped over again.

She broke the kiss. "Let me do it, Pandora."

Her voice was thick and melodic. I blinked, staring down into the eyes of Hera. Queen of the Gods. Wife of Zeus. Her hand slid down between us as panic shot through me. This was really, really wrong. The King of the Olympians would not be happy to be cuckolded by me.

"Wait, Queen Hera!" I gasped as she slid my cock down through her bush until it nuzzled into the folds of her pussy.

"No waiting," she moaned. "Fuck me! I want that cock in me. Ram that dick into my cunt this moment, Pandora."

"But your husband!"

"If he can have his dalliances, then so can I." She smiled. "Besides, I promised to take no other *man* into my bed. You're no man. Now ram that girl-dick in me so I can give you my gift."

"Gift?"

"Of motherhood. Your seed shall find fertile soil wherever you plant it, Pandora." She rubbed me into her folds. Her pussy lips slid around the tip of my cock. They were thicker than Aphrodite's. "Now ram that cock into me, Pandora!"

"Y-yes, Queen Hera!"

I thrust my cock into her pussy and cuckolded the most powerful being in the universe.

I shuddered at the forbidden delights of Hera's cunt. Her pussy clenched around me. I groaned as inch after inch of my dick slid into her delicious sheath. I would feel her jar with all my seed. Her flesh squeezed about me. She held me tight as I went deeper and deeper into her married depths.

It was incredible to be in her. To be on her. Our bodies were pressed tight. It held an intimacy that being ridden by Aphrodite and fucking Athena's asshole lacked. I *made love* to Hera. I kissed her on the mouth, our tongues dancing as I pumped my cock in and out of her juicy twat.

My virgin cunt clenched every time I thrust into her. She felt incredible around my cock. Her pussy gripped me. That wonderful heat wreathed me. I groaned, my body shuddering on hers as I pumped away at her pussy.

Our nipples kissed.

We groaned into the other's lips.

Her hands roamed my back, her fingertips stroking fire across my skin.

Her touch inspired me to thrust harder and faster. To pound into her married pussy with harder and harder strokes. Her cunt clenched around me. Her wonderful twat swelled that naughty ache in my ovaries again.

I would flood her married pussy with my cum. I would cuckold the King of the Olympians with my futa-seed.

I thrust faster and faster at Hera's pussy. She moaned beneath me, her lips working on mine. Our breasts rubbed together as our bodies heaved. Her hands slid down my back. She grabbed my rump. Her fingers bit into my flesh.

She broke the kiss and licked along my lips. "Mmm, yes, yes, you know how to please a woman. Ooh, Pandora, your futa-dick is amazing. Yes, yes, keep driving it into me. You shall receive the gift of motherhood."

"Thank you, Queen Hera!" I moaned, driving my girl-dick deep and hard into her pussy.

"Just Hera," she whispered and licked my ear. "My sweet, delicious Pandora. Mmm, my son made something special in you." Her hands grabbed my rump. "Harder. I want to cum on this cock!"

"Yes, Queen Hera!"

I thrust with all my might into her pussy. She bucked her hips up to meet my thrust. Her face contorted in delight. Her pussy clenched about my girl-dick. Our nipples brushed. Sparks flared. The bed creaked from our passion.

Her fingernails bit into my ass. She held me tight, pulling me into her cunt. I groaned with each plunge into her twat. I buried to the hit in her, my virgin pussy aching, wishing to be filled by a futa-cock the way I filled her jar. My ovaries quivered. My orgasm hurtled closer.

"Pandora!" she gasped as her pussy rippled around me. "Receive my gift!"

She kissed me, her cunt spasming around my futa-dick. A wave of heat washed through me. I groaned, feeling it settle into my ovaries. My pussy clenched as I drove my cock into her married pussy. Tongue dancing with hers, I erupted.

My cum fired into her convulsing pussy. I flooded Zeus's wife with my cum. I cuckolded the King of the Olympians with every spurt of my girl-jizz flooding into Hera's spasming pussy. She shuddered beneath me, kissing me hard. Her tongue danced with mine.

The pleasure slammed into my mind. I rode that wonderful delight. My virgin pussy convulsed. I kept erupting. More and more of my cum fired into her twat. It was incredible. I filled her jar with my cum. Every last blast sent ecstasy slamming into my mind while rapture washed from my cunt.

She broke the kiss and moaned, "Fill me up with your cum. Flood my vessel with all your seed!"

"Yes, Hera!" I moaned, trembling on her. "I'm filling your jar with all my spunk!"

"Yes, you ar—"

Thunder rumbled. Lightning flashed, painting the room in harsh brilliance. I bucked on top of her. She gasped as a figure loomed over us, beard bristling. A strong hand seized me by the back of the neck and ripped me off his wife.

Zeus held me in his terrible grip, lightning zapping from his eyes. "You *dare* cuckold me, Pandora!"

Terror struck me. I gibbered, legs kicking.

"I came to give my gift and found you giving it to my wife instead!" he growled. His eyes sparkled.

"Do not kill her!" gasped Hera. "Please, my lord. I am the weak one. Punish me, not her. She is a woman. Not a man. She has not cuckolded you. Not truly."

I whimpered, my heart thundering in his grip.

"It is time for *my* gift, Pandora!" Spittle flew from Zeus. "I curse you with tragedy, Pandora. It will befall on you the day you break your hymen. On the day that you uncork your virgin jar, you shall bring suffering and pain upon all the mortals. They shall curse your name for all time for what you shall do to them."

I whimpered.

"You are banished from Mount Olympus. I send you to the care of Prometheus!" A cruel smile spread upon his lips. "Can you control your appetites, Pandora?"

"I..."

The world blurred. It whirled past me. I gasped as a mountainside rushed by me. I fell from the heights of Olympus, hurtling toward the mortal world below, naked and scared. I fell towards a house. A lone cottage in the hills above a town.

I crashed to the earth and darkness overtook me.

To be continued...

Pandora's Futa Passions Awakened

Pandora's Naughty Futa Box 2

by

Reed James

Pandora's Futa Passions Awakened

Prometheus, the titan banished to live among the humans, stared down at the woman who'd fallen from Mount Olympus and now lay before his house. She was naked, lying on her side, her black hair in a braid.

"The gods sent her to us," Prometheus's wife, Hesione, said. She stood at the fiery-haired titan's side. The tall and busty woman had a fall of blue hair that gave her a striking appearance. Though she looked human, she was an oceanid, a naiad of the sea. "Is she a gift?"

Prometheus groaned. "Never trust gifts from Zeus. They are always poisoned."

"But she's hurt," Hesione said. She bent down and put a hand on the young woman's forehead. She stroked away a lock of black hair. "And... Oh, my, she has a cock."

Prometheus frowned. She did. What was this strange creature that had fallen from the sky? All the instincts in him screamed to leave her where she lay. He glanced up at the great mountain that towered over the world.

He could feel Zeus smirking down on him. He hated Prometheus for stealing fire from the gods and gifting it to the humans. With a growl, Prometheus bent down and picked up the young woman. The titan knew that she would bring some calamity. Some danger to him.

But she was hurt. Cock or no, she had hit the ground hard. She was lucky to be alive.

* * *

Pandora

I felt soft sheets about me. A mattress.

I was in the palace of my creator, Hephaestus. My father. That terrifying fall, being caught by Zeus in bed with his wife, and cuckolding the King of the Olympians must have been a dream. A strange nightmare. There was no way Hera would have awakened me in bed and cuckolded her husband with me.

I fluttered my eyes and stared up at a tall and brawny man with fiery hair. He had arms folded before him. He felt like Hephaestus, but this wasn't the broken and ugly visage of my creator. This man was too handsome. His body too whole. I swallowed as I realized I was in a room constructed out of wooden logs. It had a rustic feel to it. I wasn't on Olympus nor was I in Hephaestus's workshop beneath Mount Etna where he had created me.

The first woman with a cock. The first futanari.

"Who are you?" asked the man standing over me.

"Pandora," I said, her body aching. I felt so tired. I wanted to slip back into sleep. "Who... are you?"

"Prometheus."

I blinked. "The cursed titan?"

"Zeus is a jealous god," Prometheus said. "He does not enjoy competition."

Flashes of that dream, which must have been real, appeared in my mind. How Zeus had grabbed me. How he cursed me. Something about how my jar must never be opened. That I must be a virgin or tragedy would befall the world.

"No," I said. He had been furious to find that I had made love to Hera. She had given me the gift of motherhood. Many of the Olympians had bestowed gifts upon me. Aphrodite gave me beauty before she made love to me.

I had cuckolded not just Zeus, but my creator. My dick twitched, remembering the delight of those two goddesses as well as Athena's asshole. The virgin goddess had given me an understanding of engineering. I knew how the walls of this house were constructed. The ceiling.

"Are you able to eat?" a woman asked.

Stepping up beside Prometheus was a blue-haired and busty woman wearing a brown toga. The sight of her sent a throb through my cock and a clench of heat through my pussy. She was so gorgeous. Just a beautiful woman with a broad smile on her lips.

"Yes," I said, my stomach growling. "Thank you, madam."

"Hesione," she said. "I'm Prometheus's wife."

A third figure watched from the doorway. A girl my own age. She had brown hair that fell about her curious face. Blue eyes watched. Her slender form, wrapped up in a light-blue toga, sent a thrill through me. My cock twitched even more, tenting the blanket over my naked body.

Hesione sat down on the side of my bed. She held a bowl before her full of steaming broth. She stirred it up and fed it to me, a large smile on her face. I chewed at the hunks of goat, the warmth seeping through me. I groaned, my body sore. Sleep dragged back down on me.

"What are you, Pandora?" Hesione asked.

Prometheus grunted.

"Futanari," I answered. "Hephaestus created me."

"That runt," spat Prometheus. "And why did Zeus throw you to earth? Because you have that cock?"

"Cock?" the girl asked.

Prometheus glanced over his shoulder. "Run along, Pyrrha."

The girl swallowed then vanished.

Prometheus turned back to me. "My brother Epimetheus's daughter. She is staying with my wife and me."

"He takes in strays," said Hesione. Her deep, blue eyes held a sparkle to them as she spooned up more goat stew. "Mmm, so you have a cock."

Prometheus gave his wife a look then grunted under his breath, "Poisoned gifts."

I didn't know what that meant, but I smiled at Hesione. "Thank you. Your stew is delicious. But..."

"Yes, yes, sleep," she said and stood up, color spotting her cheeks. "You need your rest. A pretty, young thing like you needs to recover."

I closed my eyes. Hesione was so gorgeous and sexy. Aphrodite had shown me the delights of a busty woman, and then Hera had cemented those delights. Though my cock was hard, aching for passion, I couldn't stay awake. I fell into sleep.

* * *

Over the next few days, I grew stronger and stronger. I slept less and less. Hesione was such a comforting woman. The titan's wife always had a warm smile as she brought in her cooking. She had a skilled touch, her presence always excited me.

Not that I had the strength to do anything to her. Yet. I could see it in her eyes. Aphrodite had blessed me with beauty. She had made me into a creature of sublime perfection for the pleasure my girl-cock had given her.

That wasn't the only gift I'd gotten from the Olympians. Ares had given me stamina. Strength.

It kept me hard much of the time. Horny. When I wasn't sleeping, I was aching to stroke my cock and cum. As my strength returned to me, I played with my cock as I lay recovering in my bed. The first time I had cum, such delight had rushed through me. That warmth of passion. My seed had fired up beneath the covers, making them all sticky.

I should have asked to have them changed, but I then fell into an exhausted sleep, drained by the act of masturbation.

It was a week before I finally had recovered enough that masturbating didn't send me back into sleep. I had just cum and lay reclined on my pillow against the headboard of my bed. It was finely carved by Prometheus himself, the mattress stuffed with goose down. I stared up at the ceiling, my cum cooling on my breasts.

I hummed. Apollo had given me the gift of song. The melody rose in me and then the words. They flowed out of my mouth as I idly traced the drying spunk on my round breast. I bathed in the delight of my orgasm, my finger swirling the jizz around my nipple.

The stars were shining outside of my window. Night had fallen over the world. My sleep was so irregular. I spent hours and hours sleeping between bouts of wakefulness. Day and night had lost all meaning for me.

I scooped up the cum and smeared the salty delight on my lips in a break of my song. Then I resumed, loving the salty taste of the cum on my lips. My toes flexed beneath the covers. My dick twitched and throbbed. I was always hard.

I slid my hand down to my pussy. I rubbed at it through my brown curls. What had Zeus meant when he'd said, *"I curse you with tragedy, Pandora. It will befall on you the day you break your hymen. On the day that you uncork your virgin jar, you shall bring suffering and pain upon all the mortals. They shall curse your name for all time for what you shall do to them."*

I caressed over my hymen. I shuddered and pulled my fingers away from that naughty hole. Part of me ached to find out what it was like to be penetrated. Both Aphrodite and Hera had enjoyed my large futa-cock plundering their cunts. My dick throbbed again. I felt the urge to masturbate again rise in me. My song trilled from my lips, a passionate strain swelling in.

I grabbed my cock and worked my hand up and down it. The delight rushed to my pussy. I ignored that naughty hole. I had to focus on my clit-dick. I could enjoy that as much as I wanted. I didn't need to have my pussy penetrated.

Then my door creaked open. I glanced over to see Pyrrha peering in. I hadn't seen much of Epimetheus's daughter. She kept out of the room. She was staring at my naked breasts covered in cum and my hand pumping up and down my cock. She bit her lip as I grinned at her.

"Come in, Pyrrha," I said. "Don't be shy. I won't bite you."

"Prometheus doesn't want me to come near you." She stared at me with those blue eyes of hers.

"And?" I asked. "What do you want to do?"

She slipped into the room, wrapped up in her sky-blue toga. She had this look of fear and lust on her young face. She closed the door behind her, breathing quickened. She stared at my hand pumping up and down my girl-cock.

"You have both," she said. "Don't you? A cock and a pussy."

"I do." I sat up, feeling my strength rising. For the first time, I rose out of my bed. My legs were weak, trembling, but I didn't care. I had this beautiful virgin here.

She had a hymen that could be broken.

I sauntered to her. My breasts swayed back and forth. Her eyes locked on them. On the pearly spunk that covered them. I felt my cum running over my breasts. She quivered there, this look of scared lust on her face.

"I... I shouldn't be here, Pandora," she said.

"Shhh," I told her, so horny. I needed her. A woman. The three goddesses had awakened passion in me. I cupped her face, stroking her silky skin. "It's okay, Pyrrha. I won't hurt you. I just want to love you."

"We're women," she groaned. "We're not supposed to love each other."

"I have a cock that was made to love women, Pyrrha." I leaned in and kissed her lips.

Her mouth, warm and soft, melted into mine. She moaned, hugging me tight. My breasts pressed into her toga, smearing my cum into her clothing. My cock throbbed, pinned between us. I ached. My pussy clenched as I kissed her with hunger.

The way Aphrodite had kissed me.

I thrust my tongue into her mouth as my hands roamed her back. I slid up and down her body, gripping her rump through her toga. She whimpered into the kiss. Her tongue played with mine. She was such a sweet and delicious thing.

I broke the kiss with her. She panted, her blue eyes glassy. She stared up at me with a look of awe on her face. She licked her lips and shivered. She must have tasted the salt of cum on me. I grinned as her gaze fell down to my breasts.

"Enjoy," I told her. "That's my seed. I spilled it all over my tits."

Pyrrha whimpered. Then she ducked her head down and licked at my cum on my breast. Her pink tongue slid up to my nipple, brushing it as she gathered up my pearly futa-spunk. She sighed at the taste of my salty seed.

I smiled at her and then began unwinding her toga. She stared up at me, her eyes so wide. She knew what was coming. That she had wandered into the hungry lion's den. Artemis, the Goddess of the Hunt, had bestowed on me the gift of trust. That my prey would never fear me. Not that I would hurt Pyrrha, but I wanted her passion. Ached for her flesh.

Hers and Hesione's.

Her toga fell away. She had a slender body, her breasts small mounds. She was a young woman, just flowered into adulthood. She should be wedded or betrothed to a man, but I was about to claim her. I grabbed her cheeks again and kissed her.

This time, my breasts pressed into hers with nothing between us. My cock throbbed against her warm belly as my tongue thrust into her mouth. She whimpered, our kiss tasting of my salty futa-cum. That only excited me.

I turned her as we kissed. The rest of the house slept. My host, Prometheus, was charged with taking care of his brother's daughter, and yet here I was preying on her. I would take her virginity. I would pump my seed into her virgin jar.

Breed her.

My dick twitched against her belly. I wanted to breed her. Hera gave me the gift of motherhood. I pumped my spunk into her pussy. I flooded her with my spunk, and now I wanted to do the same to this virgin delight.

I pushed her back to my bed. She didn't resist. She just moaned into the kiss, her hands on my hips. Our breasts rubbed together, hers so firm and small. Her nipples brushed mine. Sparks flared down to my virgin pussy.

The backs of Pyrrha's legs hit my bed and she fell back onto it, breaking our kiss. She panted, staring up at me. Her small breasts rose and fell. I licked my lips and then fell to my knees before her. I parted her legs and stared down at her brown bush covering her virgin delight.

That tangy musk swelled in my nose. I groaned and darted my head in. I pressed my lips right into her silky curls. The heady scent grew stronger. Then my lips kissed her virgin flesh. My own pussy clenched as my tongue stroked up her slit.

"Pandora!" she gasped in delight as I licked at her. "Oh, Pandora."

I smiled up at her. My tongue caressed up and down her pussy lips. My virgin twat clenched. I ached as I brushed her hymen protecting the entrance to her depths. My hands stroked her thighs as I fluttered my tongue up and down Pyrrha's virgin flesh.

Her moans echoed through my room. They resounded back and forth as I feasted upon her. I licked and lapped at her with hunger. I wanted to drink down all her passion. She tasted so delicious. Her thighs squeezed about me as she whimpered out her delight.

"Pandora! Pandora!" Her small breasts quivered. She leaned back on her hands. "This... You... Oh, Pandora."

"Shhh," I purred. "If Prometheus hears us..."

She gasped and nodded, her blue eyes wide.

I loved her pussy. I licked and lapped at her with hunger. My tongue caressed over those folds, drinking her juices. My futa-cock ached more and more. I wanted to penetrate her. My hands tightened on her thighs, wanting to love her, too. To make her cum before I took her virginity.

I wanted to make such love to Pyrrha. Women were just glorious creatures. Like me but lacking my cock. My tongue caressed over her pussy's folds. Licked up to her clit. That was where my dick thrust from. She had a little bud that Hephaestus had grown into my cock when he made me.

I sucked on her. She gasped, liking that.

"Oh, Pandora," she whimpered as I nursed on her.

The virgin trembled as I sucked on that bud. Her breasts jiggled. And moans grew louder and louder. Her tangy flavor swelled in my mouth. Her silky curls rubbed against my face. I loved the delight. I breathed in her musk, my pussy soaking my bush. My cock ached for her.

She squirmed, her small breasts jiggling. I nibbled on her bud with my lips. I had all these instincts rushing through me. Knowledge on how to please a woman that came from outside of my own life. I swirled my tongue around her bud. She gasped. Her face scrunched up.

"Pandora!" she squealed in delight.

Tangy juices gushed out of her virgin pussy. I groaned and

183

drank down that flood. The bed creaked. I had made her climax. This surge of triumphant delight rushed through my body. I licked at her. my tongue lapped at her cunt. I swirled it around her clit. This wonderful bud throbbed in my mouth. It was such a treat to enjoy.

She groaned, her body shaking. Her moans cried out through the room. She shook her head, her brown hair dancing as her orgasm swept through her body. She whimpered, her face scrunching up with delight.

"Oh, Pandora," she groaned. "You... You're... I don't know why Prometheus says you are cursed. You are wonderful."

I smiled up at her shining face. "Pyrrha." Joy surged through me. I leaned up and cupped her face. I kissed her on the mouth, my lips coated in her pussy juices. She groaned, her tongue darting out to meet mine.

Our lips kissed with hunger as I pushed her down on the bed. My futa-cock ached so much. I had to be in her virgin pussy. Athena wouldn't let me uncork her jar, but Pyrrha would. I would break through the girl's hymen and plunder her depths.

I would flood her jar with all my cum.

She sank down on the bed beneath me, so lithe and delicious. She whimpered beneath me, her hands stroking my body. Her touch slid up and down my sides and then grabbed my ass. She squeezed my rump, digging her fingers into my butt-cheeks.

My tongue danced in her mouth as her digits gripped me. She pulled me tight against her. My dick throbbed as it rubbed into her bush. Her silky hairs slid over my cock and her pussy was so wet beneath it.

I shifted my hips, kissing her hard. I slid my cock down and pressed it right against her hot pussy lips. She groaned beneath me. She squirmed and whimpered. The tip of my dick pushed into her folds and found her hymen. That barrier.

I needed to be in her. She was ready. I could tell from how she kissed me.

I thrust.

She groaned as I pushed against her hymen. I would uncork her jar and fill her up. Her fingernails bit into my rump. Pyrrha squirmed beneath me. Her maidenhead stretched before my cock. The elastic barrier held me back for one more heartbeat.

Then it tore.

I plunged into her cunt. Her hot flesh slid around me. That silky, amazing, wonderful sheath gripped me. She groaned into my lips, her eyes widening. Her fingernails bit hard into my rump this time as my girl-dick bottomed out in her.

I broke the kiss and moaned, "Pyrrha."

"Pandora!" she gasped. She stared up at me with such awe in her eyes. "I... You... This..."

"I know," I told her. I smiled down at her as she squirmed, her pussy shifting around my futa-cock. "I know. You feel amazing."

She kissed me again, her deflowered pussy clenching around me. I drew back, loving the tightness of her cunt. It was like Athena's asshole but wetter. Silkier. I groaned as I thrust back into her depths, savoring her flesh engulfing me, caressing me.

It was amazing. I pumped away at her. I thrust my girl-cock into her beautiful pussy. The titan's daughter moaned beneath me, her lips so sweet. My breasts rubbed against hers, our nipples sliding over each other's tits.

Sometimes they met.

Sparks flared.

It added to that building ache at the tip of my girl-cock. I plunged over and over into her pussy. I thrust into her cunt. I buried hard into this naughty girl's twat. She kissed me with her sweet lips as I plundered her cunt.

I broke the kiss and panted, "Pyrrha! Oh, yes, yes, your pussy is so sweet."

"Pandora! Your girl-dick! I love your girl-dick!"

I smiled down at her, loving the joy shining in her eyes. She grinned up at me, stroking my back. She caressed me as I thrust my dick into her twat. I buried into her again and again. I plundered her, loving every second of being in her cunt.

It was a delicious treat. A wild joy. I buried into her again and again. Her pussy clenched about me. She held me tight. Her twat squeezed about me, building and building that pressure in my cunt's depths. My cum had to flood her jar.

"Pyrrha," I groaned.

"Yes, yes!" she gasped. "I'm going to... to... to have that good feeling again."

"You're going to cum?" I purred, rubbing my nose against hers.

"Yes, yes, cum!" she gasped, squeezing her twat down around my dick. "I want to cum again!"

I groaned into her twat with hard strokes. She gasped, her pussy clenching around me. That swelled the ache at the tip of my girl-cock. It was amazing. This wonderful delight rippled through me every time I plunged to the hilt in her jar. Her juicy twat squeezed about me, gripping me.

My own pussy clenched, savoring the heat swelling down my cock. It flowed from her pussy to mine, my dick drinking it all up. I came closer and closer to cumming, my sensitive nipples rubbing into her breasts. I groaned as I slammed into her.

"Pandora!" she squealed. "Yes!"

Her hot pussy went wild around my cock.

"Oh, Pyrrha!" I moaned as I thrust into her cumming depths.

Her rippling flesh sucked at my cock. The pressure in my ovaries swelled as I felt the suction on them. I groaned as I buried back into her spasming twat. Her silky flesh massaged me. The tip of my clit-dick burst with pleasure.

I fired my futa-cum into her pussy.

I basted her fertile depths with my blessed seed. I groaned, my virgin pussy convulsing and spasming. I shuddered, two different delights spilling through me. Bliss rushed from my spasming cunt and euphoria fired from my spurting futa-cock.

"Oh, Pyrrha!"

"You're flooding me, Pandora!" she moaned, trembling beneath me as her pussy writhed around my spurting cock.

"I am!" I moaned. "Oh, yes, yes, I am. And you feel so good. You're such a wonderful delight. Oh, you're making me feel so good."

I kept spurting in her. I kept firing my cum into her pussy. The pleasure slammed through my mind. It was amazing. I groaned at it, my heart pounding in my chest. I shuddered, sparks sizzling through my thoughts.

And then her pussy wrung out the last of my cum. I had filled her sweet jar with all my spunk. I groaned, panting. I rolled off of her, my dick popping out of her naughty flesh. The room spun around me. A sudden exhaustion fell on me.

"Pandora," moaned Pyrrha, snuggling against me. "Oh, that was wonderful."

"Uh-huh," I groaned, staring up at the ceiling. "You were amazing."

"I loved you being in me," she said, her voice goring distant. I faded, drifting towards sleep. She kissed me on the lips.

The drowsy bliss tugged me further and further from this world.

I had strange dreams of futas fucking other women. There were so many of them. Just pounding them with their big girl-dicks. The women all gasped and moaned, crying out in ecstasy. It was such a wonderful sound to hear.

It made my dick so hard to dream of it.

I throbbed. Ached. The dream was so real that when one of the women fell before me and sucked on my cock, I felt it. My pussy clenched. My cock throbbed. The nursing pressure on my futa-cock dragged me out of my dreams with its intensity.

My thoughts rose up into my body. I felt the bed beneath me. I heard the birds chirping outside of my window. I groaned at the mouth around my cock nursing on my dick. I shuddered at it. My eyes fluttered open at the wonderful sight.

"Pyrrha," I groaned, staring up at the ceiling. It was morning. Daylight flooded through the room. "That's amazing."

The mouth slid off my cock. "I'm not Pyrrha."

I gasped and sat up. Hesione lay between my thighs naked, her blue hair spilling about her beautiful face. She had a mature grace like Hera had. A woman fully blossomed and ripened. She licked her lips and ducked her head back down to my cock.

"No!" I gasped, this fear rushing through me. The memory of Zeus flared in my mind. "You're married. What if Prometheus catches us?"

"He is not here," his wife moaned. "Oh, I've wanted this cock since I saw you lying there. A nymph from the heavens. You're

187

gorgeous."

The sea nymph sucked my cock into her mouth. I groaned at the oceanid's hard sucking. My toes curled. My pussy clenched. Her mouth worked up and down my cock. She sucked with such intensity. I glanced at the door. It was shut.

What if Prometheus caught us? Would he throw me out like Zeus had? Of course, he would. Where would I go then? The world out there was strange to me. Alien. I didn't know anything but my creator's workshop beneath Mt. Etna. Until a week ago, I had spent my whole life there.

Now I had this place of safety, but it would be jeopardized if I cuckolded my host. However...

His wife sucked hard on my cock. Her warm mouth nursed on it. She slid her lips up and down my girl-cock. The pleasure rushed through me. This heady heat blazed through my body. My pussy clenched at the fierceness of her sucking.

She wanted my cum.

I whimpered as she loved me. Her blue hair rustled as she blew my cock. She moaned, her passion humming around the tip. My toes curled and pussy clenched. I groaned, my breasts jiggling as she sucked hard on my dick that had taken Pyrrha's virginity. Not that the two women were related, but it was sexy knowing Hesione could taste another pussy on my cock.

"Yes," I moaned. "Hesione! Oh, you wicked wife."

She purred around my cock.

Then her fingers slid down through my bush. She stroked at the folds of my pussy. She caressed at them, exploring around them almost like she couldn't believe I had both. My twat drank it in as she pushed into my folds and brushed my hymen. She stroked it.

Fear flashed through me.

"No, no, don't touch me there!" I gasped. "Not my hymen. I have to keep my jar corked."

She stared at me for a moment, not sucking. Then she shrugged and nursed hard on my cock. I could tell what she truly cared for. I groaned, biting my lip as she worked her mouth up and down my futa-dick while her fingers just stroked my labia. My toes curled, the pleasure rising faster and faster.

I couldn't hold back. It was so hot being woken up by this sexy wife's blowjob. Cuckolding my host sent such a wicked thrill through my flesh. I had fucked Zeus's wife and lived. I could get away with this.

"That's it," I moaned. "Oh, yes, yes, Hesione. I... I... Yes!"

I came and flooded her mouth.

My futa-dick unloaded my salty cum. The pleasure slammed through my body. The heat crashed into my mind. It burst over my thoughts. Stars showered across my expression. I groaned, my pussy convulsing. Juices bathed her fingers caressing my twat.

"Yes, yes, Hesione!" I groaned. "You wicked wife!"

She nursed with hunger on my futa-cock. She sucked out the cum firing into her mouth and gulped it down. She moaned as she did, her intense, blue eyes glassy with her passion. The bed creaked as I squirmed. I hit that peak of pleasure, unloading my last blast into her.

She kept sucking. Kept nursing. She moaned around my cock like she wanted to draw out just one more spurt of my cum. I groaned, my cunt clenching. My dick ached in her mouth, that itch growing at the tip again. Ares's gift of stamina suffused me.

She slid her mouth off my cock. "You're not going soft."

"I don't," I said. I hadn't really tested it, but since Ares had blessed me, I hadn't really ever gone soft.

"You are that virile?" she asked and rose.

"Yes," I said.

I groaned, seeing that she was naked. Her large, motherly breasts swayed over me. She straddled me, grabbing my cock and holding it up. She aimed it at her pussy and then sank down on it. Her pussy swallowed my futa-dick. Her hot flesh slid over me, engulfing me in her wet passion. I would flood her married jar with all my futa-seed.

She would brim in it.

She gripped me with her cunt. She arched her back. The married oceanid's breasts heaved forward. Her big boobs bounced and jiggled as she worked her twat up and down my dick. I gasped, savoring her working up and down my dick.

"Hesione!" I gasped.

"Pandora!" She squeezed her pussy down on my dick. "This cock is amazing. You're so huge. You dwarf my husband. A titan." She slammed her cunt down my futa-cock. "Oh, this is amazing. You're a girl with a big dick. Pandora!"

Her moans echoed through the room. Her tits smacked together as she rode me. Her thighs flexed. I shot my hands up and grabbed her boobs. I cupped her soft, yet heavy, breasts. I cradled them in my hand, loving how they jiggled. The way they quivered in my grip.

It was amazing.

My fingers dug into her flesh. I kneaded her tits as she worked her cunt up and down my clit-dick. She gripped me as she slid up and then slammed that hot and juicy pussy back down my cock. Her married flesh massaged me. Built my orgasm.

"Pandora, yes!" she moaned, staring down at me, her blue hair swaying about her face. "Oh, yes, yes, this dick... Oh, this dick is amazing.

The door creaked open. Pyrrha watched us.

Hesione had no idea the girl watched us. She just worked her cunt up and down my cock with her passion. I squeezed her tits. Her hands shot down and grabbed my round breasts. She dug her fingers into my flesh, kneading them. A smile crossed her lips.

She slammed her cunt down my cock and slid back up my dick. The ache swelled at the tip of my shaft. That spongy crown drank in the friction of her silky cunt. She felt amazing. My virgin twat clenched, the heat swelling in my ovaries.

"I'm going to cum in you!" I moaned.

"Good," she panted. "Mmm, fill my jar with your cum. I want to brim with your impossible seed, Pandora!"

"Such a wicked wife!" I groaned.

"Yes!"

She rode me faster, her fingers digging into my flesh. Pyrrha, squirmed as she watched, the door creaking open more. I could see her hands roaming her body through her toga. She bit her lip. I loved it. I thrust upward, driving my cock upward into Hesione's pussy as she plunged it down.

She gasped. Pyrrha shuddered on her busy fingers.

I thrust up again and again, my tits jiggling in the naughty wife's grip. She dug her fingers into my boobs as she slammed her cunt down my cock. Then I bounced her up. She slid her cunt fast up my cock, squeezing about me. My ovaries brimmed.

Hesione plunged down my cock. She gasped as my thrust met hers. Her boobs jiggled. She cried out at that moment. Her pussy went wild. Her hot, married flesh sucked at my cock, as hungry for my cum as Pyrrha had been.

"Yes, yes, yes!" the climaxing wife moaned. "Oh, Pandora, flood my jar with your futa-cum! Fill me up!"

I groaned and shuddered, my legs spasmed on the bed. Then my futa-cock erupted. My hot cum fired into her pussy just like she wanted. I groaned at that moment. The pleasure rushed through me. This heady, intense delight.

I knew that I bred her married pussy. That Hera's gift of motherhood had activated once more. I shuddered, knowing that I had thoroughly cuckolded Prometheus. I pumped his wife's pussy full of my fecund girl-seed.

That thought rushed such rapture through me. "Yes!" I groaned, dizzy from it. "Oh, yes, yes!"

Pyrrha stepped into the room, watching me cum in Hesione's pussy. I bred the older woman like I had the younger girl last night. It was so intense. My pussy convulsed harder, juices flooding hot down my thighs.

The girl licked her lips. Her hands squeezing at her breasts as she watched in awe. I groaned, pumping my cum into Hesione's pussy. Naughty ideas flooded through my mind. Something imparted along with Aphrodite's gift of beauty, perhaps. Other knowledge she slipped into my mind.

As I fired the last of my cum into the bucking Hesione, I rolled the wicked wife over. she moaned, ending up on her back as her pussy rippled around me. I groaned and then pulled my cock out of her, panting.

"Oh, yes, Pandora," moaned Hesione.

I smiled. "Mmm, look at all that cum I pumped into your jar. It's leaking out. We need to clean that up, right, Pyrrha?"

Hesione gasped and turned to see her young houseguest staring at us and groping herself through her toga. The wife scrambled to cover herself until she noticed what the girl was doing. Then Hesione stopped moving.

"When I heard you and Pandora last night, I just couldn't resist any longer," she said. "I don't know what there is between you two, but don't tell your uncle. He would not understand."

"I won't," whispered Pyrrha, her eyes locked on Hesione's pussy. "You're... That's..."

I grasped the girl's toga and unwound it from her as I whispered. "Go, feast. Enjoy her. I know you like the taste of my cum."

"I scooped it out of my pussy after you fell asleep," Pyrrha moaned as I finished unwinding her. "It was deliciously seasoned with my juices and... and..."

She threw herself down between the married woman's thighs. The nubile girl leaned down, her brown hair falling over Hesione's pale thighs. My futa-cock throbbed at the lesbian sight before me. Women loving women. It was such a beautiful thing. It filled me with such awe.

Hesione shuddered, her large breasts jiggling as the naughty girl feasted on her. It set my lusts on fire. This wicked heat that throbbed through my cunt as I watched the naughty fun. My clit-dick throbbed. I grabbed it, stroking myself as I licked my lips. My cunt blazed with fire. This heat would consume me.

Pyrrha's rump wiggled back and forth as she licked my cum out of Hesione's pussy. The girl drank my futa-jizz pouring out of the married woman's jar. It was so hot, and her ass was so cute. I smiled, remembering how Athena preserved her maidenhead.

I crawled onto the bed behind Pyrrha. Hesione smiled at me, her hands kneading her breasts. The motherly oceanid bit her lower lip and groaned. It was this deep and throaty sound as the girl licked her pussy.

"Fuck her, Pandora," she moaned. "Pound her pussy. Pump that cum in her. Make sure you bred her."

"Oh, she's bred," I groaned, staring at the girl's rump. I grabbed her butt-cheek and parted it. Her brown hole peeked out above her brown bush. "I think..."

She gasped. "You're going to do what those Athenians do. Sodomy? The way men fuck men?"

I smiled. Of course, Athena had taught her city about anal sex. I nodded and pressed my cock against Pyrrha's asshole. The girl gasped. She lifted her head from Hesione's pussy and threw a look over her shoulder, lips gleaming with pussy cream.

"Pandora?" she asked.

"Shhh, you'll enjoy this," I said. "Athena loves it. Mmm, and you've got such a pretty bottom."

I pushed my clit-dick against her asshole. The girl squealed as her anal ring parted. Her eyes widened. Then she let out a throaty moan as her sphincter spread wider and wider open. The velvety flesh slid over my futa-dick's thick tip.

"Oh, Pandora, you're sliding into my butt!" she groaned. "That's so wicked."

"Yes, it is," Hesione said, her eyes sparkling. "Does it feel good?"

"Yes," the girl whimpered as I slid deeper and deeper into her bowels. "It's different, but it feels... nice. Better than nice. Naughty!"

"So naughty," I groaned, her asshole swallowing my cock. The velvety friction sent this heat melting down my dick. "Mmm, that's good."

I bottomed out in her, my black bush rubbing into her rump. My hair, not braided but loose, swayed about my face. I stroked the girl's sides as I savored the tight delight of her hot bowels wrapped around my girl-dick.

"Mmm, don't stop licking me, Pyrrha," Hesione purred. She grabbed the girl's brown hair and pulled her head down. "Just eat my pussy. Mmm, I need it. Just lap up that jizz from me. I want to cum on my mouth and there's still plenty of futa-cum to drink out of my jar."

"And your yummy pussy cream, Hesione," Pyrrha moaned, her bowels clenching around my clit-dick.

She nuzzled back down. I couldn't see her licking, but I could see the effect on Hesione. The busty wife shuddered. She moaned, her face contorting in bliss. I loved it. I gripped Pyrrha's hips and drew back my cock. I slid my cock out of her bowels. Her hot flesh gripped me. That wonderful pleasure spilled over my dick. It was amazing to experience.

I slammed back into the girl's asshole. I felt her bowels squeezing around my cock. She felt amazing wrapped about my clit-dick. Her hot bowels massaged me as I pumped away at her. My round breast bounced.

"Oh, yes, yes, Pyrrha," I moaned, reveling in her bowels. In my domination over the two women. They both had surrendered to me. Thanks to Aphrodite's gift, they couldn't resist me.

And thanks to Ares's gift, despite having just cum moments ago I had the stamina to fuck the girl's asshole. Hard. I pounded her with my powerful strokes. I buried my cock into her with passion. I slammed to the hilt in her. I buried deep into her hot flesh. It was amazing to feel.

Her velvety flesh squeezed about me. That wonderful, delicious, and amazing sheath gripped me. I groaned, savoring every moment of her cunt clenching about me. I slammed deep into her. Hard. My dick plundered the girl's bowels with powerful strokes.

"Pandora," she moaned. "Oh, wow, Pandora!"

"I know," I groaned, savoring that delicious feel of her bowels squeezing about my cock. "Yes, yes, just enjoy that dick in you."

"I am!" she gasped out, voice muffled by hot pussy. "Oh, Hesione, you taste so good."

"Mmm, and your tongue feels amazing. Yes, yes, lick at my clit! You naughty girl."

Hesione arched her back, her tits jiggling. She squirmed there, her face contorting with delight. She ground her cunt against the girl's mouth. She humped against her in time with my powerful strokes. I buried to the hilt in her hard. Fast.

I slammed my cock deep into her bowels, my pussy growing hotter and hotter. She moaned louder and louder, her head moving as she feasted on Hesione's pussy. The naughty wife squeezed her big boobs as she squirmed on my bed. Her passion echoed through the room.

"Oh, Pyrrha!" Hesione groaned.

"Is she going to make you cum?" I asked. "Because her asshole is massaging my cock. I'm going to fire so much cum in her bowels."

"She is!" Hesione shuddered. "Oh, Pyrrha! Pyrrha! That's good. Oh, you're such a good pussy licker."

"You just taste so good!" she moaned. "And... and... I'm going to cum on your cock. Your dick feels amazing in me, Pandora!"

"Good," I groaned.

I thrust hard at her. Fast. Her velvety flesh swelled that ache at the tip of my dick. My dick drank in her delicious bowels. The friction burned hotter and hotter with my every thrust into her bowels. My every plunge into her hot flesh. My ovaries clenched. My virgin pussy brimmed with heat. I couldn't take much more of this.

I slammed hard into Pyrrha's asshole. She squealed out in delight. Her hot bowels rippled around my cock. The girl orgasmed like Athena had from my big clit-dick. I groaned, slamming into the girl's bowels, loving how she rippled about me.

"Pandora!" she moaned into Hesione's pussy.

"Oh, yes, yes, make me cum!" gasped Hesione. "Oh, Pyrrha, you wicked girl. Yes!"

A creaking sound drew my attention. As Hesione cried out in orgasmic delight, cumming on Pyrrha's hungry lips, I looked over my shoulder and saw Prometheus staring at us through the open door. The titan looked stunned as he witnessed me driving my cock into Pyrrha's asshole while his wife writhed on the bed.

"Oh, Pyrrha, yes, yes!" gasped Hesione. "You licked all of Pandora's seed out of me and made me cum."

Prometheus just stood there and watched as the women of his house writhed in my bed. I groaned, savoring this moment. His eyes blazed with a feverish light. He licked his lips and watched me drive my cock into Pyrrha's spasming asshole.

"Oh, yes, yes, Pandora!" Pyrrha moaned. "Cum in me. Like you did last night."

"When I bred you!" I groaned, slamming hard into her. "Just like I bred Hesione. Hera blessed my futa-cock. I fucked her, too."

"Oh, yes!" Hesione moaned. "Your dick is amazing, Pandora! Cum in Pyrrha's asshole!"

Prometheus squeezed at his toga, at his own growing arousal. Then he fled from the room. I smiled and slammed into Pyrrha's asshole. My futa-cock erupted. My hot cum fired triumphantly into her asshole.

I basted her bowels with my cum. I fired blast after blast of jizz into her asshole. The rapture zapped through my body while the delight rippled out of my spasming cunt. The two ecstasies met in my mind. They swirled through my thoughts, leaving me dizzy with delight.

"Oh, yes, yes, you're both mine!" I groaned.

"Yes!" Pyrrha gasped, her bowels wringing my cock dry.

"You... Pandora..." panted Hesione. "I... I... I want to be yours, but my husband."

"Isn't contesting this!" I groaned. "He saw us and fled. So you are mine."

Hesione smiled and nodded as she quivered there.

I pulled my cock out of Pyrrha's asshole. I fell down on the bed beside Hesione. The girl snuggled up on the other side of me. I had them both snuggled up against me and leaning in to kiss me. My virgin pussy clenched. I wanted a big dick to fuck me, too.

Not that there was a cock I could fuck in this house. Prometheus held no interest for me. He was too male. All those hard muscles. The hair on his face. He shaved it, but he had that shadow clinging to him. I didn't want the titan, but my pussy... my pussy ached for a girl-dick.

Then, from the knowledge that Athena gave me, a concept emerged. An artificial cock. A dildo worn by a woman to please others. She had mentioned it, hadn't she? How she fucked her devotees. I shivered, my pussy clenched.

I could make one. But... I couldn't let my hymen be broken. I would unleash tragedy on the world. Right? That's what Zeus claimed, but... What would be the shape of that tragedy? How bad could it possibly be?

Is hook my head. I couldn't think these thoughts. I had my futa-cock. I had Pyrrha and Prometheus's wife. I didn't need my pussy filled when I had their holes to enjoy. Their bodies pressed against me.

I pushed down those wicked thoughts and pulled them closer to me. I was still hard.

To be continued...

Pandora's Naughty Curiosity

Pandora's Naughty Futa Box 3

by

Reed James

Pandora's Naughty Curiosity

Prometheus watched Pandora claim his wife and niece. The futa, thrown down from the top of Mount Olympus by Zeus, had seduced both the women in Prometheus's house. Now they writhed together on the bed in the most depraved act.

Pandora's braid of black hair bounced down her back as she drove her cock hard into Prometheus's wife. Hesione gasped and moaned, the oceanid taking that futa-dick with enthusiasm. Her moans, muffled by Pyrrha's pussy, echoed through Prometheus's ears.

He had lost his wife and the girl he was supposed to care for. Fighting seemed pointless. Pandora, despite having a cock, was a woman. Where was the honor in killing a woman? He slunk out of the room, leaving Pandora to her continued enjoyment of the two women.

"Zeus and his poisoned gifts," muttered the Titan. The sounds of their passion echoed through his home, built of logs in the shadow of Mount Olympus. For the last hour, he had heard those moans.

Pandora was insatiable.

* * *

Pandora

Things had changed. Prometheus had watched me fuck his wife and his brother's daughter without complaint. He had known that my futa-dick was superior to his own. Hesione had milked my cock with her pussy and asshole. So had Pyrrha, the girl who was my own age. Eighteen and nubile.

I enjoyed them for hours before my passions were spent and I collapsed on my bed. Hesione and Pyrrha had no idea that Prometheus had watched us from the doorway. That the Titan had witnessed my prowess and said nothing.

I had cuckolded my host, but his wife had come to me. She had awoken me with her sweet mouth. She had sucked on my cock and then rode me hard. The oceanid's blue hair had bounced around her mature and gorgeous face. The busy wife had cried out in orgasmic delight, milking my futa-cock.

The women could not resist me. The Olympians, before Zeus had cursed me to never lose my virginity, had given me many gifts. Aphrodite had given me beauty. A perfect countenance that both young Pyrrha and mature Hesione had not been able to resist. Ares gave me the stamina to keep enjoying my passion. Apollo gave me the gift of singing and Artemis the gift of stealth. Athena taught me engineering and Hera, whose embrace had earned me Zeus's wrath, had given me motherhood.

I knew that my seed had quickened in both Hesione's and Pyrrha's wombs. That their pussies were brimming daughters. I felt it the first time I had cum in their pussies. It had been incredible. It made my virgin cunt clench.

I still had my hymen. Zeus had cursed me. If I ever uncorked my virgin jar, tragedy would befall mankind. I ached to know what it was like to be fucked like I had fucked Hesione and Pyrrha. How I had reveled in Aphrodite, Athena, and Hera's holes. I had the knowledge to fashion a dildo and the harness so one of my lovers could wield it.

I was so curious about what it would be like. My pussy itched through the evening, everyone pretending that I hadn't fucked Hesione and Pyrrha today in a wild threesome. Prometheus acted like he had not seen it. His wife pretended she didn't have a womb full of my seed as she served the evening meal of lamb stew and flatbread.

All through dinner, I itched to have my pussy touched. I had a cock. A big, throbbing dick. It was wonderful to fuck Hesione's pussy and Pyrrha's asshole. To pound them hard and fast. I didn't need to have my cunt fucked.

I just had to ignore this curious itch.

Night had fallen. The hearth died down to coals. Only a ruddy twilight lit the house. Prometheus and his wife retired to their bedroom. I followed them, my dick throbbing more and more. My pussy clenched. Young Pyrrha, her brown hair falling about her round face, gave me these doe-eyed looks as she headed to my bed.

I could just enjoy her. Let Prometheus have his wife, but she wasn't happy with his cock. She liked mine. She had enjoyed my dick. Why should she suffer without me? My cock throbbed beneath my toga.

I was finally well enough from my fall from Mount Olympus now. I marched to the Titan's bedroom, my futa-cock tenting the front of my toga. I threw open the door. Prometheus bolted upright. His wife gasped, lying naked beside him, prepared to do her wifely duty.

"P-Pandora," Hesione said, her large and soft breasts bouncing. She had such a motherly maturity about her even though Prometheus had never quickened a child in her. But I had. That made her my woman, didn't it?

"What are you doing, Pandora?" Prometheus asked, his voice full of resignation. He knew why I was here. He stared at me, his brawny chest rising and falling. He was a god, too. A Titan, the generation of gods who had come before Zeus and his Olympians. He was the Cursed Titan, banished by Zeus to live like a mortal.

"I'm claiming my woman," I said, unwinding my toga. The cloth fell from about my body, revealing my round breasts. My braid of black hair swayed down my back. Hesione's eyes widened. The oceanid, a type of nymph from the ocean, shuddered. She licked her lips, her hands cupping her breasts. "She's ready for me."

Prometheus glanced at his wife. She flushed and quickly pulled her hands down.

"No, no," Pandora moaned, her cock throbbing. "Don't stop kneading your tits. I excite you, don't I?"

"Yes," moaned Hesione. She glanced at her husband and flushed. "I'm sorry, my husband, but..." She dug her hands into her tits. She kneaded them before me. "She makes me so wet. From the moment I saw her lying before our house, she had captured my heart."

"I know," Prometheus growled. He rose from the bed. He had a weariness about him. A resigned acceptance. He stared at me, at my cock, then he marched past me and out of the room.

"You don't want to watch?" I asked, sauntering to the bed where his wife waited for me. "You enjoyed it this afternoon. For an hour, you witnessed me enjoying Hesione and Pyrrha."

Hesione gasped. "My husband?"

"I'm not your husband," growled Prometheus. "You are making that clear."

Hesione swallowed. Then she glanced at me. After a moment, she rolled over onto her hands and knees. She presented her pussy covered by her sapphire curls. Her juices beaded on them. She wiggled it, her hands clutching the sheets.

"Claim me, Pandora," she moaned. "I'm your woman. You were sent to please me. To please Pyrrha and me, weren't you?"

"She was sent to be a curse on the world," growled Prometheus. "If I had any sense, I would snap her neck."

"I'm not a curse," I said, angry. My cunt clenched. "I'm just different. Zeus doesn't like that. He likes being able to make every woman wet." The words rose out of me, bursting through a dam holding back my frustration. "I didn't beg his wife to slip into my room. Just like I didn't beg for yours, Prometheus. They made their choices."

"Yes," Hesione moaned. "Please, please, Pandora, I need your cock in me. That big girl-dick."

"I'm not going to be ashamed of what I am," I declared and marched forward. "Zeus sent me to suffer, to torment me with his curse. Well, I won't let him have any satisfaction."

I reached the bed and mounted it. Prometheus watched. I felt the Titan's eyes on me as I lined my cock up at his wife's pussy. She dripped with her excitement, so ready for me. It was exciting having him watching, knowing that his wife wanted me more. It was empowering. Exhilarating.

Hesione chose *me*.

I thrust into her pussy and made her utterly mine.

"Pandora!" Hesione moaned, her head throwing back. Her cunt clenched down on my cock. She squeezed about me. She held me tight in her cunt. I groaned at that tight grip clenching about me. This wonderful twat squeezing about my dick.

I grabbed her hips and savored her pussy around me. She was no longer Prometheus's wife. She was mine. I reveled in that delight. My hands slid up her body to those large, swinging breasts. I gripped them, kneading the oceanid's boobs.

"Pandora," she moaned, squeezing her cunt around my cock. She stirred her hips in slow circles, her pussy sliding around my futa-dick. I groaned at that wonderful delight. I would make Zeus regret throwing me down to this world.

He thought the mortal women lusted for him. Well, they would lust for me more. Just like his wife, Hera, had. I smiled at that thought as I kneaded Hesione's breasts. I drew back my cock, savoring her juice pussy squeezing about me.

Prometheus let out a ragged breath as I slammed back into Hesione's pussy. The Titan watched me slam into her cunt again and again. I buried into that wonderful pussy, the pleasure rushing down my cock to my own virgin twat.

My depths ached to be filled like this. My braid of black hair swayed down my back. It bounced and danced as I buried my girl-cock into Hesione's cunt. I thrust hard. Fast. I slammed into her with passion. I buried hard into her cunt. I loved that wonderful snatch squeezing about me.

"Yes, yes, yes, Pandora!" Hesione moaned. "I love this cock. It's the best I've ever enjoyed. Fuck that big dick into me. Oh, your girl-dick is amazing!"

"Hesione!" I groaned, burying into her, showing Prometheus the passion I inspired in his wife. "Oh, Hesione, you're so hot. So delicious. Mmm, your pussy... I love your pussy. I'm so glad I bred you."

"Yes!" she moaned, slamming back into me. Her butt-cheeks rippled from the impact of my crotch. I groaned, my dick throbbing in her cunt. "Oh, Pandora, that's so good. That's amazing."

Prometheus panted. I could hear the rhythmic stroke. He found it arousing watching us. Beautiful. He knew that my girl-dick gave his wife more pleasure. I buried into her juicy depths, her cunt growing hotter and hotter around me.

My fingers worked down her tits to her nipples. I pinched her nubs. I twisted those wonderful delights. She gasped, her cunt squeezing down around my cock. It was a magical delight to feel. I reveled in her snatch gripping my futa-dick.

She held me tight.

I groaned, slamming into her cunt. I buried hard and fast into her twat, her pussy so juicy about me. The ache swelled at the tip of my cock. The slap of my flesh into her rump echoed through the room along with our moans. My breasts heaved. I tugged on her nipples.

"Pandora!" she squealed. "Yes! I'm cumming!"

Her pussy went wild around my cock. That hot and delicious twat sucked at me as I drew back. My cunt squeezed down in envy, aching to be filled. This wonderful heat swelled in my ovaries. I groaned through my clenched teeth and slammed to the hilt in her.

"Hesione!" I moaned and erupted into her spasming twat.

"Yes, yes, flood me with your futa-cum!" she gasped.

Prometheus groaned and grunted. I knew his smaller cock spurted cum as he watched me flood his wife with my seed. Her pussy spasmed around my dick. She milked me. My pussy cream spilled down my thighs from my virgin twat.

I wanted to uncork that jar.

I hit the peak of my pleasure. I fired the last of my cum into Hesione's already bred pussy. The delicious oceanid worked me dry. She panted there while I swayed, my ecstasy dying down to a simmering boil.

Then I pulled out of Hesione and slipped off the bed. I faced the Titan. He stared down at the floor where his seed pooled. Then he looked up, panting. His wife grabbed my arm. She clung to me as we walked towards the door. Prometheus stepped aside.

I took Hesione to my room where Pyrrha waited naked and ready. The young girl licked her lips, eager to devour my cum out of Hesione's pussy. I closed the door and smiled as my two women came together and kissed.

* * *

The months passed for me at Prometheus's home. The Titan would often watch as I enjoyed his wife and ward, standing in the door to my room stroking his little cock while my big dick buried into my women's pussies.

During the day, I helped with the chores. I learned to garden, to make cheese from the goat milk, and to bake flatbread with flax seeds. My women's pregnancies progressed. Soon, they both had gentle curves to their stomach. Pyrrha's small breasts grew plumper, her nipple larger.

The idea of uncorking my virgin pussy tingled in the back of my mind. This curious itch I could never quite reach. But I could ignore it. So long as I had a hot pussy, a warm mouth, or a velvety asshole around my girl-cock I didn't have to worry about it.

About a month at Prometheus's, I went to the nearby town. There were other women here. Purely mortal women. Greek beauties with bronzed skin, their hair various shades of black and dark brown. Long, straight, and curly. They had beguiling figures that made my dick throb and ache.

It wasn't long before the wives of the town discovered my attributes. They sensed that I had something special beneath my toga and wanted it.

The coppersmith's wife blew my cock while he repaired a cookpot, working her mouth up and down my dick. She stared up at me with this feverish hunger in her eyes, her lips working up and down my dick to the pounding beat of her husband's craft. Her hands gripped my naked hips, my round breasts jiggling and my virgin pussy clenching.

"Euthalia," I groaned, savoring her fervent sucking at my girl-cock. The wonderful heat of her mouth around my dick. "Yes!"

She swirled her tongue around the tip of my cock, her black curls dancing around her face. She sucked and slurped, her husband unaware. The sounds of his hammer keeping him from hearing the wanton sounds his wife made.

She nursed with hunger, her eyes feverish. My pussy clenched, my dick throbbing. My cum rose in my ovaries. The pressure swelled and swelled. The ache grew at the tip of my dick.

"You're going to drink it all, aren't you?" I purred.

She nodded, nursing with such wild hunger on my dick. She felt incredible. Amazing. I loved every heartbeat of it. My virgin pussy clenched, that itch to be penetrated swelled in me. I focused on my cock in the wife's sucking mouth.

I erupted.

I pumped my cum into her hungry mouth.

"Yes, yes, yes," I gasped as I splashed the back of her mouth with my cum.

She gulped it down. She swallowed all my load, her eyes squeezing shut. She trembled as she nursed with hunger. The pleasure slammed into my mind. My breasts heaved. The coppersmith's hammer rang from his forge.

"Euthalia," I groaned. "Yes."

She slid her mouth off my cock and rose. She kissed me with my own seed on her lips. I fucked her on her counter beside the dough she had been kneading. I pumped her pussy full of my cum and left her dripping when I paid for the mended pot.

Hesione would be happy. It was her favorite.

I sodomized the miller's wife as he filled a sack of flour Hesione needed. His wife's tight bowels squeezed about my cock as I rammed into her over and over again. My fingers stroked her belly, knowing it had quickened with life the last time I had fucked her.

"Pandora!" she whimpered as my cum pumped into her bowels, her asshole spasming around my futa-dick.

The women sought me out. I ravished farmer's wives while their husbands were in the fields, tilling their women's fertile pussies with my seed. The town elector's wife rode my cock while her husband talked about local regulations with a group of craftsmen. Her pussy milked out every drop of cum in me.

205

When I walked through Dion, the women would appear in their doorways, begging me to come into their homes while their husbands worked in fields or shops. The butcher's wife and the mason's lay atop each other while I went back and forth. I came all over the ropemaker's wife. Just coated her and her pregnant belly with my spunk.

I needed more. Hesione and Pyrrha were always at home to satiate me. They were my wives, but that itch grew and grew in the back of my mind. They would come with me to the village sometimes, joining in my romps.

Watching a pregnant Hesione devour the miller wife's bred pussy dripping with my cum was a sight. Especially when the miller's wife was licking Hesione's cunt, their round bellies pressed into the other's large breasts.

It was such a sight. Such a distraction, but... That itch.

* * *

It was walking back from the town, the supplies on the donkey, and my mind full of the weaver's pussy I had flooded with cum, that I spotted the piece of wood. It was an oak branch, a section the length of my arm from elbow to fingertip. It was thick. In good condition. The idea blossomed in my mind.

I could make a dildo with this.

Athena, the virgin goddess, had her female devotees fuck her ass with dildos. She had gifted me with the art of their construction. I froze, staring at the branch, my virgin pussy clenching. It had been six months now since I had fallen to the world. Summer was fading away. Autumn was descending on the world.

It was the perfect piece of wood. I bit my lip. Zeus *claimed* I would unleash tragedy if I ever let my cork be popped, my pussy filled with a cock. But what if he meant that it had to be a man who uncorked me? Did a dildo actually count? Was it truly losing my virginity with a piece of wood?

The weaver had gasped and moaned as I fucked her bent over her loom. I pounded her hard from behind, her pussy squeezing around me. She had loved it. Cum so hard from the friction. What must that be like? I was a woman. I had a dick, yes, but I still had that desire to have my pussy filled. To be reamed out by a cock.

Not a man's cock. But a woman's like mine. Or the nearest facsimile.

"This is wrong," I whispered, my curiosity blazing through me. I picked up the piece of wood and shuddered. "You're only going to practice your woodcarving. You're not ever going to use it, right?"

My pussy clenched.

"I bet Hesione and Pyrrha will love playing with it," I muttered, tucking the stick into the pack harness. I grabbed the bridle and pulled the donkey onward. "That's it. I'm making it for them. I'm not ever going to use it."

I kept telling myself that as I headed up the trail. The first touch of autumn stained the leaves, oranges moving out from the edges, driving the green back to the center. I kept glancing at the stick, the smooth, polished shaft forming in my mind.

Prometheus had all the tools. The copper chisel. The knives. I would use the sand by the river to polish it smooth. I would make it into a work of art. It filled my mind as I made my way up to the home where I lived.

Smoke rose from the chimney. A pregnant Pyrrha plucked carrots from the garden, setting them in a basket after shaking dirt of them. When she saw me, she rose, clutching her belly full of my child. Would she be a futa, too?

"Enjoy any wives?" asked Pyrrha, a naughty gleam in her eyes.

"The weaver," I said.

She giggled. "Have you bred every woman in the town."

"I think so," I said. "Mmm, and look at you, just so adorable. I'm going to fuck you first tonight."

She beamed at me and waddled up to plant a kiss on my lips.

Hesione was inside working on dinner at the hearth, her pregnant belly swollen. I put away the supplies and went to help her. I had new wool to make new winter togas. I kissed her and patted her belly, feeling my child move. I smiled, excited.

I forgot about my project. For a while.

The women distracted me. I fucked Pyrrha and then Hesione before we settled down to sleep. The two women on their sides cuddled up to me. I couldn't find sleep, though. The wood beckoned. It was a long, long night.

I started working on it the next day. I used the chisel to gouge it out into the rough shape and then different knives to trim off more and more of the wood. I worked with care, forming a cylindrical shape that rounded at the tip. Finer knives took off less and less material. I kept having to sharpen the copper blades, but I made them work.

It took most of the week, but I was soon polishing with sand held in a rag, sliding up and down the shaft. It was like stroking my cock. It was a delight to make. As big and thick as my own shaft with the base shaped so the harness could hold it.

"What are you making?" Pyrrha had asked on the second day. She had squatted down in her toga, her pregnant belly looking so sexy.

"What does it look like?" I asked her, showing it off. It was still in its rough shape.

"A cock?" she asked.

I winked at her.

"But you have a beautiful cock," she said and grabbed mine through my toga. She stroked it. Played with it. Soon was blowing it.

Hesione would often pop in to watch me work. She would smile every time. I think she knew why I was constructing it. I would hold it up and she would stroke it. "Not yet." Every day, I polished for hours and she would come around, caress it, and shake her head.

Finally, after four days of polishing it with increasingly fine sand, she stroked the tip and beamed at me. "This is ready."

I winked at her.

I fashioned the harness the next day out of strips of leather. I trimmed them off, cut them to shape, and riveted them together with copper rivets. I had fucked the coppersmith's pregnant wife again while he made them for me. She had cried out so loudly.

He had to know that I had bred her. All the men were intimidated by me. They knew I had something better that their wives craved.

208

That night, after supper, Prometheus retired to his room. He only watched us once or twice in a week. He never complained. Never said a word. He was resigned to his wife and brother's daughter sharing my bed. They were my wives now.

I closed the door behind me and smiled at the two pregnant beauties. Hesione and Pyrrha both clutched their bellies as they lay on the mattress. They stared up at me with such delight in their eyes. A twinkle.

I grinned at them, my pussy clenching. It itched. I held the toy that could satisfy that curiosity. Uncork me. I knew my lie of having them fuck each other with it was out the window as I stared at them. My petite Pyrrha and my busty Hesione were gorgeous Their pregnant bellies rubbed together as they stared at me.

"Who gets to wear it?" asked Pyrrha. "I want to fuck you with it, Pandora. You always have so much fun fucking us."

"Yes, yes," Hesione purred. "I know why you made it. You wish to feel complete."

My cunt clenched. I had never told them about my curse. They didn't know what would happen if I uncorked my jar. I bit my lip, the ache to lose my virginity rising. Then Hesione rose. Her blue hair swayed about her face. Her pregnant belly thrust out before her, that swollen curve proof of my potent seed. My Hera-blessed cum.

She took the dildo from me. "Mmm, let me wear it, my beloved." Her dark eyes quivered. "Let me love you, Pandora. Like you've loved us."

"Yes, yes, and you can fuck me at the same time," moaned Pyrrha. She rolled over onto her hands and knees. She wiggled her tight rump at me. Her brown bush peeked between her thighs hiding that pregnant pussy.

My dick throbbed.

Hesione stepped into the harness. She slid it up her body. I had attached little copper buckles so it could be tightened. Fine craftsmanship. The coppersmith knew his job. The wooden dildo bobbed before her, the oak wood gleaming with its smooth polish. She cinched it about her waist.

"Is the base pressing on your clit?" I asked her. "That's where it's supposed to go."

"Yes," Hesione said. She stared down at her pregnant belly. It thrust out long enough she should be able to see the tip. "Oh my, this is amazing."

"It is," I told her, loving the sight of her. My pussy clenched. This was it. I would have that curiosity satisfied.

I moved to the bed. I knelt down on it, my dick bobbing before me. I smacked it down on Pyrrha's cute rump. I grinned as I smacked from butt-cheek to butt-cheek, making her flesh ripple beneath my cock.

My pregnant wife giggled. She threw a look over her shoulder at me, such delight and love in her eyes. "Pandora, I need you in me. Mmm, do you know how wet I am all the time thinking about you fucking other women? I need to go into town with you again. I want to fuck you with the wooden cock while you fuck Diokles's wife. She's so sexy."

"Yes, she is," I groaned. "Sure. We can do that."

Pyrrha beamed at me.

"Mmm, slide that cock into her pussy," purred Hesione. "Just pound her hard. I'm going to fuck you with this." She moved up on the bed behind me, the hay-stuffed mattress shifting. She poked the tip of her wooden-dick into my rump.

I shuddered. My cunt clenched. I slid my dick down to the girl's pregnant muff. I slid through her wet curls. I shuddered, loving being in a pussy that I had bred. I pushed my cock right against her twat, her flesh wet and hungry for me.

I thrust into her. Pyrrha moaned as I plunged to the hilt in her. I buried my cock into that wet heaven. It was incredible. I groaned, my face twisting in delight. I sank all the way into her cunt. Her pussy squeezed about my dick. My breasts bounced and heaved as my crotch smacked into her rump.

My hands slid around her body. I stroked her pregnant belly, my virgin pussy clenching. Her twat squeezed about my cock. She moaned, her curly, brown hair swaying. She was so delicious to be inside. I leaned over her as Hesione moved that tip down my butt-cheeks towards my pussy.

My cunt itched.

My curiosity swelled.

I would find out. She would uncork my virgin jar. She would plunder my cunt the way I had Pyrrha's. I shuddered. The polished tip slid down my taint and through my bush. She rubbed on my pussy lips. She was there. Ready to deflower me. At my hymen.

She pushed. My hymen stretched.

"Wait!" I gasped, a wave of fear washing through me. "My asshole. Fuck my asshole! I want it in there."

"You're sure?" Hesione asked. She pushed a little harder on my hymen. The membrane stretched. She was so close to uncorking my jar.

"Yes, I'm sure!" I gasped. "My asshole. Fuck my asshole."

"Okay, Pandora, my beloved," she purred. Hesione slid the dildo up my taint and between my butt-cheeks. She nuzzled it into my asshole. I would finally be penetrated. I wanted this so much.

She pressed the smooth dildo forward. The fake dick didn't need to be lubed, that was how much I had polished the shaft. I groaned as my anal ring stretched and stretched. I whimpered as that thick shaft penetrated into my bowels.

She sodomized me.

"Hesione!" I gasped as the dildo slipped into my bowels.

She went deeper and deeper into me. She filled me up. I groaned, my hands rubbing over Pyrrha's pregnant belly. Hesione's swollen stomach pushed into my rump and back. I bent over, letting her stomach slide over me as the dildo bottomed out on me.

I quivered there, penetrated by her dildo. She filled me up. She felt incredible in me. I squeezed my bowels down around the shaft. I stirred my hips around the fake toy, groaning at the feel of the dildo in me. The heat swept through my body. I shook. My breasts swayed together. They smacked and bounced and rippled. My dick throbbed in Pyrrha's pussy.

Then Hesione drew back, groaning, "Pandora! This is so exciting."

"Yes," I purred, following her.

I chased her dildo. My cock slipped out of Pyrrha's silky cunt. Her bred twat squeezed about me. Pleasure rushed down my cock and melted out of my asshole. The two delights met in my cunt. They swirled around each other.

I loved the feeling of fucking and being fucked.

Hesione thrust the dildo back into my asshole. She buried to the hilt in me. I gasped as that drove me deep into Pyrrha's cunt. My hands held onto her pregnant stomach. My finger dipped into her navel. She gasped, her cunt squeezing down on my cock.

"Oh, yes, yes, Pandora," moaned Pyrrha. "I can feel Hesione slamming into you. Ooh, she's driving your cock into me."

"Uh-huh," I moaned, my futa-dick throbbing in Pyrrha's cunt. Her pussy massaged me. The feel of her twat was incredible.

Hesione pumped away at me. She thrust into my asshole again and again. She set the pace. Her hands slid around and groped my tits. She squeezed them, her pregnant belly rubbing across the top of my rump and pushing into my back. It was so hot.

My bowels drank in the friction of the smooth shaft. It filled me up again and again. My virgin pussy clenched, loving it. My futa-cock pumped in and out of Pyrrha's cunt. Her twat gripped me. She moaned, her hips undulating, stirring her twat around in me.

"Yes, yes, yes!" she moaned. "Oh, Pandora, you're making my cunt melt."

"Good," I groaned, feeling her wet heat around me.

"Mmm, and what am I doing to your asshole?" Hesione moaned. "Huh, Pandora?" She slammed hard into me.

"Making my asshole melt!" I gasped.

Pyrrha giggled. "I bet. I love it when you fuck me in my asshole or my pussy. You always make me feel so good with your futa-cock."

"A gift from the Olympians!" moaned Hesione. "You're not a poisoned gift at all, Pandora. You're amazing. I love you."

"Love you!" Pyrrha whimpered, her pussy squeezing about my withdrawing cock.

Joy surged through me, mixing with the pleasure. "I love you both. My sweet, pregnant wives!"

Hesione moaned and thrust harder at my asshole. She slammed her hips forward, gasping out her own pleasure. I knew the base of the dildo pushed on her clit every time she drove into my bowels. It gave her pleasure.

I wanted her to have pleasure. To cum so hard. My own orgasm built and built. I didn't need her to fuck my pussy. My asshole was enough. Athena maintained her virginity this way. So could I. I shuddered, squeezing my bowels down around that girl-cock while my pussy juices dripping down my thighs.

My orgasm built and built.

Every thrust of my cock into Pyrrha's pussy, very plunge of Hesione's wooden-dick into my bowels, fed the growing flames. I groaned, loving every moment of it. My face twisted in rapture, my ovaries drinking in heat. My cum approached that boil.

"Oh, yes, yes!" I gasped and erupted.

Hesione's thrusts rammed my spurting cock to the hilt in Pyrrha's pussy. My futa-cum fired into her twat. The pleasure blazed out of my cunt and burned to my mind. Sparks burst across my vision as the rapture exploded out of me. My asshole spasmed around the wooden cock withdrawing and then thrusting back into me.

"Pandora!" Pyrrha gasped. Her pussy convulsed. Her hot flesh spasmed around my cock. "Oh, yes, yes!"

"Cum in her!" moaned Hesione. She rammed that hard cock into my spasming bowels. She buried her wooden dildo into me. I groaned, the pleasure burning hot through me. It was amazing. My mind melted beneath the rapture. I loved every moment of it. "Flood her."

"Oh, yes, yes flood me!" Pyrrha gasped.

"I am!" I moaned, my pussy spasming, aching to be filled, craving the same delight as my asshole. I pumped more and more of my cum into Pyrrha's cunt. I filled her up.

My orgasm hit that peak as Hesione slammed into me. Her fingers squeezed tight into my boobs. Her pregnant belly rubbed into my back as she trembled. She gasped out her rapture, joining us with her own climax. The dido stirred around in my writhing asshole.

It was incredible. The pleasure burned through me I groaned, my eyes fluttering. I loved every minute of this amazing rapture that burned through my body. It was fantastic. My body trembled, the flames dying down.

"This dildo is amazing," moaned Hesione, her fingers kneading my tits.

"Mmm, it is," I moaned. "Oh, yes, yes, it is."

I sucked in deep breaths, dizzy. Pyrrha crawled off my cock with a wet plop. She turned around on her knees, her pregnant belly and plump breasts jiggling. Her flushed face beamed at me. She cupped my face and kissed me with hunger.

I groaned into it and slumped forward. I broke the kiss, my asshole sliding off the dildo. I twisted and fell on my back, my pussy on fire. My cunt burned. I had to know. I had to find out. I squirmed there, Pyrrha shifting around, bringing that pregnant twat to my mouth so I could lick her clean.

Hesione panted there, the dildo thrusting out from her waist. That big, thick shaft had made my asshole feel so good. I shuddered there, my face contorting. I wanted to beg her to slam that dildo into my cunt.

"A gift from the Olympians! You're not a poisoned gift at all, Pandora. You're amazing. I love you," echoed through my mind.

What could possibly happen?

I had to know. I had to find out what it was like to have my jar uncorked. To have it filled it with a hard cock like I had filled Pyrrha's moment ago. She settled down on me, her vessel brimming with my salty futa-cum.

"Fuck me, Hesione!" I moaned. "Take my virginity. Ram that dildo into my jar!"

"Yes!" Hesione groaned.

"Oh, Pandora, you'll love it," Pyrrha panted. She settled her pregnant pussy right on my lips, her wet bush sliding over my cheeks and chin. My nose nuzzled into her taint. Salty cum and tangy pussy cream flowed into my mouth, dripping out of her twat. "I loved it when you uncorked me."

Hesione moved in. I felt her pregnant belly brushing my throbbing clit-dick, the curve sliding into my hard cock. The dirty dildo pressed into my bush and kissed my virgin pussy lips. That made this all the better. My tongue thrust into Pyrrha's cunt. I was so ready for this new passion.

Nothing would happen. I *wasn't* a poisoned gift. I brought happiness to all those women in town. Gave them the pleasure their men lacked. They would all have my futa-daughters. New dickgirls that would spread out and make more and more women happy.

I *deserved* to have my jar uncorked. There was no futa to fuck me, but I had the next best thing.

Hesione thrust.

My virginity stretched and stretched. I swirled my tongue through Pyrrha's cunt. I licked out that salty cum and her tangy juices. The two flavors mixed together as I squirmed. Moaned. A burning heat swelled around my maidenhead.

The membrane popped.

The thick dildo slammed into my virgin jar. I shuddered at the feel dirty shaft buried into my juicy pussy. My futa-cock throbbed against the curve of Hesione's pregnant belly. I tensed, waiting for Zeus's curse to fall on me.

Nothing.

I laughed my triumph, squeezing my cunt down on that big dildo. It felt so right in my pussy. I loved the delight of the dildo being in me. She reached into my depths, filling me up. Finally, I experienced all the delights of a dickgirl. My futa-cock throbbed against her belly.

She drew back as I licked my cum out of Pyrrha's pussy. She squirmed on me and grabbed my boobs. She kneaded them as she ground her furred muff on my face. I stared at her curving rump and sleek back, watching her brown hair dance as she enjoyed me.

"Pandora," she moaned as I scooped the cum out of her pussy. I licked and lapped it out of her, loving the taste of her. That wonderful flavor soaked my mouth and spilled over my lips. "Ooh, yes, yes, Pandora, lick me clean."

"Mmm, lick all that yummy jizz out of her pussy," Hesione moaned, thrusting the dirty dildo back into my cunt. My twat squeezed around it. My futa-cock throbbed and pulsed against her belly. It moved with her, aching as she pounded me. "Yes, yes, lick her clean, Pandora."

"I plan on it," I moaned, my pussy melting around the dildo.

It was incredible. As good as fucking. I loved it. My pussy was meant to have her girl-dick reaming me. Meant to have this pleasure surging through my body. It was amazing. I loved every moment of it. Fires built in me. I humped against her, my futa-cock throbbing and aching. The pleasure rippled through my body.

It was just delicious. Just the best. I groaned, my hips wiggling from side to side. I stirred my snatch around the dildo. I loved every thrust. The pressure built in my ovaries from it. My cock ached, precum leaking down the shaft. Pyrrha's hands massaged my breasts, my nipples aching against her palms.

"Oh, yes, yes," she moaned, her tangy pussy sliding over my mouth. More cum poured out. I pumped so much in her. "I love being in you. I love it so much. It's just the best."

"Mmm, it is," I groaned, savoring the cum and pussy cream coating my tongue. I thrust it deep into her pussy.

I loved feeling that wonderful dildo slam into my cunt. Those hard strokes plunged that wooden-dick deep into me. Hesione pounded me. My body trembled. I climbed towards my orgasm. My legs gripped her waist. I humped against her, meeting her strokes.

Precum dripped on my belly. It spilled off my cock as it twitched and bobbed. I whimpered and plundered Pyrrha's cunt with my tongue. I searched for every drop of spunk I could find. I wanted it all. She tasted so good. The flavor of her melted down my tongue. I groaned, licking and lapping at her. I loved every moment of it. I savored every last bit of passion that I sucked out of her.

My tongue thrust into her pussy. I swirled it around in her. I licked and lapped at her with such hunger. When I couldn't taste any more of my salty jizz, I sucked at her pregnant pussy. Her hands tightened on my tits.

"Pandora!" she moaned, her tangy cream spilling into my mouth. "I'm going to cum."

"Yes, yes, drink all that sweet nectar from her jar!" groaned Hesione.

"Yes, yes, drink it!" squealed Pyrrha.

The dribble of her pussy cream became a flood. Her tangy delight gushed into my mouth. I drank down her passion, loving the taste of her cream. It spilled into my mouth. I groaned, licking and lapping it up.

"Ooh, my clit is melting," Hesione moaned. "I love this strap-on. I love fucking you with it! Pandora!"

She slammed into me and gasped. I could hear the passion in her voice. My pussy clenched down on the dildo. It stirred around in me. The pressure surged to the tip of my cock. I gasped and moaned, my body bucking.

My pussy clenched on the wooden dick. My futa-cock erupted.

"Yes, yes, yes!" I squealed, my pussy finally cumming around a shaft for the first time. The pleasure rushed out of my body. I bucked on the bed.

"Jizz!" gasped Pyrrha. "Ooh, your cum is splashing my belly."

"Yum!" moaned Hesione.

I just moaned into Pyrrha's cunt. I licked and lapped at her as my cunt writhed around the dildo. Waves of bliss washed out of my twat, so much more intense than normal. My dick spurted, but I hardly felt it before the joy of having a dildo in my pussy.

A cock.

I was a full dickgirl now. I loved it. I trembled through my pleasure. Stars danced before my eyes. It felt so incredible. I groaned, feeling something new growing and growing in me. I gasped as a pressure swelled in my pussy.

"Oh, Pandora," moaned Hesione. She pulled the dildo out of my pussy. "That was—"

The dildo popped out.

A great surge of cold darkness rushed out of me. I gasped as I felt something *trapped* in me erupting from me. Energy flowed out of my cunt. A great tide of darkness. Pyrrha screamed and fell backward off my face. Hesione threw herself to the bed, whimpering.

I shuddered as my body bucked through my orgasm. *Evil* passed through me. It spilled out of my jar me with my gushing juices. Three shadows formed in the air. Entities that Zeus had trapped in me. It was all so clear now. My virginity had sealed them away.

Lust, Envy, and Wrath.

They were shadows that floated in the air, feminine, futanari like me. They weren't my progeny. I was merely the seal. I trembled as they laughed in delight, mocking me. All I had to do was keep my virginity. Zeus had warned me.

Now I had unleashed tragedy on the world. The shadows zipped off in three directions, passing out of the house and into the world. Lust. Envy. Wrath. I shuddered, the ground beneath the bed shaking. The world itself groaned.

"W-what is that?" gasped Pyrrha. She hugged me from behind.

"I'm cursed," I gasped, squeezing my thighs shut. I stared at Hesione. "I *am* a poisoned gift."

"What?" she gasped, sitting up.

"I just unleashed *evil* on the world. True evil." I felt it when the passed through me. The depths of their depravity. They were darker than anything in this world. They would bring strife. They would inspire suffering. They would torment mankind.

Why? Because Zeus hated that I cuckolded his wife. That I was a human woman with a big dick. Now three evil futanari were out there. Prometheus was right. He should have left me to die. All I had to do was not be curious.

"I'm the worst being that has ever existed," I sobbed. "He told me... He warned me... Cursed me. It was my punishment. Now I have to live with this. My selfishness will cause so much harm."

"Pandora!" Pyrrha hugged me from behind. Her breasts and pregnant belly rubbed on me. "Don't talk like that."

"I'm terrible!" I shouted. "Worthless! If Hephaestus had never made me, then that evil wouldn't be in the world."

"No!" Hesione hugged me. "Don't ever say that. You're not terrible. She pressed her forehead into mine. Her eyes filled my world. "You're amazing. Beautiful. You brought us pleasure. Delight. Love. I had never felt anything like this until you. You're my gift. I love you, Pandora. Never, ever say you are terrible. You are not worthless."

She kissed me.

"That's right," Pyrrha said, hugging me so tight from behind as Hesione kissed me with passion. "You've touched not just us, but the other women in the village. You are a miracle, Pandora."

As they showered me with their love, something sprouted in me. A seed. Small, a kernel, but it had the potential to sprout into something amazing. Something glorious. Hope grew inside of me, fed by their compassion and joy. Their affection and passion.

I had to stop this evil. It came from me. So it was up to me to undo it. I broke the kiss with Hesione. "Thank you. I love you both so much."

I didn't want to leave them, but my mistake had to be undone. Hope kindled inside of me that something better could be created. A bright future. I would find it. I would make sure it happened.

I would tame Lust, Envy, and Wrath.

To be continued...

Pandora's Futa Satisfaction

Pandora's Naughty Futa Box 4

by

Reed James

Pandora's Futa Satisfaction

Lust smiled as she came across another village. The naughty entity hummed as she strode through the sleeping village. The moon shone down her. She stretched her back, thrusting out her breasts before her. Her large futa-dick bounced in time with her steps.

There were people awake. They were sharing their passion in the dark. She could feel it. The sexual pleasure swelled and swelled. Irritation flooded her as she felt one person approaching their climax. The pinnacle of their grunting and thrusting.

The end of their lust.

She couldn't have that. Lust could never end. Her power flooded out of her.

* * *

Pandora

I stared with guilt at the destroyed village.

Another one.

Smoke rose from half-burned buildings. Bodies lay amid the rubble. The people had gone wild and torn each other apart. This was the third village I had found like this. I must be on Wrath's trail. Zeus had bottled up three evil entities inside of me. So long as I kept my virginity, didn't allow my jar to be uncorked, they would have been contained.

I had succumbed to lust. After months and months of enjoying women with my futa-dick, not just Hesione and Pyrrha, but all the women of the village near Prometheus's house, I had succumbed to temptation. I had loved them. Bred them. My girl-cock had pleased all of them more than their husbands possibly could. I had fun, but it wasn't enough.

I grew envious. My lusts swelled. I grew angry that *I* couldn't be fucked.

I wanted to know how it felt to have a cock entering me. So I used the knowledge Athena had gifted me. I constructed a dildo, a polished shaft of wood strapped to a leather harness. I gave it to Hesione, Prometheus's wife and my lover, and she took my cherry.

It had felt incredible.

Now the world suffered.

Zeus was such a petty god. Angry that I had cuckolded him and fucked his wife, Hera, he had thrown me from Mount Olympus. He tortured me by torturing the world. I hated him, but that would do little to stop this evil.

For though I had released it, I had hope that I could stop it. Pyrrha and Hesione believed in me. The two women I loved had faith that I could stop it. I clutched to that as I passed through the ruined village, Mount Olympus looming behind me.

What did Zeus think about this destruction? Did he even care? Or did he hate the humans who worshiped him? Like he hated me for having a superior cock. His wife came to my bed while I slept. She slipped in, sucked my cock, and then gave me the gift of motherhood as her pussy came on my clit-dick.

Shaking my head, I passed out of the ruined village and kept moving onward. Wrath, Envy, and Lust had escaped me. Three nasty and deadly entities. I had to be on Wrath's trail. How else to explain the wanton destruction that I'd been finding. I walked as fast as I could on my sandaled feet, my toga whisking around me. I had a satchel that held food—goat cheese, flatbread, raisins, and salted mutton—I shifted to pull out my waterskin. I drank from it as I pressed on.

The day wore on as I moved through the hilly land around Mount Olympus. I would stop the evil. I wouldn't let it destroy the world or spread any more suffering. I nibbled on some goat cheese as I walked, not willing to stop. My maker, Hephaestus, had given me the pinnacle of human strength and endurance.

I caught glimpses of another village. It didn't look destroyed. My hope swelled. I was in time. I smiled and felt energized. I would save them and tame Wrath. Her anger would not be allowed to rampage any longer.

"Yes, yes, yes," moaned from the bushes to my right.

I blinked at the sexual sounds I heard.

"Oh, that's it." It was a woman. "Come on. You can do it. you can cum in me, Evaristus! Do it! Be a man and cum in your wife!"

"Trying, Kallisto!" a man groaned.

"CUM!" the woman screeched. She sounded half-mad.

What was going on?

I found a small trail that led off the main road. I followed it back to the grunting and groaning, passing a small field growing wheat. Some of them rustled. I spotted the long, dark hair of a woman swayed between the stalks. Her head moved up and down. I caught glimpses of her naked back. I dropped my satchel and hurried to them.

I reached the gap in the rows to find a woman riding a man's cock. Her ass clenched as she rode him. Her voice gasped and grunted. The gleam of sweat coated her pale skin. Her fingernails clawed at the man's chest. She left blood furrows in his skin.

"Cum in me right now, Evaristus!" she screeched, sounding mad. "Give it to me. I need your cum!"

"I'm so close, Kallisto!" he growled, his face flushed and drenched in sweat. "You just have to squeeze that cunt harder. Zeus's beard, woman, use that pussy. I'm so close."

"Such a failure!" the woman, Kallisto, hissed. "What sort of man can't cum in his wife's pussy?" She beat her fists on his chest. "I need it. I need to cum. Give it to me!"

She kept riding him. I stared in shock. What was going on here? Her husband bled. She'd hurt him in her frustration. She sounded wild. Insane. I had never seen this. What was going on here? Something felt so wrong about this.

I had to stop this.

"Hey," I shouted as Kallisto raked new furrows down her husband's chest, tearing across his muscles. "Stop that!"

I grabbed Kallisto by the waist and hauled her off her husband's cock. He popped out of her with a wet plop. I threw her back. She stumbled and then landed on the small trail in a puff of dust. Her round breasts, gleaming with more sweat, heaved. She stared up at me, legs spread wide She had no pubic hair. I'd learned that Greek women would pluck or burn away their pubic hair when trying to have a baby. Her pussy lips gaped open, juices spilling out of her and trickling down her rump.

"What are you doing?" I demanded. I felt the wrongness of it.

"I have to cum!" Kallisto hissed. She stood up and stared at me with wild eyes. "Can you make me cum?"

Before I could react, she threw herself at me. She grabbed the front of my toga and ripped it open. My round breasts spilled out into her hand. My braided hair swung down my back. I stumbled, fighting to hold my balance as she unwound the cloth wrapped around me.

My futa-cock swayed into view, already half-hard from the sounds of their fucking. I could smell Kallisto's pussy. A tangy musk rose in the air. My pussy clenched as Kallisto's hands grabbed my breasts. She squeezed them.

"Maybe a woman can make me cum where my *husband* has failed!" sneered the woman, her fingernails biting into my tits.

Pain flared.

"Stop that!" I hissed and knocked her hands away. "I will not permit you to—"

"What is this?" gasped the woman. She shot her hand down and grabbed my girl-dick. "You have a cock and a pussy?" Her other hand cupped my snatch, rubbing at me through my bush. Awe spilled across her face, cutting through the maddened lust for a moment. "What are you?"

"Futanari," I moaned, my dick swelling hard in her hand, growing thicker and longer.

Her eyes widened as she fondled me. "Your girth. Your length. I have never seen a man with a cock this big. No man in our village has one. It would be gossiped about." Her gaze shot up to my face. "You are what I need!"

The frenzied lust appeared on her face, a wild look as if she were a woman caught up in a bacchanalia, drunk on Dionysus's wine. She threw herself at me and kissed me. Her naked breasts pressed into my tits. I groaned as her tongue thrust into my mouth while I stumbled back and fell to the ground. The soft loam cushioned my fall.

Kallisto pounced on me. She kissed me again, thrusting her tongue into my mouth. She swirled it around in my mouth and kissed me with such a frenzy. She still held my cock and pushed me against the shaved folds of her married pussy. I groaned at the feel of her silky twat. With no pubic hair, she felt so smooth down there. So exciting. She guided me to her hole and pushed her cunt down it.

She broke her kiss to moan, "Yes! Finally, a cock! A real cock! This dick will make me cum!"

"Yes, yes, make my wife cum," groaned her husband. Evaristus knelt over me, jerking his cock. "Please, please, make her cum. It's been so long."

"Yes, yes, yes," moaned Kallisto. She rose up and rode me like she had her husband. Her round breasts heaved, gleaming in the afternoon sunlight. Her black hair fell about her youthful face. Pleasure crossed it. "Oh, futanari, your dick is amazing. So huge. You're stretching me out. I feel like a virgin."

Her hands groped my breasts. I felt her fingernails, but they didn't rake my tits. I shuddered, realizing I had to make her cum. Somehow. If I didn't, she would attack me like she had her husband. I didn't understand what was happening, but I knew how to make women cum.

I slid my right hand around her hip and down her rump. I felt her flesh flexing beneath my touch. My fingers dipped into the crack of her ass, sliding lower and lower as the beauty rode me. She worked that tight, hot, juicy cunt up and down my dick.

"Such an amazing cock!" she moaned. "Zeus's beard, that's good."

"Yes, yes," panted her husband. He stood over us, stroking his cock. "Cum on her dick, Kallisto. Explode. You need it."

"I do!" she moaned, squeezing her pussy around me. "Now that I have a real cock. Not your little thing!"

The humiliating words only spurred her husband to stroke faster. I cuckolded him. He was like Prometheus, reveling in the degradation of his wife wanting my cock more than his. It swelled the ache at the tip of my clit-dick.

I didn't fight my building orgasm. I could cum and cum and cum. I would spurt my jizz into this woman's fertile pussy as many times as I could. She wanted a baby, too. I would give her a futa-daughter and make her explode.

My digit found her asshole. I pressed my middle finger against it. She gasped, her back arching as her anal ring parted for my digit. I sank it into her flesh. She shuddered and whimpered, her velvety sheath engulfing my finger.

"Yes, yes, that's it!" she gasped. "She knows how to please a woman. Mmm, not like you, husband. Oh, yes, she's going to make me cum!"

"Good!" he panted, stroking his cock.

Her fingers slid up my breasts. She grabbed my nipples. I gasped as she pinched them. The sensation shot down to my cunt. My pussy clenched. I groaned as the tingling delight met the silky heat melting down my shaft. The pleasure from her married twat built and built in my snatch.

In my ovaries.

I plundered her asshole as fast as she rode my clit-dick. Her pussy worked up and down my thick, long shaft. She sucked at me. The pleasure felt incredible. I groaned, loving every moment of it. The heat built and built. I would have such a huge explosion of bliss. Just a mighty burst of ecstasy in her.

She needed to cum, too.

As she twisted and pulled on my nipples, I thrust my pointer finger against her asshole. Her face twisted in pleasure. She arched her back, tits heaving above me, as her sphincter swallowed my second finger. I worked two in and out of her asshole.

"Oh, yes, yes, yes!" Kallisto howled.

"Are you going to cum?" her husband asked.

"I need her cum first!" the wild wife moaned. Her eyes shot down to me. Her fingers pinched my nipples hard. "Give it to me. Cum in me, futanari-slut! I want that dick erupting in me! Now!"

Her asshole clenched down on my digit. Her pussy squeezed about my cock. She slammed down me hard. I groaned at the feel of her snatch. My dick twitched. Throbbed. Her hot pussy swelled the ache in it.

She twisted my nipples. Stretched them out. My breasts jiggled. Flares of pain met the bursts of pleasure. All those naughty sensations rushed through me to my cunt. My pussy drank them in. My ovaries grew tighter while her cunt slid up and down my dick. The pressure built at the tip of my futa-cock.

I whimpered. Moaned. She slammed her cunt down my cock. Every inch of her twat massaged my shaft. I nuzzled into her cervix. She rose up me, her pussy sucking at my clit-dick. Her fingers tweaked my nipples.

I erupted.

My futa-cum fired into her pussy. Titanic blasts of ecstasy shot through my body as I flooded her cunt with my passion. My fertile girl-seed flooded her married twat. Her cunt slammed down me, engulfing my erupting cock.

"Yes!" she howled. Her pussy went wild. "I'm cumming! Oh, Evaristus! I'm cumming on her girl-cock!"

"Yes, yes, yes!" groaned her husband. Then his cock erupted.

As Kallisto's pussy writhed around my dick and milked out my spurting futa-jizz, her husband's pearly seed splashed across her heaving breasts. He groaned in such relief, erupting over and over and over again.

Pleasure hammered my mind as my cum pumped into his wife's cunt. He groaned, stroking his small cock. I couldn't believe how much he fired. He covered her tits in the jizz. Spunk ran over her breasts and down her stomach.

"Yes!" I groaned as I hit the pinnacle of my orgasm. I fired my last spurt of cum into Kallisto's writhing cunt.

She kept bucking on me, her pussy rippling and writhing around my cock. Her husband kept erupting. His balls still held more cum, like he was unloading days' worth of jizz in one go. He shuddered, his face twisting in pleasure, his abused chest rising and falling.

"Evaristus," moaned the wife. Her voice sounded slurred. Her pussy's spasms slowed. "I finally came."

"As did I, wife," panted the man.

The wildness in Kallisto's face faded. Now she looked exhausted but satisfied. She rose off of me, my cum spilling out of her pussy, and grabbed her husband. She kissed him with a gentleness while I lay there panting.

"What is going on?" I groaned, sitting up. I was so confused. This was clearly suffering caused by the entities, but I thought I was wrath's trail. Kallisto certainly had been angry, but it was more out of frustration than fury.

The couple broke the kiss. Kallisto gasped at the sight of her husband's chest. "Evaristus, I'm so sorry. You're hurt."

"It's fine," he said, staring down at me and my cock. "We fled our village to escape the madness."

"Madness?" I asked.

"For two days, no one has been able to climax," said Kallisto. "Two days of every woman growing increasingly frustrated with their men. No orgasm. No seed fired into us. And we're all so horny. Evaristus and I managed to flee, holding off, hoping we could get away from the madness. We got half a day and then... Then I attacked him." Horror crossed her face. "I would have killed him if he didn't make me cum. Then I would have gone searching for more."

"You would have destroyed everything in a frenzy," I whispered. "You would have torn each other apart until everyone was dead."

Kallisto nodded, tears beading in her eyes.

"Lust," I groaned. "I have to go." I grabbed my toga and pulled it on. "I will save your village."

The two looked at me, shocked.

I just smiled at them and said, "I am Pandora. The hope to stop this evil. I unleashed Lust. I will bottle her back up."

I headed down the road, moving at a brisk pace. The sun was sinking down towards Mount Olympus, Apollo's ride across the sky almost complete. I moved at a swift pace, my braid of black hair swinging down my back. I nibbled on salted mutton as I passed more fields and then orchards of olive trees. The village I had been glimpsing came closer and closer.

It didn't look destroyed.

I could hear the sounds of lust. The gasping, moaning, frenzied screeching of the frustrated women who needed to cum. I stopped at the edge of the village and sat down my satchel. Not wanting my toga torn, I unwound that from my body and draped it over my satchel. My cock thrust out hard before me. The sun vanished, darkness engulfing the village.

I marched forward to find Lust and stop this madness.

A woman gasped between two men. They fucked her pussy and asshole, pinning her between them as she berated them to cum in her. She hissed her fury, clawing one man's back as they slammed their cocks into her.

One woman spotted me. She pounced on me before I could go two steps. I gasped as the motherly woman pushed me to the ground, mounted my cock, and rode me. Her face twisted with delight. She cried out her rapture.

"Finally, a cock that can make me cum!" she hissed. Like Kallisto, this motherly woman was out of her mind with lust.

I groaned, letting her ride me. I thrust up into her twat, my orgasm building fast. I didn't hold back. I knew what she needed. She gasped and groaned, slamming her cunt down my dick. Her hair danced around her face.

When I erupted, her pussy went wild around my cock. She howled out her rapture, her cunt writhing and rippling around me. I groaned as the pleasure slammed through my mind. My thoughts boiled beneath the delight.

Then she collapsed on me, mewling in satisfaction.

I rolled her off of me. She breathed regularly. Passed out from exhaustion. I sat up, shaking my head. Others were rutting around me. A woman took a cock in her mouth and pussy, kneeling between the two men. Two other women were eating each other's pussies. A third was pinned against a house, getting fucked hard in the ass.

"Ass fuck me harder!" the woman hissed. "You have to be better than my husband. I have to cum! I need satisfaction!"

Satisfaction...

That was what was going on here. Lust had kept all these people stuck in the act of rutting, but never let them find their climaxes. Kept them trapped in a circle of desire and need that they could never escape. Perpetual horniness.

Didn't Lust know the joy that orgasms brought? The sweet release that was the achievement of all that pent-up passion?

No. She didn't. She wasn't a complete entity, was she? She was just a thing with a singular focus. A thing that needed to be stopped. I had to reach her, but I would never get to her if every woman in this village pounced on me.

I had to use stealth.

Artemis, Goddess of the Hunt, had granted me a gift. Most of the Olympians had. Ares had given me my sexual stamina, Athena my knowledge of engineering, Aphrodite had given me irresistible beauty, Apollo taught me to sing with poetry, Hera had granted me motherhood, and Artemis had given me stealth. My prey would never know my approach.

I understood it. I stared at the village, spotting the deep shadows I had to move through. Knew the way I had to step. I padded towards the nearest one, blending into the darkness, and made my way through the village.

Wood crashed in one building, a woman screeching in fury. "MAKE ME CUM!"

I winced, wanting to rush, but I couldn't. If I was spotted, I would only save one woman. I could make her cum, but there were a hundred or more women in this village and just as many men consumed with frustrated lust.

I could feel the pressure rising in the village. Lust permeated it. Like a bloodhound on the scent of game, I tracked it. My cock throbbed harder and harder. I moved past the homes. I crept through gardens. I passed through goat pens. I came closer and closer to the source, passing rutting.

"FUCK ME HARDER!" hissed a woman getting pounded bent over a fence, her big tits heaving. She was a mature woman. A young man fucked her, his chest drenched in sweat. "DO IT, BOY!"

I hurried down the side of another building, moving in its shadows, and peered around it. There, sitting against the village's central well, was Lust. Large breasts swayed beneath her, as big as my Hesione's. Black hair fell in curly ringlets around a flushed face. She stroked her futa-cock, pumping her hand up and down it. Her other was busy fingering her pussy.

"Yes, yes, yes," she moaned. Her head snapped to the right, looking away from me. "Yes, you feel that desire. You want it! Revel in it! Embrace it!"

Lust stood up and watched a woman being fucked by a man. He fucked the woman from behind, slamming into her like she was a bitch in heat. She clawed at the dirt, her hips thrusting back into the thrusts.

"Fuck me!" she snarled. "Make me CUM!"

"But he can't!" Lust said. She fell to her knees, stroking herself. "Why would you want to cum? Savor that desire. That need. Oh, yes, yes. Unending ache. Hunger that never ceases. You'll never be truly satisfied. Why bother with it? You'll just get horny again."

Fury rippled through me. The satisfaction might fade, but that just meant you could share in it again. I loved sharing it with Hesione and Pyrrha in our bed. My pregnant women gave me such joy. I would show her.

I watched Lust fingering her twat, her digits pumping in and out. Her ass clenched. Her right arm pumped away, stroking her clit-dick. Her back arched as I stalked towards her. My futa-cock throbbed as I set every sandaled foot just right.

No noise.

I crossed the paved stones of the square. I moved up on her, my futa-dick throbbing before me. Lust shuddered, her black hair swirling as she watched the rutting couple grow more and more frustrated.

"You will die feeling that passion," Lust moaned. "It'll be beautiful."

I pounced on Lust.

I fell on her from behind, my cock thrusting out before me. My clit-dick swayed and bobbed. I fell to my knees behind her and thrust my shaft right at her ass. The crown slipped into her crack before she could react.

"What?" she gasped, twisting around. She stared at me in shock. "You're not a man! How do you have—"

My cock found her asshole. I thrust, my tip lubed by pussy cream and my own precum.

"NO!" she gasped as her anal ring parted for me. I slipped into her with surprising ease. I bet she had fingered her bowels and got herself all loose and ready. "You can't be here! What are you doing?"

"Fucking your ass," I groaned as I sank my cock into the depths of her anal sheath. I shuddered, her velvety flesh squeezing around me. I groaned at the feel of her bowels gripping my dick. "Oh, yes, yes, that's good. That's fucking amazing."

She squeezed her flesh around my girl-dick. She wiggled her hips from side to side, stirring her bowels around my cock. I groaned, loving the way she did that. The pleasure surged through my body. I shuddered, my twat clenching.

My hands grabbed her big breasts as I drew back and then rammed into her asshole. I pumped away at Lust's bowels. My fingers dug into her tits. She gasped and whimpered, making such sweet sounds.

"Oh, yes, yes, that's good," I whimpered. "You like that?"

"Of course I do," Lust moaned, her bowels clenching about me. "Mmm, yes, yes, ram that cock into me. I can feel that desire in you. That aching need for release. Isn't it delicious?"

"Yes, it is," I panted, my nipples rubbing into her back. My pussy drank in the heat that plowing into her bowels generated. "It's fantastic. I'm going to enjoy cumming in your asshole."

"Cumming?" Lust groaned, her bowels squeezing around my dick. "Where is the fun in that? That's what ends it."

I nuzzled into her ear and licked it. She shuddered in my embrace, her breasts jiggling. Her bowels squeezed tight about my thrusting dick. "Is it?" I whispered. "Is it the end of the fun, or the beginning of something better."

"What can be better than this?" she moaned, her bowels gripping me. "Then the delight of my asshole massaging your clit-dick, Pandora?"

"The climax."

She laughed. "A few moments of shuddering pleasure can't compare to unending bliss. Oh, yes, yes, just fuck my asshole. Pound me for eternity. We can say locked like this. Don't pretend your cock doesn't enjoy my asshole."

"I love it," I moaned, my cunt clenching. The velvety heat of her bowels built the fire in my ovaries. My futa-cock ached every time I buried into her tight depths. "Your asshole is amazing. I'm going to cum so hard into you."

"Why?" she moaned. "Then you have to stop enjoying my asshole. Stop giving me this bliss. Ooh, I love your girl-dick fucking me, Pandora. Ram that futa-cock in me. Yes!"

She groaned, the slap of her hand stroking up and down her girl-cock increasing. My fingers digging into her tits slid up and found her nipples. I seized her nubs. I pinched and twisted them. She gasped, her bowels gripping my cock with velvety tightness.

I tweaked her fat nubs, loving the way it made her gasp. My own nipples rubbed into her back as I fucked her hard. My crotch smacked into her rump. I plowed my dick into her bowels with force. Power. I rammed hard and fast into her.

She groaned, squeezing her asshole down around my dick. The pleasure of that moment swelled in me. I drove into her hard and fast. I fucked her with passion. I slammed with all my might into Lust's asshole.

"Yes, yes, yes!" she moaned. "That's so good. Let's do this for all eternity, Pandora."

"No!" I groaned, pinching her nipples.

"No?" she gasped. "Why not? Don't you love my asshole?"

"It's amazing!" My cunt clenched. Juices soaked my bush. The heat in my ovaries swelled. "It's the best asshole I've ever fucked."

"Mmm, then why stop?" she moaned.

"Because I want to do this!"

I buried into her and surrendered to my body's lust. I erupted.

I fired my cum into Lust's asshole. Spurt after wonderful spurt of cum erupted from my girl-dick and flooded her bowels. The heady pleasure rushed over my mind. It rippled out of my cunt and fired from my futa-dick. The pleasure slammed into my thoughts. It was incredible. I enjoyed every heartbeat of bliss.

"What are you doing?" she moaned.

My pussy convulsed, aching to be fucked. My jar desired to be filled with futa-seed like I filled her asshole. I pumped her full of my cum. I shuddered, the ecstasy slamming into my mind. Stars burst across my vision.

"That's such a waste!" groaned Lust. "You climax! Why would you cum? Now you can't fuck my asshole any longer. You're going to become soft. Limp. You're going to want to cuddle and sleep. Do all that boring stuff. Your pleasure is over."

"Mmm, but it was so *satisfying*," I moaned. "I feel even better now than when I was fucking you. My body brims with bliss."

"Liar," she hissed. "Ooh, you're so annoying, Pandora. If you don't want to enjoy my gift, fine. The rest of these humans do. Listen to all their pleasure."

"They're frustrated because they can't cum."

"I know." Lust shuddered, her bowels clenching around my aching dick. "It drives them to fuck even harder. To desire with even more fervor. It's beautiful!"

"It's cruel. It's torture." I shivered. "You need to experience a climax to know."

Lust snorted.

I ripped out of her asshole and spun her around. She gasped, facing me. Her hands stroked her girl-dick and fingered her pussy. Her juices ran down her thighs. Precum dripped from the end of her futa-cock.

"There's nothing you can do that can make me cum," Lust said. "That would be the end of me. My death. Why, why, why would I ever want to give this up?"

"Because there's nothing sweeter than the climax," I purred. "Than the finale. That one moment of pure ecstasy. When you're utterly open to everything. It's worth anything. You are suffering and don't even know it."

She laughed. "I am *pleasure!* Unending bliss."

"You don't know what bliss is." I smiled. "You will."

I ducked my head down and sucked on her girl-cock. I slipped my lips over her futa-dick. She gasped and shivered. Her face twisted in delight. She stopped stroking her shaft as my lips sealed about her. I stared up at her and sucked.

Her breasts jiggled. She groaned, letting me nurse and suck on her. The salty flavor of her precum spilled over my mouth. I hungered to taste her girl-cum. To drink it all down. I would show her. I would give her ecstasy.

I bobbed my head, sliding my lips up and down her girl-cock. I rocked there, my breasts and clit-dick swaying beneath me, as I loved her. My braid slipped off my back and dangled off my right shoulder. I sucked. Slurped. Drool ran over my tongue.

"Oh, that's a delicious pleasure," moaned Lust. "Not as good as you fucking my asshole, but it's lovely. Yes, yes, suck my futa-dick."

I winked at her. My tongue swirled around her crown.

"I like that," she gasped, her clit-dick throbbing in my mouth. "Ooh, that tongue thing is lovely. You are full of surprises, Pandora."

I sucked with hunger. I nursed on her, wanting to drink her cum. She fingered her twat with her left hand while her right grabbed her nipple. She twisted it and moaned, her face twisting in delight. My tongue swept around her cock, stroking her. Giving her pleasure.

I knew it wouldn't be enough, but it was a start. I sucked on her. Nursed. I worshiped her girl-cock with all my might, letting her enjoy it. Building her passion. I would give her such bliss. I groaned, reveling in sucking my first dick.

It was so much fun.

Pyrrha, Hesione, and the women of the village all loved sucking on my girl-dick. I understood why. This was delicious. Amazing. It was a fantastic delight. I nursed with all the hunger I had in me, wanting to make her cum.

My tongue slid over her crown, brushing her slit, then I slid down her shaft. She groaned, pinching her nipple. Her cock throbbed in my mouth. The taste of her precum grew saltier. She shuddered, biting her lower lip.

"Yes, yes, you can suck on my cock until the end of time," gasped Lust. "Oh, Pandora, you have such a sweet and succulent mouth."

This would not work. I would never make her cum this way. I closed my eyes, enjoying sucking her cock for one more moment, savoring that salty delight. Then I slid my mouth off her girl-cock. I popped off with a wet plop. It made such a naughty sound.

"No! she hissed as drool spilled over my chin and ran down my lips. "Don't stop! Keep sucking me! That was delicious!"

"But I want to do something different," I purred. I stared up at her, licking my lips. I rose, my tits swaying before me. I grabbed her shoulders and pushed her back. "I want to feel that cock in my cunt. I want to have my first futa-dick in me."

"Yes!" moaned Lust. "I can feel it. Your need. It's why you sinned. Why you released me in the first place. That lust to cum, that envy of the other women who enjoyed your cock, that anger at Zeus for cursing you. I felt it all while I slumbered in you. It's time. Enjoy your desire for the rest of eternity. Ride my cock!"

She stretched out on her back, her fingers sliding out of her cunt. I grabbed her wrist and brought those digits to my mouth. I sucked on them, cleaning off the spicy flavor of her twat. She shuddered as I did that.

Her other hand grabbed her clit-dick, holding it upright for me. I straddled her, and then I lowered myself. My cunt nuzzled into her futa-cock's tip. My shaft throbbed as I ground my pussy lips into her spongy crown. My labia parted around her.

I sank down her futa-dick.

"Yes," she moaned. "Oh, Pandora, let's revel in this desire for eternity."

I pulled her fingers out of my mouth as I sank further and further down her clit-dick. I shuddered as I bottomed out on her, my futa-cock throbbing over her stomach. "Eternity? Doing one thing? That sounds boring."

"Boring?" she gasped as I squeezed my cunt around her clit-dick and rose up her shaft. "What is boring about *this?* Your pussy feels amazing about my dick. And I *know* you love this."

"I do," I groaned, savoring having a real cock in me. Not a wooden dildo, but a throbbing, living, fleshy futa-dick. My cunt gripped her shaft as I rode her. The friction rippled through me. "It's amazing. I love it. I'm going to cum so hard on you!"

"No!" she moaned. "Why do that? Why stop the fun?"

I winked at her and slammed my pussy down her girl-dick. It

237

was such a delicious shaft. My own girl-cock smacked into her belly, adding this exciting burst of stinging pleasure to the mix. My precum splattered her tits before I rose back up her, savoring that girth.

I loved fucking her cock. It was amazing. I arched my back, my boobs bouncing before me. I squeezed my cunt down around her cock. I gave her all the pleasure I could. She gasped and moaned, her face twisting in delight.

She was gorgeous. Her cheeks were delicate. Her lips plump and red. She had bewitching eyes. I could stare into them for eternity. She didn't feel evil despite all the problems she caused. She just felt... incomplete. She was missing something vital.

I would give it to her.

My pussy squeezed about her futa-dick as I rode her faster. When I slid up her cock, my twat clung to her throbbing shaft. I reeled in the silky friction as I slammed back down her, my cock smacking into her belly.

"Why would you ever want to stop this?" she moaned, her face twisting in delight. "Oh, Pandora, your pussy... Your pussy is amazing. I want to enjoy it until the end of time."

I grabbed her boobs, squeezing them. "There's something far, far better than this. Lust is wonderful, but satisfaction is the reward. The prize. The wonderful delight that desire brings. It might be fleeting, but it is wondrous. Embrace it, Lust!"

"No!" she whimpered. Her hands grabbed my rump. She squeezed my butt-cheeks as I slid up her again. "I won't. I love *this*. Your pussy. I love your cunt. I will stay in your cunt forever."

"Fine," I said, leaning over her. I gripped her hips as I stared into those intoxicating eyes. "If that's what you want."

She smiled up at me. "Pandora!"

I shuddered, my orgasm building and building. I slammed down her girl-cock. I groaned at the feel of her thick girth spreading me open. She felt incredible in me. I arched my back, loving every moment of this bliss. I groaned, my hips wiggling from side to side. The pleasure swelled to that explosive pinnacle.

I couldn't hold out too much longer. Not on my first futa-dick. Lust's cock was amazing. Just a delight. I shuddered, my pussy squeezing about her cock. The silky friction fed the pressure in my ovaries.

SMACK!

My futa-cock cracked into her belly. The thudding impact sent shivers of delight shooting up my shaft to my pussy. "Yes!" I moaned, rising up her. "I'm going to cum, Lust!"

"What?" she cried out. "No!"

SMACK!

I bottomed out on her and climaxed.

I threw back my head, my cock spurting jizz that splattered her big breasts. My pussy writhed around her girl-dick. I shuddered, my boobs heaving. Pleasure blazed across my mind as I coated her tits with my spunk. I bathed her in my seed.

"No, no, no!" she moaned as my cunt writhed around her clit-dick. Sucked at it. "You liar!"

"I didn't lie!" I gasped, the pleasure melting through my thoughts. The dual delights rushed through me. It was so amazing to cum on a real futa-dick. I loved every moment of it. I groaned, stars dancing before my eyes.

It was amazing. Incredible. I groaned, loving every last second of this bliss showering my thoughts in passion. I quivered atop her, my cunt writhing about her delicious snatch. I hung at the heights of ecstasy, my cum firing a last time.

"You! You!" Frustration rippled across Lust's face. "Why would you cum? We were having fun!"

"We were," I purred, squeezing my thighs tight around her. Then I rolled us over onto my back. She gasped as she settled atop me, her cock shifting around in my cunt. Her cum-splattered boobs pressed into mine, hers so soft. She smeared the jizz across me. "Look, now you can fuck me. A new delight to enjoy."

"But..." She shivered. "Your pussy... It..."

"Mmm, found satisfaction," I purred. "More pleasure in those few heartbeats then you gave me for the rest of my ride. You are missing out."

Her brow furrowed. Then her face hardened. "I'm not!"

She thrust her girl-cock into my cunt. I groaned as she plowed into me. I shuddered beneath her, loving the way her cum-splattered

239

tits rubbed against mine. She smeared the cum across my boobs. My cock throbbed between us, pinned by our stomachs.

Her cock pistoned in and out of my cunt. My twat gripped her. I shuddered, knowing that I would have such a huge orgasm on her girl-cock. My hands stroked her back as I stared into her eyes. I caressed her.

"So beautiful," I whispered. "You are gorgeous, Lust."

"So are you," she moaned. "And your pussy... It's the best. I love being in you."

"Mmm, you're amazing, too," I purred, my hands grabbing her rump. "Thrust faster. Really stir me up. That will make me cum so hard."

She bit her lip. She paused in her thrust for a moment, a hesitation, then she groaned and thrust harder. Faster. She pumped at my cunt, driving that thick dick to the hilt in me again and again. My dick throbbed between us, pulsing with the delight of her cock slamming into me.

She gasped and moaned, her dark eyes glassy with her delight. She thrust into me. She buried hard. Fast. She plunged her cock to the hilt in me again and again. I loved it. My cunt gripped her. I loved every moment of being beneath her. Our nipples rubbed together, the cum coating both our tits now.

A sticky mess.

"Mmm, that's it," I purred. "Make me cum, Lust. I want it. I want to climax on that big dick of yours again."

"Pandora," she groaned but kept thrusting. "Don't. Don't surrender."

"Mmm, but I want to. I want to feel that little death shuddering through me. I want to milk your futa-dick. I want to feel you cumming in me, Lust. Fill my jar with all your futa-seed. Unleash your full passion."

"No!"

She pounded me. Her dick slammed into me. My pussy rejoiced. My futa-cock throbbed beneath her. I trembled, climbing so fast to that orgasm now. I shuddered beneath her, clenching my twat down around her clit-dick.

The pleasure built and built. Every thrust swelled it. The feel of her body on mine. Her nipples sliding over my breasts. My cock pinned between us. All these delights swirled through me, feeding the pressure in my ovaries.

"Yes, yes, yes, Lust!" I howled as she slammed into me.

I came again.

Another amazing orgasm burst through my pussy. My flesh writhed around her. She gasped as she felt my cunt sucking at her girl-cock pumping away at me. My dick erupted, spurting cum between our bodies while she plowed into me again and again.

Mighty waves of ecstasy washed out of my cunt. Jolts of lightning fired from my cock. The two pleasures mixed and met and swirled in my mind. The rapture drowned my thoughts. The euphoria electrified my brain.

"Oh, Lust, cum in me!" I begged as she thrust into me. "I need to feel your jizz in me. Please, please, you're amazing."

She groaned, thrusting away at me. She pumped hard and fast. I bucked beneath her, rubbing our tits together. My cock kept erupting, splattering our breasts in fresh spunk. I coated us as my orgasm kept rippling through me.

Her face twisted. She groaned, her eyes squeezing shut as she hammered my spasming cunt. My flesh writhed around her. Sucked at her. My cum hungered to for her cum to jet into me. I hugged her tight.

"Cum in me, Lust," I moaned. "Please, please, I need it."

Her eyes snapped open. "I'm scared." She buried her girl-dick into me. "I feel like... Like I'm going to fall. I'm on the edge of a precipice."

"Fall," I purred. "I'm here to catch you."

I kissed Lust.

She melted into my mouth. She buried her cock into me. Erupted.

Her cum pumped into my pussy. For the first time in my life, seed filled my jar. My cunt writhed around her spurting futa-dick. I milked her, eager for every drop. Lust moaned into my lips. She shuddered atop me, her breasts rubbing into mine.

More and more of her cum pumped into me. She unleashed a torrent. Another orgasm burst through me. New pleasure rushed through me. More spunk fired from my clit-dick. I soaked our bodies as she filled my womb.

Around us, I heard every man and woman in the village joining us in climax. They finally had their release.

Lust broke the kiss. "Pandora! Pandora! Yes, yes, this is amazing. Bliss!"

"Satisfaction!" I purred. "Enjoy."

I watched her buck and tremble through it. Her face squeezed shut. She fired the last blast of her cum into my pussy. Then she collapsed onto me. She hugged me tight. Her cheek rubbed into mine. Her hair spilled like silk over my face.

"Thank you," she whispered in my ear.

And then she became black smoke. She spilled over me, flowed into me. I closed my eyes and shuddered as Lust flowed back into me. I hugged her vaporous body to me. There was nothing wrong with Lust. She had her place in my heart.

She just had to be controlled.

I sat up and looked around. The people of the village were collapsing into an exhausted stupor. They had their release. They would wake up tomorrow, their desires once again under their control. I smiled as I felt Lust inside of me.

Satisfied. Happy.

I hummed to myself and laid back down on the stones. I stared up into the night sky. As I fell into sleep, I smiled. One down.

To be continued…

Pandora's Envious Passion

Pandora's Naughty Futa Box 5

by

Reed James

Pandora's Envious Passion

Envy sauntered into the next town naked. Her big boobs jiggled before her and her large futa-cock bounced. Every man and woman turned to stare at. Their envy swelled. Jealousy arose. She had bigger breasts than all the women and a bigger dick than all the men. She shuddered at their attention, reveling in it.

They swarm around her, wanting her attention. Wanting to be her. She reaches the heart of the village. "Bring me a chair!" she cried. "The best chair in this village!"

Men raced to fetch theirs. The argument began quickly. Who had the best chair? Then she hungered. Women screeched over who had the best food. The best cooking. She licked her lips, wanting it all. Wanting everything.

Then Envy grew horny. Who had the best pussy? The competition began.

* * *

Pandora

I found another town ruined. More victims of the evil that had escaped me when I lost my virginity. Zeus's curse ravaged the world. The cruel and petty god wanted me to suffer and didn't care how many other humans paid the price.

I had come across two other towns like this one. The men had hacked each other down with swords, knives, axes, and various farming implements and tools of trade. Whatever came to hand that they could use as a weapon. Many had their cocks severed, the severed bits lying in the mud. Women had clawed or bludgeoned each other's faces, ruining beauty. They had disfigured the other's bodies. Scattered around them were signs of a feast. Dishes set out on tables, the food all rotting or feasted on by the scavengers.

At first, I thought it was Wrath I was on the trail of. But I had thought that with Lust, the first of the three evils I had tamed and taken back into me. They had escaped me, shadowy emotions manifested with flesh by Zeus's powers.

Lust, Wrath, and Envy.

Was this Envy I tracked? The food was strange. I couldn't imagine people would be setting out food for Wrath. It was almost like a competition, the villagers going mad to prove that they were the best, consumed with envy for what their neighbors had and then ruining it out selfish destruction, leaving all that pain behind.

And then Envy would move onto the next town.

I had to hurry. I had to move faster. I was the only hope for the world. I held that in me after the evil escaped. The hope that I would save them all and return to my Hesione and Pyrrha. My pregnant women awaited. The village near where they lived was still safe. Hopefully. It was full of the women I had bred.

All those wives that I had loved.

I wanted to protect them all. I had to stop these evil incarnations from their rampage. This couldn't be allowed to continue any longer. I pushed myself as long as I could before I had to stop and camp by a field of wheat. I curled up on my blanket and fell asleep.

I didn't sleep well. The drive to stop this next evil pressed on me. I was close to her. The destruction in that last village had been fresh. I shuddered at that. I couldn't let the next one fall into evil. I had to stop Envy and Wrath. My own selfishness was partly to blame.

Zeus had cursed me, but I gave in to my own selfish desires. My own lusts to have my virginity taken and a cock filling my pussy, my envy at all the women I fucked who got to enjoy that delight of my dick delving into their twats, and my anger at Zeus for his curse that denied me the pleasure that they received. I had succumbed. Made the wooden dildo.

Let Hesione uncork my virgin jar and fuck my pussy with the fake cock.

The next morning, I was on the road. I neared a village. As I descended from the road, I could see them all gathered in the center. Hope blossomed in me. It wasn't too late for this one. I could stop Envy from destroying them. Tame her. Take her back into me where she belonged. Then I could control her. Stop her from harming others.

I passed into the outskirts of the village, passing the mud-brick huts. They all had doors open. The sounds of the villagers all shouting rose as I came upon the town center. A square with a well in the middle they all drew water from.

On a raised dais, sitting on a chair above all, was a busty, black-haired woman. She had tits as big as Lust's. They were pillowy and soft. Her cock thrust up from her crotch, a mighty futa-dick. She sat with her legs open, showing off her hairless pussy to them all.

"Look at my wife!" one man shouted. He had his woman naked beside him. "Euphoria is the most beautiful woman in this village. Look at those breasts! They're magnificent."

"No, no!" another man roared and shoved his naked wife forward. She had smaller breasts, her body slender, her legs lithe. "My wife is the true beauty of this village. She's the woman who deserves to fuck your cock."

"She doesn't even deserve to fuck your cock, Leontios!" roared a third man. "Your dick is smaller than mine. Look at this cock. You know you wish to have a cock that big. Your wife does! Sostrate loves my cock!"

"She's never touched your cock!" roared Leontios, gripping his wife, Sostrate, against him.

"You sure? She wants a real cock."

"She wouldn't touch your cock then, Antigonos!" a fourth roared, a burly man with a square-cut beard. He stroked his own cock. "My wife knows my cock is the best."

"Because she's fucked every man in the village!" another shouted.

"Look at my tits!" a woman gasped, shaking them at Envy. "They're so big and lush. I'm the most beautiful woman. You have to fuck me."

"No!" screeched another. She broke from her husband, her round breasts jiggling. "I'm more beautiful than her. You want me! Me!"

"As if you can compare!" the first said. "Look at these tits. You know you wish you had these tits!"

The two women stared at each other with hatred. Looks of jealous passion twisted their expressions. Envy sat above them all, smiling at it. Others were arguing over the food, women declaring theirs the best. Men held up tools, crafts, furniture, all boast that their work was superior while staring with rapacious hunger at what others had.

I could feel it building and building. While everyone proclaimed they had the best, they wanted what the others had. Men lusted for each other's wives, wanting the prettier women for themselves. Women stared at each other's bodies, wishing they had those plump breasts or curving hips or lush lips. They were about to burst into violence to steal what others had.

I had to put a stop to this.

How to soothe them? How to calm them down and capture their attention? I had been given gifts by the Olympians. Not all of them, because Zeus caught me in bed with his wife, Hera, before they were all handed out. I cycled through them in my mind. My sexual prowess from Ares and my beauty from Aphrodite wouldn't do it, nor my knowledge of engineering from Athena and hunting skills from Artemis. Hera's gift of motherhood, too, was not what I needed.

Apollo's gift... That might do it.

I unslung my satchel and unwound my toga. I stripped naked, my hard cock, thrusting from my black bush, twitched before me. My breasts swayed, round and perky. A braid of black hair fell down my back. Hephaestus had given me the greatest gift of all.

He had made me. A futanari.

I drew in a deep breath and sang. The words poured from my heart as I strolled forward. Poetry given song. My perfect pitch rose over the shouts and cries. Over the arguments. All the eyes turned toward me. They blinked as they stared at me.

The women shuddered. Lust for me kindled in their eyes. Aphrodite had made my body irresistible to women. Beautiful. Perfect. My breasts, my hips, my big futa-dick, my delicate cheekbones, my plump lips, even the folds of my pussy were all desirable to them. They shuddered. Their argument over who was the most beautiful lost to me.

The men could see that I had the biggest cock of them. The one that could satisfy women the best. My song poured over them. The words rising out of my heart. Sharing. Supporting. Taking joy in what others possessed instead of coveting their possessions and hating them. Envy glared at me as she sat on her throne, no longer the center of attention.

Perfect.

I reached the middle area, stepping on the rugs that had been set down in offering to Envy. All of finely woven wool, made in interesting patterns when they were still upon the loom. Skill had gone into them all. I admired them.

"My wife!" Leontios said and pressed slender Sostrate forward. "You must see that my wife is the most beautiful woman in the village."

I smiled and took Sostrate's hand. I pulled her towards me. Everyone watched me as I walked around the woman, my voice trilling out my song. The pure poetry serenading from my lips, something only a god should be able to compose, had soothed their hearts.

For now.

I squeezed both of Sostrate's plump butt-cheeks. She shuddered, my cock nuzzling into the small of her back. I kneaded her rump, my fingers digging into her flesh. My dick smeared precum across her skin as I moved around to her front again.

"Aren't I beautiful?" asked Sostrate as I came before her. She had brown eyes and long lashes, her face round. Brown hair fell in a curly fall down her back. Her small breasts rose and fell. They were perky delights, topped by pink nipples. She was young, eighteen, and yet to be a mother.

That would change.

"You are beautiful," I said, my hands sliding up to cup her breasts. "Mmm, such succulent tits."

Leontios nodded his head in agreement, arms folded as I fondled his wife's tits.

Sostrate smiled in delight as every man and woman watched me duck my head down and suck on her breasts. Envy did, too. She folded her arms beneath her big breasts and glared at me as I nursed on a small, pink nipple.

The wife groaned. Her nipple filled my mouth so wonderfully. I loved them all. Women had so many delights to enjoy. How could I think one was best? My tongue swirled about her nub. I caressed over her areola with my hungry strokes. She groaned as I did. I sucked and nibbled on her.

"Oh, yes, yes," she gasped. "Stranger!"

I popped my mouth off. "I am Pandora."

Envy ground her teeth. "I'm better than her. Look at my dick. It's big. Someone, come and suck it."

"It's okay," I told the women. "Enjoy her cock. I can't please you all at the same time. But I will get to each of you, so don't you worry. You are all beautiful. Sostrate might be first, but that's not because she's better. Mmm, you're all gorgeous."

I sucked her other nipple in my mouth as one of the other women broke from her husband and went to Envy. The incarnation of jealous emotions glared at me even as she got what she wanted. A hot, wet mouth sucked on her cock. The woman standing before the raised throne had bent over and thrust her plump rump out in my direction.

A black bush peeked out between her thighs, so enticing.

My dick throbbed as I watched her blow Envy out of the corner of my eye. The entire time, I sucked on Sostrate's nipple. I nursed on her, loving her. I sucked with hunger on her while she moaned. The women and men watched me, whispering, shifting, getting horny.

I popped my mouth off Sostrate's nipple and fell to my knees before her. I grabbed her hips and stared at her pussy. She had plucked all her hairs away, as was the custom for a woman who wanted to have children. It would increase her fertility having no pubic hair.

I pressed my face forward into her pussy lips and licked at her cunt. Her spicy juices spilled over my tongue. The married woman gasped, her cute breasts jiggling over my head. I loved sexy wives the best. They were so much fun to fuck.

To cuckold their husband with my big futa-dick.

"Pandora!" moaned Sostrate as my tongue caressed over her folds. Her spicy cream spilled into my mouth. "Oh, yes, yes, that's so good."

I loved the sounds she made. I was so glad to give them to her. I caressed up and down her slit. I licked at her. Teased her. I fluttered my tongue up and down her folds. The sounds she made were so delicious. So wonderful to stir from her.

I thrust my tongue into her cunt. I licked and lapped at her. I teased her with my hunger. She groaned, her cunt clenching down on my dick. It was fantastic to experience. She moaned, her hips wiggling from side to side, grinding her cunt on my mouth.

"Leontios," she gasped. "Oh, she's the best. Oh, yes, yes, she knows just how to lick."

Women moaned around me. They murmured around me, their words flowing over me as I feasted on Sostrate's cunt. "Good at pussy licking?"

"Mmm, how wonderful."

"What a delicious creature."

"That dick of hers is amazing, too. Boobs, pussy, and a dick."

"I want her."

Envy hissed in annoyance even as the married woman sucked hard on her cock.

I thrust my tongue into Sostrate's pussy. I swirled around in her. My tongue danced and swirled, caressing that delicious snatch. I loved every moment of it. My tongue plundered her cunt. Her juice soaked my taste buds.

I shuddered, my cunt clenching. The heat washed through me.

It was fantastic to experience. I thrust my tongue into her cunt. I fluttered in fast circles around in her snatch. I stirred her up. She moaned, her breasts quivering.

"Oh, Pandora," she moaned. "Oh, you're going to make me cum."

"Yes, yes, make my wife cum," Leontios groaned.

I loved that. My dick throbbed harder. When husbands begged me to enjoy their women... That was a treat. A delight. Their actions were the opposite of envy. It was them taking joy in their wives' pleasure. That they were glad I could make them feel amazing.

I danced my tongue through Sostrate's married depths. I swirled around in her, churning her up. She tasted so good. Her spicy delight felt amazing. Her hairless folds rubbed on my lips and cheeks as I feasted on her.

She shuddered. Her hands grabbed her breasts. She pinched her small nipples, twisting her wet nubs. She whimpered, face blazing with delight. My hands gripped her plump rump, pulling her pussy tight against my face.

I found her little clit. Sucked on it.

"Pandora!" she gasped. "I'm going to cum. Oh, Leontios, I'm going to explode! She's nursing on my clitoris."

"Good," groaned Leontios. "Cum on her face, my wife."

The other women squeezed breasts or fingered pussies as they watched. I felt their hungry eyes on me. They all wanted this. Ached for it. Envy wasn't a bad thing so long as you didn't let it turn into jealousy. If you didn't try to take what others had but instead let it inspire you to improve yourself.

I nursed on Sostrate's clit. She gasped. Her body bucked. Juices gushed out. I drank down her spicy flood. I closed my eyes, reveling in her wonderful, spicy delight. I gulped it down as she moaned out her delight.

"Yes, yes, yes!" she moaned. "Lord Zeus! Lady Aphrodite! So good!"

I drank her passion. I feasted on it, my futa-dick throbbing. Aching. I had to be in this woman. She wanted a child. I would give her one. Every woman I fucked, I bred. I would plant my babe in her married depths.

"Oh, yes!" she moaned, swaying.

I pulled her down to the rugs. She sank down on them, spreading her legs. Her body quivered there, her pussy ready for me to fuck. I settled between her thighs, her pussy cream running down my throat. She stared up at me with lidded eyes.

"You're so beautiful, Pandora!" she moaned, her hands shooting out to grab my futa-dick. "And your cock... Your girl-cock is gorgeous. So big. Ooh, I want this in me. I love big cocks."

Antigonos chuckled nearby.

Sostrate pulled my cock to her pussy. She pressed me right against her wet folds. I groaned at the contact. It felt incredible. Her hot folds smeared juices across my dick. I felt the entrance to her cunt. I pushed forward, eager to be inside her.

I slid into her with ease.

I groaned as I penetrated into her pussy. I loomed over her, my round breasts swaying as inch after inch of my cock vanished into her cunt. She groaned, her pussy squeezing around me. She wrapped her arms and legs around me and held me tight as I vanished into her depths. It was incredible to feel. An amazing delight to enjoy.

I bottomed out in her. Every bit of my cock was buried in her married pussy. Her husband watched in awe, stroking his smaller shaft as I filled his wife's pussy with my clit-dick. My back arched, my boobs jiggling. Women groaned.

"She's so gorgeous!" a woman groaned.

"Yes!" another wife whimpered. "Those breasts!"

"Beautiful breasts!" panted a third.

Then two women were falling down on either side of me, one with her black hair in a long braid, the other wearing hers loose. They ducked their heads down and sucked my nipples into their mouths. I gasped as they nursed at me, the pleasure shooting down to my cunt.

"No!" Envy hissed.

"You should fuck my wife!" another man said. He pushed his wife forward. "My Zenais has big breasts. Bigger than hers. She is more deserving of your cock."

"They are big breasts," I moaned, thrusting away. "But that doesn't make her more deserving. All your women deserve it equally.

Some have bigger breasts or cuter faces or tighter rumps, but you're all beautiful in your own way."

"Don't listen to her!" Envy moaned, grabbing the head of the woman sucking her cock and ripping it off. "I bet your wife is a better cock-sucker than this woman."

"You are an amazing cocksucker," I gasped to the woman who stumbled back, looking stunned. "I'll let you suck my dick when I'm done fucking Sostrate!"

The woman shot me a grateful look even as Zenais's husband ushered his busty wife over to suck on Envy's cock. He squeezed his wife's rump as she leaned over and sucked on the futa's big dick, nursing on it.

I bet the two women had the same level of skill. Both would be delicious cock-suckers. Envy needed to learn that choosing who or what was the best was subjective. There were so many different pleasures out there to enjoy. Different delights to experience.

I thrust my cock hard into Sostrate's pussy. She gasped and moaned as she squirmed on her back, her brown hair fanning over the rug. Her face twisted as my futa-dick plowed into her cunt. I fucked her hard. Fast. I buried into her again and again.

"This cock is amazing!" Sostrate whimpered. "Oh, you all are going to love her fucking you."

"I have the stamina to fuck you all!" I moaned. "Every last one of you!"

The women sucking at my nipples nursed with even more delight. The pleasure shot bliss through me. I groaned, thrusting with passion into Sostrate's cunt. The other woman cheered their excitement, pressing around them.

Ignoring Envy.

I heard her hiss in frustration even as Zenais sucked hard on that big futa-dick. She put her all into it, but did that satisfy Envy? No, it didn't. I could feel his eyes on me, coveting what I had. The delights that surrounded me.

"Yes, yes, yes!" Sostrate moaned. "I'm so lucky to get this big futa-dick fucking me. Oh, yes, yes. Pandora! Your girl-cock is amazing!"

"Make her cum," her husband groaned.

"Yes, yes, make her explode so you can fuck me!" a woman moaned.

"She has to let me suck her cock first!" whimpered the woman who'd been blowing Envy. She licked her lips.

"Yes, yes, Herais needs to suck Pandora's cock!" another woman moaned.

I smiled at that, thrusting so hard into Sostrate's pussy. The two women nursed harder on my nipples. They sent such delight down to my cunt. My twat clenched, the aches forming in the depths of my ovaries. The need to erupt. To fire my cum and flood Sostrate's pussy. It swelled in me with every thrust into her married snatch.

I came closer and closer to breeding Sostrate. I reveled in the tightness of her pussy. In how she gripped me. That wonderful snatch squeezed so tight about me. My face scrunched up. My cunt grew hotter and hotter.

I slammed into Sostrate's pussy. I couldn't hold back any longer. Not with those wonderful mouths sucking at my nipples. I threw back my head and gasped out in ecstasy. My futa-cock erupted. My cum fired into Sostrate's snatch.

"Lord Zeus!" she gasped and then her twat rippled around my cock. "Leontios, she's cumming in me!"

Her husband groaned as I spurted blast after blast of cum into her pussy. Sparks burst across my vision as I shuddered through that wonderful delight. My head threw back. Juices gushed out of my cunt and ran down my thighs.

Sostrate milked my dick with her pussy while the pleasure rushed through me. Stars danced in my head. I cried out in ecstasy. The women suckled at my nipples, adding that tingling delight to the roar of bliss firing from my cock and the wash of delight rushing from my twat.

"So good! You're all so amazing!"

Herais fell too her knees beside Sostrate, licking her lips. She wanted to suck my cock. I fired the last of my cum into Sostrate's pussy and rose. I withdrew my futa-cock out of that hot cunt and stood up, pulling my nipples from those hungry mouths. My dick dripped with juices. I grabbed Herais's head and rammed my cock right past her waiting lips.

Herais sucked on me. She nursed with hunger on my girl-dick wet with Sostrate's cunt. Herais didn't mind the taste of another woman's cream. She nursed and stared up at me as she worshipped my cock. One of the women suckling at my nipples grabbed my butt-cheeks and pressed her head in between my thighs from behind.

"Pandora's pussy," she moaned before she nuzzled up and licked at my cunt.

Envy growled her frustration.

I savored the tongue lapping at my cunt while Herais sucked on my cock. She bobbed her head, working her lips up and down my dick. She groaned as she did. She sucked hard on me. I loved the way she did, her passion delicious.

"Oh, Apollonia, that's so wicked," Sostrate moaned. "Yes, yes, lick Pandora's cum out of my pussy."

A collective groan rose from the watching men at the sapphic sight. I smiled. I had seen Hesione and Pyrrha enjoy that delight so many times. I had done it, too. Licking my cum out of a woman's pussy was a delight.

I shuddered, the woman licking my pussy swirling her tongue through my depths. She stirred around in me, teasing me. Her tongue fucked in and out of me. Herais, at the same time, bobbed her head. She worked her plump lips up and down my cock.

She was eager for my cum. Eager for me to spurt my jizz into her mouth. I groaned, rising towards that moment with her every suck. The tip of my cock throbbed in her mouth. She had such skill at blowing dicks. Envy was a fool.

"Yes, yes, yes," I moaned. "Ooh, that's nice. That's beautiful. Ooh, you're going to make me explode, aren't you?"

She nodded, staring up at me with such hunger in her eyes.

"Yes, you are, Herais," I groaned.

"My wife's an amazing cock-sucker!" a man shouted with pride.

"She is," I purred. "I've yet to meet a woman who wasn't. They're all wonderful, Envy."

"This one is the best!" Envy hissed. "Right, Zenais. Unless... You... Eirene. Come suck my cock. I bet you're even better."

I shook my head. "You'll never be satisfied if you're always chasing the best."

Zenais stumbled away and then glanced at us. She darted over, her big boobs heaving. She threaded through the other women watching and went straight for my right boob. She smooched at it, her tongue licking and lapping.

"Mmm, yes, yes, you're just delicious, Zenais," I purred. "Don't listen to her. She's a fool."

"Yes, she is," Zenais said. "Not happy with my mouth? I would have made her cum hard."

"I know."

She sucked my nipple into her mouth. I groaned at how amazing that felt. My pussy clenched down on the naughty woman probing my depths. My dick throbbed in Herais's mouth. She cleaned off all of Sostrate's pussy cream.

I groaned as Herais slid her mouth further down my cock. My spongy cock pressed into the back of her throat. I shuddered and then slipped down her gullet. She swallowed me with ease. My eyes fluttered.

Her lips nuzzled into my bush and kissed at my labia.

She had taken every bit of me.

"Zeus's beard!" I gasped in delight.

Herais hummed around my cock. She moaned, the pleasure rippling around my dick. It was an amazing delight to enjoy. I groaned, my face scrunching up. I smiled, the bliss rippling over my features. My heart pounded, pumping hot blood through my veins.

My pussy grew hotter and hotter. My orgasm swelled and swelled. The woman who licked my cunt stimulated my naughty sheath. Her lips kissed at my folds while Herais slid her mouth back up my clit-dick. Zenais's mouth suckled with hunger on my nipple.

"Oh, you wonderful delights," I moaned. "You're all going to make me cum. Herais will get a yummy treat."

"Cum in her mouth!" moaned Sostrate as she humped her pussy against Apollonia's mouth. "Yes, yes, just flood Herais's mouth with your cum."

"It tastes so good," moaned Apollonia.

"Yes!" I gasped and then I erupted.

My pussy convulsed around the married woman's tongue. My

futa-cock pumped jizz into Herais's mouth. Zenais sucked at my nipple while Envy hissed in annoyance and frustration, clearly not satisfied by Eirene's sucking.

Not like I was by these women worshiping me. They gave me such bliss.

My mind blazed with the passion. I trembled, the rapture bursting through me. It was fantastic. My hips wiggled back and forth. I smeared my twat into the woman's face. She drank my juices while Herais gulped down my cum.

I hit that wonderful peak. "Oh, that's amazing. Who wants to be fucked next?"

"Can you fuck me?" the woman who ate me out moaned.

"Of course!" I gasped.

I turned around, pulling my cock from Herais's mouth and my nipple from Zenais's lips. The woman who ate me out had her black hair gathered in a thick braid draped over her shoulder. Her large breasts swayed. She pivoted on her knees and bent over, thrusting that curvy ass at me.

I couldn't resist.

I placed my cock against her asshole and purred, "I'm going to fuck you Athenian style!" Anal was something Athena had taught me. It was how she preserved her virginity. "How does that sound?"

"I just want to enjoy you futa-cock, Pandora!" she moaned.

"Fuck my Pherenike in the ass!" her husband groaned.

"Mmm, share that cum with me, Herais," Zenais moaned in the background as my futa-dick pressed on Pherenike's asshole.

The woman's anal ring surrendered to my cock. I groaned as I slid into her bowels. I savored the heat of popping into the warm, velvety embrace of her asshole. The pleasure rushed through my body. I groaned, my head tossing back. The pleasure felt incredible. Another explosion of jizz that I would fire into her asshole built in my ovaries.

"Yes!" I moaned.

"Oh, Pandora!" Pherenike groaned as her bowels swallowed every bit of my futa-dick.

I gripped her hips and drew back. I groaned, my breasts quivering at how tight and delicious her bowels felt. Pussy juices trickled down my thighs. The air brimmed with the passion. My breasts quivered. Envy was already calling for another woman to suck her dick.

None came.

I slammed back into Pherenike's bowels. I buried to the hilt in her. She gasped. I fucked her hard and fast. She moaned, her bowels clutching about my cock. She wiggled her hips, stirring that velvety sheath around my dick.

My boobs heaved as I fucked her. I pounded her, gripping her hips as I rammed my clit-dick into her anal sheath again and again. I savored every moment of it. Every last second of thrusting into her bowels. It was amazing. Delicious. A rapturous delight that would have me exploding in ecstasy. I groaned with each plunge.

The woman cheered. They fingered each other. Some were kissing friends. Married women loved each other while their husbands watched. The excitement of this swelled my orgasm. I hammered Pherenike's bowels with powerful strokes.

"Pandora!" she squealed. "Yes, yes, yes, I love you in my asshole. I'm going to cum!"

"Zeus's beard, do it!" I howled and buried my cock to the hilt in her tight anal sheath.

Pherenike's bowels writhed around my cock. That wonderful sheath massaged me. I threw back my head and groaned out my pleasure. I fired my cum into her bowels. I pumped her spasming asshole with my jizz.

"Yes, yes, yes!" I howled, my mind melting beneath the bliss.

"Pandora!" she groaned, her bowels rippling around my futa-dick. She worked out my cum.

It was incredible.

When I pulled out of Pherenike's asshole, every woman wanted my cock. "I have plenty of cum for you all!"

Their men cheered me on as I bred their wives' pussies. I rammed my dick soaked in cunt cream into their asses. Other women nursed me clean of after those wicked encounters so I could fuck them in their twats.

Women rubbed their boobs on my body. I ate their cunts, sometimes full of my own jizz. They rode me. Fingered me.

Devoured my pussy. Rimmed my asshole. Mouths found my nipples and nursed. The day passed as I satiated all the beauties of the village.

Envy glowered on and on. Her face grew puce and then looked sickly green as she sat on her throne. She lorded over us all, and yet I was the one the women turned to for satisfaction. I didn't rip them off my cock and say they were terrible. I didn't demand only the best, I just wanted to love them all.

Every woman in the village had their charms.

"You have the best cock, Pandora!" gasped the women.

"Your tits are ripe and perfect, Pandora!"

"You have such a yummy tasting pussy. This must be what ambrosia tastes like!"

"Your cum is perfect. I love drinking it!"

"Ooh, your ass is so gorgeous. I could just kiss it all day long!"

"Can I ride your perfect futa-dick, Pandora?"

The cheers and gasps and compliments showered over me as I pumped my cum into woman after woman. They dripped with my seed. They humped cunts dripping in my futa-jizz against my thighs. They jammed fingers into my cunt and asshole. My cock penetrated all their holes.

"WHAT MAKES YOU THINK YOU'RE BETTER THAN ME!"

The roar of Envy cut through the celebration.

I smiled as I pumped my load of cum into Zenais's pussy. I bred the busty woman. She shuddered, her pussy milking out the last of my futa-jizz from my ovaries. I stood up amid the writhing women, their men around standing us. They all were hushed.

Envy stood up on her dais, towering over all. Her big boobs quivered. Her large cock throbbed with her angry heartbeat. She had a bigger clit-dick than me. Her boobs rivaled those of Aphrodite in their size. Envy had perfect beauty.

"WHY?" she demanded. She shook her cock. "This dick is superior to hers! Why aren't you all fighting over mine? And these tits...? Why aren't you men salivating over my tits? Why are you offering up your wives to her and not me?"

"I'm not better than you," I said. "You're right. Your cock is superior. Your tits are bigger. But here's the problem, Envy, no one likes it. It's one of the ugliest emotions in the world. It's better to share. Look."

Sostrate and a woman named Eirene were sucking on the tip of my cock now, licking off Zenais's pussy cream. They fluttered their tongues around it, their cheeks pressing tight together. Then a woman pressed her face between my butt-cheeks and licked at my asshole. I cupped a fourth woman's pussy and thrust my fingers into her depths, her furry bush tickling my palm. Apollonia's twat clenched on my digits.

"Look, Envy, don't you see?" I asked.

"I see them all ignoring me for *your* inferior body!" Envy hissed.

"No, they're sharing. Sostrate and Eirene are enjoying my cock. The other woman is reveling in my asshole. These women are all writhing together. Look, Herais is licking at Zenais's pussy. It's a beautiful thing. You could have come and joined in instead of just pouting."

"I'm not pouting!"

"Yes, you are!" I shook my head. "Why don't you come down here and we can share Apollonia's pussy together. We'll both fuck her cunt."

Envy frowned. "Why would you want to do that?"

"Share her pussy with you?" I smiled. "Because you deserve to have fun, too. You're beautiful in your own way, Envy, just not when you're being a spoiled brat."

"But she'll see that my cock is better," Envy said and strode off the dais. "It'll prove my clit-dick is superior to yours, Pandora. Then they'll all want me!"

"Why does one have to be better?" I asked. "And even if yours is, I'm still happy with what I have. My cock has given all these women pleasure. And it's given me so much bliss. Even if they like yours better, who cares. I'll still get to make love to them. And so will you."

The men parted before Envy and her huge tits. Apollonia trembled, her cunt clenching down on my fingers. She bit her lip as she stared at that big dick. Then she glanced at me, her brown eyes glassy with desire.

"I'll get you both in me?" Apollonia asked. "Because your cock alone in my pussy was amazing, Pandora. I came so hard."

"Yes, you did," her husband called.

"It's your lucky day, Apollonia," I told her and then kissed her on the mouth, my dick throbbing as Sostrate and Eirene licked and lapped at the tip. Then they pulled away, letting me enjoy Apollonia instead of jealously clutching to my dick.

Kissing the sexy wife, I pulled Apollonia down to the rugs. She moaned, her tongue playing with mine as we stretched out on our sides. Her round breasts rubbed into mine. Her hand grabbed my cock. She whimpered, stroking me.

Envy sank down, her big boobs jiggling. She stretched out on her side, too. Apollonia broke the kiss with me and rolled onto her back. She grabbed Envy's even bigger dick and shuddered. A smile spread on her lips.

"Ooh, this will be amazing," the married woman purred.

She rolled over and kissed Envy, their breasts pressing together. Around us, the other women of the village fell into their own embraces, licking, lapping, and fingering each other. Their men formed a ring around us, watching the passion of their wives.

Apollonia pulled my cock to her rump as she kissed Envy. Their breasts pressed together. Envy moaned. Then she gasped and thrust forward. Apollonia groaned, and I knew that Envy had entered that hot and juicy sheath.

It was my turn.

Apollonia pressed the tip of my cock into the base of Envy's shaft. My tip slid up the incarnation's cock until I felt the wet lips of Apollonia's pussy. I pushed against that juicy twat, my breasts rubbing into her back. She let go of my cock and whimpered.

She broke the kiss with Envy to moan, "Yes, yes, slide your cock into me. I need it!"

Apollonia's pussy lips spread and spread over the crown on my cock. She trembled between us, her back rubbing into my breasts. My nipples throbbed and ached. They burst with delight. Pleasure shot down to my cunt. My dick throbbed with passion.

I kept pushing against her labia, almost in her. She gasped and shuddered. She whimpered as I pressed into her. Her body trembled, her nipples rubbing into my back. She gasped as my cock popped into her cunt's depths.

"Oh, yes!" the married woman moaned as her pussy stretched around the two futa-dicks. Her cunt squeezed me tight against Envy's girl-cock.

"That's tight," gasped Envy as my dick slid down her shaft. "Yes, yes!"

"A delight that can only come from sharing," I groaned, sliding my cunt deeper and deeper into that twat.

I reveled in it. I savored the joy of sliding into this pussy. I trembled, my cock throbbing as I bottomed out in her. Hot cunt squeezed me against a hard futa-dick. Apollonia moaned and trembled between us.

Her passion echoed through the air. She whimpered and groaned. The sounds she made were so naughty. Especially when Envy and I pulled back our hips. Her pussy gripped us as we drew out of her. Then we rammed back into her, our shafts moving together in near unison.

"Lord Zeus!" howled Apollonia. Her cunt clamped down on us. "This... Oh, by the Twelve! This is amazing!"

"Yes!" I panted, thrusting away at her, my futa-dick burying into her cunt and sliding past Envy's big cock.

Our dicks quickly fell out of sync. We were thrusting in and drawing out at different rhythms. The sensitive crown of my cock slid down her shaft and brushed her tip. Sparks flared every time, my pussy drinking them in. My twat grew hotter and hotter as I shared Apollonia's married snatch with Envy.

The incarnation thrust away hard and fast. She moaned in delight while Apollonia groaned. The married women trembled between us, her pussy squeezing tight about our clit-dicks. The silky friction swelled my orgasm.

"Zeus's beard!" I moaned, my nipples aching as they rubbed against her back. "This is incredible."

"Amazing!" gasped Apollonia. "I'm going to explode. My mind is going to melt. Two huge futa-dicks in me. Yes, yes, yes!"

Her pussy clenched around our cocks. She squeezed us tight.

Envy's futa-dick massaged my shaft as we thrust away into Apollonia's depths. I shuddered every time our crowns caressed past the other. It happened over and over again, the pleasure rushing down to my pussy.

The other woman moaned around us. Sostrate and Eirene devoured the other's pussy, entwined in such a naughty position. Some women fingered cunts or assholes, licked twats, fingered buttholes, and sucked on nipples. They shared in their bodies instead of envied what each other had.

It was a beautiful sight, stirring me to thrust harder and faster at Apollonia's cunt. To ream her with all my might and make her explode. She would cry out with such passion. Her pussy would writhe around our futa-dick fucking her.

"Yes, yes, yes!" Envy groaned. "That's it! You love my cock!"

"Love both your cocks!" Apollonia moaned, her pussy gripping us. Massaging us.

It was all such a perfect delight. A wonderful thrill to enjoy. I savored every moment of thrusting into her. My orgasm built and built, the pressure at the tip of my cock swelling to an explosive release. It slid past Envy's again and again, brief smooches that sent jolts of lightning shooting down my clit-dick.

My pussy brimmed with passion. I groaned, thrusting forward hard and fast. I buried into her cunt again and again. I reveled in it all. This was amazing. I never wanted this to stop. I wanted to enjoy this forever and ever and ever.

"I'm going to cum in this pussy!" Envy moaned. "Yes, yes, you've earned my spunk!"

"Cum in me!" Apollonia gasped. "Both of you, fire your seed into me!"

"Yes, yes, let's flood her bred pussy!" I moaned. I had bred every woman in this village. They would all have my futa-daughters. "Oh, that's amazing. Just fantastic. Yes!"

Apollonia gasped. Then her cunt squeezed down around our girl-cocks. Her pussy spasmed. Her orgasm surged through her. She shuddered between Envy and me. The married woman's cunt sucked at us both.

"Yes!" I gasped, driving my cock to the hilt in her spasming twat.

"Rapturous grace!" gasped Envy and did the same.

Both our cocks filled Apollonia's cunt to the hilt. Then we erupted. My dick pumped hot cum into Apollonia's pussy. Envy's futa-shaft pulsed against mine. We filled her with our girl-seed. She gasped, her pussy sucking harder at us.

"You're both flooding me!" Apollonia moaned, adding her cries to the women writhing around us. "Yes, yes, yes! You're filling me up with all your girl-spunk!"

"I am!" Envy groaned. "You're taking my superior seed! You love it the most!"

I trembled through my orgasm. My pussy convulsed, juices soaking my thighs. The air brimmed with the heady scents of women's passion. My mouth salivated over it. I breathed it in as I pumped spurt after spurt of my cum into Apollonia's cunt.

"Pandora! Envy!" groaned the married woman. She whimpered, her pussy wringing me dry.

I reached the utter heights of ecstasy, soaring above Mount Olympus even. My mind melted from the bliss of it. From the shuddering bliss of this moment. I smiled, savoring it. This was something delicious. Something utterly rapturous.

"Oh, that was amazing," Apollonia groaned.

"It was," Envy said. "Mmm, and my cock was the best, right?"

"Best?" Apollonia sounded half-dazed. "Mmm, it was wonderful."

"But it was better than Pandora's, right? It had to be better. I'm bigger. Longer."

"You are? I can hardly tell. You're pretty similar." Apollonia sighed. "But you both were amazing. Who cares which of you were better? You both made me cum so hard. I loved both your futa-dicks being in me. So why choose which one I liked better? What's the point? Wasn't the pleasure we shared the point?"

Envy gasped in shock. She stared at me over Apollonia's shoulder. "You might be bigger, but we still give women pleasure. That's all that I care about. Why waste all that time on being better? On negativity? Isn't positivity better? Isn't pleasure and rapture superior?"

Envy shuddered and then I could feel it happening like it had with Lust. I opened my soul up and welcomed back Envy into me. She melted away into smoke and poured over Apollonia. The woman gasped, her pussy suddenly clenching down on only one dick.

Envy suffused back into my soul. I hugged her tight to me. We all were envious of what others had to some degree. But it was how you dealt with that envy. You could enjoy their success. You could inspire yourself to reach higher.

You could stand around in a circle and watch your wives engage in lesbian passion knowing you would soon be pounding them, too.

I rose from the women. I had one more sin to find. One more dark part of me that had escaped and needed control. Wrath... She must be causing the most amount of destruction of all of them. I swallowed.

As the men of the village went to their wives, all inspired to fuck them hard, I left them behind. I had to find Wrath before she caused more problems. Hope swelled in me. I had tamed two of them. I could collar the third.

I would control my darkness instead of letting it destroy.

To be continued...

Pandora's Naughty Passions

Pandora's Naughty Futa Box 6

by

Reed James

Pandora's Naughty Passions

Wrath arrived.

The final incarnation that had escaped Pandora's jar had arrived. She descended on the village with all the fury that brimmed inside of her. Angry at everything, hating everything, she sent her fury into the men and women.

She engulfed them in her passion.

* * *

Pandora

There was one more of the sins that had escaped me to find and tame. I had once again mastered Lust and Envy. I had reclaimed and reabsorbed them, and they again resided within my soul instead of the mortal world. But I hadn't succeeded before a great deal of damage had been inflicted upon the world.

Zeus's curse had left so many dead and suffering. The vindictive god had punished me for cuckolding his wife. He knew I couldn't resist having my virgin jar uncorked. I ached to have a cock, even a fake one made of wood, ram into my pussy and give me that pleasure that other women experienced.

I had made love to Hera, and he hated me for it.

My Lust and Envy had manifested from me, escaping me to wreak havoc upon the world. Wrath was still free, and I had to be close. I had found her trail. Like with the previous two, she left villages devastated in her wake. I worked my way out from the shadow of Mount Olympus across the Greek landscape.

I passed through another one of the villages that Wrath had ravaged. I didn't know what to make of them, though. Everyone was dead, but there was no sign of violence on any of them. People just lay scattered around the heart of their villages.

It made no sense. I had seen the destruction Lust and Envy had left behind. The people had gone mad and murdered each other. Lust made it so they were so sexually frustrated and unable to cum that they eventually went insane. Envy made them all jealous of each other to the point they ripped each other apart.

I expected the worst violence from Wrath. So what was going on?

I kept walking, my sandaled feet whisking across the hard-packed dirt of the roads. My toga hugged my body. I adjusted my satchel as I approached the next village. I could see it on the hill before me. It had a low wall around it. That was more common out here on the plain. Farmland surrounded it, including orchards of olive trees. I peered at the village, afraid of what I would find.

Would I be too late?

I resettled my satchel on my shoulder, my supplies dwindling. I marched on ahead. I had been walking for over a month by now. I had traveled far and wide. I was ready for this misery to be over. Hope burgeoned inside of me that I could stop the suffering. I had to keep a hold of that golden emotion. I had to embrace it.

I climbed the hill. The gates were open. They were wooden and set in the wall. It was only a little taller than me. I reached the top and peered into the village. I didn't hear any sounds of industry. No sign that anyone lived in here. I swallowed, my fear building and building.

Then I heard a woman shrieking. She shouted at the top of her lungs. I frowned; was this her? Had I found Wrath? The woman sounded so angry. This had to be the incarnation of my fury at Zeus's curse. Or was this just the last survivor ranting and raving amid her dead neighbors. Had the people screamed themselves to death?

The shouting grew louder and louder as I moved through the village's streets. It was the largest one I had come across. The streets twisted about the homes as I headed for the center. Then I rounded the corner and saw people just sitting in the heart of the village.

A woman marched among them, screaming at them. Her voice shrill. Her entire body trembling with her fury. She had black hair that tumbled about her face in wild locks. Unkempt. Unmastered. Her large breasts bounced and heaved as she darted right and then left. Her futa-cock thrust out hard before her.

She grabbed a woman by the hair and yanked her head up. "You god's cursed, shit-eating bitch! Look at you just sitting there with that blank expression on your ugly, bloated, miserable face! Move those crap-eating lips, you maggot-ridden corpse! Huh? MOVE! Don't just sit there like you don't give a fuck about anything? Move that putrid husk!"

Wrath let go of the woman's face and screeched her fury. She darted to her left to a man sitting blankly. She backhanded him. His head snapped to the right then slowly drifted back to look forward, a bruise rising on his face.

"Hit me back, you goat-sucking coward!" she hissed. "Come on! Be a man! Stand up and slam those fists into my face! Show me that you care! That there's an ounce of passion in that heart of yours! Don't just sit there like a sack of rotting curds and stare at me with all the expression of a donkey-sucking bastard! Huh! Your wife's a flea-ridden whore who fucks anything with a cock no matter how blighted and diseased! She crawls around with her fly-bitten cunt on display just hoping for a real man to fuck her! Not some limp-dick pansy who won't fight back like you. Come on! Give a shit about something!"

I stared in shock at this. She had stolen all their passion. She had taken from them everything that gave them the will to live. She had fed on their anger at the world, their outrage at injustice, their passion for everything. Wrath, Pandora was beginning to realize, was passion taken to its most extreme. It was unrestrained. Uncaring. No morality. No consideration. Just outpouring of the most basic of emotion. Feral. Animalistic. No logic. No thought.

Just stumbling around in wild, pointless screeching.

How to stop her? How to tame this wild beast of a futa before me as she ranted and raved? She kicked dust in a woman's face. She spat in a man's eye. They didn't care. She had devoured every bit of what made them human.

Passion.

They didn't care about anything, not even their own survival. Those people I had seen dead had just sat down and died of hunger and thirst, not moving once. It was horrifying. Lust had denied people release, keeping them locked in a cycle of ever-increasing arousal with no satisfaction. Envy had driven them to the worst excesses of competition in a pointless drive to prove themselves superior. Now Wrath just swallowed everything that animated the human soul.

Zeus was a cruel god. I despised him more and more.

I moved out to Wrath. I had an idea. A way to tame her passion. Rewards for good behavior. Not punishment. Oh, no, I couldn't punish her. I had to show her an outlet for all that fury and rage and unbridled emotion. I had to evolve it from its most base and predatory, mold it into something useful and productive.

I had to tame the beast.

Wrath snapped her head around and saw me coming. She froze as I unslung my satchel and began unwinding my toga. Her gaze struck me. I shuddered at the intensity of her passion. It boiled over me. So strong, so forceful, it almost snuffed out my own passions like a candle.

But that hope inside of me shone bright. The light that drove back the suffocating darkness of her night. I was wrong about her rage feeding on them. Her presence was just so extreme, her fury just so strong, that she snuffed out the fires burning inside of everyone else. A fire so strong, it consumed all the fuel and left nothing for the others.

My hope burned strong, too. I had defeated Lust and Envy. I had tamed and mastered them. I would do the same for Wrath.

She bristled. Her hands balled into fists. Her large breasts jiggled as she stared at me. Her nostrils flared. Her feet stamped on the ground. I could feel her anger building and building at me as I dropped my toga. My braid of black hair swayed down my back as I bent down to my satchel. My boobs jiggled. My cock swayed. I was hard. Erect for the coming challenge.

I pulled out the one thing I would need, holding the coarse fabric, and stared at her.

"You festering pile of walking shit!" Wrath snarled and marched at me. Her foot struck a man in the chest, pushing him on his back. She stepped on him. He made not a sound of complaint as she rose up and then came down on the ground, her boobs heaving and futa-dick bobbing. "You think you can stand there and not pay for being a fucking cunt. Oh, you have a dick, too. A putrid shaft that spews vile crap! All the women puke after you've lain with them. They claw out your tainted cum and go find a real cock to fuck! You couldn't satisfy a Priestess of Aphrodite whoring herself out to the entire town!"

"Is that supposed to make me whimper?" I asked. "Am I supposed to weep because an unhinged lunatic said a few bad things to me?"

Wrath blazed hotter. She swelled up, her entire body shaking. "I can smell the pus dripping from your maggot-ridden cunt! You don't have a pussy. You have an incubation for filth! Your tits are saggy sacks of watery mush that disgust every man who sees them. You revolt me with your presence. You just stand there thinking you're worth something, but you're not. You have no value. You're just another whore crawling on all fours begging for a dick to slam into that cunt and give you a few seconds of bliss so you can forget about the miserable mire that is your shit-ridden life."

I snorted in laughter. "Really? That's the best insults you can hurl." I patted her cheek. "That's sweet. You're trying so hard to be mean, but—"

She swung a fist at me. She wound up so much, that I had no problem side-stepping her. The fist blurred past me as she screeched her fury. No one had ever talked back to her. I doubt anyone had ever talked to her. She was wild. Feral.

I grabbed her wrist as knowledge filled my mind. Many of the Olympians had given me gifts when Hephaestus had first brought me to Mount Olympus to show me off. He was proud about what he had made. A human woman with a cock. He had been so proud.

The goddesses had been so wet.

Athena, the virgin goddess, had come to me and, after I assfucked her, had given me an understanding of engineering. She had taught me about points of leverage. Fulcrums. Angles. Limits of different construction techniques. That included the human body.

I twisted Wrath's arm behind her back, putting stress on her joint. She screeched in fury as I bent her arm in a way that it wasn't meant to go. I put pressure on her joint and used it as leverage to control her body's movement.

"You whore-mongering bitch!" Wrath screamed. "You release my wrist right now, or I will claw that smile off your plague-ridden face!"

"Just one moment," I said and uncoiled the rope I had taken from my satchel with my one hand. It wasn't the easiest thing in the world to do, but I had Athena's knowledge of engineering. How to build things. Secure things.

How to tie a knot swiftly around a woman's wrist with one hand. It took some skill, but she had given me all the knowledge I needed with her gift to execute it. The rope went taut, the knot secure. The fiber rope bit into her flesh.

She screeched.

"I know, I know," I said. "You're going to slap the smirk off my putrid lips or some nonsense like that."

"Nonsense?" she snarled.

"Yeah," I said. "All this pointless shouting and ranting. It's tiresome. There have to be better ways for you to spend that energy. Ways that give you pleasure instead of just make you hoarse as you scream out whatever disgusting insults you can."

She twisted around to try to bite me. Her teeth snapped at me. But I had the rope. I yanked in just the right way to twist her arm back. She gasped at the spike of pain. Then I swept her leg, striking at just the right spot with the right force to yank it out from her. She collapsed to her knees before me.

I fell down to my own and seized her other arm. I levered it back and tied her wrists together. Her hands were bound at the small of her back, fingers splayed over her cute rump.

She shook her shoulder violently. Her boobs heaved. I wrapped the rope around her waist, using it as an anchor to build my bindings. I braided the rope up her torso, binding her arms even more securely as I crisscrossed the rope, forming a pattern up her stomach. I reached her large breasts.

Her face twisted in fury. Her boobs heaved. I looped the rope around both her tits and pulled tight. I squeezed her boobs into two mounds that thrust out before her. They turned red from the trapped blood, looking swollen.

"Mmm, does that hurt?" I asked.

"Yes!" she snarled.

"Now isn't that something worth being angry over?" I asked. "Something real. Not just your pointless screeching. You can't just be belligerent over everything. You'll never get any happiness if you do that."

"When I escape from these ropes, I'm going to strangle your scrawny neck with them, you shit-sucking bitch!"

I sighed and kept working. I pushed her legs apart and then tied a stick between her ankles, keeping them forced open. Then I stood back. She was bound tight, ropes wound about her body, including her thighs. Her futa-dick thrust out from the thick tangle of black pubic hair hiding her pussy lips.

I stepped up before her and shook my cock at her. "Suck it."

"What?" she snarled.

"Suck my cock," I said, stroking it. "Lean forward and suck on my dick. If you do, you get a reward."

"Reward?" she demanded.

"Yes, a reward. For using all that passion for something worthwhile. Giving something to another person is a rewarding thing." I smiled down at her. "You can find such a great deal of satisfaction from doing something kind to another. You have all that emotion. Let's put it to good use. You'll be rewarded. Handsomely."

She snapped her teeth at my cock.

I sighed. "Very well."

I fell to my knees before her and slid my own lips around the tip of her girl-cock. She gasped as I sealed my lips tight around the base. And then I nursed. I sucked hard. I worshiped that big dick with all my might. My cheeks hollowed. I wiggled my hips back and forth, my pussy cream soaking my bush at my excitement.

Her swollen breasts jiggled above me. She spluttered her outrage as I gave her pleasure. I danced my tongue around her spongy crown. I savored the taste of the salty precum flowing from her tip. She had this beautiful dick. She could have been using it to love the women of this village instead of insulting them.

"What?" she gasped as I nursed on her. I gave her pleasure for the first time. Something to soothe that bleak anger. "You're... That's... Of course, you would suck my cock like the depraved slut you are! Just a futa-whore worshiping my big clit-dick."

I was. I put my all into loving it. No shame would hold me back. I sucked hard on her. She gasped, her breasts jiggling, swollen and ripe. Her nipples thrust out hard. The taste of her precum spilled over my tongue. I breathed in.

Smelled a spicy musk.

The black curls of her pubic hair beaded with dew as I nursed on her. I loved her dick and knew her pussy grew hotter and hotter. I shuddered, my own futa-dick throbbing. Aching. I thrust my fingers up between her thighs spread apart by her bondage and found the curls surrounding her pussy lips.

I thrust two digits into her cunt.

"You filthy whore!" gasped Wrath. The ropes binding her rasped. "You're just a nasty cock-sucking slut."

I sucked hard on her cock, loving her girl-dick in my mouth.

"Yes, yes, just a whore. Mmm, that's it. You're just a fucking slut who... who..." Her face contorted. Her pussy clenched down on my fingers. "Zeus's beard, what are you doing to me?"

I danced my tongue around her cock's crown. She shuddered, ripe boobs jiggling. She shook her head, black hair tossing. I thrust my fingers in and out of her cunt. She whimpered and moaned. Her face scrunched up.

The flavor of her precum grew stronger and stronger on my tongue. I swirled about it. I savored the salty flavor. Her pussy cream dripped down the back of my hand. I plundered her juicy sheath, watching her face twisting with delight above her bound tits.

She groaned. I could feel her pleasure building and building in her. An outlet for her wrath. A new way of her to feel emotions. She shook her head. She squeezed her cunt down on my cock like she could fight it.

"No, no, what are you doing to me?" she snarled. "Stop sucking my dick like the disgusting futa-whore you are! I don't need your nasty mouth nursing on my dick or your dirty finger plundering my cunt!"

I thrust a third fingering her cunt. She gasped, her pussy clenching on my digits. Despite her protests, her body loved it. She moaned, her dick throbbing in my mouth. The flavor her precum spilled over my tongue. Her snatch grew hotter and hotter. I felt her orgasm building.

She gasped and whimpered. Her head tossed. That moment hurtled closer and closer. She clenched her jaws. Her pussy clamped down hard on my digits. I nursed on her clit-dick with hunger, my cheeks hollowing. I felt the moment of eruption nearing.

I ripped my mouth off her cock and my fingers out of her pussy.

"You fucking bitch!" she snarled, eyes snapping open. "Why did you stop? I was about to... to..."

"Cum like a dickgirl-whore?" I asked in amusement. I licked my fingers, tasting her spicy juices. "Mmm, that's good. That is delicious cunt cream you have, you know? Just yummy."

"Get back to sucking my dick!" she snarled. "Or I'll bash my head into yours! Now!"

"Tut, tut," I admonished, rising up. I shook my girl-cock. "Are you going to do something nice to me in return? I made you feel good, so it's your turn to make me feel amazing. You do that, and I'll make you—"

She spat on the tip of my dick.

I smiled and swiped up her spittle. I popped it into my mouth. I smacked my lips. She tasted delicious. "I can't wait to kiss you. So, not going to suck my dick?"

She shook her head. "You're going to suck mine! You're going to make me feel that bliss. I could feel it building in me."

"That's your reward. You get that if you make me feel good." I smiled at her. "You see, all that anger, the constant fury, it's so pointless. That passion can be used for so many other things. Like pleasuring your lover. Giving her bliss and then receiving it in turn. So, are you going to suck my cock?"

"I'll rip it off and fuck it in out of my cunt until I feel that good pleasure, you dick-teasing slut."

"Oh, I haven't begun to dick-tease," I purred.

I stretched out on my back and then slid my head between her thighs. I stared up at her pussy. I seized her girl-cock with one hand and then grabbed her thigh and yanked her down to my face with the other. Her silky bush slid over my lips followed by the wet contact of her pussy on my mouth.

Her spicy musk filled my nose. I licked out through her folds. I caressed her cuntlips. I ran my tongue over those juicy folds while stroking her girl-cock. She shuddered atop me. She groaned, her hips humping forward and back, smearing her cream on my lips. I savored the ticklish feel of her bush on my face.

"That's it!" she hissed, her butt-cheeks clenching before my eyes. I stared up at them, her fingers twisting. "Eat my cunt, you pussy-licking whore. Yeah, you're just a slut for my cunt."

"Mmm, I'm a slut for every woman's cunt," I groaned. I thrust my tongue into her twat. I swirled it around in her. At the same time, I fisted her clit-dick. I stroked her, feeling her throbbing, aching.

"Aren't you insulted?" she hissed. "I call you a whore. You're a complete tramp for my cunt and cock."

"I know!"

"How can you be proud of that?"

"Because I'm giving you pleasure." I nibbled on her labia, loving how she gasped. "I'm sharing my passion. It such a better use of my time."

"Why? You're not getting anything out of it."

"I will."

"I'm not sucking your diseased and putrid futa-cock!"

"Mmm, it's got all that yummy cum I just know you want." I thrust my tongue into her snatch and swirled it around.

"I'm not a cum-hungry whore like you!"

277

"Mmm, sure you're not," I groaned.

I devoured her cunt, savoring her spicy juices. I fisted her dick. She had such a big one, like me. Bigger than any of the human males. My tongue danced around in her. I swirled it about, loving the taste of her. That spicy delight filled my mouth. I groaned, savoring the flavor of her cunt.

She groaned, her butt-cheeks clenching. She shuddered, grinding her furred muff on my face. I plundered her cunt again and again. I loved it. It was so much fun to thrust my tongue into her snatch and dance around in her. I savored every moment of it. My futa-dick throbbed and ached as I pleasured her.

"Oh, yes, yes," she moaned. "Mmm, eat my cunt with that whore-mouth! Ooh, yes, yes, I'm going to erupt. I'm going to jizz all over that nasty dick of yours. It'll never be sucked. No one wants to put that foul thing in their mouths. They're not whores like you."

"You sure?" I sucked on her cunt, drawing out her spicy juices.

She gasped, her cunt cream warm and delicious. Her body shook and shuddered atop me. I loved her moans. Her passion channeled away from wrath. She still had that anger. She wanted me to be consumed by it. She wanted to belittle and insult. To tear me down because she was so empty.

Anger didn't sustain. It devoured. Destroyed. Left nothing inside but echoing pain.

I would give her something better.

I stroked up to the tip of her futa-dick. I massaged her spongy crown with my thumb. She shuddered. Her body bucked. She groaned and gasped, her pussy cream tasting so wonderful as it flowed into my mouth. I nursed on her, listening to her moans.

"Yes, yes, yes!" she gasped. "You stupid cunt. That's it. That's what—"

I slid out from beneath her.

"NOOOOOOO!"

I rose and faced her, fury blazing across her expression. She shook, ropes creaking and her swollen boobs smacking together. Frustration brimmed. She wasn't like Lust who never wanted the moment to end. Wrath craved something to fill her. She needed it. She just refused to give in.

I'd wear her down.

"You stupid whore, I was almost there! Again!"

I turned around and shook my cock at her. "You know what you have to do. You want to cum, you have to give in. You have to do something for someone else. Take all that passion and channel it into the best blowjob in the world."

She snorted, her eyes staring at my dick. Around me, people blinked. They shifted. Someone scratched their nose. I smiled as Wrath just stared at my dick. Her tongue flicked over her lips. She shuddered, nipples so hard.

"It's easy," I said. "You just open your mouth and suck. You put all that anger burning in you into nursing out all that cum for my clit-dick."

She leaned forward, trembling. Then she snarled and lunched her head at my cock. I jumped back. Her teeth snapped together. She bent over, her momentum carrying her face to the flagstone of the town square. That thrust her ass up into the air. She howled her rage.

"Just make me cum, you fucking whore!" she snarled. "You want to. I can tell. You want to devour my spunk. You want to guzzle down every drop of jizz I have. Why aren't you?"

"Because I want to cum, too," I said. "I want to feel delicious. Amazing. I want us to share in it."

I moved behind her and spread apart her butt-cheeks. I exposed her brown sphincter. I licked my lips and ducked my head down. I kissed right at that earthy hole, tasting the dirty flavor. She gasped in shock as I licked it.

"What foul deed is this?" she demanded, her butt-cheeks squeezing about my face.

"Rimming." I swirled my tongue around her asshole. "Mmm, I want to give you pleasure so much, I'm willing to do this dirty act. It's kinky, right?"

"Yes," she said, sounding... confused. "That's a dirty spot. What sort of kinky, foul slut are you?"

"One who likes the taste of your asshole." I danced my tongue around her sphincter.

Her moans were such a delight to hear. I savored them. She trembled on the ground, her moans echoing through the air. I danced my tongue around her naughty butthole, licking and loving and teasing her. I soaked her asshole and savored her dirty flavor.

Kneeling down, my pussy cream ran down my dick. I was so horny. So aching to get my satisfaction. I wanted to cum, too, but I held off. I controlled myself so I could deliver rapture to her. It was difficult, but I wanted to give her pleasure.

I wanted to tame Wrath.

I thrust my tongue against her anal ring. She gasped as she felt her sphincter parting. That naughty hole opened. My tongue pressed into her bowels. The sour flavor increased. My own butthole tingled as I swirled my tongue around in her velvety sheath.

"That's so dirty," moaned Wrath. "And it feels so good, whore. Mmm, just a dirty, nasty, ass-licking tramp. Yeah, yeah, you love the taste of my ass."

"Mmm, it's good," I purred. I kissed at her sphincter. Then I thrust my tongue back into her dirty sheath.

She gasped. Her bowels squeezed around my naughty tongue. I swirled it in her. I savored the feel of her around me. I stirred her up. She groaned, her asshole squeezing about me. It was such a fantastic delight.

A true treat. I shuddered, my heart pounding. This was amazing. She tasted so yummy. I swirled my tongue around in her while my dick ached more and more. I shuddered. This would take all my self-control, but...

I stood up.

"I wasn't even close to cumming that time," Wrath hissed. "You're such a failure at teasing me with that pathetic..." Her words trailed off. "What are you doing?"

"Taking you Athenian style," I purred, pressing my futa-dick against her asshole. "Just like the virgin goddess loves it."

I thrust my girl-cock against her asshole. Her anal ring parted. She gasped, her bound hands fighting at the ropes holding her tight. Lubed by my spit and my precum, her asshole surrendered to me. I groaned as I slid into her velvety sheath.

She moaned as I suck more and more of my futa-dick into her tight asshole. Her flesh squeezed about me. The pleasure race down my shaft to my cunt. My pussy grew so wet and juicy as I went deeper and deeper into her.

My breasts swayed from side to side. They jiggled as I drove into her. I gripped her hips, groaning as I sank to the hilt in her bowels. My black bush rubbed against her butt-cheeks. She squeezed her sheath around me.

"You ass-fucking whore, yes!" gasped Wrath. "Finally, you're doing something right. Yes, yes, fuck me with that nasty cock!"

I gripped her hips and drew back. Her hot bowels squeezed around my cock. I savored that wonderful pressure. Her grip was amazing. She massaged me. I thrust back into her, my boobs heaving. My crotch smacked into her rump. Her flesh rippled.

She moaned. Her whimpers echoed through the air. I shuddered, loving every second of it. This was incredible. I pumped away at her. I thrust my girl-cock into her bowels with hard strokes. My crotch smacked into her rump.

The pressure built at the tip of my cock. My pussy grew hotter and hotter. My ovaries brimmed with my seed. I would fire so much into her. I would baste her bowels with all my spunk. I shuddered, my boobs jiggling from the hard plunges I rammed into her ass.

She wiggled her hips. She stirred that wonderful asshole around my cock. The ropes binding her flesh creaked as she humped back into my strokes. She gasped and moaned as I sodomized her with passion. I fucked her hard.

"Oh, yes!" she hissed, clenching about me. "That's it! Oh, fuck my ass with that dirty cock, slut!"

"Dirty?" I stroked her back, sliding over the bonds. "You love my filthy clit-dick fucking that naughty ass, don't you?"

"Yes, yes, yes!" she gasped.

I thrust my hand beneath her. I grabbed her girl-cock. I squeezed it. I stroked it. She whimpered, her bowels clenching down hard on my futa-dick. I shuddered at how amazing that felt. I reveled in the grip of her asshole around my shaft.

"You want to cum on this dick, don't you?" I cooed, pumping my hand up and down her hard futa-cock. "You want to erupt. I can feel it."

"I'm so close!" she moaned. "You've teased me, you fucking bitch! Now make me cum! Ass-fuck me, whore! Yes, yes, ram that cock into me!"

I could feel the shift in Wrath. The people around me were waking up. Blinking. Shifting. They still looked bored, but they turned heads. Stretched arms. It was progress. I buried to the hilt in Wrath's asshole. Her bowels squeezed about me. She held me tight.

It was such a treat to feel. I groaned, my own orgasm building.

Her asshole swelled my bliss. I slammed hard into her, my pussy getting wetter and wetter. My ovaries brimmed with the cum to tame her. I threw back my head, my breasts jiggling. I shuddered, savoring the heat.

"I'm going to explode!" Wrath hissed. "Finally, you're doing something useful with that whore-dick! Zeus's beard! Yes!"

I slammed to the hilt in her. My pussy clenched. I was there. I just needed to fuck into her one or two more times and we would be cumming. I gritted my teeth, let go of her cock, and did the hardest thing in the world.

I had already tamed *my* lusts.

I pulled out of her bowels.

"NOOOOOOOOOOOO!"

Her shout shook the town. Her fury burst out of her. Every villager slumped over, so smothered by her anger. Then it turned into something else. Whining, begging, pleading need. The people around me started sitting up. Men and women both blinking, shaking heads.

I rushed around, seized Wrath's black hair, and yanked her head up. I thrust my dirty dick into her mouth. I shuddered as her warm lips slid over the crown of my futa-cock. I savored the feel of her wrapped around me. This was it. This was the moment that I needed.

I ached for her surrender.

She sucked.

She channeled her passions. It was incredible. My dick throbbed. Ached. I shuddered as she nursed on me. It was amazing to enjoy. My pussy clenched at the feel of her hungry mouth nursing on my cock fresh from her asshole.

"That's it," I moaned. "Mmm, Wrath, that's it. You're going to get that release you need. Just make me cum."

I gripped her head and fucked my dick in and out of her succulent lips. She whimpered and moaned. My boobs jiggled as I slammed into her mouth. My futa-cock buried to the back of her throat. She sucked as I pulled back, the pressure at the tip of my dick swelling.

It was incredible.

She nursed with such passion on my clit-dick as I pulled it

back. With such force. I groaned as she sucked her own asshole off her cock. She polished that dick with such fervent delight. I shuddered as I thrust into her.

"That's it," I cooed, gripping her head. "Mmm, yes, yes, put that anger to good use. I can feel your fury. It's why you're sucking so hard."

She growled around my cock.

"I know!" I groaned. "I'm such a whore. A bitch. But you love it. You savor that sour flavor of your asshole. You're just as kinky as me. Just as much a wicked and wanton whore."

She glared up at me.

I smiled back at her. "You love it. I can tell by how you're sucking. You can pretend, but I know the truth."

I reveled in mouth-fucking Wrath. I buried my clit-dick into the incarnation's mouth again and again. I loved the way her mouth sucked at me. She nursed on my futa-cock hungrily. Her passion was stirring. Amazing. My cunt clenched, juices dripping down my thighs.

I would have such a huge orgasm. Just a mighty burst of rapture. I shuddered, thrusting into her mouth with hard strokes. Powerful thrusts. I buried into her again and again. I slammed to the hilt in her. It was incredible.

"Yes, yes, yes!" I moaned, pumping away at her. "You love that, don't you? Yeah, you do. Mmm, you're going to make me cum. Oh, yes, yes, you're going to gulp down every drop of jizz that's brimming in my ovaries."

I thrust to the back of her throat. I pushed against her gullet.

"You're going to take every bit of my cock and love it!"

My boobs heaved as my next thrust slammed my cock down her throat. She squealed as her lips slid into my bush. They nuzzled against my labia wrapped around the base of my girl-dick. I shuddered, my cock buried to the hilt in her mouth.

My pussy clenched as she moaned. She sucked. Her tongue swirled around my dick. She buffed me with her passion. She gave me such delight. I could feel the strength of her ardor working on me. She would have me spurting into her snatch. Just flooding her. It would be incredible.

"Yes, yes, yes!" I moaned. "Oh, you are channeling all that passion. You're going to make me cum! Mmm, just polishing my futa-dick clean. I love it, Wrath!"

She moaned as I drew back. Her vibrations massaged the crown of my cock. The pressure swelled and swelled. My cunt clenched, juices trickling down my thighs. I buried back into her mouth. I slammed to the hilt in her. I groaned at the way she sucked at me. How she nursed so hard on my futa-dick. Her tongue danced around the spongy crown.

I shuddered and thrust back into her.

My boobs heaved as I buried my girl-dick back into her mouth. I slammed hard into her. I shuddered, savoring the way her mouth nursed on my girl-cock. She sucked at me with hunger. It felt amazing. My face contorted with delight. The pleasure spilled over my features.

"Yes, yes, I'm going to cum!" I moaned, drawing back.

Her face contorted. She hummed, her vocal cords massaging my futa-dick. I shuddered as my crown popped into her mouth. Her tongue danced around it. She sealed her lips and sucked with such hunger.

She desperately needed to taste my futa-cum. I could feel the anger behind it. The fury that compelled her. She wanted to cum. She ached for that reward, so she gave me all the pleasure she could. It was the start. I smiled, loving it.

"Wrath!" I groaned. "Yes!"

I came.

My pussy convulsed as my futa-dick erupted into Wrath's hungry mouth. She squealed around my cock as she sucked out my girl-cum. My jizz flooded her. I spurted blast after blast of my seed into her hungry mouth.

Cream spilled hot down my thighs. The watching villagers all moaned. They moved. They made sounds as they watched. Women stared at me with desire in their eyes. Men with envy. I shuddered as I pumped load after load of my cum into Wrath's mouth.

She gulped it down. She swallowed every drop of spunk I had. I shivered, the pleasure rippling through me. It was incredible to enjoy. I shuddered, loving every second of it. This was amazing. Just a delight to enjoy.

"Yes, yes, yes," I groaned. "Oh, that's good. That's wonderful. It's so delicious. Just perfect. Mmm, yes, yes, that's awesome."

She moaned around my cock. She stared up at me with such eager delight in her eyes. I grinned at her, loving to see her staring up at me with all that heat in her eyes. That wonderful bliss. It was fantastic to witness.

I ripped my clit-dick out of her mouth. She panted, cum and drool running down her chin. "I need it! I need to cum!"

"And now you've earned it," I told her. "You did something amazing for me." I sank down on my rump, spreading my legs before her. I grabbed her cock and pulled her towards me. "Mount me, Wrath. Pour out all that passion into my pussy. Fuck me!"

She groaned and fell on me. With her hands behind her back, her tits pressed into mine. Those swollen mounds felt so firm and plump on my breasts. Her nipples brushed mine. She moaned, her face twisting with aching need. Glassy eyes stared down at me.

My futa-dick throbbed between our stomachs, trapped by our silky flesh. I pressed her girl-cock into my pussy lips. I ached to have her in me. It was such a delight to feel a real cock. I would miss this. Men held no interest to me.

But dildos were fine. I made a delicious one for Hesione and Pyrrha to fuck me with.

With a hard thrust, Wrath rammed her girl-cock to the hilt in me. My clit-dick throbbed between our stomachs as my pussy welcomed in that amazing shaft. Her girth stretched me out. My toes curled. I moaned, hugging her to me.

I kissed her, tasting my salty cum and her spittle on her lips. I shuddered as her mouth worked on mine. Her hips thrust forward. She buried her girl-dick into my cunt. She pumped away at me with hard strokes.

Powerful plunges.

My cunt clenched about her girl-dick. I held her tight. My body trembled. I groaned, humping against her. The pleasure of this moment rushed through me. I groaned, my heart pounding in my chest. She slammed hard. Fast. She buried her clit-dick into my pussy.

My twat squeezed about her cock. I shuddered, savoring her girth in me. She had such a huge dick. I moaned into her kiss. My fingers slid over her bound arms and the ropes. She groaned, pumping away at me with passion. Hard strokes.

Around us, the villagers were becoming aroused. They were watching. The men drew out cocks. The women squeezed tits and rubbed at cunts. They were all trembling, moaning, witnessing Wrath's passion channeled into something positive.

I broke the kiss. "Wrath!" I gasped. "Oh, Wrath, you're melting my pussy with your futa-cock!"

"You're feeling good?" she gasped, thrusting into my cunt. "No, no, this is my pleasure. I blew you, now it's my turn."

I grabbed her rump, squeezing her ass. "That's what is amazing about love-making. We *both* can feel good when we share our passion. Mmm, you feel it. The joy. The bliss. All those other emotions that passion can become!"

"Yes!"

She kissed me again, thrusting her girl-dick into me. I trembled beneath her, savoring her channeled emotions. Her anger turned into rapture. Rage to ecstasy. She slammed that girl-cock into my cunt with hard strokes. Bold ones. My pussy clenched about her, drinking in the friction. My futa-dick pulsed between us, aching to cum.

Her nipples slid over my breasts. They brushed my own nubs. Sparks flared. Wondrous delight showered over us. It splashed on my mind. I enjoyed it. I groaned into the kiss, my tongue dancing with hers. The rapture was incredible. It built and built with her every thrust into my cunt.

I broke the kiss. "Wrath! By the gods, I'm going to cum! Yes, yes, ram that girl-dick in me!"

"Mmm, your pussy is so hot! You're so wet, Pandora! You're going to make me cum! I want to! I want to feel this wonderful delight!"

"Let's cum together!" I moaned. "Just keep slamming into me. Don't stop. We're almost there!"

"Yes!"

Wrath kissed me. Her lips hot. Hungry. Every thrust into my pussy built and built my orgasm. I climbed towards it, my cunt squeezing about her girl-cock. My twat worshiped her clit-dick. My own swelled with pressure. I hovered there, on the brink of my eruption.

She buried into me. I exploded.

My pussy went wild around her girl-cock. I moaned into the kiss with her. I shuddered beneath her, my cunt writhing and convulsing. My futa-dick basted our bodies with spunk. Jizz fired between us. She buried to the hilt in my spasming twat. Moaned.

Her cock erupted into me.

Her jizz splashed against me. She bathed my cunt with her passion. The pleasure gushed through me. Ecstasy burst in my mind. Rapture washed out of my cunt and splashed my mind with bliss. I trembled beneath Wrath, my cunt working out every drop of cum she had in her. I milked her.

She broke the kiss and howled out, "Pandora! Yes, yes, yes! This is amazing! I love this! I love cumming! I love feeling... happy!"

She stared down in me. Stars burst across my vision as my body trembled. My cock spurted the last of my cum between us while my twat worked her clit-dick dry. She smiled down at me. Her eyes sparkled.

I had tamed Wrath.

She melted into black smoked. The rope binding her fell loose across my naked, cum-splattered body. Wrath's essence flowed back into my soul. I lay there, smiling. Peace descended over me. I had broken Zeus's selfish curse.

I had mastered all the negative emotions that had surged through me after he had flung me from Mount Olympus. Around me, the people of the village moaned and gasped. The women surged in at me, enchanted by the beauty of my body, Aphrodite's gift to me.

As they licked the cum off my belly and tits, I smiled. I thought of Hesione and Pyrrha waiting pregnant for me. My wives. I would return to them, traveling the breadth of Greece. I would savor the pleasures of this world. Zeus might have cursed me, but if I had controlled myself, the tragedy never would have happened.

But I had learned. Grown. I was a new woman. Reborn. I had tamed the darkness and brought peace.

* * *

Pandora returned to Hesione and Pyrrha. It was a slow journey. She enjoyed many men's wives, leaving her seed planted in fertile soil. By the time she reached Prometheus's home, her two women were near delivering her daughters. And they weren't the only women pregnant.

All around ancient Greece, women Pandora had encountered had a bit of her hope in them. A spark of new life that grew inside of them. The jealous spite of Zeus had caused something new to happen. Pandora, with the gifts of the other gods, had spread her seed far and wide.

She had planted something that would change the world.

While not all of Pandora's children were futas, enough were. When her futa-daughters came of age, they took wives of their own. Generation and generation passed before Zeus witnessed his folly fully realized.

Pandora was the Eve to a new world. A world without men. A world of futas that would remember Pandora and, thanks to a mistranslation, the "box" she had to never open. The one that curiosity had driven her to peek inside and unleash evil upon the humans. But they also remembered that hope that was inside of her.

The hope for the future. The hope that the darkness inside of us could be tamed, mastered, and utilized to build something better.

Pandora didn't know what she had done. She just settled down to a life with her family happy that she had corrected her mistake and spited Zeus.

THE END

About the Author

Reed James is a thirty year-old guy living in Tacoma, WA. "I love to write, I find it freeing to immerse myself in a world and tell its stories and then share them with others." He's been writing naughty stories since high school, furiously polishing his craft, and finally feels ready to share his fantasies with the world.

"I love writing about women who want to be a little (or a lot) naughty, people expressing their love for each other as physically and kinkily as possible, and women loving other women. Whether it's a virgin experiencing her/his first time or a long-term couple exploring the bounds of their relationships, it will be a hot, erotic story!"

You can find Reed on the internet at the following places:

Twitter: https://twitter.com/NLPublications
Facebook: https://www.facebook.com/reed.james.9231
Blog: http://blog.naughtyladiespublications.com/wp
Newsletter: http://eepurl.com/4nlN5